Le

Mike Lunnon-Wo
cated in Australia
Middle East for te
and has a young so .... reflect his interest
in the sea, adventure and human heroism.

MIKE LUNNON-WOOD

LET NOT THE DEEP

HarperCollins*Publishers*

HarperCollins*Publishers*
77–85 Fulham Palace Road,
Hammersmith, London W6 8JB

A Paperback Original 1994
1 3 5 7 9 8 6 4 2

Copyright © Mike Lunnon-Wood 1994

The Author asserts the moral right to
be identified as the author of this work

A catalogue record for this book
is available from the British Library

ISBN 0 00 647590 6

Set in Linotron Meridien by
Rowland Phototypesetting Ltd
Bury St Edmunds, Suffolk

Printed in Great Britain by
HarperCollinsManufacturing Glasgow

Dedicated to my son Piers, to Rodney Terry, the real coxswain of the St Mary's lifeboat, who spent many hours with me, and to the brave men and women of the RNLI who turn out when the night is dark and the tempest rages. Their courage leaves me humble.

PROLOGUE

Fiona was born on 20 September.

For a full week the sun had beaten down on the South Atlantic, six hundred miles off the coast of Liberia. The air was sluggish and the sea had taken on a strange, oily calmness.

Now, the surface layer of water had been at twenty-seven degrees for twelve hours and at noon small clouds began forming over the area. The air began to stir from its torpidity, gentle zephyrs that would still barely have raised the telltales on a sail, had there been one there.

By two in the afternoon the clouds had become larger, swirling. Below their bases, dark and heavy, the wind began to gust and within an hour several small groups had formed together, gathered by the increasing air movement into huge towering anvil shapes. The warm gusts became one and, above, the air began to move faster, fed by the warmth from the water.

The collection of giants began to shift, whirling around a centre, as if the vast movement were choreographed by the gods – its massive performers travelling across a hundred-mile front, gaining power as their slow revolving dance of destruction began to increase in tempo.

With the barometric pressure falling and the winds near the centre already at storm force and gaining strength, she moved westwards, building huge waves only to snap their crests away into flying foam like the gigantic malevolent destructive bitch that she was.

Fiona was a hurricane.

By dawn the next morning she had travelled one hundred and twenty miles to the west and during the dark hours her whole enormous mass of energy had sucked in yet more storm clouds and she had tightened her massive coils. Her eye, now a mere twelve miles across, was the calm centre of a vast weather system of shrieking, howling winds that gathered up huge waves into seventy-foot monsters that could swallow a coaster.

A twelve-thousand-ton Cypriot freighter en route to Lisbon barely survived her fury and stood head into wind, under steerageway, for a bruising, battering ten hours.

At the Weather Center in Atlanta, Georgia, the men who had tracked her birth with a satellite the day before now watched her move westwards. The next twenty-four hours would be critical. In that time she would establish her path. If she followed the normal route of others like her famous brother Andrew, then the Center would issue warnings to ships at sea and the coastal areas of the Caribbean and Lower Eastern seaboard.

She could, however, swing northwards around the Azores high-pressure area and eventually run out of energy over the colder northern waters and be downgraded to a storm. But then, the supervisor mused, as he studied the satellite pictures, an old hurricane slamming into the polar zone could make for an interesting warm occluded front and that could have problems of its own.

He was right.

Fiona wasn't going to go all that way for nothing.

ONE

Nichols took his eyes off the stevedores and the derricks and looked back down towards the stern of the ship on which he was proud to be chief officer. Not for the British Steamship Company the informal title of mate, although that is what he was. Wiry and lean, he was just under six foot tall with friendly brown eyes that were emphasized by a dark tan, the result of years of exposure to salt and sun.

Four hundred and seventy-two feet from her raked bows to her cruiser stern, the MV *Caledonia*, once a proud cargo liner plying the Africa and India routes, was now just a tired old lady. Built in the fine traditions of the *Uganda* and the *Kenya* she was designed as a sister ship to these vessels, but was sold on the slip of a Clyde builder's yard only days before her completion.

Fourteen and a half thousand tons' registered weight, she was of the three-island configuration of centre accommodation and bridge superstructure, separated from the raised poop and quarterdecks at either end by four good-sized holds, two for'ard and two aft. Her seven-thousand-horsepower single-screw diesel engine could still give her a respectable fourteen-knot cruising speed and rattle her along at sixteen if pushed.

Nichols brushed his dark hair out of his eyes and scanned the bridge windows. The captain was due aboard. Harry Wellbrook, master of the *Caledonia*, was from the old school. When in port, he wore his uniform whites and insisted his officers did the same. Nichols, however, was in working kit of khaki trousers and heavy sweater. He wasn't going to ruin another set of whites in the hold, and he wasn't going to stand and watch this load aboard from the deck either. Not steel plate.

Like most merchant seaman he had his likes and dislikes with cargo. Some were easy, some were tough. Some were light and easy to handle, some were awkward. The loading was an issue, but as long as a cargo was easy to secure it was acceptable. Bulk loads like coal and wheat and fertilizers now moved on specialist ships, leaving the traditional mixed cargo to conventional vessels. Traditional cargo like steel plate.

Nichols hated steel plate. It was heavy. Its sheer mass made it difficult to move and, once below, it didn't fill out the cargo spaces nicely like crates or pallets might. It sat mid-hold with lots of room around it, room to move, room to shift. Even with the big two-inch chain and inch wire rope strops securing it, steel moved. It scraped and groaned and sometimes, in a blow, the scraping became a shriek and someone had to go below and check the big shackles and bolts. As chief officer, that was his job. He was ultimately responsible to the captain for the cargo, and he wanted this load tied down nice and tight. If a crate broke free and shifted that was one thing. If a thousand tons of steel plate began to move, then you had a real problem.

Nichols didn't like that kind of problem. It was the kind that sank ships and that was why, even with three other competent officers aboard and a bosun of twenty years' service, it was still his responsibility.

Overhead, the dockside crane moved into view with another load of the rusty plate slung on the hook. One of the Icelandic stevedores hung on a rope to steady the load as it was lowered into the number one hold. The bosun, Jarvis, made his way for'ard to Nichols. He was a big man, his hands huge beneath the leather gloves he wore. His jaw was lopsided, the stories said, after being shattered by a swinging crane hook years before, and he bore the marks of a lifetime at sea. One old jagged scar ran round his neck from below his left ear to his Adam's apple, the remnant of a night in Singapore when four Koreans had tried to relieve him of his pay packet. They didn't get it. One died beneath his deck boot and he split the skull of another with a marlinspike.

His name was, so he thought, the best kept secret aboard. In reality most of the crew knew it, although none of them would call Cecil Jarvis by his given name. He ruled the lower decks with his fists if he needed to, but with the Filipino crew it was largely unnecessary. They were all professional seamen.

'How's things, Bos'?' asked Nichols.

Jarvis grunted. 'I hate fuckin' coal. I hate fuckin' rice. But I really fuckin' hate steel plate.'

Nichols laughed softly. 'Me too, Bosun, me too.'

'Trust the bastards to get the wrong fuckin' spec.'

'What's that?' Nichols asked.

'Wrong spec. Lads on the wharf said. They needed nine-mil plate and they got eleven. So this load of shite has to go back, and we have to carry it.'

'You know what they say,' Nichols said. It was an old line they had.

'Aye, who'd wanna be a sailorman anyway?'

A minute of silence passed as they watched the load beneath the crane boom lowered and secured.

'Right, I'm going below,' Nichols said. 'Start them on number four with the rest.'

'Aye aye.'

Nichols spent the next twenty minutes checking the load and when he arrived back on the main deck Captain Wellbrook was making his way along the rail towards him. Wellbrook was a chunky, solid man in his fifties with big bushy eyebrows. His muscular torso was covered in dark hair that peeped over his collar in places and he had a booming voice which, when needed, could be heard from one end of the ship to the other. Usually, however, he spoke in carefully modulated bass tones. He had served

11

the British Steamship Company man and boy for thirty-five years and was, Nichols thought, an outstanding seaman.

'Well, mister?' he rumbled.

'Finished here, sir, just started aft,' Nichols answered.

'The tug will be alongside at eighteen hundred hours.'

'We will be ready, sir. What of our other cargo?'

'They will be back aboard at four thirty. If they look like being late, get someone ashore to round them up.'

'Young Fripp can use a run ashore.' Nichols thought aloud.

Fripp was the cadet, a likeable seventeen-year-old.

'Make sure he is dressed like a ship's officer, Number One,' Wellbrook said dryly, running his eyes down Nichols's faded sweater and work pants.

'Aye aye, sir,' Nichols answered, accepting the expected rebuke good-naturedly. He wasn't trying to make light of it. The old man hadn't been the same in the last few months. Not since the accident. This was the first time his old dry self had been evident since the funeral and the chief officer was delighted that his captain's wounds were healing.

'Carry on then, Mr Nichols.'

The on-deck formality was all part of Wellbrook's style. Other masters allowed a far more relaxed air but not he. Only in the officers' mess did he allow the dropping of rank, and only in his cabin were two individuals allowed to use his Christian name. Those were McDermott, the chief engineer, and Nichols himself.

Nichols brushed the fine streaks of rust from his sweater and moved aft along the port rail past number two 'tween deck hold, now converted along with number three to accommodation. Those two holds had been chosen because they both abutted the centre accommodation island and could be converted to allow access from below decks. That was for the other cargo he had asked the captain about. Twenty-one students and their master. One of

12

the students was accompanied by a policeman, a member of the Diplomatic Protection Corps, who was accommodated in a small cabin in the officers' quarters. He was also the reason for the two policemen at the foot of the gangway on the wharf. An educational trip by sea to study the geology and geography of Iceland was a chance that few schoolboys could resist and this boy was no different, even if he was the Prime Minister's son.

David Lawler was a tall, gangly, likeable boy set in the image of his father and he detested the fact that he needed to be treated as different. Once upon a time the Prime Minister's son could have gone to school alone like any other student in the country, but since the IRA had stepped up its operations on the mainland there had been threats. Some were new and some residual from the days when his father had been Northern Ireland Secretary. Now, everywhere he went, he was accompanied by a police officer.

The 'tween deck holds had been converted into two dormitories, four studies, a classroom, a recreation area and a dining area that also served as a cinema. Showers and toilets were limited and for those the boys had to walk through into the main accommodation.

The crew quarters were also stretched now as the passengers required looking after. The extra crew included a purser, three more men in the kitchen and two extra stewards. It was lucky that one of the existing stewards had once been a nurse and was qualified in advanced first aid, or they would have had to find room for a medic as well.

Nichols moved aft, the bored policemen on the wharf watching him as he crossed above them. He looked at his watch. It was now noon. The loading into the aft hold, number four, was going well so he crossed the deck to the seaward side to check on the problem of the day. Thankfully it was McDermott's problem and not his. On the run into Reykjavik the main engine had been having difficulties and the chief engineer was fairly sure it was caused by fuel tanks contaminated from the last refit. The yard had rebuilt one side of the main fuel bunker and he suspected that minute amounts of steel filings and welding debris had been left in it when the top had been lowered down and welded into position. He had set about flushing the tanks the moment they arrived and by now should be transferring the fuel back aboard from the holding tanks ashore, behind the handling sheds.

Nichols could see the thick bunkering pipe throbbing and pulsing as he approached and he looked to the Filipino crewman standing by the coupling. The man flicked something over the side and looked a little sheepish.

'Fuel coming aboard?' Nichols asked.

The man nodded. 'Nearly full, sir.'

'Good . . . The next time I catch you smoking during refuelling I will tell the bosun. After he has beaten the fuck out of you I'll send you back to fucking Manila in a fucking box. Understand me, sailor?'

The man went white and stammered a reply but Nichols just kept moving. Later he would tell the bosun. He would also tell him he had dealt with it. Better that way. Jarvis was an old-time bosun and this way at least the man still had a job and all his teeth. Most of the crew owed Nichols one in this fashion and this was partly the reason for his popularity amongst the men in the quarterdeck crew's accommodation. He was aware of the fact, but also knew that there could only be one soft touch on a vessel this size, and if the bosun had been any other than Cecil Jarvis he would have changed his style to reflect it.

He moved downwards to number four to check the loading. They were now using the new alloy shackles from the store and he wanted to make sure they were screwed down good and tight. He didn't trust new alloys, no matter how good the makers claimed they were, especially when shipping four thousand tons of steel plate.

*　　*　　*

14

Captain Wellbrook stepped into his cabin and, sliding his jacket off, hung it neatly on a hanger behind the door. The steward would brush it later and return it to the wardrobe. Wellbrook was a meticulous man and, although his wife loved him dearly, she usually breathed a sigh of relief when his shore leave ended and her household could return to normal. Not so this last time, however. This departure had been from a silent house and a grieving woman. Her picture, taken with his two children as a Christmas present, stood proudly on the shelf above his desk. He looked at it and his eyes misted over. The smallest of the three figures, tousle-haired and freckled and all of thirteen on the day the photo was taken, had died, broken and tangled, in the smashed and buckled frame of his bicycle four months before. The car had taken a hundred yards to stop. Wellbrook didn't pray any more. Once he had believed. Not any more. Wellbrook was a man who had lost his faith.

He settled at his desk and began to complete his own paperwork in time to sign off that of his subordinates before they sailed. There would be victualling invoices and the same for bunker fuel and oil, paint, rope and stores. They would go ashore in the company bag before they sailed, along with manifest copies and the other official papers that would allow them to clear the port of Reykjavik. The cargo had been a bonus. He didn't like steel plate any more than anyone else, but he ran a tight ship, a profitable ship, and the load would make a nice margin for the owners.

In these days of specialist carriers and containers, times were hard for what few traditional cargo liners were left. That was why she had been converted. A lucrative four-year contract to provide educational cruises in the North Atlantic that also allowed her owners to take on cargo at ports of call was too good to pass up. The refit had been long overdue, and the British Steamship Company's head office had seen fit to splash out on some new bridge electronics as part of the package. Wellbrook, a traditionalist, had insisted it was installed against the rear bulkhead and snorted at it when it malfunctioned, even for a millisecond. But even he had had to admit the new Navitex was a wonderful gadget, when he had watched with hooded eyes as the new cadet fumbled inexpertly with his brand-new sextant on the bridge wing.

'What,' he rumbled, 'is that?'

'A sextant, Captain,' the junior answered, confused.

'It's plastic!' Wellbrook said incredulously.

'Yes, sir. Japanese,' the junior, Fripp, added proudly. It had cost him a quarter of what a steel one would have done, but still accounted for most of his savings.

'Mr Nichols,' Wellbrook called.

Nichols had stepped out on to the wing.

'If that horrible object appears on my bridge again I shall throw it and its handler into the sea.'

'Right you are, sir,' Nichols said, as the lad's crestfallen look verged on tears.

The next day a solid-brass hand-tooled sextant was left on the boy's bunk with a terse note that read, 'Use it well and it's yours by voyage end.' Wellbrook's name was scrawled across the bottom. It wasn't an offer. It was a command. Nichols had smiled the first time it appeared on the bridge and he tried not to let the old man see him. Wellbrook wasn't fooled.

'What the hell are you grinning at, Mr Nichols?'

'Nothing, Captain.'

'Well . . . couldn't have the young bugger trying to take a sighting with plastic,' he said, trying to justify his gesture. 'Never learn pride in one's craft that way . . . anyway haven't taken the bloody thing out for years.'

Nichols knew that was nonsense. It had been kept in a walnut case and polished regularly by its meticulous owner.

As a master mariner, Wellbrook had trained many young officers over the years and each had received his particular mix of discipline, firm handling and encouragement. The first thing they learnt was pride in their ships and that came from pride in themselves and their own standards.

The *Caledonia* was spotless. From the polished brass nameplate over the bridge door to the depths of her bilges, she was pristine and immaculately kept. The story went that Wellbrook, once dissatisfied with the standard of cleanliness on the bridge, had taken out a tin of Brasso and, in front of a mortified group of deck officers, had put a gleam on the brass screw heads peeping out from the spokes on the old-fashioned teak ship's wheel. When he had finished he turned to the group and said, 'The next time I have to do that, you will all be staying ashore. Understood?'

The wheel in question was his own. He had found it on a rotting hulk halfway up the river-mouth entry into Bangkok harbour. He had stripped down the layers of garish paint to the natural grain and begun to sand and polish. When finally satisfied that it was as good as it would ever be, he had had the steel wheel removed from the bridge of the *Caledonia* and the old teak trophy mounted on the pedestal. In fact, she had automatic steering and only in harbour manoeuvres or heavy weather did anyone actually physically steer the vessel. Even so, as people passed the old wheel, their hands would stray across the old polished spokes, a momentary journey of pure tactile nostalgia.

It wasn't that Wellbrook was overly fastidious. He just loved his ship. This was his third command and he had loved each of them in his own special way, but for him there was no ship quite like the old *Caledonia*. She was his and, during rough weather, when she put her mighty forefoot into the huge waves, he spoke to her like another might talk to a horse or a favourite dog, encouraging her, sharing the ordeal and, when the tempest was past, he would cosset and fuss about her like a doting father.

There was a rap at the door and he sat back in his chair.

'Come.'

Nichols stepped through the opening. He was now dressed in uniform with the steward-pressed creases sharp. This was traditional. Before each voyage Nichols and the chief engineer, McDermott, joined the captain for an appropriate drink in his cabin. Now in mid-afternoon it would be tea, or, for McDermott, the harsh sweet Turkish coffee he favoured. Wellbrook was a strict timekeeper. The sun went over the yardarm of his ship at eighteen hundred hours local. Nichols had never seen the rule broken and any man aboard the *Caledonia* who took alcohol before that time suffered his wrath.

'Ah, Johnny. Come, my boy, sit down.' Wellbrook indicated an easy chair away from the window. The one by the open scuttle was his. That was the only way he could allow his visitors to smoke, a habit he knew they both enjoyed, but he personally found unpleasant.

'How goes the loading?' he asked.

'We are finished, Harry. Tied down good and tight. Two thousand tons in number one and the other half in number four. Won't be hogbacking too much with a bit of luck.'

'Good. Our young lads aboard yet?'

'Not quite. Saw them fooling around on the wharf not long ago so they are making the best of the space while they have it, I think.'

'Nothing dangerous?' Wellbrook asked.

'Good Lord, no. Playing cricket with a bit of four-by-two and a rock sample.'

Wellbrook grunted and, pushing the papers away, stood and moved across to the easy chair as the steward entered with a tray laden with cups, saucers, milk jug and tea pot. Balanced across the top was a plate of gingernut biscuits.

''Ere we go, sirs. Mr McDermott will be five minutes, Captain. I'll bring his coffee then, shall I?'

'Yes. That will be fine.' Wellbrook peered at the biscuit plate. 'No chocolate digestives, Parsons?'

'Sorry, Captain. Scoured the shore I did. All I could find

was a few plain and they are likely broke into pieces. Not easy shopping 'ere, sir. All they 'ave is 'errings,' he muttered sadly. 'That's why the buggers go to Sainsbury's in Glasgow. Like I said . . .'

'Yes, all right, Parsons, you may go. Thank you,' Wellbrook interrupted.

The steward left and as he closed the door, Wellbrook stood and crossed to a small cabinet by his bookshelf. He bent and rummaged around in it.

Nichols took the opportunity to look the cabin over for the thousandth time. A matching pair of polished steel cases held barometer and chronometer. Mounted on a walnut base they hung over a bookcase that contained many volumes. Travellers' tales mixed with stories of the sea and encyclopaedias, reference books for everything from signal flags to remedies for gout and how to lay down good wines. Beside the picture of the family was another of a much younger Harry Wellbrook during the Korean War, standing proudly by the binnacle on the bridge with a group of other youthful officers. On the wall was a photograph of the *Caledonia*, white superstructure, black sides down to her waterline, and the blue stripe of the company along her waist. The red ensign snapped out from her staff and the bow wave showed she was steaming at what would have been her top speed back then. The cabin was a warm room, one that had many stories to tell.

Wellbrook was still fishing in the cupboard. 'A sad day when a master has to steal his own biscuits to make sure he has one with a cup of tea . . . Ah, there we are.' He held a packet of chocolate digestives aloft with a flourish, a boyish grin across his broad face.

'You be mother, Johnny, and tell me what you think of young Master Lawler. You're a Conservative, aren't you, lad?'

Nichols smiled. 'I suppose I am . . . although I've never voted. I like the boy. His head is screwed on right. Popular enough with the others in the class.' He bent forward and began pouring the tea, strong and dark the way they both liked it. 'Very dry sense of humour. Had his minder going for a while yesterday.'

'Did he?' Wellbrook laughed softly, taking the cup from Nichols's hand. 'Wouldn't have that job for the world. One minute you're a serving copper and the next, bodyguard to a schoolboy.'

'I promised him some bridge time on the trip back to Southampton . . .'

A sharp rap on the door and in strode McDermott. He was a tall, lanky Scotsman in his fifties, wearing clean, pressed white overalls. Sometimes belligerent, sometimes dour, he was never boring. His small dark eyes glanced at the plate on the tray.

'Gingernuts again . . . sodding things.' Then he looked across at the captain. 'Afternoon, Harry . . . young John . . . got your cargo loaded, have you?'

'Aye, Archie,' Nichols said, grinning. McDermott and Wellbrook went back twenty years together, but, even so, McDermott's familiarity with the captain, even given the closed door, always surprised him. Technically the chief engineer outranked the chief deck officer but McDermott had never questioned Nichols's traditional right to second-in-command status. He was lord of the engines and that was all that interested him.

'How's the fuel problem?' Wellbrook asked.

'Bloody refit,' the Scot muttered, taking one of the biscuits he had recently slandered and bypassing the offered packet in the captain's hand. 'I've seen better refits on river scows. I have flushed the reworked tank and the lines and nothing is coming into the filters now, so we should be all right. Should have seen it. Filings, weld droplets, even a bloody cigarette butt came through. Disgraceful. Wait till I see the foreman at that yard.'

'The engine fit for sea?' Wellbrook asked. His tone had changed and McDermott's did too.

'As best we can tell. Yes, sir,' the Scot replied.

20

What McDermott didn't know was that the yard fore-man, thinking he was doing his best, had also made spot repairs to seams in the bunkers on the other side and his amendment to the work report had been mis-filed in the office. No one on *Caledonia* was aware of it.

'Good.' Wellbrook relaxed. 'Johnny has just been giving me his impression of young David Lawler. Met him yet?'

'I have. Had the lot of them on a grand tour of my engine rooms. He's not difficult to spot. Not with his father's ears and that bloody rozzer at his shoulder the whole time,' McDermott answered, pushing the whole biscuit into his mouth and reaching for another.

'The minder? He's all right. If you were in the mess more often, Archie, you would have had a chance to have a drink with him,' Nichols said.

'You know me, boy, don't drink often, but when I do it's a real one,' he replied, his mouth full. 'Anyway, it's the bulge under his armpit that bothers me.'

They were interrupted then by the steward bringing McDermott's Turkish coffee and they remained silent till the man left.

'I suppose we were "vetted" or whatever they call it?' the Scot asked. 'Sounds like a trip to de-knacker a tom-cat.'

'No. That wasn't deemed necessary. He's not royalty,' Wellbrook answered.

'Royalty.' McDermott shuddered. 'I wonder what they cost us. Royal weddings . . . and divorces!'

The other two smiled at each other. Archie McDermott's chief complaint in life was the wealthy classes, but in reality he loved the Royals as much as anyone and in fact had once got into a fight with an American who had called the Queen Mother an old hag. Archie McDermott had leapt to his feet, bony fists balled and said, 'Hag this, bastard!' He had then proceeded to give the unfortunate individual a Liverpool kiss, the hard surface of his forehead slamming down across the bridge of the other man's nose. A pair of his engineers had dragged him clear of the Boston bar before the police arrived. Nichols had ragged him about it and McDermott had said, 'They may be a bloody anachronism, but they are our bloody anachronism.'

'If he were the son of a Labour PM he wouldn't have a copper with him,' he muttered. Wellbrook smiled. This was vintage McDermott.

Twenty minutes later they were finished and Wellbrook was pleased to see the two officers leave his cabin. He wasn't feeling well. Must have eaten something, he thought.

Nichols was on the bridge wing as the students came aboard in gaggles of two and three. Phillips, their master, trailed behind with the last pair of boys. Sergeant Carstairs, bodyguard to David Lawler, walked with his youthful charge, taking the gangway in long strides, his ever-watchful eyes on the move, his hands free and his jacket unbuttoned.

Nichols smiled to himself. No ordinary copper, that's for sure, he thought. Knows which spoon to use as well as how to clear a jam in his weapon.

He looked at his watch. The tug would be alongside in an hour and, any minute now, McDermott would fire up the main engine. As if on cue, the deck vibrated beneath his feet and a belch of smoke cleared the funnel stack and the old *Caledonia* shivered along her waterline as if anticipating with pleasure the prospect of putting to sea.

Towards the stern the seamen were gathering, pulling on leather work gloves and sweaters to ward off the chill wind that was now blowing across the bay. Jarvis moved amongst them, delegating jobs. Nichols reminded himself to mention the man he had seen smoking during refuelling. He turned and walked on to the bridge. The place was getting busy. The second mate and both the thirds were present as they should be and even Cochran, the radio officer from Marconi, was out of his hidey-hole. Nichols liked Cochran. In these days of modern electronics, most ships had dispensed with radio specialists, looking instead for electronics officers who could maintain equipment. Ordinarily Wellbrook did the same, but they had agreed the specialist with the charter operators, and in reality it was easier to have one man operate the gear in the tiny radio room than have the duty officer fumbling about. It became noticeable when they were deep sea, over the hundred-fathom line. Close to the shore the VHF was easy and effective, but out in blue water a skilled radio operator could make all the difference between a message getting in or out and nothing at all.

Everyone stiffened slightly as Nichols arrived on the bridge from the wing. If below decks belonged to Jarvis and the engines to McDermott, then the bridge was his domain and all deferred to him except Wellbrook himself. Only Rodriguez by the helm, a picture of studied indifference, seemed unaffected. The two number three mates, one lanky and one short, stood silently like Laurel and Hardy. Chafney and Jeffries were both in their early twenties, and of the pair Chafney was the natural sailor, his father being the master of a P & O bulk carrier.

Scott, the second mate, had just risen from his bunk and still looked sleepy. He would return as soon as they were clear of the bay and take the watch from midnight to four.

On the bulkhead above the new Navitex machine was a wall charger unit and in its sockets were a set of Motorola hand-held radios. He scooped out three and, holding them, walked across to the navigation table where, above the laid-out charts, written up on a small blackboard, was the frequency used by the Reykjavik port tugs. There would only be one for *Caledonia*.

Nichols had served as a very junior number four on a big passenger liner years before and loved the bustle as three, sometimes four, powerful tugs muscled and shoved the mighty *Canberra* up to or away from the wharf. Once, in New Zealand, he had watched a tiny harbour tug, more a work boat than anything else, being driven backwards by the force of wind against the ship she was trying to stop running aground in a freak storm in the big bay. Her little hooter was shrieking, crying for help to others of her own kind. From across the bay came the huge deep-sea salvage tug from the Shell terminal, engines running flat out, shouldering aside waves impudent enough to try to slow her. She had caught the swinging bows of the light crude carrier only seconds from driving the little tug aground on the rocks. The sea boiled under her broad transom as thirty thousand horsepower was transferred into her four big screws and they bit and slowed the swing. Then, foot by foot into the teeth of the gale, the tug called *Betsy* powered her consort backwards, the wailing of her big bass horn answering the shrieking poop from her smaller worried sister. Harbour tugs. The stuff of small boys' stories and hard work and sometimes, just sometimes, real drama.

He set the frequencies and handed them to the lanky cadet.

'Mr Fripp. Take these two down to the bosun. Then you stay and watch him work. Watch in particular the way he takes the bowlines off. Note that when the ship leaves the wharf, miraculously it is not tied on any more. No bits of string tied to big bits of metal on the land.' The youngster blushed. He had made a complete cock-up of the departure from Southampton, much to the jeering delight of the watching dock workers. 'Then perhaps you can do it next time.'

'Yes, sir.'

'Right, on your way, lad,' Nichols said. 'If it means anything, we have all made a hash of at least one departure. The secret is not to do it twice.'

'Aye aye, sir.'

'Tugs coming, Mr Nichols,' a voice called.

'Thank you. Give the captain my compliments and tell . . .' Nichols began.

'I am here,' Wellbrook interrupted, stepping on to the bridge. 'Take her out, Mr Nichols.'

24

'Aye aye.'

He stood on the bridge wing, the radio to his lips. From there he could watch the sailors in the bow and stern and also see the men on the wharf who would let go the massive six-inch nylon lines. In the bows, Jarvis and three able seamen were passing a line to the tug. As they let go from the wharf and, with just enough power to get under way, the tug would pull their bow round away from the dock.

'*Kavic*, this is *Caledonia*, are you ready for us?'

'*Ja*, we are ready. Line is fast.'

'Thank you. Let go for'ard . . . let go aft.'

With shouts and hand signals from the seamen to the men on the dock, the lines were lifted clear of the bollards and were quickly hauled aboard.

The schoolboys were all scattered in gaggles along the rails, some waving to people on the shore, some on the other side watching the *Kavic* as she towed them out. One lone individual had his hands against one of the big vents, feeling the vibrations, and yet another strutted with a hand over one eye and a stiffened leg like a pirate captain.

'*Kavic*, we are clear.'

There was a crackle of static by way of acknowledgement and the tug's screws bit and, with the strain taken on the line, the bow began to swing. As they cleared the dockside Nichols spoke again.

'Bridge, slow ahead, starboard twenty,' and, with a last look at the wharf and a wave to the few watchers, he stepped back into the bridge. As the ship, pulled by the tug, swung her bows into the wide bay, Nichols moved to the centre of the bridge. The number three, Jeffries, stiffened slightly as the chief officer came close. He was pleased that it had been the cadet who had taken the roasting and glad it was not he who had been up on the foredeck with the bosun, under Nichols's watchful eye. He had been down that road and hated it.

'Midships the helm.'

The Filipino seaman repeated the order back to him and

a minute later the tug slipped the line and Nichols gave the order for full ahead.

Nichols watched the tug as she increased power and swung away to the left out of the *Caledonia*'s track, the stubby little boat giving a farewell toot of her siren.

'Thank you, *Kavic*, and good day.'

'You are welcome, *Caledonia*. Safe voyage.'

Nichols crossed to the rear of the bridge and dropped his radio back into the charger unit. Fripp bounced on to the bridge with the bosun's radio in his hand.

'Come on to two eight three degrees.'

'Two eight three it is,' a moment later from the helmsman.

Nichols turned to the cadet.

'Mr Fripp, plot a course for once we clear the heads.'

'Done, sir. One fifty three degrees,' he answered confidently, desperately eager to please.

Nichols nodded. 'Very well. You agree, Mr Scott?' he asked with a wink.

'Aye, sir,' Scott replied seriously before stifling a yawn.

As the second officer, it was Scott's job to lay off the courses but Nichols had the cadet work every calculation every time. If they agreed with Scott's then all very well. If not they did them again till they did.

Fripp didn't have to repeat his work very often. He was a very competent navigator, a perfect throw-back to the days when the Royal Navy had a ranking deck officer who simply navigated the ship, the pilot. Nichols also knew the course was accurate. He had worked the calculation himself only an hour ago. It wouldn't do to tell Fripp that. He must believe his chief had sufficient confidence to trust the plot.

'Mr Jeffries, I believe I have the pleasure of your company on this watch?'

'Aye, sir.'

With the luxury of an extra officer, the four-to-eight watch, normally the chief officer's alone, would have the extra third on the bridge. Given the choice he would rather have taken Chafney. He didn't like Jeffries. Nothing he could put his finger on, just instinct and a couple of incidents that were unsettling. Nastiness and sarcasm with crew were unnecessary and Nichols disliked it. He had discussed it with Scott during a routine evaluation and the number two thought he was being a bit harsh.

'You have the bridge. I shall be in number one hold.'

Nichols looked across at the captain who had remained silent the entire time.

'Good enough, Mr Nichols,' he rumbled.

That was as near a compliment as one would receive in public from Wellbrook, and Nichols shielded a smile as he left the bridge to check the cargo for the first time of many. As he went, the Navitex, a machine that looked like a large office facsimile machine, started to hum and the latest four-hourly weather reports began to print off.

Jeffries glanced at the printout and the accompanying satellite picture and then he tore off the printout and clipped it on the board above the standing-orders book. The forty-eight-hour forecast was for largely fine weather with odd areas of rain. Nothing to worry a sailor there.

The deck vibrated beneath their feet as the increased engine revolutions began to shake the old hull and, with the smells and sounds of the land dropping behind them, *Caledonia* headed for the open sea.

There were fifty-six people on board.

At that moment four large tugs were manoeuvring the ultra-large crude carrier, *Pegasus*, towards an offshore discharge terminal six miles off Rotterdam. The *Pegasus* was a leviathan. Over four hundred thousand tons, she was owned by the Mobil oil company and she would spend the next two and a half days discharging her load of Saudi crude. Her master, James Hawk, was an American, and command of a ship like the *Pegasus* was the culmination of a career. Modern and fast, she and others like her held the world's commerce together, delivering crude oil to refineries in a score of countries. Oil that would power industries, heat homes, fuel cars and work machines.

Hawk didn't like congested shipping lanes and it was always a relief to feel the massive mooring lines secured after a journey up the English Channel. Ships the size of *Pegasus* were built for the open ocean, where they had room to move and where they were truly the queens of the seas. Here, in the shallows off the Low Countries and in the approach up the hectic narrows of the Channel, her power was curtailed and her size was a hindrance amongst the crisscrossing ferries, trawlers, bulkers and smaller ships.

The Royal Fleet auxiliary, HMS *Drumbeat*, and the destroyer, HMS *Defiant*, were amongst seven Royal Navy ships concluding an exercise in the western Mediterranean and would soon be heading to their home port of Falmouth on the southwestern coast of England.

At the Maritime Rescue Coordination Centre at Falmouth the coastguard officers, charged with the safety and movement of shipping in their area of the Channel approaches, were changing shifts. Big radar screens allowed them to view the closer shipping movements and others, further out, were plotted on a big map. It had been a quiet shift and the weather reports were for calm conditions.

Across the Atlantic, however, in Miami, the National Hurricane Center had received forecasts from the Atlanta Weather Center and was carefully watching Hurricane Fiona, now just over a day old and already as big and nasty and malevolent as she was ever going to be.

TWO

St Mary's. Scilly Isles

The man stepped on to Hugh Street from his front door and, pulling it shut behind him, walked across the road and down towards the gap between the houses that led to the beach. He walked with the gait of one who had spent his life on moving decks and, dressed comfortably in old blue working pants, a heavy sweater and a sailcloth smock, he looked like a fisherman. He wore a peaked cap to keep his head warm and draped over his arm was an old paint-stained anorak. A pipe jutted from his mouth and he puffed gently, keeping the tobacco alight, as he threaded his way through the last of the year's tourists.

He was of medium height, clean-shaven and, other than a few lines across his forehead, he looked younger than his years. His clear grey eyes told of a man who rarely drank and his skin was ruddy from wind and sun and salt.

Hal Carter was a boatman, a Scillonian and a Tresco man. Apart from a spell in the Royal Navy as a young man, he had spent his entire life in the Scilly Isles and would be happy nowhere else. He had never owned a car or a bicycle because he had never needed either. But he had lost count of the number of boats that had been his. From small dinghies to bigger work launches, fishing boats and the beautiful sky-blue-hulled Falmouth oyster dredger that he had restored with his brother and his son during the long summer evenings.

He wouldn't call himself a romantic. He would also say

that boats were more than just his livelihood, they were a way of life, and his big hands, callused by years of salt and rope, told the tale. He loved each of his boats in his own way. He could, with a glance at the sky, tell what tomorrow's weather would bring and watch visiting yachtsmen gingerly avoiding sandbars, a full cable distant, that he could plot to the last shifting foot.

He had been one of the last crew ever to turn out to a wreck in a pilot gig. That had been in the mid-fifties and the Bryher men had launched the slim fast gig *Sussex* into the bay and pulled round to the windward side of Tresco. With six of them on the oars the gig snapped along at ten knots.

Six men pulling in a gig was the limit for the design. The rule dated back to the days when His Majesty's Customs decreed that to be the maximum allowable number of men pulling oars, in case their own cutters were out-paced by smugglers. Smugglers who weren't above using the pilot gigs to run the odd load ashore. There, aground on Golden Ball bar, was the *Mando*. The water was fouled with grain and rope and flotsam and the motor boat that turned out had to heave to, lest she foul her intakes or her propeller. The gig had gone in and pulled back out to deeper water, towing the ship's boats, crowded with men. Each man had earned twelve pounds in salvage from Lloyd's, payment for the one empty boat they had saved.

The following year Hal Carter had borrowed money and bought a share in a crab boat and courted and married Jean. They had two children and winter nights were spent overhauling gear and making and repairing pots. The children were grown now. Simon was twenty-three and crewed on a launch out of St Mary's. Helen was just twenty and a nurse at the hospital in Penzance.

He walked the alley down to the beach and, bending, slipped the knots on the mooring line for the little dinghy that was just being lifted by the incoming tide.

Further along the beach two men, stripped to the waist

in the weak September sunshine, were painting the hull of an upturned clinker-hulled boat. It was a lazy peaceful scene, the talk easy, and the smoke from hand-rolled cigarettes curling up from dry lips into the still air. One lifted a brush in greeting.

Carter waved back and, pulling the line to get the little dinghy closer, he walked down to the water's edge and deftly climbed in, still puffing on his pipe. He bent and dropped the small outboard propeller into the water and pulled the starter cord. It fired and, without sitting, he turned the throttle and steered the boat out into the bay where his heavy sixty-foot work boat tugged sluggishly at her mooring line.

She was beamy and heavy and her gunwales were chipped and scarred from years of handling small loads and pallets on to the low rock jetties and quays of the out-islands. She would deliver anything from a small parcel to pallets of fertilizer or drums of fuel or even schoolchildren. Occasionally she brought people to the doctor and once she had carried a body. She worked to a schedule where possible, but the tides determined her success. This morning's run across to Tresco would see her inch over the sandbars, scraping her old hull in places, the engine barely idling, allowing the incoming tide to do the work.

He cut the motor on the dinghy, threw a line over the big samson post and crossed over the high freeboard on to the main deck. John Timson, one of his crew, was bent over the engine hatch.

'Morning, John.'

The man looked up. He was a giant, barrel-chested with thick powerful arms and hands like hams. The thick blond hair covered his great leonine head and was long enough to be tied back in a ponytail. His cheeks were bearded, leaving his eyes to peer out of all the hair like those of a squirrel. In one earlobe he sported an earring and his laugh was accompanied by flashing white teeth.

'Morning, Hal. The lads on the quay are trying to round

31

up the crane driver, but I think his missus gave birth last night.'

Carter nodded. If necessary one of them would operate the crane. They had all done that job over time and the new quay at St Mary's was a casual affair, run rather like a club. If you were a Scillonian and a boatman you would just be left to get on with it.

'Aye. I heard. A girl.'

Timson stood and, wiping his hands on a cloth, walked for'ard to the mooring line as Carter started the engine on his lady love.

'I see Henry has got his boat up and is giving it a coat of paint,' Timson mused.

Carter smiled. 'Using a two-inch brush. He should be finished by the spring.'

Timson threw back his head and laughed as his skipper eased the throttle forward and began to move the launch in towards the wharf where he could see their morning's cargo ready for loading.

The crane driver arrived then and, hurrying so as to be loaded and clear of the quay before the big car-carrying *Scillonian* arrived, they took aboard three new generators, bright orange and shrink-wrapped. There were also two pallets of cement, a skip full of bricks and a mixed load of plumber's piping and builder's six-by-six joists. Lastly there was a new Mercury outboard and a group of six cardboard boxes of something for Mrs Clements at the shop.

With the load secured and the other member of his crew aboard, Carter eased his launch back away from the high walls and, with the water churning under the scarred transom, he pointed the bows towards the end of the quay and St Mary's Road for the first drop of the day over on Tresco. From there they would head on round to Gugh.

A group of yachts were anchored in the area between the moorings and Newford Island and Carter cast his eye over the anchor position of one boat in particular. Her anchor line dropped straight down from her bows. Way too short to allow her to move. With the tide coming in it would shorten further and then if the wind changed direction she would be unable to swing with the others and they would be crashing and bumping into each other.

Visiting yachtsmen were the bane of the professional boatmen. They came into the quays at the busiest times, fouled mooring lines, and generally got in everyone's way. They were however genuinely well intentioned and always ready to please once shown the error of their ways. Unfortunately that was usually just after having missed being trampled underfoot by a ten-ton barge when they were moored in the wrong place, or when they continued tacking away happily, expecting power to give way to sail, when common sense should have told them just to get out of the way.

He looked at the sky. The wind would freshen over the afternoon and the yacht would be causing grief by dusk. He looked across to make sure that no one had moored too close to his other lady because then he would have to stop and see things put to right.

She was the *Maeve Corrigan*.

Fifty-two feet of flared planing hull with almost a thousand horsepower delivered from two big Caterpillar diesels. She was state of the art. Her hull was divided into twenty-six watertight compartments and her wheelhouse was airtight and crammed with every electronic device a seaman could want and then some. She was fast, responsive and safe, even in the worst storms the Atlantic could throw at her. She was the St Mary's fast-afloat self-righting Arunclass lifeboat and Hal Carter was not just a Scillonian and a boatman. He was also coxswain of the *Maeve Corrigan*.

There had long been a lifeboat on St Mary's and, over the years, her lifeboatmen had saved six hundred and twenty-seven lives. There were older stations but few more picturesque than the old granite boathouse on Carn Thomas.

Painted in white on the boards which hung around the

eaves was a record of each service, the lives saved and the boats towed to safety. Old sepia-tone photographs were scattered around the walls, images of nineteenth-century men, most bearded and standing in formal poses by the boats of the day, wearing old cork life jackets and oilskins.

In the days when the men of St Mary's were provided with a slip boat, the maroons would summon the crew to the boathouse and they would board the lifeboat up on the slip. Then, sometimes with others helping to push, the boat would run down the ramp and hit the water with a crash, engines running, and put straight to sea on service. When safely home and refuelled, she would be winched up the ramp, no man going home till she was ready for service again.

Then came the afloat boat. The big fast Arun now moored out in the bay. Now the ramp was used to launch the small tender that the men used to get them out to the *Maeve*. They all disliked that part of the job. The tender was too small and they were all drenched to the skin even before boarding the lifeboat, the nylon waterproofs being ineffectual. Water came in at the sleeves, round the neck, everywhere.

The crew, all Scillonians, would once all have been boatmen but, these days, there was a shopkeeper and a local businessman on the crew list. The Royal National Lifeboat Institution, who provided the boats, gear and training, liked to see six men crewing an Arun-class boat, but Hal Carter would leave with a couple short if he had to. The RNLI provided the salary for a full-time mechanic and, provided he was aboard, with the second coxswain and at least one other man, then Carter would launch to a casualty. He had nine men to choose from and he would launch with the first arrivals as long as his core crew was present. They all knew that and the competition was fierce, but they all also knew that the boat could operate without them and no one would die just because they were out of touch or late once the maroons had gone up.

It was different, of course, for Hal Carter. Hal took his responsibilities very seriously, which was one of the reasons he was coxswain. He never went anywhere without his wife knowing where he was and, if they were out together, then the coastguard always knew where to find him.

There was usually some warning these days. Modern communications had seen to that and, invariably, the crew were already assembled at the boathouse when the decision to launch was being made by the RNLI's honorary secretary and the coxswain. Even so, sometimes the first word of a casualty was a Mayday message received by the coastguard and men would be called from their beds and their firesides. Each kept a bag by the door, sweater, warm trousers and their personal things.

Big John Timson, one of the St Mary's crew, scorned the yellow yachtsmen's deck boots and always wore training shoes. He preferred wet feet that gripped the deck. Another always arrived with food in his bag. He disliked the meagre rations aboard the lifeboat, all donated by the manufacturers, cup-a-soups and instant coffee, rich tea biscuits and boiled sweets. He was the source of much mirth aboard during the training sessions. Dry-humoured and laconic, he would bemoan the fate of the traditional English fare of fish and soggy chips and curse the invasion of hamburgers and French fries. When McDonald's arrived in the Scillies, he said, he would burn it down and be damned.

Victor Collier was a businessman. In the days of pulling lifeboats and later, in the early engine-powered boats, the entire crew were local boatmen or fishermen and for good reason. Fishermen could not go out if the weather was rough, and were forced to sit back and spend their time making repairs to pots and nets. That made the winters long and money scarce, so when, in the mid-nineteenth century, the secretary of a fledgling society to rescue seamen from wrecks offered rewards and medals to boatmen and others for their services in rescues, there were hardy men ashore who needed the work. The hourly pay was welcome and the boats later supplied by the institution were good and strong.

The other obvious advantage of using local men was local knowledge. A man who had skippered a fishing boat for twenty years knew more about the rocks and reefs than anyone. He could predict tidal flow, drift and how much water was over any given rock at any given time. This inshore knowledge was critical when the majority of ships they launched to were foundering on a lee shore, in the very waters the fishermen and boatmen knew so intimately.

If the coast of Cornwall was famous for its wrecks, then the Scilly Isles, twenty-eight miles off Land's End, was equally deserving of the reputation. It was, for seamen, a perilous place of sharp reefs, sometimes exposed above the water, but more often just below the surface. Huge jagged rocks that could rip the hull from a ship. Fast tides confused things further and any ship sailing westwards along the south coast had either to turn to seaward and give the Scillies a wide berth, or run through the passage and risk a lee shore and Wolf Rock. Seamen dreaded the very mention of the reefs: the Crim, the Retarrier, the Bishop, the Rosevear and the Gorregan, a barrier ten miles wide that for centuries had no lights and was largely uncharted.

The worst single night had been in 1707 when a fleet led by HMS *Association* and totalling fifteen ships met tragedy. The *Association*, the *Romney*, the *Eagle*, the *Firebrand* and the others had foundered on the Western Rocks. Two thousand men were lost. There were many more wrecks in the next two hundred years and many times the island men, pulling oars in fragile gigs, went to the aid of the shipwrecked. One night in 1910 the SS *Minnehaha* struck Scilly Rock. The Bryher men put to sea in their gigs and saved all sixty-six passengers and as many of the crew as they could.

In early times, gig men who brought news of a wreck

to Lloyd's would be paid five shillings each. The wrecks brought other benefits too. Rope and barrels, timber and paint, flour and tea, all washed ashore, made life easier for the islanders. But they never forgot that lives came first.

Hal Carter knew the rocks and reefs of the Scillies. Bob Cameron, his assistant coxswain, knew them also but not as well. Although he owned his own crab boat, the type of local knowledge required took more years than a man of only thirty-seven could muster. So Hal took it upon himself to vary the training run every week, to offer something new to a crew that one day would need to launch without him, just as he had learnt from the last coxswain. Cameron was good on the helm. He could take the Arun at top speed through the big breaking waves with a feel for trim and balance, his right hand caressing the twin throttles, his left on the big wheel, making the big fifty-two-footer dance. He could feel a broach coming on seconds before it happened and already be correcting the angle, feeling the wave beneath them. The others were comfortable with him at the helm. That was important. In the black of night with a gale blowing and visibility down to yards through driving spray and with the boat doing eighteen knots, her hull planing, the man on the wheel had to be trusted. He had to be, quite simply, an outstanding seaman, one in whose hands the others were prepared to put their lives.

Hal would take them into the Western Rocks this Saturday, run the boat in and out, ride the swells and get the feel of the place that had claimed so many ships and men. Hope for a bit of a gale, he thought, and give Bob the helm and then run back after dark past the Gorregan and Melledgan and in through Smith Sound. They would be back in time for a pint at the Atlantic, he and Ernie and the two boys.

Ernie Coutts was the engineer. He was a short, roly-poly man, who found something to smile about in every situation. He was the only full-time employee on the boat. He and Bob Cameron were thick as thieves, a curious relationship based on just two common denominators, a love of the sea and the lifeboat. Ernie checked the engines daily and ran them up in the winter, charging the bank of batteries on days between services or training sessions. He was also responsible for day-to-day maintenance and he kept the *Maeve* spotlessly clean. He had a sea-station behind and to the left of the coxswain, with duplicate engine instruments on a panel set into the bulkhead, but he was normally to be found down in the engine space, wedged in between the huge roaring diesels.

Comfort aside, he could only do half of his job from the seat up in the wheelhouse and felt he should be down with his babies. He had been caught once sitting in the wheelhouse when the boat had capsized and, as she had righted herself, the engines had stopped. It had taken him seventeen seconds to get them running again and half that time was getting down past the survivors into his engine space. He swore to himself it would never happen again. Down in the confined spaces of the engine compartment, he could work miracles and he knew it. He could strip one of the Caterpillar engines blindfolded and then rebuild it. He could listen to the throaty burble become a roar as the coxswain hit the throttles and could see, in his mind, every part working in perfect harmony. He could diagnose a problem by smelling the exhausts, and run his hands over the casings and know by feeling them exactly which bearing was hot and how to fix it.

Once, after they had been out to find a yachtsman, he had reappeared in the wheelhouse with a cut on his head after being thrown against a sharp edge. He flatly refused to remain in his chair when Hal had spoken to him on the next trip out so they had compromised. Now, hanging on a clip in the engine space was a motorcyclist's helmet and, if he insisted on remaining below when the boat was jumping waves, then he was to wear the device.

The others called him Evil Ernie the stuntman, but they

appreciated his professionalism and Ernie just smiled and laughed and secretly remembered the time they had gone over, each second of silence from the engines seeming like an eternity, the huge waves tossing the Tyne-class boat about like a cork, beam on to the sea and in real trouble.

The last of the foursome who enjoyed a pint after a run in the boat was Carter's son Simon. At twenty-three, he was by far the youngest on the crew, but like his father he had been brought up in boats and was a natural, be it in the oyster dredger, the launch on which he crewed or on the *Maeve*. Carter always said there were two kinds of men on a boat. Those who saw things about to happen and went to it first and those who waited and watched and then did something. Simon was one of those who always saw it about to happen and went towards it. John Timson was a wait-and-watch type, and together, on a pitching deck, they moved in harmony, one covering for the other.

Simon was a good-looking, confident, laughing young man with a reputation as a prankster but, when the chips were down, he was there, time and time again. For Hal Carter there was no nepotism involved in his decision to add his son to the crew list. When he had taken over as coxswain he had looked for the best crew he could muster and actively sought out younger men, men who could gain experience and crew the boat for years to come.

The older men who had retired had laughed when he had looked for youngsters to replace them on the crew but, in the last two years, John Timson and Simon Carter had earned their places on the boat. John had pulled three French kids in over the low waist of the boat with a hand that later proved to have six broken bones. It had been caught between the hull of the *Maeve* and the casualty yacht when he had slipped as they were thrown together by a wave. That was why he never wore the yellow sea boots any more. They had let him down.

Simon had swum with a line to a couple trapped at the

base of a rock after their glass-fibre motorsailer had gone aground and broken up. Pulling an inflatable after him into the shallows, he had loaded them and had launched back into the big surf to get to the lifeboat, the couple terrified in the centre thwarts. Simon Carter had his mother's good looks and his father's down-to-earth attitude to life which meant that he didn't think he was good-looking. For the girls on St Mary's that combination made him irresistible.

John and Simon shared a house up by the church and every now and then Jean Carter would take matters in hand and walk up the hill, buckets, mops and dusters in hand, and stand over them while they cleaned the place up. Then she would have them both down to eat their evening meal at the Hugh Street house, a change from the pizzas and sausages which were all they seemed to have in their freezer. There, in what was once the kitchen, but was now an eating and sitting area, warmed by an Aga stove, they would sit and talk over the day. John Timson was almost part of the family now that he was walking out with Simon's sister Helen. The truth of it was that none of them really expected much to come of the relationship in spite of what they all might wish. Helen was nursing in Penzance and liked the discos and the nightlife on the mainland. She was, her mother knew, also seeing a young man more than she ought to if she were serious about John. He was an estate agent and wore suits to work, owned a car and had a mortgage on his own house.

Helen had explained it once: when she was on St Mary's, John Timson was right for her. He was a boatman, like her brother and father, a Scillonian, respected by the other men on the quay and on the fishing boats. When the wind brought waves over the sea wall down by the Mermaid and threw spray high over the rooftops on Hugh Street, when being an islander meant feeling safe in a storm, then it was John Timson's arm she wanted linked through hers.

But not on the mainland. Not in a city. Not in the real world. He had come to Penzance once to visit her. They had driven up to Falmouth and he had hated it, hated the crowds and the noise and the traffic. The trip had been awful and they had returned to St Mary's in silence. It was that night, when Jean Carter had listened to what her daughter had to say, that she finally accepted that Helen was not going to come home to the islands. Not to stay. She would visit, but she would not marry a local boy and raise a family in a house nearby.

Jean had told Hal as they lay in their old bed in the upstairs front room, the bed in which both children had been born. Hal had said that he knew. He always had done. That had been six months ago and it now made each visit all the more precious. Helen was due to arrive for a few days that night, so when the last of the load was on the quay at St Agnes, Hal turned the launch for home, eased the power settings forward and called the coastguard on the radio, letting him know where he was and his approximate arrival time.

Up on the deck John coiled a rope, a whistle on his lips and thoughts of Helen in his heart, his big hands gentle as if he were handling cut flowers and not the wet nylon warp.

I have to tell him sooner or later, Hal thought. He's a good lad with a heart as big as a house and he doesn't deserve to be frigged about by any woman, my daughter or not. The wind had veered and was cold. He zipped up his anorak and reached for his pipe, taking the tobacco from the flat tin and rubbing the flake back and forth in his callused hands, the boat rolling sluggishly beneath his feet.

Helen's bags were cluttering up the hall as Hal Carter stepped through the door from the street, hung his anorak on the peg by the front-room door and slipped his boots off. It was a small terraced house like the others on the older St Mary's streets, with a small front room, a hall and a kitchen on the ground floor. It had been converted a few years before and an extension held a new kitchen while the old became a family room with the television and bookcase, a pair of easy chairs and a small dining table pushed against one wall. A photograph of two young men in a sailing boat stood on the mantel and a print of a Trinity House lightship adorned one wall. It was a friendly room and in the winter the old Aga stove kept it warm as toast.

Helen was in the kitchen helping her mother, chattering about a car she wanted to buy and dipping her fingers into the chocolate sauce while she talked. Then, hearing her father come through, she walked across and kissed him fondly on the cheek.

'Hello, Dad.'

'Hello, lass. What time did you get in then?' He held her back to look at her. A shock of brown curly hair framed a soft pretty face and rosy cheeks.

'Came on the chopper. Saw the Johnsons and Mrs Conran, and Millie's new boyfriend was on it as well.'

Jean came over and handed him a cup of tea and he sat back in stockinged feet.

'Simon will be coming over for dinner,' Jean said to her daughter, 'and I think John will expect to walk you down to the Atlantic this evening.'

'Still drinking there, are they?'

The locals regularly changed their loyalties to the pubs and she found the Atlantic overcrowded and smoky.

'Perhaps if you ask John he will take you somewhere else,' her mother answered dryly. She knew that John would have taken her to the moon if she asked.

Hal looked up. Good a time as any, he thought. 'How long are you going to keep that young man waiting in hope?'

'Dad,' she said exasperatedly, her voice meaning, let's not bring this up again. Jean stepped through from the

42

kitchen, her own cup of tea in her hand, and sat at the small table.

'Your father is right, Helen. If you are not serious about John, then tell him. It's not fair on him. You come over one weekend a month if we are lucky and he waits here like a faithful dog for you.'

'I know . . . he's a very sweet man. It's just that . . .' She trailed off. 'I don't want to hurt him. I'll tell him soon . . . I promise.'

The conversation stopped then as Simon arrived, slamming the door with a crash behind him. Helen grinned and darted for the broom closet. It was an old game they played; she would hide and jump out at him.

'Hello, hello,' he bellowed. 'Don't hide, girly. I know you are here. Mrs Conran has told the entire street you are back.'

She stepped out of the closet, disappointed, as he entered from the hall.

'You always hide in the same place anyway,' he said as she came across for a kiss.

'Spoilsport!' she said. 'You need a haircut. You look like a yob.'

'Better than some Penzance skinhead,' he retorted.

'Only just,' she said.

'Hello, Mum, Dad,' he said, turning to face his parents. 'What's for dinner? I asked John if he wanted to come down. He is doing his hair and splashing on the Old Spice. Christ knows what for,' he added with a grin. 'A yacht down in the pool is causing problems.'

'Blue hull and white roof?' Hal asked.

Simon nodded. 'Aye. You saw it then.'

The conversation turned to the old favourite of visiting yachts and Helen watched them in silence as the two islanders, father and son, talked of the day, allowing her to arrive home slowly.

In the quiet front room with its small suite and glass-fronted cabinet, the room that was kept 'for best', for celebrations and visitors, six framed vellums hung on the walls. They were citations, given by the Royal National Lifeboat Institution for bravery.

David Parnell listened to the woman with all the interest he could muster. Flowers weren't on his list of riveting conversational topics, but any hope of shutting her up was long passed, so he nodded every now and then and tried to finish bandaging her knee as quickly as he could. The evening clinic was usually quiet but tonight had been a busy one and there was still a teenage visitor needing stitches in his foot in the next cubicle.

He finished off, handed over to the sister, and stepped through the curtain. The smell of suntan oil and beer wafted towards him and the young patient grinned weakly up at him.

'Stepped on a broken bottle, didn't I,' he said. 'Like a mug. Me first day here too.'

'Let's get you patched up then,' Parnell replied. 'When was your last tetanus injection?'

'Dunno. A couple of years ago maybe,' the lad answered too casually.

'Let's be safe then. I'll give you another.'

'Shit. I thought you would say that,' he said with an apprehensive look on his face.

'And you were right. Don't worry. I won't tell your girlfriend you are a wimp with needles.'

He got on with it and was finished twenty minutes later. With six neat sutures in the wound and with a nurse finishing the dressings and reading the riot act about getting it wet or walking on the foot, Parnell took off his white coat and slipped out of the back door.

He had been at the hospital on St Mary's for three months now and had seen the peak of the season come and go. He had arrived as a locum for the regular doctor and now the chap wasn't coming back and he had been offered the full-time position. It was a nice little hospital as they went. There were sixteen women's beds and eighteen for men, a small casualty and outpatient clinic and a very basic theatre where he could perform minor surgery. There was also a delivery room and a midwife. While they had no anaesthetist and no specialists of any kind, they did have a first-rate team of nursing staff, and fine nurses, he knew, could cure where specialists gave up. They had been pushed lately, short-staffed, but there was, apparently, another sister due tomorrow and that would put the team at full strength.

The doctor, whoever it might be, lived in a house next to the hospital, but the other man had yet to move out, so Parnell had taken a small bungalow one hundred yards up the road. It was a tatty place with a glassed-in porch pretending to be a conservatory and a tin roof that leaked in the rain. The garden was overgrown, tufts of grass growing up the sickly pink clapboard wall. The place was generally neglected but the rent was reasonable and it was close.

He walked up the gravel drive and, pushing his way in through the back door which he never locked, dropped his coat on the kitchen table and walked to the fridge. There, in company with a small piece of cheese and a sad-looking lettuce, was a single can of beer. He pulled the ring opener and walked through to the sitting room and dropped back into a chair. A big black cat appeared from nowhere and threaded itself through his legs.

'Hello, you big black bugger,' he said. 'Have you had a good day here in the Fortunate Isles?'

His accent was southern Irish and soft as was fitting for a man from the right side of Dublin. A dark shock of black hair dropped over his eyes every now and then and he swept it back with hands that could have been those of an artisan. They were strong, capable, the nails cut short. His cheeks showed the five o'clock shadow of men who are born in the Mediterranean, but the eyes gave away his ancestry. They were blue, the piercing blue of the Celtic and Norse blood that was present in most of the Irish.

'I suppose you want to be fed,' he said, taking a sip from the can. 'That's all you do, isn't it, eat and sleep and shit out there in that jungle of a garden?' He ran a hand down the cat's back and the animal arched its spine in pleasure and made a crying noise. The cat had been at the house when he arrived and slipped through the door ahead of him when he had opened it for the first time. Its look had said, I live here, pal, so who are you? They had made a truce then and it had held so far. He would feed it, stroke it, love it, take care of it, and, in return, the cat would do nothing whatsoever, other than eat, sleep and shit in the garden like it always had done. That was fine. They understood each other.

He got up and walked to the small pantry and, finding a tin of cat food amongst the other items, opened it and dumped the entire contents on to an old, chipped, blue saucer. The cat jumped on to the bench, dropped his big scarred head and tucked in.

There was a knock at the door so, carrying the can of beer, Parnell walked down the hall, stepped over a pile of Wellington boots, wetsuits and a windsurfer, and tugged at the handle. The door was warped. He tugged again and it swung open with a jerk.

'Sorry,' he said to the figure standing on the overgrown path, 'I don't use it very often . . . Can I help you?'

The man was tall and gaunt with thinning hair and horn-rimmed spectacles. A shapeless old tweed coat hung off his shoulders and he carried a soft leather briefcase.

'Dr Parnell, is it? I am Jeremy Dickerson, Honorary Secretary of the RNLI here on St Mary's. We spoke the other day on the phone . . .'

'Yes, yes, of course. Please come in.' He swung the door back and indicated that the visitor should enter. 'Sorry about the mess.'

'Oh,' Dickerson said, 'don't apologize. I'm rather glad to see you are the athletic type and like water.'

His eyes had a twinkle as he said it and he smiled thinly.

'Why might that be, Mr Dickerson? I thought you were here to touch me for a fiver.'

'Oh, good Lord, no ... Any donations gratefully received, of course, but it's another issue that brings me to your door ... yes, another issue.' He smiled again, peering at Parnell, who felt like a rare butterfly under a dropping net.

'What can I do for you, Mr Dickerson?'

'Call me Jeremy. Fancy walking down to the Bishop for a drink? In truth, Dr Parnell, I have a proposition to put to you and quaffing an ale would ease the way.'

My God, Parnell thought, quaff? Haven't heard that since someone re-ran a Peter O'Toole movie. Suddenly he liked the professorial old chap in his hall.

'Quaff a few, do you?' He grinned. 'Yes, let's go quaff an ale and hear your proposition.'

They walked down the hill in the dying daylight and soon were sitting at a small table in the Bishop and the Wolf public house.

'Know much about the RNLI, Doctor?' Dickerson began, with his ale in front of him, now all business.

'A little. Seen the boat on the water here. Volunteers who go out as needed.'

'Good enough. That lifeboat has seats for a crew of six.' He stopped there to take a sip of his drink. 'There is also room for a doctor. Ideally we would like a doctor on every service but we accept that that is unrealistic. However, when the time comes that we think a doctor should be aboard, are you prepared to help? Turn out with the crew?'

Parnell sat back, his mind racing. The old boy had gone straight for the throat! On the bloody lifeboat! Jesus!

'You will want to think about it, of course ... Normally the weather is awful and obviously there is some element of risk, but the coxswain, Harold Carter, is a man whom I would trust with my life and the boat is as good as they come.'

'Did my predecessor ... ?'

'No, sadly not. He is a man in his fifties, as you know, portly and he gets seasick. Puked just thinking about it.' Dickerson grinned like a lean old jackal. 'But not you, lad, windsurfer in the hall, wetsuits on the floor. You are a natural for it!'

Parnell studied him for a few seconds. The noise increased as others gathered at the bar and a wave of laughter rolled across towards them. Dickerson looked back at him, his eyes unwavering.

'I know why they made you the honorary secretary. Because you get people to do things, don't you?' Parnell said resignedly.

'Damn right, boy.' He laughed then, a dry crackle like brush burning. 'I may look like a doddery old fool, but don't treat me like one. Tell you what. There is a training run coming up soon. I'll talk to Hal and get him to give you a ring. Go out with the boys and see what you think.'

Better tell Hal not to overdo it, Dickerson thought to himself as he sat back. Don't go surfing the boat down the front side of waves, or allowing her to broach. Let's get the chap hooked on it, nice and slow. He had been out himself once on a full training run with no holds barred. A gale blowing and big seas. He had been terrified from start to finish, every time the boat had gone up the side of a wave, it seemed it would never come down. But it did with a crashing, jarring, bone-numbing fall over the wave. Great, huge, steep-sided walls of grey, green, spume-laced water that seemed to be reaching out for them as they fell, trying to crush them in their arrogant little cockle-shell boat. He had never gone out again and, to compensate, he had redoubled his efforts ashore.

'Sometimes out there . . . there are people hurt. Injured. Very often by the time we get there they are already dead. Drowned. For those that have survived that long, it can be a rough ride back to shore. They need more than our first-aiders can manage.'

Parnell had been thinking in the last few days. He wasn't

sure he wanted to stay on the island. He had come to heal himself as much as anything. Immerse himself in something new, a new place and new people. Get over her. It had worked. The wound was healing well. Just some nights he sat alone now, fighting the memories, and, less often, he eased the pain with the bottle of Jamesons in the cupboard.

The tranquillity had been welcome then. But now it was too quiet. Too many old ladies with skin problems and people who came to surgery because they were lonely. He had been in a small community before. The gossip which amused him at first became boring and, finally, an irritation. Everyone knew everyone else and there was no privacy, none of the wonderful anonymity of a bigger place and none of the kind of medicine he liked. The kind that was worthwhile. Now this. It was the sort of commitment he didn't want to have to make. He looked across at Dickerson as the realization set in. He was a doctor. If they needed him before he finally left for sunnier climes, then so be it.

'All right. Get your captain to give me a call, but if it conflicts with the surgery hours or . . .'

'Oh, dear me, yes, of course. Perfectly understand . . . Coxswain.' Dickerson added. 'He's called the coxswain.'

The Right Honourable James Lawler, MP, Member for Chichester, Prime Minister and leader of the Conservative Party, ran a hand through his hair, lit one of the thin cheroots he favoured, and looked down at the papers spread before him. He still had the contents of the dispatch box to read once he was home, but if he could get through this material compiled by the Foreign Secretary, then he would be well briefed for the two meetings that would run back to back until eight thirty or nine that night. The first was with a team from the Foreign Office and the second, but still dealing with the same issue, was with his Secretary for Defence. Both of those were preliminary

49

to the main cabinet meeting scheduled for Monday morning.

If things went well, he could be home by ten thirty or eleven. Not upstairs at Downing Street, but at the family home outside the tiny village of Cocking in Sussex.

It was the deal he had made with Heather the day he had stood for his first seat twenty-five years before. Home for the weekend. It had become tougher in recent years, since his move down to the front bench in the House. He had held the portfolios of Secretary for Northern Ireland, Trade and Industry, and Defence and each function had brought its own stresses and demands. Only rarely had he broken the deal and on each occasion Heather had understood. She was the perfect wife for a politician. Attractive, supportive, tactful, clever, articulate, well educated and sensitive to the nuances that could fuel the tabloid papers in their irregular feeding frenzies.

Their home, a listed farmhouse on the edge of the village, was beautifully maintained, the gardens famous in themselves. They were, as modern couples go, as happy as they could ever hope to be. They did want more children, but when their son David was born there were complications and further conceptions became impossible. Heather got over her disappointment and, in time, became the patron of a group seeking funding for development work on the condition, prepared to forgo her own privacy in the effort to give the group some support. She also threw herself into the raising of their son. With his father away at Westminster, so much of the burden fell squarely on her shoulders and she relished the task.

She stood now in the spacious kitchen of that beautiful house, a big pair of scissors in her hand. Spread across a scrub-top table in front of her were flowers from the garden, the last blooms of the late summer, which she was cutting and arranging in a deep crystal vase.

She would finish and then put the kettle on for the boys at the gate. The police detail didn't expect coffee and biscuits but she felt it was the least she could do. She had, however, trained them enough to overcome their embarrassment at having the Prime Minister's wife make them coffee and they now came willingly to the kitchen door at seven each evening to collect the tray.

It was a habit the press had caught on to but thankfully had not publicized. They said the nation would love it, but the police didn't want anyone knowing that at times, however briefly, there was only one man at the gate and so the press had agreed to keep it from their pages.

Heather Lawler was tall, with brown hair that had shown grey streaks since her early twenties, and a figure that still kept her husband interested. She considered herself fortunate. Gifted with health, a husband who loved her, her wonderful son David and a beautiful home. She considered herself so fortunate that she sometimes worried that something seemed bound to give. Fate was not that kind.

If this person, who considered herself blessed, had a fear that she could confide to her husband or herself, it was the fear of losing David, of something happening to him. It was with that in the front of her mind and telling herself that every parent worries that she agreed to his joining his classmates for an educational cruise to Iceland. She couldn't refuse. She knew the peer pressure on each of the boys was equal, the need to be there, to be seen and to be a part of it all. Anything rather than be different, the odd one out. After all Sergeant Carstairs would be going along. It was a big ship. A British ship. What could happen?

John Timson and Helen and Simon Carter threaded their way down to the end of the bar at the Atlantic. John had a stool that he customarily headed for, the last along the bar nearest the big picture windows that overlooked the boats and the pool. From the stools, drinkers could look out and see the boats tugging on their moorings and past them to the *Maeve*, her orange wheelhouse standing out in the dying light and her sharp flared bows into the wind. Along the back wall there was a fireplace, now filled with designer marine memorabilia for the tourists – nameplates from famous ships, old wheels, anchors, the obligatory photographs of wrecks – and a row of small tables for those who chose to eat from the menu.

John stood a good head higher than anyone else in the room and as he moved forward towards the end of the bar, proudly holding Helen's hand, his face wore a huge grin. He winked at the barmaid as she approached.

'Mine's a pint,' she called, giving a very credible impression of his voice and mannerism.

John smiled. He had been saying that as his first line here for years now. 'And a gin and tonic and a pint for Simon.' He offered Helen the stool but, knowing him and his ways, she opted for the one beside it and sat down for an evening of being adored, something she thought every woman should have at least once a week.

The place was filling up and, although it was mostly locals up at the bar, there were a few visitors scattered around the tables. Simon saw two girls sitting at the fireplace table. Their faces were soft in the muted red light that bathed the area. One blonde and curly and the other with dark straight hair that shone and moved like a living thing whenever she shook her head.

'That's me,' he said.

'Which one?' John asked, knowing full well which it would be. They had been friends for years and he had seen Simon on the chase many times. Asking was simply good form.

Before Simon could reply Helen answered. 'The dark one. He likes that Italian look . . . all very well now but wait till she has had a couple of kids and four thousand pizzas . . .'

'I'm not going to marry her. Just buy her a drink,' he replied innocently.

'Bed her more like it,' Helen replied, laughing. 'Oh, go on for God's sake. We will see you later.'

The following morning when Parnell arrived to do his ward rounds she was there. The new sister. But not just any sister. It was she.

She of the flashing green eyes and the rich brown hair, of the sweaty crumpled sheets and fierce lovemaking, of the spitting anger and soft compassion, of his dreams and his despair, of scratches down his back and long legs and a laugh like pealing bells, of Sunday lunches and long walks, of stories of her home in the Aran Islands, of open fires and welcoming arms, of the taste of her tears, of going to America and leaving him. Hannorah Madden.

The senior sister went to introduce her.

'Dr Parnell, this is Sister . . .'

'We have met,' he said, without taking his eyes off her. 'Hello, Norah.'

THREE

Nichols threw his cap down on his bunk and walked across to the small night stand with its iced water jug. His quarters were smaller than Wellbrook's, a day cabin with two easy chairs and a desk, and a night cabin with a single bunk, wardrobe and bedside locker. Just off the night cabin was a very compact but complete bathroom. It was spartan in comparison to the captain's. The walls were bare except for a pair of faded framed prints.

A couple of motor magazines lay spread across the locker top. A shelf of paperbacks ran along one bulkhead and a lone Polaroid photograph leant against the mahogany panelling. The picture was of a blonde sitting at a restaurant table, a woman in her thirties, an impish smile on her face. He poured himself a glass of water and sat back on the bed, sipping it slowly. The steward would be along with a tray in a minute and after a cup of tea and a smoke he would shower and get something to eat. He began to strip off his clothing, the deck moving beneath his feet as the ship met the big Atlantic swells bow on.

Fifteen minutes later he was in the officers' mess where they were serving breakfast, the one meal that the galley on the *Caledonia* prided itself on. A smart white cloth on the table, old-fashioned toast racks and butter balls were the order of the day. Large china plates, sporting the company crest, came laden with eggs, bacon, tomatoes, mushrooms and baked beans for those who wanted them. There were also sausages, devilled kidneys and, on Sunday mornings, eggs benedict. Coffee was served constantly and the toast rack was restocked with hot slices every five minutes.

Jars of old English thick-cut marmalade sat beside more exotic preserves in the centre of the table. On the sideboard there were jugs of chilled juices, bowls of fruit and boxes of cereal. In the colder months porridge was served with cream and brown sugar. Someone had once suggested a Continental breakfast of rolls and ham and cheese and had received such a look from the chief cook that he had never mentioned it again.

Nichols took his usual chair with its back to the scuttle and reached for the two-day-old papers from Reykjavik. He had read them three times already but there was nothing else. Jeffries and the second engineer would be in any moment. They too had finished their watches.

'The usual, Mr Nichols?'

'Thank you,' he said without looking up. The plate arrived a moment later, grilled tomatoes on toast with three rashers of crisply cooked bacon. He began to eat and only looked up when the second engineer sat down opposite. Eamon Colly was a tall thin man with a protruding Adam's apple and a nose that looked more like a beak. When he laughed, it sounded like a donkey braying. Nichols liked to watch him eat. He would take huge forkfuls of food and, as the mound approached, his mouth would begin to open, the lower jaw seeming to dislocate like that of an egg-eating snake. The maw would close and the Adam's apple would bob once or twice and then he would swallow without seeming to chew. Nichols found the entire performance endlessly fascinating.

'Good shift, Eamon?' he asked.

'Aye, not bad. Boat davit's all greased up but the for'ard winch is only halfway there.' As second engineer, his day-to-day responsibility was preventative maintenance. 'Bloody kids leaning over me shoulder.'

'They are about early,' Nichols said. He had seen them from the bridge, the group with slick wet hair from their showers, moving up the gently pitching deck towards the bows. It was an excursion, the long route to breakfast.

Pushing and jostling each other, they were enjoying the fresh air and the bite of the breeze.

'They are that.' Colly signalled to the steward and looked back at Nichols. 'With a bit of luck they will all get seasick and remain in their bunks till Southampton,' he finished.

'You are a cheerless bastard, Number Two,' Nichols replied.

'I came to sea to get away from the little buggers. I've five at home, you know. Eggs and bacon, please.'

Jeffries arrived then, his hair wet and combed, dressed in jeans and a sports shirt with a sweater over the top. He was now off watch like his two seniors at the table and looked like he should be shopping in a high-street Sainsbury's somewhere.

He moved to the sideboard and began heaping bran cereal into a bowl before covering it with fruit.

'Anyone fancy a movie?' he asked, sitting down.

'Got any new ones?' the second engineer asked.

'No. Thought we could chuck *Blade Runner* on again.'

'Jesus. That must be the fiftieth time.'

'What about *Working Girl*?' the junior offered pleasantly.

Eamon Colly looked up, his watery eyes suddenly showing interest in something other than the food he could see making its way towards him in the hands of the steward. 'Is that about prostitutes?' he asked quickly.

'No. It's not. It's about a secretary who makes it big,' Jeffries answered patiently.

'Oh,' Colly murmured disappointedly. His plate was put in front of him and Nichols sat back to watch the performance. It reminded him of *Wildlife on One*.

'What about you, Mr Nichols? Fancy Melanie Griffiths?'

'No, thanks. I'm going to get my head down for a bit.'

Opposite him the maw opened again and an entire fried egg, half a slice of toast and a rasher of bacon disappeared. The gullet moved and the fork was coming up, loaded once more.

Incredible, he thought. It's like a rubbish compactor.

He looked back at Jeffries who was watching him watch Colly.

The youngster grinned.

'Tell you what we have got. *Jaws*,' he said, with an expression that suggested that butter wouldn't melt in his mouth.

Nichols coughed a laugh into his napkin, drained the last of his coffee and stood up to leave.

Back in his cabin he pulled the blackout curtain across the closed scuttle and settled back on the bunk, a paperback from the small ship's library in his hand. He tried the first page but his mind was on other things and he dropped it back across his chest and looked at the photograph standing on the bookshelf.

Her name was Susan and he had met her at a party at the home of a friend of a friend. He had arrived and within minutes was bored by the talk of house prices, poll tax and the commuting time up to London. The noise level was rising and couples were pairing off. Finally he had seen the small balcony overlooking the garage on the quiet suburban street and, stepping out to escape, he had found her there.

She had looked across at him and smiled. It was a hard, bitter expression.

'You too?'

'Sorry?'

'You too. Bored to death by it all?'

He smiled then. 'Yes, I'm afraid so.'

'I'm surprised you aren't upstairs then.'

'Why? What's upstairs?' he asked.

'A woman I know,' she answered a little sourly, 'and some of the others, and some "special" videos they're watching.'

'Ah . . . sorry. Not my scene,' Nichols answered.

'Oh. I thought you were one of the inner circle,' she said dryly.

'No.'

'What are you then? You don't fit with this crowd down-stairs and you aren't with the hedonists upstairs.'

'Just a guy on leave. That's all.'

'Army?'

'No. Merchant marine.'

'Ah, "Home is the sailor, home from sea . . ."'

'". . . And the hunter home from the hill,"' he finished.

'My God. A well-read sailor too. I thought you all just spiked marlins or something.' She was smiling now, the hardness gone.

'Gosh, no. These days we can write and everything.'

She laughed then. It was a throaty, sexy laugh that came from deep within, the laugh lines round her eyes creasing gently. The eyes, he noticed, were blue, as blue as the light waters over a reef. She was, he thought, quite beautiful.

'*Touché*,' she offered gallantly.

They talked for a while, the verbal jousting relaxing into a gentler art and finally he drained his drink and turned to leave before stopping and turning back to face her again.

'I don't suppose . . . ?'

'What?' she asked, the hardness back.

'I was going to ask if you would like to come into town and have something to eat.'

'So the gang bang wasn't your thing but candlelight seduction is?' she flashed sarcastically.

He looked at her and stiffened, his eyes narrowing.

'No. I haven't eaten all day. So I am going to. I thought you might like to eat as well. I spend most of my time cooped up in a ship with the same group of people. I thought this might make a pleasant change. It was a simple invitation. No more, no less.'

He turned and began to walk towards the doors into the lounge.

'Wait. I am sorry. That was very rude of me.' She walked towards him. 'If the invitation is still open, I would love to come.'

He looked at her and finally smiled.

'My name is John Nichols.'

'Susan Farmer . . . Susan. Not Sue.'

'OK, Susan not Sue.'

'I won't come to bed with you. You have to know that,' she said quickly.

He didn't know what to say to that so he just nodded and led the way past the noisy drinkers and passionate embraces and on down the stairs.

They found an Italian restaurant up a narrow side street, complete with the obligatory candles in Chianti bottles and checked red tablecloths. The fake rafters were festooned with plastic grapes, and a poster of Venice was stuck with tape to a bad attempt at stucco plaster on the walls.

'Jesus,' he said, looking around, 'this looks awful. Shall we move on and find something else?'

'No.' She smiled. 'Don't you dare. You have found the best cannelloni in the south of England. The decor is, as you say, awful but the food here is great!'

'How do you know?' he asked sceptically, raising an eyebrow at the surroundings.

'I have a friend who is a food and wine writer. She rates it.'

During the meal, a roving photographer stopped at the table and took a picture of them and they finished the evening walking along the seafront towards her flat. At the door she stopped and studied him for the hundredth time.

'Where are you staying?'

'Not sure,' he replied. 'I'll find something.'

'Have you got a toothbrush even?'

He laughed. 'Yes. In a bag in a locker at the station. Thanks for having dinner with me.'

'Thank you,' she said, her expression softening.

He turned and began to walk away and, after a long moment, she called after him.

'Shit! Look . . . I have a sleeping bag.'

'Sorry?' He had stopped and turned to face her from

twenty yards away beneath the glow of a street light.

'I have a sleeping bag . . . the couch is quite long if you chuck the cushions on the floor. You can stay the night . . . in the drawing room.'

He smiled. His mother used to call it the drawing room. He thought for a second or two. The station was a good two miles away and the chances of a taxi were remote at this hour with the pubs spilling out their patrons.

'Thanks,' he said, moving back towards her. 'It will save me a walk.'

She had thrown him the sleeping bag with a forced formality, a frostiness that suggested she had already regretted making the offer. He settled back on the long chintz-covered sofa, lit a cigarette and studied the room in the soft light from the hall. It was filled with an odd collection of things from many places, some patently expensive, while others, like the faded postcards in a collage, were there purely for their sentimental value. He could hear her in the bathroom. It was a pleasant normal sort of sound of running water, teeth being brushed, bottles moving on shelves. It was all so unlike the ship with its cramped quarters, constant vibrations and motion. Suddenly her head popped round the door. The make-up was gone and her hair was back in an Alice band. Without the make-up she was startlingly attractive in a healthy farm-girl kind of way. She seemed relieved to see him in the sleeping bag, as if she were safe to come in.

'Coffee?' she asked.

'If you are.'

'I've only got sweeteners.' She said it as if that might put him off, maybe even send him off down the road.

'Sit down, Susan.'

'I told you that I wouldn't . . .' she began defensively.

'I know. Sit down.' He pointed across to the chair opposite. 'Over there where you are safe in case I leap up.'

She sat. On the edge of the chair.

'What is the problem?' he asked.

She snatched her cigarettes from the table and lit one, puffing hurriedly.

'No problem. I just shouldn't have offered you the night here, that's all,' she said, blowing smoke.

'Look. We met tonight. We chatted. We had something to eat. I actually enjoyed your company because every now and then you forget you hate the whole world and relax, and then, Susan Farmer, you are a nice lady. But then you get angry again and that isn't much fun. I don't know what happened to you. But whatever it was wasn't my fault.' He stood up, dropped the sleeping bag down his legs and reached for his trousers, completely unselfconscious in his underwear. 'There's a hotel near the station. I'll spend the night there.'

As the door closed behind him, he thought he heard her begin to cry, deep racking sobs that came from her very soul.

Nichols had checked in and slept the sleep of the dead. His shore leaves were regular enough and he loved the break in the watch system which allowed him to sleep normal hours. This time, however, he rose early and had taken a walk and was back at the hotel in time for the dining room to open. He ate a full cooked breakfast, mulling over what to do with the day and then the next three days, before he was due back aboard *Caledonia*. He had no relatives left to speak of, a brother in Canada, an aunt in London whom he barely knew and a cousin somewhere in Malta. With no family pressures on his time, he used it to travel, usually around the south coast.

Born and brought up in Falmouth, ships were his life just as, to his family, they were something to be avoided as far as possible. His father had been a bank manager in the town. His mother was an uncertain woman who seemed to welcome growing old as if she need no longer worry about her looks to keep his father happy. He had had his dalliances over the years, turned up to the Rotary lunches and joined the local golf club and had been thoroughly bored by the entire first forty years of his life. One day he had announced himself sick of his job and the golf club. He told Rotary what to do and made plans to sell up and buy a nursery. He had ended his days an eccentric widower talking to pine seedlings.

Born late in their lives, Nichols had watched all this, one eye on his parents' unhappiness, the other eye on the ships that sailed away from the port and on out to the world. He had joined as soon as his age had allowed and, within the next five years, had visited every major port in the world and never once regretted his decision to go to sea. It was his love, as much as that of Drake or Nelson.

What to do with the next few days, he wondered. There was a village in Cornwall he rather liked. Perhaps he should head down there. He was reaching for the coffee pot when the waitress came to a halt at his table.

'Are you the gentleman in room 34?'

He nodded, his mouth full.

'A call for you. You can take it at the reception.'

Shit, he thought. Some bugger is sick and I'm back to sea on the tide.

'Thanks,' he said.

He walked through to the reception and took the phone off the desk where it sat.

'Nichols.'

'John?' It was a woman's voice.

'Yes.' Not the company. The superintendent of operations had a secretary but he made the recall calls himself. Then he suddenly remembered that he hadn't phoned in yet with his contact number.

'It's Susan . . . Susan Farmer.'

'Oh . . . hello,' he said, surprised that she would call, that she would bother to track him down, look up the number. For what? To feel threatened by him again?

'I wanted to apologize. For last night.'

He knew it was difficult for her to say that. Difficult to admit.

'That's OK. Forget it.'

'I'm driving up to Arundel today. Got to see someone . . . I thought that you might . . . well . . . if you aren't doing anything . . . maybe you would like to come for the ride.'

He smiled to himself. An olive branch.

'Love to,' he said. 'Perhaps we can stop somewhere and have a ploughman's and a pint.'

'I know a place . . .' she said, some caution still in her voice.

'Done then.'

'I'll pick you up in an hour.'

They had seen much of each other over the next three days. She told him she was a journalist and worked for ITN and, like him, didn't have parents. On the last night she cooked a barbecue on a small gas unit on her balcony and had invited a couple over. They sat and talked and joked. The other two assumed that they, too, were a couple, partners, the girl half of the other pair studying him with frank looks as if evaluating him and his suitability.

The whole arrangement had had an odd feeling because Susan would not allow him close. The moment he came within inches of her, she seemed to stiffen, battling some urge to fight or flee. When the time came to go and Nichols had to leave to get the last train to Southampton, the atmosphere suddenly became forced, Susan distant and tense.

'Thank you,' he said. 'I enjoyed the weekend very much, hogging your time like that.'

'My pleasure,' she said briskly.

'I come ashore here regularly,' he said. 'Would you like to do something next time?'

'If you like.' Again the briskness, the defensive shield.

'No. What would you like?'

She said nothing and it was time for the goodbye kiss so, playing safe, he brushed his finger across his lips and ran it down her nose.

Later when she was tidying up she found a sweater of his behind the sofa and began to fold it neatly the way her mother had taught her, but then something inside her cracked and the strength ebbed away and she sat on the arm of the chair and hugged it close, smelling him, his aftershave, his strong French cigarettes. Cuddling him close as if he were still there.

Please phone, please phone, please be different, please be good to me, don't be another bastard, and she began to cry again. Ten minutes later she straightened her shoulders angrily, brushed the tears away and threw the sweater against the wall.

The last man she had let come close had left her seven thousand pounds poorer, with her teeth loosened and her cheekbone cracked. She had confronted him about sleeping around and he had attacked her. The evidence was irrefutable. You don't find photographs in a jacket pocket and ignore them.

He stayed the next two days. The longest two days of her life, beating her in a drunken rage, using her brutally as he saw fit. Afterwards she felt degraded, abused and soiled.

Her body had healed but her trust and her pride and her heart were still tender. She began to cry, wondering if she would ever trust again.

He put the book down on the bedside locker top. Susan was attractive and, even better, she was interesting. Not the run of the mill at all. He had had his share of fleeting romances but the lure of the sea had prevented any of them ever becoming too serious. They all made the ultimatum eventually. Me or the job. Why can't you do something on land like normal people? To her his having a job that demanded things of him seemed acceptable and yet there was something else there. Something had hurt her, because that amount of caution wasn't natural. She would be worth the effort to get close to because, if he managed it, he knew instinctively that deep down she could be twenty-four-carat gold.

He felt the easy roll of the ship beneath him and, in the warm bunk, the motion was soporific. He switched off the reading light and settled down to sleep.

Down the passage Sergeant Robert Carstairs relaxed in slacks and a plaid shirt. The boys would not be breaking for a while yet, but he checked his timetable to make sure. Down in the 'tween decks classroom they would be in a double geography period. He grinned to himself. He had hated geography at school. The only thing about the subject that was the least bit interesting to him was the maps bit, because he knew he wanted to travel. The geology side was dreadful. Knowing that he wanted to join the Metropolitan Police, he had forced himself to understand mathematics, physics and English because without those he would never have got into university and the graduate entry programme. Now he was fast-track material and in the next year, back in Special Branch proper, would make inspector. For now, he mused, he was half bodyguard and half social secretary to a fourteen-year-old. He couldn't pretend he didn't get along with the Prime Minister's son. David was a likeable relaxed fellow, sometimes a bit quiet and distant, but all there nevertheless. And not such a child any more. One or two of the girls in Reykjavik had displayed interest and he had enforced the curfew several times. Since the bomb the previous year his full-time job was ensuring that the lad arrived home in the same healthy state he had left it in.

Carstairs thought back to the first time the boy had confided in him. It had been on a delicate issue when David had announced, quite unsolicited, that he thought a certain cabinet minister was a complete prat. He had then smiled disarmingly and said, 'You won't tell my father I said that, will you?'

Carstairs had assured his young charge that his secrets were safe and sometimes, in the evenings, when he had finished a bit of unofficial tutoring on some mathematics or physics homework problem, the boy would begin to talk to him about his life, the extraordinary circumstances of a teenager who was not allowed to be a normal teenager, and yet not allowed to be an adult either.

The staffing levels surrounding the family varied according to his father's duties and increased when they were resident at Downing Street where he was exposed to the other support staff, the private secretaries, the political advisers and the protection team, now a large group since the increased IRA threat. This had recently manifested itself as seven kilos of Semtex under a bridge the family used to cross when travelling into Chichester. Then, last year, there had been the man found loitering near the school. His republican background had worried everyone and Special Branch had confirmed that he was on their list of suspected active IRA members.

On the passage north the boy had confided that he liked the gruff manners and no-nonsense attitude of the protection men and found the patronizing manner of others boring. Carstairs had smiled and said that so would most young men of his age.

But most young men of his age didn't have to live up to his father's legend. A few months before, David had again confided in his bodyguard, who was driving him back home for an exit weekend.

'Problems?' Carstairs had asked casually, the boy's face miserable.

There was no answer so he sat quietly, knowing that it would come out in a few minutes. The boy, like his father, only spoke when he was ready and then held strong views on most things.

'Who am I?'

Carstairs looked across at him.

'What's brought this on then?' he asked.

David said nothing, the rules on telling tales as strict in his group as any other.

'Well, who do you think you are?' Carstairs tried another tack.

'I'm not the son of a bloody tradesman with a gong!'

'Ah . . . and who said you were?'

'Hacking's aunt,' he said miserably.

Hacking was one of the boys in the group and one of those close enough to have been invited to the family home last Christmas.

Carstairs knew of Hacking's aunt. A champagne socialist who had divorced her penniless peer husband and married a millionaire industrialist, presumably, he thought, so she could criticize the world in comfort. What the boy didn't know was that his father, as a bachelor, had constantly spurned the woman's interest back in the late sixties.

'She said this to you?' Carstairs asked.

'No. Hacking heard her say it to someone.'

'Well, I shouldn't worry about it. I'm afraid it comes with the territory. Everybody thinks you have an easy time of it. We know different, eh?'

'What do you really think . . . honestly?'

Carstairs studied the boy. He was obviously quite upset by the remark.

'Really?'

'Yes . . . please.'

He had been briefed to expect this kind of thing and had been warned not to take a stand on any issue. Keep your distance, they said. Remain impartial and do your job. Leave the formulation of young minds to those charged with their development. You just make sure he is safe and doesn't make any solo trips. Remember that until three years ago he led a relatively normal life. No bombs. No terrorist threat with his name on it. But Carstairs had become fond of the boy and he felt he deserved an answer.

'It's your circumstances, David. A kid out of the Gorbals is labelled by his accent and his attitudes. A kid from a middle-class family in Denver, Colorado, is the same. You have a different label to any of them. You happen to be the son of one of the most powerful leaders in the Western world. But you are young. It will take some getting used to. By the time you do, you probably won't need it . . .' Carstairs grinned then. 'Unlike those other kids your role is determined, for the time being anyway, and no one ever said it would be easy. People will say things about your father, about your family. Anyone awarded a medal like your father deserved it. Irrespective of their background. Anyway, he's hardly a tradesman.'

'Sometimes . . .' David began, then trailed off.

Carstairs smiled. 'What?'

'Sometimes I feel that people expect me to be the same as him.'

'They will. It's natural enough. You look like him. Talk like him. Every son is measured against his father. Usually by idiots.'

'I'm afraid that when the time comes I will let them down.'

'Who? Your folks? That's crap, David. They will love you whatever you are.'

'I don't mean that,' he said, almost to himself. 'I mean the medal thing. I wonder, will I be as brave when my turn comes?'

Carstairs thought about that for a second or two.

'Courage is relative, David. The fireman who goes into a burning building is well trained, well supported and experienced. To the observer he is brave. To his colleagues he is doing his job just like they are.'

'But my dad wasn't a fireman,' the boy said.

'No,' Carstairs said, 'he wasn't,' regretting having used the fireman analogy.

It had happened years before. A car had hit a tractor

and trailer on a bend, overturning them both, the vehicles ending up together on the verge. The trailer, a hundred-gallon tank on an axle, contained paraffin and, when the car began to burn, the people that had stopped to help heeded the tractor driver's screamed warning from the ground where he lay.

Lawler, twenty years old, had pulled to a stop fifty yards from the scene and had run back. A woman was shouting that there were still people in the car and over the noise he could hear the screams from the Rover. He ran through the flames three times, his coat over his head, to drag each of the injured occupants clear in turn.

Both of the adults had died of their injuries, the shock and the dreadful burns. The girl, seven years old, with the resilience of youth, had survived. Lawler, his left hand, arm and neck badly burnt, had also been taken to hospital. One of the people at the scene, a stringer for a local paper, had a camera and had taken pictures. Another witness had been the wife of the local magistrate. The story, human drama in its purest form, made the national press and the following year the young man received the George Medal, the nation's highest civil award for courage, from the Queen. Although he never mentioned it himself, the tale was still told and his courage and his modesty had endeared him to the nation.

'It was a very brave thing to do. But don't worry about living up to it. Thankfully, very few people ever find themselves in those circumstances . . . Anyway, Hacking's aunt is a prat.'

The boy looked across at Carstairs, delighted that he had used his word and smiled, feeling much better.

He now walked in and threw his books on his bunk. As a prefect he got the only 'study' while the others had to sleep in the dormitory of the main accommodations. It was useful and meant that his bodyguard could share with him.

'What now?'

'Oh,' he answered, 'a tour of the engine room and then

back in for physics. I think I'd like to see the bridge tonight. Could you ask the chief officer if I could?'

'You did the engine room on the trip north, didn't you?'

Carstairs knew full well they had. He also knew what was planned by the teachers every minute of the day. But showing interest simply by asking was important.

'Yes, but this time we are looking at delivered power. Torque,' David explained.

'Ah, I see.'

'What about the bridge tonight? Will you ask Mr Nichols? Please? He said I could have some helm time and see how the Navitex works.'

'Certainly will. Come on then. Let's go see the engines.'

'Engine,' David corrected. 'There is only one.'

Jarvis, the bosun, dressed in blue working trousers and a heavy sweater, stepped through the coaming and moved down the passage into the crew's mess. The air from the ventilation system seemed canned after the fresh blusteriness on the deck.

The mess was small, three formica-topped tables dominating the floor area, with a video and television up on a high shelf. A counter ran along the for'ard end, separating the tables from the crew galley. The food passed across the shiny stainless steel surface.

He would have the place largely to himself now and he liked that. Years ago, when he had gone to sea as a boy, the entire crew would have been British, but now with costs the way they were, things had changed. Now deck hands and able seamen came from Sri Lanka and India, and, in the case of the *Caledonia*, the Philippines. He didn't dislike the new ways. He simply found that he had little in common with most of the Filipinos and, while he was a loner by nature, he did miss the easy camaraderie of his fellow countrymen. He was the only one left down here now. In the galley there was a wok where once a frying pan had held pride of place.

They did look after him, however. If he ever felt the dishes in the crew galley weren't to his taste, he would just have to give the steward a nod and he could have something brought from the officers' galley – but that was a rare day and the three Asians in the crew galley now had pies and stews and heavy puddings down to a fine art, just for him. They seemed to enjoy the challenge and watched, beaming over the counter, as he tasted each new offering from the *Woman's Weekly* cookbook which one of them had found.

He walked across to the big urn and, taking a tea bag, dropped it into a china mug and watched the scalding hot water course over it. He jiggled the bag once or twice and then slopped in a goodly amount of long-life milk straight from its cardboard carton and finally sat down on the long upholstered bench along the aft bulkhead. Behind his head there was a rack, with two stacks of magazines loosely grouped as 'general interest' and 'ships' but, having read everything before, he ignored them.

A lithe figure, dressed in a pair of old trousers and a clean pressed shirt, stepped through the door and walked directly to the urn.

Jarvis nodded his greeting. Ed Reyes was one Filipino with whom Jarvis did have something in common. They had sailed together on the company ships for seven years now.

Four years before, while the ship was docked in Manila, Jarvis, feeling disenchanted with the West and Western women, had met his match. Seventeen years old, tiny, elegant, enchanting and feminine, she had wrapped the big Yorkshireman round her little finger and her heart. Florry and Cecil Jarvis were married at the end of a week. Jarvis had, for the first time in his life, worn a bow tie and frilly shirt and, although he had felt a complete fool, he would have done anything for Florry. Amid the tears of family partings he had taken her home to England and installed her in a small terraced house in Southampton where she was, much to everyone's surprise, blissfully happy. She was a stalwart of the Catholic Church, and helped run the Mission to Seamen, Filipino section. The man who introduced them, Ed Reyes, now Jarvis's brother-in-law, moved across to join him, a mug of tea in his hand.

'Morning,' he said, sitting down.

'Thought about it then, Ed?'

'Sorry?'

'Christmas.' The bosun rubbed a massive hand across his lopsided face where it itched. 'You've got days off, right?'

'Yes.'

'Florry would love to have you. You know that.'

Florry had made the suggestion on his last leave and he knew just how much she would love to have her big brother to her home for Christmas. She had sat up naked on the bed after they had made love, the two baby girls shrieking and giggling downstairs, and read him out the menu she was thinking of – a rich rolling feast of turkey and ham and fresh pineapple and spicy fish, a spanning of two cultures.

'I know she would.' Ed grinned. 'The trouble is I'm still waiting for an extra day's request to come through. If it does, I want to get back to Manila if I can.'

Jarvis knew that Ed's own family, three sons and a daughter, would be expecting him home if he could make it.

'Well, Florry finished the spare room last month, so it's ready and there if you want it.'

The ship rolled heavily over a wave and, down in the hold, the cargo gave a shrieking, steely groan and the plates shifted against each other.

Jarvis listened for a second. 'I fucking hate coal, I fucking hate rice, but . . .' and Ed joined in, so they chorused '. . . I really fucking hate steel!'

They both laughed and Jarvis drained the last of his tea and stood up.

'Right. See you later.' The itch on his face persisted. He put his hand up to scratch. He looked at the sky as he stepped out on to the deck. The itch usually meant a bit of a blow coming, but the sky was clear enough. He thought nothing more of it and moved forward to check the two men working with the fourth engineer on the winch.

He had been born in the Yorkshire town of Bridlington. His father had been a fisherman, running a small trawler out into the grey slate waters of the North Sea, coming home every three or four days to the small terraced house of two rooms up and two down. He had three brothers and two sisters and, in the bleak post-war years, he had shared a bed with two of his brothers and worn hand-me-down clothing. His father was often drunk, but to everyone's relief never beat anyone; it was not like the family next door. There was running water in the kitchen and a bathroom had been added later, after he had left, when there had been a particularly good season's catch. Before that, it had been a tub in the kitchen by the stove, his vast big-breasted mother presiding over family bathtime like a jailer.

He, as the youngest, had got everything last including the bathwater and it was with some pride that he had had a second bathroom put on to their home in Southampton in the last year.

He had gone to sea at fourteen, partly to escape the family obligation to help crew the boat and partly because, with the herrings gone and the cod way too far north for them, he knew the boat could never support them all.

At fourteen he was bigger than most men and, having had to fight for everything he ever had, he was more than a match for those he came across on the lower decks. Down there, away from the discipline of the weather deck and the eyes of the officers, he survived and prospered. He learnt his craft, drew his pay and by the time he was twenty he was bosun on a small freighter, plying the routes between Singapore and Jesselton as it was then and down through the Indonesian islands and the Philippines.

He went home occasionally but when his parents died the annual trips to Yorkshire stopped and when he found and married Florry he chose Southampton to be their home. Not only was it home base for the company but people were more forgiving of foreigners than in Bridlington. He wanted her to be happy. She was, and in the first two years of their marriage, she presented him with two perfect daughters like tiny copper-skinned angels. When they were out shopping they made an odd sight, the big solid man with the lopsided face and the petite, polite Asian beauty on his arm.

Now, it was with Florry on his mind and a whistle on his lips that he moved up the gently rolling deck, casting an eye at the bridge as he crossed between holds one and two.

The forenoon watch was Chafney's, and Jarvis felt a touch of envy seeing him walking the bridge. Having left school when he did, he simply didn't have the education needed to become a deck officer. But Florry had a solution to that as she had to most things. In a bag in his small cabin he kept some books and, when he got home, he would have to show her the exercises he had done. In six months she said he would be up to the reading skills and could begin to do correspondence courses through the adult education centre. They had worked it out that in a year he could go for his third mate's ticket and in four, with his previous experience taken into account, he could sit for his master's ticket. Life was good.

Along the deck a group of the passengers, the students, pushed and jostled each other, cups of something hot and steaming in their hands. One leant back on the rail behind a lifeboat davit and cupped a cigarette to his lips. Jarvis moved down towards them, threading past the main group to the smoker.

'Not here, son.' He pointed down to the deck a few feet

away. 'That's a fuel filler and that' – he pointed to a sign – 'says no smoking.'

'Sorry,' the fellow replied guiltily. 'I say, you won't tell . . .'

Jarvis smiled. 'Through that door on the left. The bogs. No one will bother you there.'

'Thanks.' The relieved boy smiled back at him.

'Excuse me,' another said, 'but we were wondering . . .' He pointed up at the bottom of a lifeboat as it hung in its davits. 'How long would you survive in a lifeboat?'

'Never been in one,' Jarvis lied, 'but they say fully loaded, a few weeks.'

'Weeks!' With that the boys wandered away back to their classes and Jarvis moved back up the deck with his memories of the dying engineer and the four other squabbling seamen and the nineteen days they had spent drifting into the shipping lanes off the Maldive Islands. The one who had challenged him over the water ration and had decided to fight it out and lost, his head cracked open on the hard gunwale, after taking a mighty punch that would have floored an ox.

Some things were clear, crystal clear in his memory, like the graduated drinking cup and the flaking paint on the boat's thwarts, little curls of white and blue, cheerful happy colours, mocking them as they slowly dehydrated under the hot Indian Ocean sun.

Horrocks, an able seaman from Hull, a wizened little man with a bright chipmunk face and gaps in his teeth, told jokes and anecdotes for hour after hour, keeping spirits alive. Turley, the youngest on the crew. Colin Turley with his unshakeable faith in his bosun's ability to keep them alive in the boat. His hero worship of Jarvis, normally irritating, suddenly became the foundation relationship that others, more ephemeral, could rely upon.

He now ran a hardware shop in Australia and the Christmas cards came from him every year, photographs of growing children on parched lawns. Florry now exchanged letters with his wife, a pretty blonde girl who, in the photographs, seemed much larger than her husband.

Images of Turley cradling the broken head of the man who had challenged Jarvis, understanding it all with a wisdom way beyond his years, keeping the burning sun off the man's face. Images of Horrocks telling the tale of the woman from the fish-and-chip shop and a dozen others, each one coarser than the last, while Turley, coming from a strong Christian home, struggled to understand and come to grips. And the days . . . the long hot scorching days as they drifted, Jarvis cutting a notch in the aft thwart for each one as the sun dropped and the darkness brought relief.

Finally they were picked up by the Greek merchantman and helped below for rest and showers and water, lots and lots of water. The simple meals they gave them every hour and the mix of honey and milk that the Greek mate said would be best for weakened digestive systems. Horrocks saying, bollocks, just give me a cup of tea, lots of milk and three sugars, and Turley saying his silent prayers like he had done every day, but this time not for salvation but of thanks.

They were thin and wasted and they were the only survivors of the sixteen crew on the MV *Corcoran*. The other boat had got away before them, after the fire had begun to rage uncontrollably back towards the accommodation, but they had lost contact with the other men on the first night and, as far as Jarvis knew, they were never seen again. For Cecil Jarvis, going to the boats was something he never wanted to do again, but then he mused, it was only something you did when you were on fire.

The forenoon watch was drawing to a close and while Chafney would hand over to Scott, the number two, the fourth engineer would hand across to the third's shift in the engine room. The three able seamen on the watch would change also.

One of the more senior men was on the bridge, serving as lookout. Rated as a GP1, he was also qualified to helm the ship should it be required. The other two were up for'ard helping with the winch because with that job came other chores. The cable would have to be moved and the entire assembly greased and repainted once the new moving parts were in.

He would put Ed Reyes up on the bridge for the afternoon watch and Rodriguez could do the dogwatch with the mate and Jeffries.

He spoke to the two seamen with the fourth and then moved back down the deck towards number one hold's big wooden hatch covers. Nichols would want to know if the cargo had been checked when he came on watch and he could hear the plate in number one groaning and giving little shrieks as steel rubbed steel.

Caledonia had no inspection hatches, the small, square, watertight manhole covers that gave access to the hold without going through the main openings. She was of an age when the steel bar had to be removed, giving access to the battens. These were then pulled and the tarpaulin rolled back, and the nearest hatchboard had to be lifted from its setting between the king beam and the side coaming.

This Jarvis did and, judging the roll of the vessel, he then dropped down on to the steel ladder that fell to the depths of the ship and crossed to the little monkey island at the head of the stairs.

A heavy torch sat in a bracket at the top of the ladder but he ignored it and hit the grubby metal housing that held safe the light switch. Below, in the main number one hold, four fluorescent tubes flickered on. The noise of the rubbing steel was now exaggerated one-hundredfold in the hold recess.

He lifted the heavy rubber telephone handset and hit the button marked 'Bridge' and a second later Chafney was on the other end.

'Jarvis. I'm in number one. Hatchboard is up. I'll be five minutes.'

'Thank you, Bosun.'

He headed down then into the depths to begin checking the cables and chain and shackles that were holding two thousand tons of steel in place.

Captain Wellbrook stepped on to the bridge from his day cabin, his eyes taking in everything in one all-knowing sweep. Able seaman Reyes, a few feet from the helm, looking off the starboard quarter through the big pedestal-mounted binoculars and Scott leaning over the chart table making an entry in the log.

'How goes it?'

Scott looked up. He hadn't heard the captain arrive and cursed silently to himself. The old man wore crepe-soled shoes and could move like a cat.

'Fine, sir. Small problem with the Satnav, but Mr Cochran thinks he can get it fixed today.'

Wellbrook grunted and looked back at the bank of electronics that took up most of the space on the rear bulkhead. There, mounted into a teak fascia were Loran, Satnav, the new Navitex machine, the secondary radar screens, the Decca navigator, the log, a VHF radio and a panel of engine instruments.

'Mark my words, Mr Scott. Never rely on that gear. A chart, a compass and a sextant, rising tables and a watch are all a man needs to navigate the world.'

'Aye aye, sir.'

'Cargo checked?'

'Aye aye, sir. The bosun was down in number one at eleven hundred hours and finished in number four just before the watch changed.'

'Very well.'

Wellbrook stepped up to the big bridge windows behind the silent clear screen and spoke without looking at the man who was peering through the binoculars.

'Well, sailor. What do you see?'

'Trawler, Captain . . . She seems to be hove to, sir.'

Wellbrook took a smaller pair of 8 x 50 binoculars from a rack and swung them up to his eyes.

'Could she be handling a net, sir?' Scott asked.

'Possible but unlikely. She is beam on. A net would have her stern to . . . Starboard twenty, Mr Scott, if you please. Back to half ahead.'

Reyes was at the wheel and, disengaging the automatic pilot, he brought the old teak wheel over to the right till the compass swing gave him the twenty points that the captain had asked for.

Five minutes later they were one cable off the trawler's beam and dead slow ahead. She was an old boat scarred by years of hard work and she rolled sluggishly in the deep swells.

'*Heron*, sir, out of Glasgow,' Scott said. He had been looking through the big pedestal glasses.

'Signal her. Ask if she needs assistance.'

Scott moved on to the bridge wing with a loudhailer, tugging on the siren lanyard as he moved past. The *Caledonia* gave a mournful blast loud enough to wake the dead and, moments later, a head appeared over the canvas covers on the trawler's pitching deck.

Scott's voice boomed across the water.

'Ahoy there, *Heron*. Do you require assistance?'

A moment passed and a signal lamp began to flash back.

Scott walked back on to the bridge and snatched up the microphone on the VHF, his other hand flicking the dials over to channel thirty-two.

'*Heron, Heron*, this is *Caledonia*.'

'Go ahead, *Caledonia*,' a thickly accented voice crashed on to the bridge over the speakers.

'*Heron*, do you require assistance?'

'Thank you, but no. We will be under way in the next ten minutes, *Caledonia*.' Then the tone changed. 'What I will need is a clean pair of underpants. That bloody great horn of yours scared the shite out of me.'

'Thank you, *Heron*,' Scott said dryly, with all the big-ship sophistication he could muster. 'We bid you good day.'

Later, Fripp, who was working days, and not on the watch system, stood back while Nichols looked over his work.

'This figure here is your noon sight?'

'Yes, sir.'

'All right. Find the Azores chart. Pick a spot exactly sixty miles to the southwest of Horta. Plot a course to put us there at midnight on the day of your choice. Come back with heading and speed, and consider all the aspects.'

Fripp leant forward into the rack, selected the chart he needed and began to work the calculation.

As chief officer, it was Nichols's task to train junior deck officers, and with Wellbrook's ongoing commitment to the mariners of tomorrow, the captain took more than a passing interest in the progress of any cadet they had serving on the *Caledonia*.

The lad stood back ten minutes later.

'Done it?'

'Yes, sir.'

'When?'

'Four nights from now. We steam at fifteen knots.'

'Why?' Nichols asked. 'What's your rationale?'

'We are not chartering, loading or unloading, so we have no demurrage costs to worry about. Fifteen knots gives us an economical speed without spending half a day waiting.'

'Good.'

He sent the boy away to have a cup of coffee, gave Jeffries the watch and took the steps to the deck. He wanted to check the cargo before the boys arrived for their tour of the bridge and was back twenty minutes later. The bridge seemed incredibly quiet after the groaning noise in the holds.

A few minutes later two figures stood in the port bridge entry.

'Can we come in?' Sergeant Carstairs asked.

'By all means,' Nichols said smiling. 'Just the two of you?'

Carstairs nodded and Nichols began showing David Lawler around the electronics on the aft bulkhead and finally arrived back at the wheel. Nichols nodded to the seaman close by and, leaning forward, turned off the automatic steering.

'Care to take the wheel?' he said.

'Yes, sir!' the lad said, stepping forward, a broad smile across his face. He took the old teak spokes and gingerly felt for some sort of response from the ship.

'It's a full two turns for hard rudder in either direction. You will find it very solid.' He explained how to steer by the compass and let the lad chase the needle for a few minutes.

'We almost stopped earlier today. Why was that?'

Nichols had awoken the moment the engine note had changed and had lain listening until he heard the loud-hailer and the subsequent increase in revolutions again. He had checked the log when he took the watch and read the detail.

'A fishing boat was stopped in the water. We slowed down to see if she was in trouble. See if we could help.'

'First rule of the sea?' David asked, caught up in the drama.

Nichols smiled. 'Yes.'

'I've always wondered . . . what's the second?'

Nichols had to think about that.

'I haven't the faintest idea,' he replied honestly.

Hurricane Fiona had decided her track. She had veered north, her huge revolving mass sucked round the Azores high pressure area and into the North Atlantic. The Atlanta Weather Center passed the good news to the Hurricane

Center in Miami and notices to shipping went out over the single side band services and on short-wave commercial channels. She had picked up speed to a respectable thirty knots, had almost sunk a small freighter, and had jeopardized an oil rig under tow. She brought shrieking force twelve winds that were capable of tearing a house apart or picking up a loaded truck and flinging it across the street; winds that vented their anger and power on the sea itself, building monstrous waves and lacing them with spume and snatching bits of flotsam up into the sky for minutes at a time.

The European Centre for Medium-Range Forecasting at Reading had been watching her since the day before and their mathematicians had fed their computers and passed the information on to another team at Edinburgh University who began to run some of the data through a sophisticated computer model.

The model confirmed the meteorologists' belief that the old hurricane would slam into the polar air mass and create a warm occluded front. The forecasters were now studying the results and would, in the next few hours, issue a forecast to Bracknell II station for aviators and Northwood station for mariners.

'Jesus. She's a big bitch,' said one, studying the satellite photographs.

'Tight too. Christ, imagine the pressure drop in the centre of that little lot,' his colleague answered.

'Let's hope we can downgrade her.'

The other forecaster nodded in silence. They both remembered the last time a full hurricane had hit the British Isles.

The first forecast from Northwood concerning Fiona would cover Finisterre, Sole, Shannon, Fastnet and Plymouth areas and predicted her arrival for the night of 24 September.

FOUR

St Mary's. Scilly Isles

Hal Carter slipped the rope around a rusted steel pipe, and stepped out of the small punt on to the launching slip at Carn Thomas. The water was calm enough here in the pool today, which made the journey from the launch to the boathouse much quicker. On days when the water was rougher, if you wanted to remain dry, then you had to walk the beach or take the road.

The boathouse stood solidly on the carn thirty feet above the water, built of the same granite as the carn itself. As he made his way up the slipway towards the big double doors he reminded himself to have a word with Dickerson about a few tins of paint for the boathouse. The red on the roof was peeling.

Ernie Coutts was waiting at the head of the slip, a grease gun and a large refill tin at his side. Wordlessly they began to grease the rollers on the slip. On the last practice run they had proved sticky and three of them had jammed altogether, as the small light launch ran down towards the water and the waiting *Maeve*.

It was ten minutes before Ernie spoke.

'I hear that new doctor has agreed to launch with us.'

'Aye,' said Carter.

'I hear he has a wetsuit. Goes windsurfing,' Ernie said with a glint of humour in his eyes. He thought that anyone who actually swam for pleasure was insane.

'Saw him the other week,' Carter said. He squeezed the

trigger on the grease gun and watched with satisfaction as the thick glutinous green worm poured out over the bearings in the roller. 'Had the sail up and went flying across the bay there.'

'Mad Irish bastard,' Ernie said, half in amazement and half in envy at his lost youth. 'Did you see the weather report last night on the television?'

'Aye, I did,' Carter answered, pushing a glob of grease into the inside of one of the big rollers and then turning it over with his hand.

'Bit of a gale maybe?' Ernie said.

Carter looked up at the sky as he had done that morning. High ripples of cirrus coloured the heavens, the mares' tails that said much to a mariner.

'Tonight some time,' Carter said. He had looked at his barometer that dawn and the low that had moved through a few days before had left the glass climbing sharply. Now it was falling again.

Carter watched the direction of the cirrus moving on the jet stream for a moment and then looked lower at the puffs of cumulus. He had seen the sky like this before. 'From the sou'west,' he finished.

It would come in over the Bishop, the Crim and the Western Rocks and bring the sea slamming in against the wall that sheltered the new quay and throw spray high over the rooftops from the Mermaid, down six or seven houses.

'When we are done here,' he said to Ernie, 'check the batteries and top up from the hand pump.'

Ernie looked up at his coxswain then. Normally he would have been mildly offended that anyone would think that he would have to be told to run up the batteries and then top up the fuel tanks afterwards, but the look on Carter's face stopped him saying anything in rebuke. He too looked up at the cirrus, the pretty little streaks of cloud, the omens of what was to come, and felt the hair on the back of his neck rise. He didn't really understand it, but

Carter did and he didn't like what he saw up there.

'Aye aye,' he said.

Out in the pool the *Maeve Corrigan* had her flared bows into wind and was tugging impatiently at her mooring line like a thoroughbred.

In the bar at the Atlantic John Timson pulled his stool out and grinned broadly at the barmaid.

'Mine's a pint,' he said, eyes twinkling.

She walked down to the taps.

'Weather's coming,' she offered. 'Gran says the rabbits are moving up the hill and the horse is uneasy.'

'Bit of a blow coming I should think,' John said. 'Bit of a blow.' He took a sip of the beer in the glass.

'Ah, that's grand,' he said. He liked a pint with his lunch and it wasn't often the launch was in at this time, but Hal Carter had wanted to do something at the boathouse so this was most welcome. Helen would be walking down and Simon said he might drop in for a quick one. Life was good.

'What's on the menu?' he asked.

RAF Brawdy. South Wales

Flight Lieutenant Andy Hall stepped over the rolling mass on the floor and lifted his duty bag on to the dining table. The mass stopped rolling and a small head peeped out of the end of the sleeping bag. It was one of his two sons, the other no doubt further down the bag. They were playing a game they called 'snowcave'.

'Dad! Tim farted in the cave!' David accused.

'No, I didn't. It was you!' his brother retorted. They argued over who had done what for a moment until one noticed that their father was packing his bag.

'Going to work, Dad?'

'Yes. Are you two riding later?'

They chimed a positive reply and he began to read the riot act about wearing riding hats, talking to strangers and listening to what their mother said while he was at work.

The twenty-four-hour shift starting at noon rolled through into the following day and, although the boys rarely played their mother up, he always made the effort to support her in advance.

Really, no one played up Caroline Hall. Not her husband, not her children and not the Royal Air Force. He remembered some admin type giving her a problem over something at the air-day recently and she had firmly and quietly put him in his place.

He looked at his watch. It was a twenty-minute drive from the house in Haverford West to RAF Brawdy and it was now half past eleven.

'Where's your mother?'

'At the shops,' Tim said. 'She said she would be back before you go.'

'Is there wood in the bin?'

'Yes,' they called in unison.

'Coal?'

'Can we have a fire?' David asked.

'If it gets cold and your mother says you can.'

'The cave will melt,' said Tim, caught up in Antarctic adventures. 'Blizzard outside, cooking inside!'

'Don't be a dimbo!' David retorted. They began jostling each other, bony elbows finding ribs, trying to push each other off the spot like miniature sumo wrestlers.

'Cut it out,' their father said.

'He started it!'

'No, I didn't, you did.'

'Did not.'

'Did so.'

'Did not.'

'Did so.'

Andy Hall raised a finger. That was the signal. He stopped speaking and simply raised a finger. They both shut up and stood still. The rule was that they remained like that till he said they could move and they were standing there a few seconds later when their mother came in the back door laden with grocery bags.

'Lend a hand,' he said and they both charged towards their mother.

'Thank you,' she said, dropping her handbag on the table. 'You away then?'

'Yeah. Still on for the Goodalls' tomorrow night?'

'Eightish.'

'I'll head straight back.'

'Mmmm.' She put her face up for a kiss and then ushered him out towards the car. 'Boys, say goodbye to your dad now.'

They shouted farewells from the kitchen and he winked as he stepped out on to the drive.

'Mind your sixes,' she said.

He smiled. It was the old fighter pilots' way of saying 'take care' although he hadn't flown fast jets for years now. He flew helicopters. Heavy, slow and cumbersome after the fixed wing, the big twin-engined Sea King search and rescue machine had other rewards, nonetheless. It could take off into a hundred knots of wind, hover blind in darkness and lift people from cliffs and boats. Andy Hall had liked the fixed wing, but he loved helicopters.

There would be a met briefing on arrival and he would take the shift officially at twelve thirty. The crew which was standing down was going on to days off, and his relief crew was coming on to standby in case the second Sea King which was sheltered in the hangar was needed.

He arrived at the base at a few minutes to twelve and walked into the crew standby room with his partner, also a flight lieutenant, Mark Selby. Their radar operator and winchman, both master A/E operators, equivalent to warrant officers, and ten-year veterans of the rescue service, were there waiting for them.

Selby grinned at Hall.

'I'll get the met,' he said casually.

'She's married,' Hall said.

The met officer had a long-legged redhead assistant and Selby never lost the opportunity to cross into the admin block in the hope of seeing her.

'Doesn't mean I can't wish.'

They dumped their bags in the crew room. There was a small sitting area with three armchairs and a television. A notice board dominated one wall and NOTAMS, standing orders and other sundry pieces of paper, some yellowing with age, were pinned to its surface.

A door led off into two small sleeping rooms, each with two bunks, one for officers and one for the non-commissioned men. In fact they were split up because Hall smoked, as did the winchman, so they shared a room, leaving the two non-smokers the other room. There was also a bathroom with showers, a toilet and six battered old metal lockers. A second door led off from the crew room into the ops office. There was a large-scale map on the wall, a bank of communications equipment, a smaller map board with acetate overlays for up-to-date weather, and a desk crowded with other sundries. The duty officer was at the desk, the telephone to his ear. He looked up as Hall and Selby walked in and finished his conversation.

With the small talk over, they began the handover as the pilots who were being relieved woke and got their things together.

'They are getting some sleep ... spent half the night looking for some kid in his dad's dinghy. Turns out he was with a friend all night.'

'Hope he got a clout round the ear,' Hall said.

'Not half. His dad got one too. The boss said next time we would send a bill.'

Hall laughed bitterly. Their job was rescue and they hated having their time wasted.

'That's all?'

'It was,' the officer said.

'Right, well, let's get the met and the boys can go home, eh?'

Selby walked over to the met officer as Hall changed into a flight suit. His helmet, gloves, life jacket and other bits and pieces were in a big pigeonhole in the crew room and, when he had zipped the suit up, he walked straight out to pre-flight the aircraft. The start-up generator was hooked up and across in the hangar he could see the ground crew going about their routine tasks.

Ten minutes later as Selby walked back across towards him, he lifted a thumb to the other crew and they waved and drove away.

From now on they were the duty shift.

He finished preparing the aircraft and walked inside. Someone had made tea and the pot steamed cheerfully.

He poured himself a cup and sat down as Selby, who had been putting on his flight suit, entered the room.

'Fucking awful weather,' he said.

Hall looked up. 'What's left of Hurricane Fiona, no doubt.'

'She's been downgraded, but the bad news is gusts of up to one hundred knots. Storm warning. Looks like they may upgrade that to severe later. Big bitch of a warm occluded front. We will have the overlays in a few minutes.'

Hall nodded. He had been watching the hurricane's progress over the last days, unable, like most pilots, to ignore a weather report on television, and, again like most pilots, fascinated and frightened by the huge whorls of cloud in the satellite pictures. Where cheery blonde weather girls pointed to little arrows and made jokes about staying in for the night the pilots saw the reality and those who could did just what the smiling blondes said and stayed home for the night tucked up with a bottle of Scotch and a good book. There are old pilots and there are bold pilots, the time-worn adage went, but there are no old bold pilots. Let some other poor bastard fly in it, was the chorus.

Well, Hall thought, I am the poor bastard.

The met officer arrived then. If the weather was going to be a factor in the shift, then the duty met officer came across and did the overlays on the chart himself, talking through the variables with the crew. Together they plotted several courses and along the lines that radiated like spokes from the Brawdy centre point he plotted wind speed and direction and other salient information. He was expecting eighty knots of wind across the runway by the mid-evening. All flying ops would be suspended with only the search and rescue team still able to launch. Anything over eighty knots and it was the pilot in command's decision. Hall would lift off into one hundred knots, and had done in the past, but that would severely limit their range, particularly if they were flying into the wind.

Hall and Selby then copied that data down on to cellophane-covered flight maps with a Chinagraph pencil and placed the newly updated maps in the rack. They would repeat the process every four hours while the occluded front remained in the area. When they had finished, Hall looked up at the windsock across the pan. It was already up and stiff, the odd gust tugging at its length.

Caledonia

Wellbrook and Nichols leant across the table as Scott, with some skill, began to transpose the data off the Navitex on to the big chart.

Nichols had seen the first reports that morning and decided to come back up on to the bridge just after noon.

It was officially Scott's watch, but he automatically deferred command to Nichols, as did Nichols to Wellbrook when the latter walked silently across to them. He stood like a lump of granite looking at the sky and the slate-coloured waves that had, in the last hour, closed their ranks and become steeper.

'We have just got a VHF forecast, sir,' Nichols said. 'Confirms the Navitex data.'

'What do all the wonders of science tell us then?' Wellbrook asked with a half-smile. He had seen the sky, seen the change in the sea, walked across and looked at the barometer glass and made his own judgement.

'Open-wave warm occluded front, Captain,' Scott said. He pointed down to the chart where he had marked in the information.

The top whirls of lines that were the depression were slashed across their base by a rising line that peaked and dropped away in profile like a hill.

'Gale force and building soon, commencing at force eight to ten and moving up to ten to eleven. Cyclonic. Sea state very rough.'

'And the VHF?' Wellbrook asked.

'Storm warnings,' Nichols said.

The short terse wording of the reports each held a special meaning, Nichols mused.

Soon meant in the next six to twelve hours, cyclonic meant that the winds would approach from different directions depending on position and, with an occluded front, would veer and shift unpredictably. The force eleven meant a violent storm, wind speed in excess of sixty-five miles an hour, with waves at thirty feet, some over that, maybe even forty-five feet, and, God forbid, the rogues, the very big short seas that could top fifty feet.

Nichols had been in these same waters during the storm that slammed into the Fastnet Race fleet a few years before. Another warm occluded front with the familiar open wave across the bottom of the chart.

Wellbrook walked back on to the bridge from the charthouse and stood by the compass binnacle of his command. He put a hand to his sternum and frowned. Indigestion. Their planned course would take them in through the straits between the Scillies and Land's End, past the Wolf

Rock. With cyclonic winds at force eleven he could have a lee shore.

He turned to face the two bridge officers.

'Mr Scott. Rework the plot. I want to stay deep sea. Bring us to seaward and give the Bishop plenty of room.'

Scott nodded. With Wellbrook, deep sea meant just that. Beyond the hundred-fathom line or, if the bottom shelved slowly, then thirty miles offshore.

'Mr Nichols, prepare the ship for a blow if you will.'

'Aye aye, sir.'

It was all in the standing orders book, every preparation that was required, but Nichols didn't need to look.

Jarvis had, with the instincts of a long-time bosun, known the master was on the bridge and orders would be coming down. He also knew what they would be and when Nichols came down the steps on to the deck he was waiting for him.

'Batten her down, Bos'. Goosenecks, deadlights and shutters, vents and stores lashed.'

'Aye. Mooring lines are done already.'

'Good. I'm going below to check the cargo.' He could hear it groaning though the steel of the deck plates. 'Let me have one AB to do the hatch battens. Rig lifelines and then get someone below to do the same for the passengers.'

'Passage?'

'Yes, and one down the centre of the dorm and the classroom. We don't want any cracked heads.'

'Aye aye,' Jarvis said. He had rope in the stores, two-inch nylon that they could run the length of the big rooms. Give the boys something to hold on to if they had to move about. Better give out a few sick bags and buckets he thought.

'What about the steward? Shall I ask him to issue seasick tablets?'

'He should have done that already.'

'Not enough,' Jarvis ventured.

Nichols smiled. Jarvis hated vomit.

'I'll tell him,' Nichols said.

Jarvis nodded and went off to find his men. Off-duty seamen would be called on deck and all hands would prepare for the storm.

The first job was the big dorade vents. The cowls were lifted clear and wooden plugs were hammered in with a mallet, covered in canvas and lashed down. The gooseneck vents were covered and heavy deadlights were swung across the scuttles and clipped down along the entire ship's sides. Steel shutters were dropped into the hinges and swung closed over windows in the accommodation structure. Two men went for'ard and began to secure the store; the paint and rope and blocks were lashed and wedged with battens. The lifeline was rigged as near to the ship's centre line as possible, hopefully away from the reach of waves should any crewman have to go on deck during the storm.

Below in the galleys the same process was under way: pots, pans and other utensils were stored away in lockers, anything that could move was secured. Hot soup and tea and coffee were prepared and put into big Thermos flasks, and the urns drained down to halfway so scalding water could not slosh out and burn anyone.

The cooks prepared a quick hot meal for the crew who would have to remain on duty while the storm lasted, and sensible, big, simple sandwiches for everyone else, enough to last the night and into tomorrow.

St Mary's

Susan Farmer took the steps slowly. There was no hurry now. The interview was in the can and the pilot of the helicopter had agreed to take the tape back with him on the last trip of the day. It had been a peace gesture after turning them away. His apology had been genuine enough. The sick woman on Bryher needed to get back to the hospital in Penzance and Susan's ticket and those of her two-man crew were valid, but they had been the last to make the reservations so they were offloaded to make room for the patient, her nurse and the bulky wheelchair.

The Bell Rock Hotel was a row of houses that had been converted years before. It wasn't the Tregarthen, but the rooms were clean and the staff were friendly. Miraculously they had two rooms free and Susan checked into one, with the crew sharing the other. The interview had been good. The old man was articulate and dry, but so he should have been, she thought, as she unpacked her small bag. He had just been nominated for the Booker Prize and the pundits said it would be a runaway victory for the cantankerous old writer.

She wondered if she could get something to eat and began to visualize the dining arrangements: the traditional seaside hotel with its set menu and guests sitting at the same table each meal, probably rotating towards the better tables by the window as they gained seniority through length of stay.

She put a call through to her editor in Southampton to let him know they were stuck for the night, and began to look forward to the evening, quietly pleased that the ITN team in the West Country had been laid low by an influenza bug, giving her this opportunity to come down on the payroll.

He told her about the storm warnings and asked her to get local footage to include in the round-up of the flooding, damage and little dramas that every storm brings.

When she came off the phone she tried the desk and was told that they could do a pot of tea or coffee in the room but nothing more until the kitchen staff came in later. She thanked them, said no to the tea and dragged her crew out of their room.

'Come on. Let's go for a walk down the street. See if someone can do us something to eat.'

'I'm on for that,' the cameraman said. 'I could do with vichyssoise and a fresh herb omelette.'

Susan laughed. She liked Ted. Ted was gay and lived with a West Indian weightlifter. Ted was also a lot of fun.

'Not here. Might just run to fish and chips though,' she said.

The soundman, a youngster with a mop of red hair, begged off, saying he wanted to clean his gear. So, promising they would bring something back for him, they stepped out on to the pavement with Ted, the complete professional, lugging his camera with him as usual. She mentioned the editor's request for material for the storm round-up.

'Met a local stringer at the house this morning. He said a storm was coming through. Said the waves slam into the wall down below Tregarthen's. I might try for some footage.'

'Now? It's not very impressive,' she said. 'What about later?'

'Yeah. But this is the before,' he replied.

She raised an eyebrow.

'Well, it's more fun than sitting in the room,' he said defensively.

As they walked down the road, her thoughts shifted to John Nichols and she wondered if he would phone when he got in next time. He had been in her thoughts constantly since they had met, although she was still pitching the desire to see him against the pain of her previous experience. He had been good-looking too, but with a nasty streak. A sadistic bully. She remembered the blows and the drunken anger, the beatings and the blame. The money he had taken and the embarrassment he had caused.

'Who is he?' Ted asked.

'Sorry?'

'The man on your mind.'

She laughed softly and tried a denial but he wasn't having that.

'You can't kid a kidder, Susan. They are all bastards, but us girls have to stick together. It would be a dreadful world without them.'

She smiled back at him, appreciating his understanding and the overdone gayness. His normal style was as masculine as the next man's. This was for her amusement.

'He's a ship's officer,' she said.

'Ooh, a sailor!' he minced and she laughed aloud and linked her arm through his as they walked.

Parnell slept. Norah, lying beside him in the big bed, rolled over to look at him, the tangled sheet wrapped round her waist, her breasts covered in a sheen of sweat from their lovemaking.

Thank you, God. You answered my prayers and I shall not run from him again. I shall love him and honour him and, if you will it, I shall spend the rest of my life with him.

She had seen him on the street in Galway, walking with great strides, hair too long, in an old sweater and faded jeans with baggy knees. She didn't meet him till a month later when she had gone to work at the infirmary in Dublin. There he had the same long hair and jeans, but now he also wore a doctor's coat. His hands, his magic hands, were in the crushed chest of a woman who had been dragged from a car wreck on the airport road. The team around him were good and she had stopped to watch. Later she sat at his table in the canteen and, over the next weeks, deliberately crossed his path until he noticed her. Then, when he did and he asked her to see a movie with him, she surprised herself. Like a dog who had chased a cat and caught it, she didn't know what to do.

He was not just a good-looking doctor working in the same hospital. He was now something mythical, something beyond reach. She refused and refused again.

But David wasn't taking no for an answer and arrived at her flat one Sunday morning, catching her in a nightie with her hair up in a rubber band and, he later told her, bags under her eyes the size and colour of squash balls. He stood in the doorway and, with her there in the flesh, he looked like a little boy and his confidence flagged for a minute. He recovered, grinned, diagnosed her condition and prescribed fresh air and relaxation. He then held up a picnic basket.

By the end of the week she was in love and by the beginning of the following month her green card had arrived and the offer of the nursing job in Boston became a reality. Not just a two-year contract. It was the full permit, to work, reside, become a citizen. It was everything she had ever wanted since she was fifteen. America. The promised land.

She had spent the next week in a daze, wondering what to do. The offer at the Boston hospital was only open for ninety days and she had to be there inside that period. She knew his views on the litigation-mad American medical system. He had been talking in the canteen one day about a friend who had returned from California. It had got so bad that doctors were more concerned about being sued than about saving lives. The other man at the table had said that a green card wasn't a problem for an Irish-trained surgeon, not a man who passed out top of his year at Trinity like Parnell. Parnell had laughed. Fuck that, he had said. America was the last place he wanted to go.

She moved into his flat in Terenure and they slipped into an easy routine, as lovers, as friends, seeing shows and movies, eating out or in on the floor before the fire, happy in each other's company, and all the while the prospect of her departure looming closer.

She remembered it so clearly. She didn't bring it up with him. She had meant to, she said, but it had never seemed right. She just announced it as they lay in bed one afternoon, tea tray on the bed, crumpled sheets on the floor, the papers strewn across the carpet where they had landed after the first session of lovemaking. He was pouring. No tea bags for him. Leaf tea with a silver strainer that some auntie had given him, bone china cups with mismatched saucers. He was pouring when she told him.

'I accepted the Boston offer.'

He looked up, then down at the cup.

'What offer?'

'Remember I told you,' she lied, running her hand through her hair like she always did under pressure.

'No, I don't,' he replied.

'Well, I accepted it. I am going to America. Why don't you come, David . . . ?' She leant forward. 'Please, David . . .'

'When?' he interrupted.

'Please, David, you can get a . . .'

'When?'

'Tuesday,' she answered in a little voice.

'This Tuesday?' he asked. 'That's two days' time, Norah.'

'I know.'

'Jesus, how long have you known about this?'

She sat silently, her head down.

'How long,' he said.

'Three months.'

'Thanks for telling me.'

'What's that supposed to . . . ?'

'Mean?' he interrupted. 'That's easy. You could have just fucked off.'

'Never! I love you!' she retorted, not believing that he had said something like that.

'No. If you did you would have had more respect for my feelings,' he said softly. 'Did you have a good time then? What's left? Don't tell me. You will say something like, "It was fun while it lasted," or something really banal like, "Things change, David, we all move on."'

'I knew you would take it like this,' she said sadly, the tears coming. 'That's why I never told you.'

'What the fuck did you expect, Norah? I love you! You are about to walk out of my life on forty-eight hours' notice

98

and you want a brass band and a ride to the airport? You want my blessings? Well, I'm sorry! I'm not that magnanimous.'

He did drive her to the airport, her luggage on the windsurfing rack on the roof of his old Toyota. She remembered the drive as if it was yesterday. The conversation was forced pleasantries, promises to write and quiet tears and she never knew about the little velvet-covered box in his drawer, the box he had collected the day before she had told him, the box with the solitaire diamond engagement ring that he had found at an antique jewellery auction and had taken out an overdraft to buy.

America had been awful and she missed home and people who spoke proper English and could cook fried eggs and make potato cakes, and she missed her David. More than she ever dreamed she would, more than she thought possible.

The letters weren't replied to and when she phoned one day she found that he had left the week after she had. It had taken her six months to find him. The time hadn't been wasted. She had done a course in Spanish and had knitted him a sweater, an Aran sweater like her mother had done and all the women before her in their families.

The sweaters were works of love because they contained a family stitch, placed there so that the Aran women could recognize the bodies of their men if they were drowned at sea while fishing. The sweater was now wrapped in tissue paper in her bag. She would give it to him some time. A gift of love. Her stitch in the knit identifying him as her man to all. And still her search had gone on. She had written to the Medical Associations of a dozen countries and had finally found success through a friend who was a rep for a pharmaceutical company. He claimed they maintained records on every registered doctor in the British Isles and he had come up with a new address.

She watched his chest rise and fall as he slept and made a vow on the Irish saints and the cold winds that swept her Aran Island home. She was never going to let him go again. They could be happy here.

The British Meteorological Office, which had so far been procrastinating over the issuing of a general storm warning, jumped a whole stage and issued a severe storm warning. People living on the southern coast were advised to stay at home and refrain from driving as wind speeds could exceed sixty-five miles an hour.

The Royal Navy, with memories of the 1987 hurricane still fresh in their minds, when the forecasters had failed to realize its strength in time, chose the safe option and allowed their commanding officers to follow their instincts. Little ships, the lightweight fast destroyers and frigates, the slower and even smaller minesweepers were all berthed in Plymouth and Portsmouth and were vulnerable. Their captains wanted the one thing all seamen want in bad weather: they wanted sea room. So, one by one, as fast as they could decently run up engines and slip moorings they put to sea and headed for the open water where they could ride out the storm in safety, away from rocks and reefs and harbour walls and other ships that broke their moorings.

All along the south and southwest coasts others also began to prepare. Lifeboatmen from St Bride's Bay through to Dover. Men from the Mumbles and St Peter's Port, from Padstow and St Ives, from Ilfracombe and Bude. Men from every lifeboat station on the south coast checked their boats and watched the sky. In Penlee, a station that had lost a boat with its entire eight-man crew in the last decade, a new generation of lifeboatmen phoned in to say where they would be that night and the coxswain was already choosing his crew, to be ready should it come to it.

Coastguards on duty were supplemented by officers who came in from days off and by auxiliaries who turned up because they knew tonight would be busy one way or another. Others were also preparing. Police in nine counties were getting ready for the mayhem that ensued when

100

normally well-disciplined people seemed to drive with a collective death wish, a phenomenon that scientists were beginning to believe was associated with low air pressure along with the normal end-of-day stress. This, combined with the inevitable flooding of roads and intersections, would stretch their limited resources. City and county councils organized emergency crews to pump water off roads and Southern Electric made arrangements for crews to turn out as lines came down.

Ernie Coutts slipped the painter around one of the stanchions and climbed from the little punt on to the *Maeve*'s low-waisted gunwale. She rocked on her mooring line, her sharp bow into wind, the small waves that had come round the new quay lifting her with watery slaps on her deep-blue fibreglass hull.

Her serial number was painted in three-foot-high letters on her orange superstructure, 52–35, giving her length at fifty-two feet and being the thirty-fifth of the design off the maker's slips.

The Arun-class lifeboat was, for the men who crewed her, quite simply the best all-round boat ever built for saving lives at sea. There were faster boats, bigger boats, boats with shallower draughts, boats that had directional thrust from small units in the bows, but there were no better boats for the task than the Arun.

Her hull was tremendously strong and divided into twenty-six watertight compartments so that even if she were holed on a reef she could still operate. The high flared bows that cut through waves also gave her a high safe freeboard, two thirds of her length, and then dropped into her low waist, so a crewman could reach into the water and pull survivors up on to the deck, or people could jump on to her from small boats. Three steps then took the non-slip walkway up to the flat safe rear deck where access was gained through a watertight door into the main wheelhouse or up the steep steps to the flying bridge. High.

guardrails stopped lifeboatmen being swept into the sea and a strong steel bollard set into the deck meant they could tow vessels much bigger than themselves.

There were no scuppers. The flush decks ran straight beneath the guardrail so that when seas broke over her decks the water could run freely away. The watertight door had a high coaming that rose above deck height allowing crew to move in and out of the wheelhouse even with the aft decks awash. Once inside, with the door locked and sealed, the interior was absolutely airtight and therein lay her self-righting capability. The weight of her massive Caterpillar engines pulling down and the airtight wheelhouse that never allowed her to roll further than ninety degrees meant she always rolled back up. She could be knocked flat again and again and theoretically rise back again and again as long as her watertight doors and windows held.

In reality when a lifeboat capsized she was immediately considered suspect and a second boat would launch to escort her home. The RNLI's surveyors would check for major structural damage. There was usually also damage to aerials and radar and sometimes injuries where people had fallen or been knocked down in the roll.

Five armoured-glass windows gave forward visibility and each was fitted with wiper blades that would clear rain and spray as effectively as a Kent circular clear screen on bigger ships.

Each crewman had a seat fitted with seat belts. The coxswain had a seat directly central behind the big steering wheel that was more like that of a bus than a boat. Big twin throttles thrust up from a stainless-steel mounting beside the engine instruments that were set into the teak fascia. Above him, mounted on brackets that dropped from the reinforced double-ribbed aluminium roof, were a radio direction finder and a VHF radio.

A Decca navigator, now obsolete, but still perfectly functional, was mounted in the far right corner of the wheelhouse beyond the radar screen's big rubber padded day-view tube over which the radar operator would hunch to seek the casualty without the problem of ambient light diffusing the trace.

Using radar in steep short seas was almost an art form and required intense concentration and hundreds of hours of experience to learn the difference between a steep sea, a piece of flotsam atop a wave and the radar reflector on a small modern yacht.

The seat behind and to the left of the coxswain was for the radio operator where the gear made by Kevin Hughes and Furuno was mounted into the bulkhead. Behind the radio operator's seat was the engineer's position and duplicate engine instruments were set into the bulkhead beside it. To the coxswain's right, behind the radar operator's position, there was a conventional wooden chart table with a depth sounder and a Philips Professional Navigator mounted on the bulkhead above the chart light. Another seat and a stretcher position took up the rest of the space along the starboard bulkhead.

In the front left corner of the wheelhouse nine steep stairs dropped away through a hatch into a forward survivors' cabin. It was spartan. A padded bench ran each side into the bows and, along the bench, seat belts were laid out ready for use. In a storm, the seat belts were essential as the boat could rise and fall forty feet in seconds and be slammed by waves that could throw a big man across the cabin like a child's doll.

A watertight door led back into the engine space from the for'ard cabin. The great gleaming yellow Caterpillar engines that could deliver almost a thousand horsepower were separated by a yellow nonslip walkway and a pair of handrails. There were generators and circuit boards and all the engineering a man could dream of packed into that spotless little engine room.

Ernie Coutts ran his hand over the control panel and pressed the starter. The starboard engine burst into life, a sweet deep throbbing sound. He watched with satisfaction as the amp needles swung up, indicating the chargers were working. He would run each engine for ten minutes and let the bank of big batteries soak up the charge.

He stepped back into the rear cabin, a smaller area that could also seat survivors and that had an urn and a set of cups neatly stacked on a secured tray. He filled the urn and heated water for a cup of instant coffee. That done, he walked back up the steep aft stairs into the wheelhouse and ran a check on all the electronics, watching as each piece of equipment came to life.

Satisfied that all was in order, he left the wheelhouse and took the steps up to the flying bridge, checking the lashings on the life raft as he went. The bridge afforded the coxswain an alternative steering position where the height gave him extra visibility. The console was plain. A rudder-angle indicator sat beside a Seafarer depth sounder and a conventional compass. There were basic engine controls and a wheel and the coxswain stood leaning against a padded backboard. If conditions demanded, he could strap himself on to the back support with a broad kidney belt. The position was protected from the elements with only the windscreen and a canvas cover overhead.

Everything was perfect as it usually was. Ernie would simply not accept anything less than one hundred per cent operational efficiency on his boat. He thought of her like that. Hal Carter may be coxswain and drive her and command her, but, as mechanic, she was his to pamper and love and he was convinced she loved him in return.

Back down below in the wheelhouse he drank his coffee and moved down towards the rear, balancing as he went against the two gleaming stainless-steel poles that had no other purpose than to act as handholds. There were many handholds on the *Maeve*. Every conceivable place a man could want something to grab on to there was such a device, some short, some long, some wood, some steel. He dropped into the engine space and shut down the engine. Finally, he topped up the fuel tanks from the hand pump and, pulling his little punt alongside, stepped down into it and headed for the shore and his dinner. The *Maeve Corrigan* was ready. Ready for whatever the night would bring, as she always was.

East of the Scillies, the ultra-large crude carrier *Mobil Pegasus* was making her way through the English Channel. Her two-and-a-half-day offloading schedule had stretched to over four when she had developed a problem in her computerized load systems and her insurers, Lloyd's, insisted that the systems were always operational, even when in ballast, as she now was.

Engineers in smart white coats came aboard by helicopter as she waited in the roads, big as an island with sides the height of cliff faces. They had pored over the system for thirteen hours straight before finding a software bug and, as the systems were all custom-made, they had waited for back-up programs to arrive by courier from the company's main operations centre in Houston.

Now, two days behind schedule and with some considerable demurrage charges against her profit and loss statement on the internal books, her angry captain, James Hawk, paced his huge bridge. The narrow roads of the Channel were busy with shipping under a hundred flags. Coastal tramps, ferries, pleasure boats, freighters, bulk carriers, warships and tankers like the *Pegasus*. The risk of collision was ever-present. The chief officer who had the watch had doubled up on the lookouts and had his best GP1 seaman on the radarscope. Lookouts had small hand-held radios because from the bridge to the bows was a long way. As the afternoon wore into early evening and the weather steadily worsened, *Pegasus* powered her way towards the Arabian Gulf, her sheer size allowing her to remain oblivious to whatever was coming.

Hawk, pleased to be clear of the roads and at last in deep

water with room to be under way, nodded to his chief officer and left the bridge for his quarters. As in most modern supertankers, facilities on board allowed for wives, and on this trip his own, an earthy practical girl from San Antonio in Texas, had joined him. She was half Mexican, a flashing-eyed, dark-haired beauty. Her favourite foray into European culture was to take sweet pastries at a set time in the late afternoon. The chef was most obliging and served them with fresh coffee the Texas way. Hawk moved back to join her in the spacious airy cabin where he knew the wife of his chief engineer would be also.

HMS *Defiant* and her squadron's supply ship the Royal Fleet auxiliary *Drumbeat* were travelling towards the Channel from the west, moving in front of the storm, towards their home base at Plymouth. *Drumbeat*'s captain, a merchant navy officer, had agreed a plan with both the pilot and operations crew, all navy personnel, of the Wessex helicopter that sat on the raised pad on her aft deck. With the storm coming through, it would be better to fly the helicopter ashore rather than risk damaging her on the exposed area.

At 16:00 hours the pilot eased the helicopter off the deck into the wind which was now gusting to sixty knots. With a full load of fuel on board and gaining height slowly, he headed for the naval station at Portland.

RFA *Drumbeat* was moving slowly. A problem had developed in one of her two drive shafts and it had affected more than just her top speed. It impaired her ability to manoeuvre and she would continue on to Portsmouth where the yards would take care of the problem.

HMS *Defiant* signalled her intention to move ahead and raced off into the gathering waves like an impatient young gun dog, leaving her heavy old supplier plodding along behind.

Scilly Isles

Hugh Town on St Mary's was coming to the end of another working day. The tourist shops were closing, racks of postcards and novelties being pulled indoors. The Co-op where everyone bought their groceries had its last customers in the queue at the checkout and the butcher, two doors further up Hugh Street, was clearing trays of chilled meats from the glassed-in counter and cleaning surfaces. Dusk was falling and the men who had boats dragged up on the beach checked mooring and anchor lines while the tide was running out. It would rise again in the early hours of the next morning and, by then, the weather would have arrived. Already the waves were hitting the sea wall at Rat Island with a dull boom.

Boats had been arriving since early afternoon, seeking shelter in the pool, some smaller craft seeking to get in snug against the wall and being turned away by the boatmen on the quay. They knew better. When the tide rose to its turn, the waves could come over the sea wall and small boats could founder.

Visiting sailors who knew the islands well moved to get into the lee of Peninnis Head and some even into the quay at the old town where there they would be out of the prevailing winds.

Visitors, as the tourists are respectfully called in the Scillies, who were staying in Tregarthen's hotel stood indoors and watched the blackening clouds move in and the gusting winds pluck at the lone tree on the terrace below them. From the windows they could see the rocky shore and the seaward side of the wall that sheltered the new quay. They watched with morbid fascination as the waves got bigger and steeper and those that knew were impressed, for the rocky shore and the wall were almost sheltered from the direct force of the wind by Garrison Hill. What must it be like on the other side?

*   *   *

Victor Collier had his shop closed and locked by six and was in his own living room ten minutes later. That was what he liked about the islands; they weren't very big. He watched the news with his wife and then they sat together at the dining room table for roast leg of lamb followed by his boyhood favourite, bananas and custard. It would be an early night for them as was usual mid-week.

Ernie Coutts cooked himself a frozen steak and kidney pie and, that finished, he wandered down to the Scillonian Club for a pint. He was there for an hour and then, like Collier, headed home for an early night.

Hal Carter sat quietly, as usual, while Jean presided over the evening meal in their household. Helen and Simon helped themselves to vegetables while their mother doled out big portions of cottage pie the way Hal liked it, with a layer of peas between the mince and the mashed potato. A big jug of extra gravy was there and a loaf of fresh bread stood on a cutting board. That would come after. Simon liked great wedges of bread with gravy poured over it just to top up a meal that could have fed half the army.

John Timson sat mid-point at the table, showered and with his beard brushed, and tried to fool everyone that he wasn't really hungry by taking a small portion. Helen took one look, and piled another huge spoonful on his plate. I really do like this man, she thought. He is big with kind eyes and has a heart the size of a mountain. He laughs when he wishes and cares nothing for the world outside. Do I love him? I think I do. She shook it off, knowing that this normally happened after a few days at home. She became an islander again. Forgot that her new home was on the mainland. Or was it? She wasn't so sure any more.

Carter looked up at the shelf where the VHF radio sat in silence. He had bought it so that Jean could listen while he was at sea. He listened to the wind outside for a second and wondered if he should turn it on for a while but

108

decided against it. Bob Cameron normally monitored it, but he was ashore in Penzance having some major dental work done. He would turn it on later when the kids had gone down for a drink.

Dickerson, the honorary secretary, worked late in his office and then, before going home, he telephoned the local coastguard man who was about to go off duty. He then contacted Falmouth coastguard and told them he would be at home that evening.

Susan Farmer and her camera crew decided to spend the evening in the pub with the locals and ended up in the bar at the Atlantic, while David Parnell opted for a quieter evening with Norah. Wrapped in waterproofs and holding hands, they walked down the hill to the Bishop for a bottle of wine before the weather got too bad to go out in.

Caledonia

The seas were steep and short, whitecaps breaking and troughs deepening and dark. Above the water the wind collected strength and shrieked over the wave tops. On the bridge of the *Caledonia*, Nichols stood with his legs apart, braced so he could move with the ship. He put out a hand to the rail as a huge wave came in on the beam, lifting *Caledonia* and rolling her viciously. Then she slid into the trough, going the other way before finding her trim in time for the next wave. This one broke, surf coming over the deck, and she shook herself free, tons of water pouring through her scuppers, and rose to meet the next wave like an old campaigner, experienced but weary. She was moving across the wind and, as it veered, it brought the confused seas under her cruiser stern and occasionally a big breaker would come rolling over the transom, throwing tons of black water over the quarterdeck, and she would quiver along her length.

She can't take much more of this hammering, he thought. Every rivet in her dear old hull is rattling, every weld straining.

Bring her head round, let her ride it out and to hell with making port on schedule. He looked to Wellbrook. The muted light came from the glow of the compass binnacle, the instrument lighting and the warm yellow that shone over the chart table. Wellbrook turned to him at the same moment and nodded. 'That's enough, Mr Nichols,' he said.

Nichols stepped up to the seaman at the helm. They had given up the automatic steering an hour ago, preferring the eye of a good seaman to judge the sea. Now it was time just to let it blow over.

Caledonia was still moving at seven knots and Nichols knew it was fast enough to do what he wanted.

'Prepare to come round to windward,' he said, watching the seas. He wanted to judge his moment to swing her bows.

'Aye aye.'

'Now.'

The seaman swung the big wheel and *Caledonia* slowly began to turn into the teeth of the storm.

It was a full twenty seconds before the manoeuvre was complete and, when she was finally taking the big waves square under her bows, he spoke again.

'Let her ride into the wind. Dead slow ahead . . . make a log entry to that effect, Mr Jeffries.'

'Aye aye,' Jeffries replied. He was tense. Scott, who stood back in the charthouse, could see it. The third officer was frightened. He smiled to himself. When he was a junior officer he had also been afraid of his first few big blows. It seemed so long ago.

They were all on the bridge, the juniors trying to stay clear of Captain Wellbrook who stood on the port wing, legs astride, resolute in the extreme.

'When you have done that, Mr Jeffries, go below and see how our passengers are making out, will you?'

'I'll go,' Fripp said cheerfully. This was his kind of sailoring, a storm building and the normal routines dropped. 'I'll offer a few pork pies,' he finished.

Even Wellbrook smiled as he turned to his chief officer. 'Thank you, Mr Nichols. I shall be in my day cabin.'

He still wasn't feeling well.

FIVE

By ten o'clock that night the storm had reached a feverish pitch and four lifeboats in the southwest had slipped their moorings and put to sea on service.

The crew from the Mumbles had gone to take an injured man off a freighter. He had slipped and fallen down thirty feet of companionway, breaking both his shoulder and his left leg. Sennen Cove's boat had gone to the assistance of a trawler that was taking water in heavy seas. The Bude boat was slowly towing in an Irish-registered yacht that had been dismasted in the George Channel and the Penlee Arun-class boat had put to sea to help in the search for four divers in a small open boat which was now seven hours overdue.

Hugh Town on St Mary's was taking a hammering. Trees were bent over, cowering before the force of the gale that lifted roofing tiles and tore up paling fences. Most people stayed indoors, some checking the contents of their kitchen cupboards because they knew that the ferry wouldn't be coming tomorrow, and whatever the Co-op ran out of would stay out of stock till the seas abated. In other houses small children sat up in bed and listened to the howl of the wind while their older brothers and sisters debated walking down Hugh Street to where the Mermaid public house stood. The Mermaid had once taken barrels in on the first floor via a hoist and a few years ago the access door had been stove in by a wave that had come over the sea wall and across the twenty feet of roadway with enough force to smash the timbers.

A few of them gathered up the street around a corner, backs to the chemist's shop window, the braver ones ducking their heads round to view the scene, all of them finding it exciting. The police had put a barrier up to stop anyone foolish enough to try and move past the Mermaid's door and round on to the road that led to the quay. A few stalwarts leant over pints inside the public house and grinned at each other as the spray showered across the roof, and the renovated dining area with its designer wreck theme and fake riding lights shuddered beneath the force of the storm. There were no 'visitors' in the bar of the Mermaid. They were either playing games in the front rooms of the small family hotels, or in either of the other two pubs, or the handful of restaurants still open. These were locals and one by one they finished their drinks and, pulling collars close and ducking their heads down, they stepped out on to the dark noisy street and headed home to their beds and their fires. The landlord closed up early. There would be no more trade tonight and as he washed glasses he listened to the waves slamming into the sea wall, the thudding booming roar like bomb blasts on the rocks.

Caledonia

23:46 HOURS

The steward had taken a big steaming jug of cocoa on to the bridge for the duty watch and poured the thick sweet drink into pint-sized heavy china mugs. A tray of sandwiches loosely covered in cling film slid across the chart table with the motion of the ship and one by one the four men, the officer of the watch, by now Third Officer Chafney, the two lookouts and the helmsman, moved across for something to eat.

Below in the crew's mess area, the remaining men sat in wet-weather gear, drinking tea and watching a movie. They would wait inside until they were needed. No one was permitted on deck unless ordered, and then only with lifelines rigged. On *Caledonia* that meant a harness with six feet of nylon line and a climber's carabiner that could be clipped on to the rope that now ran the length of the deck.

Nichols had brought the carabiners aboard one day after a trip to a climber's shop in London and Jarvis had had to admit they were better than the usual stuff one bought in a chandler's. Jarvis was now returning from checking the battens on the rear hold, number four. Even with the wedges in they could work loose in a sea and he had come back into the mess soaked to the skin.

In the officers' mess Nichols, Jeffries, Scott, the cadet Fripp and Chief Engineer McDermott sat round the table, a similar selection of the doorstep sandwiches on a plate before them, a second jug of cocoa on the table.

Caledonia was, at times, an old-fashioned ship and her mess table had the familiar rim round the edge to stop plates and other items sliding off in a sea. Even so, Fripp, who sat nearest and stood the best chance of getting covered in the hot liquid, kept an eye on the cocoa jug as they talked.

'How are our young passengers?' McDermott asked, reaching for a hefty corned beef sandwich with one hand and the Branston pickle jar with the other.

'A couple of stalwarts still up and around, but most of them are pretty green round the gills,' Nichols answered, rubbing his eyes tiredly.

'First time I went through a blow I puked my heart out,' Jeffries said.

'Shit,' McDermott said, 'I still do sometimes.' He took a bite of the sandwich, careful not to let the pickle spill on to the tablecloth which was spotless.

'Then why are you eating, Chief?' Fripp asked respectfully.

'Because, laddie, if you're gonna throw up, have something to throw, I always say.'

'Charming,' Scott murmured.

'Don't give me your bloody high and mighty ways, sonny,' McDermott grinned. 'I've seen you on all fours wishing you were dead before now . . . I remember a storm in the Arctic Sea that went on for four days. Little vessel called the *Nord Star*. Finnish she was. Well, by the fourth day not a man on her wasn't sick including the master . . . Thought it was never going to end.'

The mind is conditioned by the environment in which it exists. What is normal and routine to one will be disturbing and intrusive to another. Even the most violent environment can eventually condition the mind to acceptance, as is the case with soldiers who can learn to sleep through an artillery barrage. Seamen eat, sleep, work and relax in a world that is constantly moving, not only with the motion of the sea, but with the vibrations of the ship's machinery. Always there is the noise. Sometimes just the hum of ventilators, sometimes the full crashing roar of the engine room, but always noise. For men deep sea on motor vessels it is a reassuring sound because there the engine is everything. It takes them home from long voyages. It powers the electrics from the masthead light to the line of dim bulbs in the shaft tunnel. But it does more for a seaman. It gives him steerageway, the ability to stay on course, to steer away from reefs and shoals. It allows him to weather storms.

It keeps him safe.

A ship under way on the high seas is a formidable thing. Thousands of tons able to move with precision, she is defiant and powerful.

Until her engine stops.

She is no longer defiant. She is no longer powerful. She is a helpless cripple. So, like the soldier who awakens when the artillery barrage lifts, the seaman is aware the millisecond the engine stops.

Down in number six bunker the fuel level that had been dropping steadily as *Caledonia* steamed southwards was now a little over half full. With her bows into wind, she was pitching, rising and falling at the head by forty feet as she met the waves.

The diesel fuel was slopping back and forth as the ship rose and fell. Gathering momentum, the fine layer of sludge on the bottom of the bunker began to move from where it had settled at the welded edge of the tank by the feeder pipe. Fine droplets of weld, shavings of steel, dust and a quarter-inch screwhead, moved back and forth, agitating the sludge. Finally, the whole cloud of contaminants rose the two inches to the feeder pipe and were sucked into the fuel lines that fed the main engine.

It was Archie McDermott who felt it first. He had been chief engineer aboard the *Caledonia* for six years and he knew every rhythm, every mood, every nuance of her engine. He was lifting his sandwich again, careful not to dribble the pickle, and finishing his story about the *Nord Star*.

'. . . Anyway the mate on the *Nord* reckoned that schnapps was the answer. A glass of schnapps could settle the gut, he would say. Can't abide the muck myself.' He bit into the sandwich.

'My sister sticks one of those things behind her ear.' Fripp smiled. 'You know those little pads. She gets sick on the ferry across to Calais.'

'Everybody who . . .' Jeffries began, then paused. He was sitting opposite McDermott who had stopped mid-chew and cocked his head sideways holding up a finger for silence.

'What's up, Chief?' Nichols asked.

McDermott had felt it. The momentary falter in one huge cylinder, five levels below them.

'. . . goes on those ferries gets . . .' Jeffries's voice faded away with an edge of uncertainty.

There was a full second of silence at the table and as the cylinder missed again, McDermott was on his feet and running to the door. The sandwich had dropped to the

116

tablecloth, the Branston pickle and corned beef fallen, unheeded, out across the white surface.

Nichols suddenly put his cocoa down and moved quickly towards the door.

'What's happening?' Jeffries asked.

Suddenly everything went dark and quiet. It was black as pitch in the mess room. The vibrations ceased, the ventilators hummed into silence. All that was left was the motion as the ship met another huge wave bows on.

'Oh, Jesus,' someone said. 'The engine's failed.'

Much happened in the next three seconds.

McDermott, who had reached the first companionway, had hooked an ankle over each handrail and was sliding down the rails as the lights went out. He knew the ship so well that he hit the first landing running and was on to the second companionway, swearing to all the ancient gods in his broad Scots accent.

The second engineer awoke the moment the engine stopped. Without opening his eyes he reached for his overalls and in two seconds was out of the door running down the passage in the dark. Someone opened another door at the wrong moment and he slammed into it, catching its edge across the bridge of his nose, giving himself a nasty cut. He picked himself up and began moving again, holding the wound closed with his hand.

Wellbrook also awoke that same instant and reached for a coat to cover his pyjamas. Considering he was not feeling well, he moved surprisingly fast towards his door.

The officers from the mess followed Nichols who ran towards the bridge, taking the steep stairs three at a time. Cochran, the radio officer, woke then, just as the auto switch in the engine room panels decided that the electric power really had stopped flowing and cut in the emergency generator. The old engine chugged and coughed once or twice then let go in a full-throated roar and the emergency lighting system came on, restoring power to the radio room and the bridge.

Sergeant Carstairs who was lying on his bunk counted to five and when the engine didn't restart he sat up and pulled on his shoes.

The crew in their mess had mixed reactions. A few sat in an awkward silence, one clutched at the crucifix at his neck. The motormen raced for the door followed by two GP1-rated seamen, those qualified to work in the engine room.

McDermott hit the top level of walkways at a run, as the emergency bulbs flickered into life. The duty motormen and the fourth engineer, torches flashing in the dim light, had the big hoist-lifted tool box moving on the rails.

'Injectors!' the engineer shouted in frustration, lifting a huge open-ended spanner and attacking the heavy bolt that held the fuel line coupling. 'The fucking fuel must be clogged thick with shit . . . We cleaned the fucking bunkers, Chiefy! We fucking cleaned 'em! Oh, Jesus Christ, we cleaned 'em . . .'

'Settle down, lad,' McDermott snarled. In truth he was just as concerned, but this was no place for a panicky man. 'Now let's get that line off there and start cleaning her up.'

He knew he didn't have to call in men. Every man on the vessel who was qualified to be in his engine room would be there to lend a hand. Even so it could take anything from twelve to eighteen hours to get the house-sized engine stripped and the injectors cleaned and re-installed.

Nichols hit the bridge as the lights came on, his mind racing. Please no. Not that. Not fuel contamination. We cleaned them. We cleaned the bloody bunkers. O sweet Jesus in your heaven, if you love sailormen like the prissy bitches at the Salvation Army say you do, then not fuel contamination. Not in a sea and shipping fucking steel plate, please, please.

'Speak. Is that you, Joe?' he snapped. In the dim lights he could barely see the watch keepers. It should be Joe Mangalo on the wheel.

'Aye, sir.'

'How are we doing?' Nichols moved straight to the compass and watched with a sinking stomach as the needle confirmed what he had felt through the deck plates. *Caledonia*'s head was falling off. Without power the ship's bows were being turned round by wave and wind. In a few minutes at most, she would lie wallowing, beam on to the storm.

'Sir.' It was Chafney. The officer of the watch. He handed Nichols the intercom phone.

'Thank you, Mr Chafney . . . Have the bosun report, please. I want a man in the passenger accommodation. Up against the hold bulkhead. I want to know what he hears. Every murmur of that steel. Right?'

'Aye aye.'

Off in the gloom, Nichols saw Captain Wellbrook arrive on the bridge wrapped in a dressing gown. In the dim light he looked ashen. Nichols kept talking.

'Mr Jeffries, check on Mr Cochran. I want the status of his radios with the emergency power on. Then ask him to report here as soon as he is ready.'

As he spoke he flicked a look up at the small VHF radio in the cradle against the rear bulkhead. Its pilot light glowed a dull red. Thank Christ for that, he thought.

'Mr Fripp?'

'Sir.'

'Ask the teacher if he would be so kind as to join me on the bridge, please. You will stay down with the boys. Reassure them. Then I want them in life jackets. Once he is back, move them up to the mess deck. Internal stairs only. Understood?'

'Aye aye . . . Sir? What about some chain off the bows? It might hold her.'

'Not enough. Not in this. On your way, lad.'

Nichols lifted the phone handset to his face, thinking, that boy is good, he will make a fine officer.

'Engine room, bridge.'

119

'Aye.'

'That you, Chief?'

'No. He's busy,' a voice said.

'Get him,' Nichols snapped. He turned and held the handset out to his captain.

'Thank you, Mr Nichols,' Wellbrook said. 'Would you be so kind as to ask Mr Cochran to advise the coastguard that we may require assistance.'

'Aye, sir,' Nichols replied.

'Mr Nichols.'

'Sir?' Nichols looked closely at the captain. His voice seemed pinched and hesitant as if he were in pain. Then whatever it was seemed to pass, because Wellbrook straightened his back and looked his chief officer in the eye.

'Not a CQ. We aren't buggered yet.'

In the early days of morse code, any call commencing with the prefix CQ was for all ships. The addition of a D meant danger. It was the forerunner to the SOS call which in turn was superseded, in the days of voice radio, by the now standard Mayday call. Nichols nodded. He looked up at the Satnav display and, jotting down the coordinates, left the bridge as Wellbrook leant forward, holding the handset to his ear.

'Well, Mr McDermott? What's happened to my engine?'

Cochran, dressed in a tracksuit bottom and a T-shirt, was sitting at his operating position in the cramped radio room, the electronics around him in a semi-circle. Jeffries stood nervously behind him, watching as he checked his gear. Cochran heard the footsteps approaching down the passage and took a deep breath. This is what I am paid for, he thought. Trained by Marconi for this day. They always said that the radio operator should be the last to leave his position and if he had to leave his ship then he did so with the captain. Last men off. The stories were legend. Water swilling round the man's chest as he tapped out his CQ

120

message, giving his ship's name, their position and requesting any help. SOS.

'How's things? You have power?' Nichols asked.

'Enough I think,' Cochran replied. 'Levels look OK but we will soon know.'

'Advise Falmouth coastguard that we have an engine failure and that we may require assistance.'

'That's all?'

'At this time,' Nichols replied, 'yes.'

Cochran nodded and leant forward and flicked the digital wave band selector switch on to a medium frequency as his first choice. He could either change to short wave or look for a VHF relay if it came down to it.

'Falmouth coastguard . . . Falmouth coastguard . . . this is the motor vessel *Caledonia*, over,' he intoned. His voice was steady and well modulated.

He waited ten seconds for a response and tried again.

'Falmouth coastguard . . . Falmouth coastguard . . . this is the motor vessel *Caledonia*, over.'

The sets hissed about him, some faint traffic coming through over the single side band speakers, so he bent forward to listen to the high-resonance speaker to his front.

'*Caledonia* . . . *Caledonia* . . . this is Falmouth, go ahead, over.'

'Falmouth . . . Falmouth . . . *Caledonia*. We have had an engine failure. Repeat, an engine failure.' Cochran looked down at the piece of paper Nichols had given him. 'We are a British-registered merchantman. We have fifty-six people aboard. Our position: forty-nine degrees, forty-five minutes and ten seconds north. Seven degrees, ten minutes and thirty-two west . . . that is approximately thirty-seven miles southwest of Bishop Rock, over.'

'Roger, *Caledonia*. We copied that. Are you declaring an emergency, over?'

'Negative at this time, Falmouth. But be advised we may require assistance, over.'

'Roger, *Caledonia*. We are standing by.'

The coastguard station at Falmouth is one of six Maritime
Rescue Coordination Centres around the United Kingdom.
In the twenty-four-hour-a-day operations room, a duty
staff of three men had already been supplemented by two
others and a further three auxiliary coastguards were now
summoned. The officer who had taken the call from
Caledonia had written the message verbatim, but the signal
had only been strength three so he pulled his headphones
off and, reaching back, rewound the tape that recorded
every communication. He listened again and then called
his superior across.

'Got a possible, Frank. Merchant with an engine failure
off the Scillies.'

'Have they requested assistance?'

'No.'

The senior officer didn't have to think about it. A breakdown deep sea was normally just an inconvenience, but in
a storm it could be lethal. With a lee shore barely thirty-five
miles away they could drift and be aground on the Western
Rocks inside twelve hours. While they were disabled, they
were also a hazard to other shipping exiting the Channel.
They could also founder.

'They will,' he said.

'I took down twenty-six people, but listen to the tape,
will you? Could be twenty-six, forty-six, fifty.'

They listened together but were unable to decipher the
word through the static hiss.

The senior man, grey-bearded and once a master
mariner himself, pulled down a register of ships' names
and scanned through the C section.

'She's a fourteen five general trader. A merchant ship.
Assume twenty-six. Even that sounds a bit over the top.
Check next time they come on the air.'

He then leant across, took the coordinates and walked
to the small powerful computer in the corner and entered

the details on to the field. The computer immediately threw back the optimum rescue solution.

'Eddie. Get on to West Drayton. Tell them we may want the Sea King from Brawdy, but tell them our little machine here says it's a long flight into a headwind. Judgement time if it happens. Then phone Dickerson on St Mary's. His boat is nearest. Ask him to have a chat to his coxswain. Who is it? Carter?'

'Yeah.'

'He may want to make a few calls. Get his lads out of their beds.'

'OK. I'm on it.'

'What about the Penlee boat? Is she back yet?'

'No.'

He stood back, crossed his arms and then ran his hands down the sleeves of his thick blue-issue sweater in a mannerism that had been his for twenty years. He watched as one of the officers put a little orange ship on the six foot by six foot plotting board. It would be changed to red if *Caledonia* upgraded her emergency and asked for help. Get your engine started, gentlemen. This is not the night to be lying ahull. Outside, the wind threw needle points of rain at the thick windows and shrieked like a banshee.

00:04

Hal Carter was standing at the sink rinsing his tea cup. Upstairs he could hear Jean moving about getting ready for bed and he put the cup upside down on the sink and reached for a tea towel to dry his hands.

The phone rang.

He crossed to it and lifted the receiver. Upstairs the footsteps stopped.

'Hello.'

'Hal, it's Dickerson.'

'Oh, aye.'

'I think we have a casualty.'

123

'Go on.'

'Falmouth have taken a message from a freighter. Engine failure. She is dead in the water thirty-five miles southwest of the Bishop. Twenty-six people on board they think. Now they haven't called for help yet . . .'

'When?'

'Pardon?'

'When did the call come in?'

'Only about four minutes ago.'

'They will still be looking for the problem.'

Dickerson paused there. He knew nothing of ships. But Carter did.

'What about a helicopter?' he asked. Jean appeared in a dressing gown and stood watching him and listening to their end of the call.

'It will take the same time as you. Headwinds or something. I think we should wait for their confirmation,' Dickerson said.

'It will take me at least two hours to get there,' Carter said.

'I still think we should wait.'

'I'll get the lads together at the boathouse. If they need help we will know soon enough and it's a long way.'

'If you think that's best,' Dickerson said evenly.

'I do. You might want to phone young Parnell. If we go we won't be waiting about.'

'I'll see you there.'

He put the phone down and lifted it again immediately. 'A ship,' he said to his wife, 'sou'west of the Bishop. Pull my bag out, will you? I'll just phone the lads and we will be away to the boathouse.'

She nodded and moved back up the stairs, taking them two at a time.

He got through to Ernie first, wishing that Bob Cameron was not still away on the mainland. This one would be short-crewed, he thought.

'Ernie? Hal. Call Vic and Henry. I think we will be away in the boat. Quick as you can, eh?'

He hung up and dialled the number for the Atlantic where he knew Simon and John Timson were spending the evening with Helen.

Caledonia

In the last four minutes the ship had been rolling viciously through almost seventy degrees, her high beam broadside on to the huge seas. Nichols was almost expecting the phone when it rang. He had just arrived back on the bridge after briefing the master in charge of the boys. Fripp was now with them in the main mess taking them through the life-jacket drills, making jokes where he could. They were frightened, pale-faced and listening intently to his casual but firm tone. Carstairs had been hanging around, getting in the way. Now he was on Nichols's heels again.

'A moment please, Mr Nichols,' he said.

'I'm busy,' Nichols said and snatched the phone up off the cradle. 'Yes.'

'Jarvis. That cargo in number one is about to go. I heard a chain snap, the others won't be far behind.'

Shit, no, please, not the steel plate. But he knew the bosun was right. That's why seamen hated it so much. It was impossible to secure. It shifted too easily and with the ship rolling like a barrel it didn't bear thinking about.

'Stand by.' He turned to Wellbrook in time to see him clutching at his chest, doubled over. As he watched, the captain began to sink to his knees, his face a picture of pain.

'Christ! Jeffries take this.' He threw him the phone and crossed to where Wellbrook was on his knees on the deck. 'Chafney, get the steward with his medic chest . . . Move, damn your eyes! Take it easy, Captain, take it easy now.'

'My God . . . it hurts,' Wellbrook hissed through

clenched teeth. 'Thought it was indi . . . aaah . . . indigestion. You have command of my ship now, Johnny. Take care of her while you can . . .'

'Don't worry, sir. You'll be OK.'

'Heart attack . . . Doctor warned me . . . Oh Christ, it hurts. Take command . . . get the boys off, Johnny. They are just children. The same age as . . .'

'Hush now, sir.'

Below them as the ship rolled back into the seas there was a mighty rumble that shook her from stem to stern. She stayed over, her windward-side guardrails in the water with fifty-odd degrees of list. The huge waves were not now crashing against her high strong sides, but on to her exposed decks and hatches.

'Cargo's shifted!' Jeffries called, his voice reaching a hysterical pitch. 'Oh shit, Mr Nichols, the cargo in number one has shifted. Oh Jesus, we are gonna sink, we are . . .'

'Shut up! Get a hold of yourself!' Nichols snapped. 'You are a deck officer, now behave like one! Now come here and sit with the captain. Move it!'

The junior crossed over and Nichols stood and moved back into the passage to the radio room. He ducked his head round the door and paused for a second to steady himself on the new angle of the floor. Don't die on me, Harry, please don't die on me. I'll get your boys away safe, just don't die on me. I need you now. *Caledonia* needs you now.

'Right, that's it, Mr Cochran. Cargo's shifted. CQ please.'

The Marconi man nodded, his face pale in the emergency lighting, and turned straight back to his panels.

'Mayday . . . Mayday . . . Mayday. Mayday . . . Mayday . . . Mayday. Falmouth coastguard, this is the *Caledonia*.'

On the bridge, as the medical steward lifted his head to ease a pillow beneath it, Harry Wellbrook, master of the MV *Caledonia* rediscovered his faith. He said a prayer for the soul of his dead son and the lives of the frightened boys gathered in the mess. Lord, you took my only son, as we took yours. Then you gave me the lives of twenty-one others to care for and keep safe. The tempest rages, Lord. Spare them and love and keep my son close to your side. Then he remembered the last student and the sealed orders in his cabin, the envelope with the police crest that was to be opened in an emergency but then the dim bridge went black and he slipped into unconsciousness.

St Mary's

Victor Collier woke instantly and took the call from Ernie Coutts. He got up and, without turning on the light, pulled a heavy sweater over his pyjama top and stepped into a heavy pair of working trousers that always occupied the same shelf in his wardrobe.

His wife sat up.

'Maroons?' she asked sleepily.

'Any minute, Ernie says,' he grunted. As he quickly pulled on socks and Wellington boots, she moved down to the kitchen to pack a few things for the boys. There were chocolate biscuits, some scones she had baked that morning and, just for good measure, she threw in some cheese, a pound of butter and two sticks of French bread.

She met him as he arrived downstairs and, handing him the bag, walked him to the door.

'Come home safe,' she said quickly.

Ernie Coutts pulled on the same outer clothing he had taken off two hours before, but added a heavy-issue sweater and moved straight into the storm. Victor would pick him up on the way past. He would get wet waiting but then, he thought, he would get wet anyway. Victor's car was an ancient soft-top MG that leaked like a sieve and then after that there would be the ride out to the *Maeve* in the tiny launch.

*   *   *

The phone was beside Parnell's bed but Norah was on that side, so she picked it up.

'Parnell?'

'No. Hold on,' she said.

She shook him awake. He looked at his watch, the luminous dial bright in the dark.

'Shit. Who is it?'

'Dunno.'

He took the instrument. 'Yes.'

'Parnell? Dickerson.'

'Who?'

'Dickerson from the lifeboat.' The voice was clipped and assured.

He sat up. 'Yes. Sorry. How are you?'

'I'm good. But there's twenty-six people who we think aren't. Get yourself down to the boathouse quick as you can. Know where it is?'

'Yes . . . God, I thought you said a training run first or a . . .'

'No time. This is the real thing,' Dickerson said.

There was a pause and Dickerson let the message sink in.

'All right . . . I'll be there in' – he looked at his watch again – 'ten or fifteen minutes.'

'Make it three,' Dickerson said and hung up.

Parnell swung his feet to the floor.

'What is it? Casualty?' Norah asked.

'Yeah, but not your kind,' he said. 'A ship or something.'

'What?' she asked into the pillow as he turned the light on.

'The lifeboat is going out. They want a doctor on board.'

She looked up. 'Lifeboat? You are going on the lifeboat?'

She had seen it the previous evening as they had walked down to the pub. 'Tonight? Now?'

He nodded. She sat up. She was an islander. She knew about lifeboats. She also knew that he didn't.

'Have you thought about this? It's dangerous, David.'

'I said I would go ... Besides,' he qualified, 'I am a doctor.'

'That doesn't mean you are qualified to crew a lifeboat.'

'What are you saying?' He began rummaging in a drawer for a sweater.

'That I have just found you again. I don't want to lose you,' she said softly in Irish.

'You won't,' he replied, smiling, and then switched back to English. 'Be back for breakfast.' He stood back with an old green polo-neck sweater in his hands. 'Better go.'

'You won't need that,' she said. She got up and took the sweater from him. He watched perplexed as she reached into her bag and pulled the tissue-wrapped parcel clear and threw it to him. 'I knitted it for bloody months. Least you can do is wear it.'

He opened it and immediately understood the significance. It was the traditional Aran fisherman's sweater.

'You are my man, David Parnell, and you will wear my stitch. Now away to your boat with you.'

He winked at her and left.

Hal phoned two others on his crew list and then went to lift the handset to try the Atlantic again. As he did so it rang.

'Hal. They have called for help,' Dickerson said.

'I'll be two minutes.'

He hung up and dialled the pub again. It was answered and he could hear the noisy crowd in the background as tired staff tried to get people to go home.

He passed the message and the publican tried to get John or Simon's attention but failed over the noise. So he reached up to the heavy brass ornamental bell and swung the clapper. The deep resonant gong stunned the crowd into silence.

'Simon Carter! John Timson! Up to the carn,' he shouted over the heads of the departing drinkers, lifting one arm, as though pointing to a flare in the sky. 'The maroons are up!'

The two dropped their glasses on to the nearest table and ran with Helen towards the door as an excited hubbub broke out amongst the crowd.

'What was that?' Susan Farmer asked someone alongside her.

'Maroons,' he said. 'The lifeboat is going to sea. Some poor bugger is in trouble. Hell of a night for it.' He shivered dramatically.

'I want to see it.'

'In this?' He jerked a thumb at the storm outside. 'You are mad, woman. You will be drenched to the skin.'

'Just tell me where!' she demanded.

'Why?'

'I am a reporter. Television.' She pointed to the camera on the floor beneath the table they stood by.

'I'll take you,' he replied gallantly, 'or you might miss them.'

'Thanks.' She grabbed her camera crew and they made for the door.

00.08

Up on Carn Thomas, Hal Carter spread the chart across the old scarred workbench and, quickly spinning his dividers across the surface, he marked the *Caledonia*'s last position. Dickerson stood beside him. As honorary secretary of the Royal National Lifeboat Institution, he had to officially authorize the launch.

'Happy with it?' Dickerson asked.

'She'll be drifting. Anyone else in the area?' Carter answered.

'You want 'em?'

'Aye. It's a long way off. A decent-sized vessel could heave to. Give us a lee.'

'I'll do my best,' Dickerson said. 'You'll launch?'

This was it. Hal Carter was coxswain. It was his decision.

130

To consider the weather, the seas, the distances, the dangers. His decision and, on the honorary secretary's authorization, his alone.

Behind them Simon Carter, John Timson and Victor Collier were pulling on bright-yellow-issue oilskins, yachting boots and their orange-issue life jackets. Only Timson left his boots on the shelf. He preferred his training shoes.

Off to one side, Helen Carter stood silently and watched her father, brother and boyfriend making their preparations. She was normally good at hiding her own fears but her father knew the signs. He fired a quick smile and looked back to the chart.

Ernie was already up in the little launch on the slipway and he bent and tinkered. The engine gave a cough, fired and began to run sweetly.

He dropped down to the slip's wooden edging and checked the quick-release shackle where the winch cable was attached to the boat's stern.

Lastly he took two of the seven-inch cardboard disposable flares from the locker by the door and stood waiting. The maroons, once fired to show the foundering ship's crew that help was coming and so much part of any rescue, were now just traditional. But tradition died hard for the crews and their communities. For them the greenish-grey flares lighting up the sky meant everything. It meant that the lifeboatmen were putting to sea on service.

Dr Parnell caught the yellow jacket and pants thrown to him by Timson.

'They should fit,' he said. 'Boot size?'

'Eleven.'

'Try these,' Timson said, throwing him a pair. 'They were mine. Should do. Life-jacket bottom strap goes under your arse. Now in the boat with you.'

'What's in the bag, Vic?' Simon asked.

'We have got scones and chocky biccies and a nice smelly Camembert with fresh bread ... well, freshish,' Collier replied, feeling the edge of one loaf. 'Twenty-six, eh? Be a tight squeeze coming home. Is the chopper coming out?'

'Dunno,' John called. 'If he's got a brain he will stay in his bed.'

Up at the workbench Carter, fully dressed, looked up at Dickerson. 'I have enough crew. We slip,' he said. 'Ernie,' he called. He stepped back from the bench and folded the chart. 'Fire 'em.'

00:12

As the flares burst and the cloud lit up over St Mary's the boathouse doors were swung back and the men clambered aboard the stubby little launch. Carter, who had squeezed for'ard through the five men and knelt by the little rubber steering wheel, shouted, 'Launch.'

Ernie Coutts leant over the stern and swung a mallet at a red painted pin in the linkage that held the boat up on the slipway. With a creak she began to move and then, gathering speed, she thundered down past the doors towards the choppy cold water as the last glows of the flare finally faded.

Carter shouted a warning as they hit the water but it was unnecessary. His crew knew to hold tight and Dr Parnell felt Timson's massive hand take his collar and hold him down. The little boat, her screws thrashing, shouldered aside the first wave and, as Carter eased the helm, she pointed her bows towards the *Maeve*. Water and spray splashed over each side and most of the men were wet by the time they clambered aboard the Arun's low-waisted midsection a minute later.

The wind that shrieked over the sea wall threw spray like icicles into their eyes as Carter led the way in with Ernie, leaving Simon to run up the deck with the launch's bowline. There he secured the smaller boat to the pink mooring buoy that would drop to the water when he let go the *Maeve*'s main mooring line.

Carter moved through the watertight door and straight

132

up to the helm and climbed into the coxswain's chair.

'Start engines,' he called.

Behind him Ernie switched the two ignition keys and pressed a thumb against the starter button for number one. Below them, the engine came to life and he counted to two and pressed the second starter button. The noise doubled and he watched the instruments settle before going below to take up his position and secure the water-tight sea doors behind him.

Timson moved up beside Carter.

'On the radar, John . . . Vic, the radios.' He leant forward and spoke into the intercom. 'Leggo for'ard,' boomed out of the foredeck speakers and Simon, judging the wave, pulled the heavy line up over the cleats and watched it drop away.

00:14

The *Maeve Corrigan* slipped her moorings and put to sea on service.

As her bows turned to St Mary's Road and the huge engines increased revolutions, she lifted on to the plane, the bright curling bow wave falling away beneath her deep hull.

She met the first waves at the end of the sea wall doing eighteen knots. As Carter edged her between Bacon Ledge and the wall, Susan Farmer and her camera crew, buffeted by the wind and supporting each other, tried to catch the action on tape, the high-technology camera struggling with the available light. Then, in answer to the cameraman's prayer, a jagged pitchfork of lightning speared the sky and there, in the viewfinder, cresting a huge breaking wave, was the *Maeve*, heading into the teeth of the storm.

'Jesus!' Ted yelled. 'I got it! I fucking got it! Oh shit, that's good stuff.'

'Let's go,' Susan said quickly. She was delighted. The footage was spectacular. Now they just needed the story.

'Where?'

'To whoever knows where they are going. They have a secretary or something.'

Caledonia

Carstairs found his way into the radio room. With the degree of list, Cochran's chair had rolled into the corner and he had left it there to stand before his console. A life jacket was on the floor. Keep him safe, they said. No one had mentioned a sinking bloody ship. He had decided to use the code. If he was incapacitated, hurt or felt the situation was out of his control and his charge was in danger, he could call in resources. No resources tonight. But they could be advised at least.

'I need to get a message ashore.'

'See the captain,' Cochran said and leant forward over the microphone.

'Just include a code in a broadcast.'

'See the captain!' Cochran said, waving him away impatiently.

'I think he's dying,' Carstairs snapped, 'so I'll stop asking. Now I'm commanding.' He flashed his warrant card. 'In the name of the law. You will include the words, "Daisy Marbles Three", and you will say it twice.'

'Oh shit. I forgot about him. Sorry,' Cochran replied. 'What is it?'

'The words are "Daisy Marbles Three". Just repeat it twice. They will know what it means.'

'That might get some bugger out of bed,' Cochran said dryly, before leaning forward again.

'Falmouth?. . . Falmouth . . . *Caledonia*.'

'Go, *Caledonia*.' They were now using a special distress channel and the formal procedures had fallen away.

'Coded message coming through. Code commences in five.' He counted to five aloud and then switched the mike on again, stating the code clearly.

'Caledonia, confirm "Daisy" as in flower, "Marbles" as in schoolboy and figure three, over.'

'Roger, Falmouth.'

'Thank you. *Caledonia*, be advised the St Mary's lifeboat is on her way. Echo Tango Alpha zero one one four hours Zulu, over.'

'Zero one one four confirmed, Falmouth.' Two hours, he thought, two bloody hours. He thought about the speed at which things had happened so far. Two hours too long.

'Caledonia . . . *Caledonia*, there is also a helicopter en route to you now. Echo Tango Alpha will be advised. Did you copy that, over?'

'Roger, Falmouth.'

Maritime Rescue Coordination Centre, Falmouth

The radio operator reached for the codes of the day. They were kept in a ring binder and updated as necessary.

He flipped through the index to the letter D and scanned down to read the entry alongside the word Daisy.

It read:

When an emergency is declared by a vessel or aircraft in British waters, airspace or within reasonable proximity of the territories of the Realm, and the code (see column) is stated twice, it signifies that a person under an escort of the Special Branch of the Metropolitan Police is a passenger, is in jeopardy, or is considered by the relevant authority to be in imminent danger.

CONTACT THE METROPOLITAN POLICE, SECTION D DUTY OFFICER IMMEDIATELY, USING THE CODE-WORD 'WARRIOR' – STATE NEXT TWO CODEWORDS (one alpha, one numeric) AND THE NATURE OF THE EMERGENCY.

He read it again to make sure he had it right.

'Oh fuck,' he said. 'Boss!'

His senior crossed quickly to the console.

'Got one of those short codes from the *Caledonia*. Looked it up.' He handed Frank the open page. 'Daisy.'

'You sure?'

'Absolutely.'

'Get on it. The number is on the wall.'

RAF Brawdy

'So you have sixty knots across the runway here and you are into a headwind all the way. It may gust well over that,' the met officer said.

'How much over that?' Flight Lieutenant Andy Hall asked.

'Difficult to say. Hundred maybe.'

'Any more and we will be flying backwards,' Selby remarked.

Hall thought for a second or two. His normal operating envelope in the Sea King HAR5, the one the manufacturers recommended, was a maximum take-off wind of forty knots. But he knew the machine was capable of much more. A valiant powerful workhorse, she would take off into one-hundred-mile-an-hour winds. The trouble was she had an airspeed of one hundred and ten knots so into any serious headwind it could take them hours to reach the casualty and then they would only have limited time overhead.

He made his decision.

'Start her up,' he said to Selby.

Thirty seconds later, seven minutes into the scramble, he was just running out of the crew room when the phone rang and the duty officer called him back.

'West Drayton control,' he said, handing him the phone.

A minute later he climbed into the Sea King. Overhead the big rotors were spinning and the ground crew were clear, the start-up unit safely beside them.

'Guess who's on the casualty?' he said to Selby.

'Who?'

'Who is on an educational trip to Iceland at the moment?'

'Dunno,' he said, running through his checks.

'Lawler's kid.'

'Really? Lawler's kid. No shit, eh?' Selby said.

'Yep! Clear right?'

'Clear.'

'Brawdy control, Rescue Romeo.'

The tower was waiting.

'Rescue Romeo, you are cleared to take off.'

'Roger.'

Hall eased the collective up, changing the pitch of the rotors, and, as they began to bite, he eased some pressure on to the rudders. Then, as he felt the weight come off the tyres, he gentled the big helicopter round directly into the wind and slowly pushed forward the cyclic control, the column between his legs. That controlled the angle of the whole rotor assembly, the 'disc' giving the aircraft forward lift. They moved along the taxiway, gathering speed into the wind and began to fly with every pound of fuel they could carry.

Caledonia

The ship was now lying, her decks exposed to the seas, with a forty-eight-degree list. Her bows were low in the water and the waves, some well over forty feet high, were washing right over her fo'c'sle.

Other waves, short and steep, but nevertheless weighing several hundreds of tons, slammed down on her exposed hatch covers.

Nichols watched through the bridge window. They can't take that for much longer, he thought. They will begin to crack or become dislodged and then we will take green seas in through the hatches. Then we are in real trouble.

He walked back towards the charthouse where Scott was trying to calculate their drift. The captain had been covered with a blanket and made as comfortable as possible on the upper leeward end of the steeply canted bridge. The steward medic had forced three aspirins down his throat and now sat with him. He had refused to be carried somewhere more comfortable and Nichols had feared a second heart attack if he forced him back into his day cabin. Jeffries, who seemed to Nichols to have barely recovered his composure, was standing beside him in the charthouse.

'Well, Scotty?' Nichols asked.

'I'd say we are drifting at a couple of knots minimum. Maybe three. Using that assumption we will be aground on the Western Rocks of the Isles of Scilly in anything between twelve and eighteen hours from now . . . if we are still afloat.'

'But surely we will have the engine running again by then?' Jeffries said quickly, the note of hysteria back in his voice. 'I mean it's . . .'

'I can't presume that,' Nichols said firmly. 'We are down by the stern already. We won't be afloat in six hours, let alone twelve.'

'The boats?' Scott asked softly. It was a question he had to ask, but he knew the answer as well as the next man. Boats were only any good in calm seas. They were difficult to launch at the best of times, but, with a list like they had, the windward boats, the ones on the lower side, were useless and the leeward boats would have to slide down the side of the hull giving even less control to the men on the davits. All of this into force ten conditions. The very prospect was appalling.

'I'd try it with crew but not with these kids. Our best bet for them is the chopper or the lifeboat.'

'How many people can fit in one of those things?' Scott asked, tapping his pencil on the chart. He was very cool and collected, the classic Hollywood image of an English gentleman under pressure.

'Not many, I wouldn't think,' Nichols answered. 'Have Jarvis unlash the rafts. Both sides. Move them aft. If we need them, we will drop them into the water on the windward edge of the transom. Hope the wind blows them safely round.'

'God, we will all be killed,' Jeffries moaned.

Nichols looked up at him.

'Mr Chafney is lookout on the port bridge wing. Relieve him and ask him to join me here,' he said coldly.

'I'm senior to him.'

'You are a coward,' Nichols replied. 'You will do as I command, my lad, or I'll see you charged with dereliction of duty.'

Jeffries turned with a sulky look and edged up the sloping floor towards the door.

'He's young,' Scott said to Nichols, looking for mitigation, 'but that was damnably bad form,' he finished dryly.

Nichols grinned for a second then jerked a thumb.

'Have a look at the area up where Chafney is. If that helicopter gets here we will need to have a place where we can hook the kids on to whatever harness they lower. Give yourself plenty of space. I don't know what diameter the blades are or how low they hover but we don't want them crashing into a samson post.'

'And the lifeboat. Where do you want him to come in?'

'If they get here and find us in this shit, then whoever is in command is good. I wouldn't dream of telling him his job,' Nichols said. 'Besides, we will be so pleased to see them they can come in through the captain's cabin window for all I care. I am going to see how the chief is getting along.'

On the bridge the wheel was locked and the duty seaman was on the exposed wing with Chafney. They had rough-wired a signal lamp from the innards of the riding light, and now sat wedged in what shelter they could find with a box of flares.

The noise was incredible. The wind shrieking past them threw foam and spray into their faces, and the waves crashing against the deck below them sounded like artillery. Their chances of seeing any vessel were remote but they had to be there to try.

As the ship shuddered, the Filipino seaman lost his grip and slipped a few feet. Chafney grabbed him by the straps of his life jacket and pulled him back into the corner of the bridge wing.

'Did I relieve you, Benny?' he shouted from ten inches away, in an effort to be heard above the noise, a grin spreading across his face.

'No, sir,' the man shouted back. The sight of one of his officers grinning gave him confidence and his fear dropped away.

It was cold and the wind cut through their layers of wet clothing like a knife as they huddled together watching the sea.

St Mary's

Susan Farmer went straight back to the hotel to change into dry clothing before moving on to finish the story. There were two messages for her, both from the office asking her to phone in. Both were marked urgent, but then, she thought to herself, they always said that, so they left for the boathouse immediately. The man who had shown them the way down to the quay had explained that

140

Dickerson, the RNLI man, normally waited there to see the boat and her crew safely home.

By the time they had arrived at the edge of the walkway up to the boathouse, they were wet through again and, as she knocked loudly on the door, she pushed her wet matted hair off her face.

The door opened. A thin, owlish, academic face peered round at them. 'Good grief. Come in, come in,' he said.

'Thanks.' She pushed her crew through ahead of her and motioned to get the camera out. 'Are you Mr Dickinson?'

'Dickerson,' he said, ' "e", "r." '

'Sorry . . .' She looked round the inside of the boat-house, taking it all in very quickly. The old photographs and panels of names made a roll of honour. Names of ships wrecked or saved.

'Are you the honorary secretary?'

'Yes, I am.' Dickerson looked down at the camera that was being lifted to a shoulder. 'What can I do for you?'

'My name is Susan Farmer. I'm from ITN. We saw the lifeboat leaving. Very dramatic. Where was she going?'

'On service,' Dickerson said abruptly. He did not like intrusions, but was mindful of the role he had to play for the public. It was their donations that kept the boats afloat.

She sensed his discomfort. Get some gritty background first. Then the story. She nodded to her cameraman and he lifted his camera to his eye. The soundman flicking on the bright floodlight he held in one hand, his microphone in the other. 'You don't mind if we record, do you?' Not giving him time to say no, she continued, 'I thought it was all done by helicopters these days.'

'Increasingly it is,' he answered carefully, 'but the deployment of the various resources depends on the nature of the emergency.'

'How dangerous is it, Mr Dickerson? Being on a lifeboat?'

'There is danger in any rescue attempt at sea. We do try to minimize the potential with careful training and good well-constructed boats.'

'But there is danger?' she challenged.

'Of course,' he replied.

'Then what takes men from their beds? From their homes and families? What makes them go out in a little boat in a storm? Surely it just puts more lives at risk . . . or is it not as dangerous as you say?'

Dickerson, conscious that Helen Carter, who had just watched every man she loved going down the slip, was still in the tiny workshop, recoiled for a second and then launched to defend those who weren't there to defend themselves. 'Turn that camera off,' he said.

'Sorry?' She was taken aback.

'I said turn that camera off.'

She nodded to Ted and the soundman and they lowered their equipment.

'Right. I'll bloody tell you how dangerous it is. A few years ago not thirty miles from here we lost an entire eight-man crew. All dead, Miss Farmer. Good men dead! In 1886 twenty-seven lifeboatmen died one night trying to save the crew of a German barque. They eventually got twelve survivors off.' He paused there and thrust his hands into his pockets. 'Throughout the history of the lifeboat service volunteers have given their lives to save others. It's not very nice so we don't dwell on it. But if you doubt the courage of these men, then you are not deserving to stand inside these walls.

'You ask why they do it? I don't know. I have never been out there in a storm but they say that, when you see the look on a person's face as you lift him or her from the sea, it's all worthwhile: the fear, and they fear, Miss Farmer, they are just men; the seasickness, yes, they get seasick. I've seen that boat come home drenched in vomit. They do it because to these men life is important, it's to be cherished. Little children sometimes . . .' He was still

142

looking for the reason, a simple reason to give her, so he repeated what he had already said. 'They say the look on their faces as they are pulled into the lifeboat is worth it all ... and they do it because they have the skill, the knowledge and the experience that no one else has ... and they care ... Now then, if you have finished your smarmy bit of gutter journalism, I will give you a statement.'

'I'm sorry,' she said, 'I didn't mean to insinuate that . . .'

'Are you ready?'

She flicked a look at her crew as Ted lifted his camera. 'Yes.'

'At 23:05 hours Greenwich Mean Time this evening a British-registered freighter with twenty-six people on board advised Falmouth coastguard that her engines had failed in force ten to eleven conditions approximately thirty-five miles southwest of these islands. At 23:14, that is 12:14 British Summer Time, the St Mary's Arun-class lifeboat, *Maeve Corrigan*, slipped her moorings and put to sea on service ... We had had some warning so most of the crew were heading this way by the time the casualty called in the Mayday. The coxswain believes he will be alongside the casualty, the MV *Caledonia*, in about . . .'

'Sorry, did you say the *Caledonia*?' she interrupted.

'Yes, I did. There is more. In about two hours. Apparently her master has had a heart attack. The vessel is now under the command of her chief officer ... ah, name of . . .'

'John Nichols. His name is John Nichols.'

'Yes.' Dickerson said. 'How did you ... ?' Then he saw her expression. She knew him.

'Stop recording,' she said in a monotone.

'What?' the cameraman asked.

'Stop bloody recording, Ted!'

She walked abruptly to the door and pulled it back

and ran to the railing where the carn fell away to the sea below. She stood, the wind slapping her hair into her face.

John.

SIX

'Come back in. You'll freeze out here in wet clothes,' a voice shouted. Susan looked up. It was a girl dressed in jeans and a heavy anorak. She shook her head.

'I've sent your guys back to the hotel,' the girl shouted. She then leant forward. 'Come inside. I want you to see something . . . come on.'

Susan let herself be dragged back into the boathouse and the other girl closed the door behind them. Susan looked around. The crew had gone and Dickerson was nowhere to be seen.

'See the names on the wall? The ships and dates? Six hundred and twenty-seven people saved. By the men of the St Mary's lifeboat,' she said, shaking the water from her coat.

'I said I didn't mean it,' Susan said.

'I know you didn't. What I am saying is these men are Scillonian. They are boatmen. Islanders. If anyone can get to the casualty they can. I mean . . . if anyone can save those poor people then my da . . . these men can . . . Your friend on the ship? Try not to worry too much.'

'Thanks . . . you seem to know a lot about it all. Who are you?'

'My name is Helen.' She smiled and then explained. 'My dad is the coxswain. My brother and boyfriend are in the crew.'

'You must be very proud of them.'

Helen smiled. 'Yes, I am,' she said. 'Look, I usually wait here for them but they are going to be a while tonight. I'm going to go home. If you want to wait with me and Mum then just come on down.'

'Usually? God! How often do they go out?'

'Well. I'm normally in Penzance. I hear about it later,' Helen admitted, grinning.

When Susan arrived back at the hotel she dried her hair and, finally, feeling a little guilty, she put through a call to the office. If the messages really were urgent then there would be someone there, she reasoned. Knowing the switchboard would be closed, she used one of the newsroom's direct lines.

'Yeah,' answered a harassed voice she recognized.

'Hi, Bernard. It's Susan Farmer. Someone after me?'

'Someone? Fuck! Everyone!' She heard him shout to someone else and then he came back on. 'Where are you? Still in the Scillies, I hope?'

'Yes. Yes, I am.'

'Good. Listen carefully. A ship is in the shit near you somewhere. Sinking or something. Anyway, our source in the coastguard says that Lawler's kid and a bunch of others from his school are on board. Apparently the local lifeboat has gone out and a chopper has left RAF Brawdy. That's in South Wales.'

'Lawler's kid? David?' Her mind reeled. 'Jesus.' She thought quickly. On John's ship? Why didn't he tell me? This would be the story of the day, maybe the week. 'Bernard, I'm close to this one . . . personal. If you want someone else you better say so.'

'Who else? I was going to say get a chopper but you are cut off out there. You are it. A bunch of kids, including the son of the Prime Minister, are on a sinking ship and you are the only hack with a cam crew in distance. Auntie Beeb will be talking to God to get the weather lifted so they can cover the story. Are you there, Susan?'

'Yes. I'm here.'

His tone changed then, the flippancy fell away and he was Bernard Aitken, the news editor. 'This is a biggy, girl. There is nothing else happening of this scale. We wait all our lives to do the exclusive on a story this size. Shake it off and get professional.'

'Easy to say,' she replied.

'Easy to do. Just decide to do it . . . Listen, if this is a personal one then you knew about it?'

She laughed. It was a bitter sound.

'Yeah. We got footage of the lifeboat going out.'

'That's my girl! Who is it?'

'A guy.'

'On the lifeboat? That was quick work. You have only been there a day.'

'Don't give me any crap, Bernie. I'm not in the mood.'

'Sorry,' he said genuinely.

'He's the chief officer on the ship that is . . .' she couldn't bring herself to say sinking . . . 'in trouble.'

'I'm sorry to hear that, but we have a unit on the way to the Falmouth coastguard base and every man I can get doing the background . . .'

'OK, OK. Look, I'll cover the story. The lifeboat will take two hours to get out there, then whatever time on the site and then two hours home.'

'It will be dawn by then.'

'We have some footage in the can already.'

'Good. Feel up to going live?'

'Piss off.'

He laughed softly. 'Write something and call me back. We will record a voice-over for some stock shots. But get ready for live because I have committed an interview at 6.30 am . . . Hang on. Something's coming in.'

She waited for a moment or two and he was back. 'Big cock-up in the numbers on the ship. Reports here say twenty-six, but one of the others has just pulled the files. There are twenty-one kids in the group.'

'What?' She paused. 'That makes the total . . .'

'Fifty something,' Bernie said.

'Oh shit . . . Bernie, the lifeboat is expecting twenty-six!'

'How do you know?'

'My source here . . . let the coastguard know, will you, Bernie?'

'Sure. How good is your lifeboatman?'

'The best,' she said, Dickerson's rebuke firmly in her mind.

'I hope you're right,' he replied.

'I'll call you.'

'Twice,' he said. 'In five minutes with a voice-over sequence, and again later . . .'

'I know,' she interrupted, 'to go live as soon as the headlines are done.'

'Bollocks. Straight in. These are the headlines.'

Maeve Corrigan

Carter felt the lifeboat crest the wave and, as they flew across the back side, he eased off on the power to stop her broaching. He was steering by compass, the radio direction finder still a good way off its effective range. Behind him, Simon lay on the floor, wedged between two of the chair pylons, the place he found most comfortable in big seas. John sat with his face glued to the radarscope and Vic manned the radios.

Parnell sat strapped in a chair, his fingers white-knuckled, holding on to anything he could reach. His view from the dimly lit wheelhouse was that of some sort of hell. Jagged forks of lightning lit the shrieking night. The seas were huge. The waves great foam-streaked monsters so big that the full power approach up the leeward side was a climb that seemed to take for ever. Then came the gut-wrenching fall over the back and down into the trough. The breakers had solid walls of foaming, churning water that slammed across the *Maeve*'s foredeck as she buried her bows before rising to the next challenge.

Inside, the roar of the engines made normal conversation impossible, so Parnell faced his fear on his own, holding his breath as Carter swung the bows to meet another breaker. This one was thirty feet high, its foamy crest falling.

'Hold on,' Carter shouted.

The boat slammed into the forefoot of the wave and rose up the side till her bows pointed to the black spume-streaked skies and shuddered as the curling wavetop fell over her, breaking around each side of the wheelhouse. She shivered, shook the water from her decks and cleared the crest.

'. . . And over we go,' John Timson bellowed with a grin, holding grab bars with two hands.

My God, Parnell thought, his breath hissing out through clenched teeth, he is enjoying this. I must have committed my soul to my maker a dozen times in the last half an hour and he is enjoying it.

A figure loomed beside him. It was Simon, standing on the rollercoastering deck, one hand holding the stainless-steel grab pole with nonchalance born of youthful bravado and considerable experience.

'Don't worry, Doc,' he yelled. 'We have done this plenty of times before.'

Parnell grinned sheepishly and Simon leant forward.

'Lie on the floor if you like. It's more comfortable.'

Across the wheelhouse, Vic Collier sat at the radio panel, his feet hooked under the footrest and his bump cap tied firmly under his chin. He looked, Parnell thought for a second, like a garden gnome. He offered up a packet of chocolate biscuits.

Parnell shook his head but Simon reached across and took two and began eating.

The feeling had relaxed in the last fifteen minutes or so. Those first miles out of St Mary's had been silent and tense. With the Crim to the right and the Western Rocks and the Bishop to the left, Broad Sound was unforgiving at the best of times. Now they were clear and in deep water with nothing in front of them but the mighty Atlantic Ocean.

Simon moved up and stood beside his father at the helm, his knees flexing as the boat shuddered and danced.

Vic sat forward quickly and turned up the volume on the medium wave and began writing on a small pad at his elbow.

'Hal,' he called.

Simon stepped back, took the message and, looking at it, gave it to his father.

'Read it.'

'It says there are more people. Fifty-six! Not twenty-six. Fifty-six!'

Carter said nothing. He steered the boat and thought about it. The makers said fifty was about the limit that the Arun could handle. If that new figure was correct then with his crew they would have a homeward-bound trip with sixty-two people on board. Where could he put them all? And then back with big following seas.

'Ask 'em if they have any other vessels nearby? We want a lee,' he shouted.

'There's more,' Simon said. 'The Prime Minister's son is aboard the casualty.'

Carter leant towards him to hear better, not taking his eyes off the seas for a second.

'Lawler's son,' Simon repeated. 'He's on the casualty.'

He saw his father nod and shrug and he smiled. He knew that, to him, a life was a life.

Drumbeat

The big Royal Fleet auxiliary was moving slowly away, fifteen miles to the east. The captain was a prudent man and in a storm like this, even if she had both of her screws functioning, she still would have been barely under steerageway, her bows into the wind to ride it out.

They had been monitoring the radio traffic between *Caledonia* and the coastguard, and her captain was on the bridge discussing the issue with his chief officer and chief engineer.

'It's now fifty-six, including a party of schoolchildren. Have Falmouth asked for assistance yet?'

'Negative, sir, but they are aware that we have our own problem. They probably don't want us adding to theirs,' said his chief officer.

'You have a solution, Number One?' Captain de Villiers asked testily.

They might have an engineering problem, but they were a Royal Naval auxiliary, crewed by the pride of the merchant marine, and it would take more than a hot shaft to stop them being anywhere when it counted.

'We can be there in an hour and a half.'

'With more revolutions,' the chief engineer qualified. 'I can only give you six knots and that will be shaking the heart out of her.'

The captain looked at them both, his decision made.

'We proceed with all due speed.'

'I can give you six,' the engineering officer said.

'Only six? Maximum revolutions on the good shaft now?' de Villiers said with one raised eyebrow.

'Eight, maybe eight and a half,' the engineer said unhappily.

'Thank you.'

He turned to a seaman who had just stepped on to the bridge with a message in his hand. 'Make to Falmouth. *Drumbeat* will proceed to the *Caledonia* and assist where possible.'

The phone warbled beside the pilot at his plotting table. He lifted the handset, listened and then looked at the captain.

'Coastguard has requested assistance for the *Caledonia*, sir. Can we make a lee for the rescue attempt by the St Mary's lifeboat.'

'There we are then.'

'There's more, sir. *Defiant* has advised they will assist.'

'Have they, by Christ?' De Villiers laughed. 'In that baby boat? They want a lee, get more bloody cover behind a lilo than behind a destroyer.'

'. . . Ah, yes, sir. Falmouth also want us to relay. Apparently there is a ULCC coming up the Channel.'

'Now they are talking. What ship?'

'*Pegasus*, sir.'

'I know her. She is big. Give a lee like Gibraltar. Relay and let's see what her master is made of.'

Twelve miles further east, HMS *Defiant* moved from her uncomfortable, pitching, downwind leg and, with the revolutions building, did a wild slewing turn back into the teeth of the storm.

Her captain, by rank a commander, couldn't resist a jab at his bigger merchant-navy-crewed consort.

'Make to *Drumbeat*, "*Defiant* is able, *Defiant* will assist, *Defiant* will be first, think what you missed."'

As his smile died he looked into the storm and thought about the people on the stricken ship.

'Have CPO Hardy ready, scrambling nets. Also prepare four inflatable rafts.'

'How about a seaboat, sir?' his senior lieutenant asked. 'I'll take four volunteers.'

'Negative, Number One. That isn't even a calculated risk. That's four drowned sailors and an officer who should have known better . . . but thanks for the offer.'

Pegasus

James Hawk, the master of the *Pegasus*, was standing under the shower when he was summoned to the bridge, very politely, by a cadet. The fact that his wife was under the same shower and was giving him her south-of-the-border steamy look as he soaped her down made it doubly inconvenient.

He pulled on a tracksuit and moved quickly up the wide silent passages. She was such a big ship that the storm was barely noticed by anyone inside her accommodation superstructure and it was only when he stepped through the heavy automatic doors on to the bridge that the noise level rose. She was pitching very gently. Fully loaded, she would have simply shouldered aside the biggest storms. Now if they had a potential problem it was with her being in ballast. She was too light and could be pushed by the force of the wind against her cliff-high sides. The automatic steering, called 'Jack' by all, had to be programmed to compensate.

'What have we got?' he asked.

It was just on midnight, the watch was changing and there were two duty officers on the bridge. The chief officer was also there, leaning over a chart. Hawk moved over to him. He was a tall lean Arizonan who wore cowboy boots everywhere he went.

'Got a request from Brit coastguard, Skipper. There's a vessel in trouble. Got a bunch of schoolkids on board. They have a lifeboat, one of these volunteer ones, going out to try and take 'em off. The master of the rescue boat wants a lee to attempt his rescue behind. Coastguard wants us to offer.'

'Where are they?'

'Here, sir.' The chief officer touched a point on the chart with a huge pair of brass dividers and lifted his unlit cigar to his lips. It was the nearest area to the tanks that a man could take a smoke but no one ever did. Not on Hawk's bridge.

'By now not much more than thirty-five miles off the Scillies.'

'Close . . . very close,' Captain Hawk said.

They were asking him to slow his colossus, turn away from the storm and bring her close enough to a vessel foundering to create a windbreak. If anything happened she was close. Close to a lee shore. Every seaman's nightmare.

His decision as master. His peers would understand, but the owners would not. The shareholders would not and neither would Lloyd's. Three hundred million dollars' worth of ship. The lives of his crew and their dependants.

He knew what his wife Juanita would say. Fiery, beautiful Juanita, who was his conscience and his judge in all things.

He could hear her words. If it were your ship in trouble then I'd want them to stop and help you. Will your ship give them what they want to try and save lives? You say yes. What choice have you? So simple. Three hundred million dollars. So? Let Lloyd's who have, you point out so often, spread the risk, take the risk you pay them for. Besides Mobil can afford another ship. They can't buy those children back. You don't even have the excuse of a load of pollutant oil on board. You are a fine *marinero*. An honourable man. You decide now.

He did.

'Come on to two hundred and ten degrees. Give "Jack" the plot. We will come off the power fifteen miles off her position, gun her in on a slow dogleg, a zigzag, if you like, and do one drift pass. Then every revolution on, hard port helm and back into wind.'

'Aye aye, sir,' the Arizonan chief officer drawled.

'Contact Falmouth,' Hawk continued. 'Get the frequencies of the others involved. I want to talk to every son-of-a-bitch within twenty miles. Once we start we are committed. They must understand that we will barely have steerageway once we take power off and it will take us six miles to build up again. Positions must be accurate and everyone stays put downwind of the casualty till we have moved through. That should give the rescue boat a minute and a half or two minutes of lee, depending. Those are my conditions.'

'Aye aye.'

'I am going to finish my shower. I shall be back. In the meantime double the lookouts and I want every light aft the bridge turned on. Nothing for'ard other than riding lights. I want to see but also be seen.'

The chief officer looked back at the chart. By now the second was also there. He had laid off the courses and the data for the steering system while his chief officer and captain had been talking.

'Captain.' The second officer looked up. 'We can drop back to slow ahead in eighty-eight minutes. The turn for the pass, 03:21 hours.'

'Very well. Let's hope we aren't too late to be of some use,' Hawk said.

Caledonia

'You haven't got yours on,' David Lawler said, as Carstairs checked the way he had secured his life jacket.

'No,' Carstairs replied, smiling, 'you are right. I haven't.'

'Don't you think you ought to?'

'Plenty of time for that.'

They were in the corridor outside the main crew's mess area, leaning against the wall, the floor beneath them steeply canted. The other boys were inside with the teacher while Fripp wandered amongst them, a cheery smile on his face, chatting with each in turn. They were all frightened but some bore it better than others. Surprisingly there was only one crying openly and, as Fripp came up to him, a Filipino seaman nudged him to one side and sat down with the boy.

'I have five sons and when I get home they love to hear a tale about the sea. Especially they like the one where the *Kunak* sank and the flying fish landed in the lifeboat.'

'You have been on a sinking ship before?' the boy asked, wiping his eyes.

'Sure,' the seaman lied. 'Three times . . . see the earring!' He leant round so the boy could see his left earlobe. 'If you have been wrecked at sea you have earned the right to wear one!'

The seaman grinned like a pirate and slapped his life jacket proudly.

'Why haven't you got three?' the lad asked, taking strength from the man's apparent wealth of experience.

'My wife wouldn't let me,' he replied, laughing and flashing a wink at Fripp. To the boy, who was from a conservative home, that was very believable and he smiled. Fripp moved on with a new respect for the Filipino seaman who had had to deal with his own fear to help the boy.

In the hall the lighting was dim, just the single emergency bulb every ten feet.

From their position in the passage Carstairs and David could hear the sound of the waves hitting the afterdeck. The crashing slam of tons of water on the hatch covers carried clearly over the howl of the wind, the ship shuddering each time.

'When the time comes I want you to do as I ask,' Carstairs said. 'My single responsibility is now your safety.'

The boy didn't answer, his eyes fixed on some point in the distance, a curious look on his face.

'Did you hear me?' Carstairs asked.

'Yes.' David looked at him. 'I was just wondering what Dad would be doing if he were here.'

'Well,' Carstairs answered, 'he would probably be helping in whatever way he could.'

'What can I do to help? I want to help.'

'Nothing. These officers are professionals. They are doing all that is possible. The best we can do is do as they ask, when they ask it, and stay out of their way.'

The boy nodded, as if he expected nothing else.

'How will we be getting off? In the lifeboats?' he asked.

'No. The seas are too rough. There is a helicopter flying out. That will lift us off. There is also a rescue lifeboat coming, but it will all be over by the time they get here. Everyone should be away by then.'

'How many people can a helicopter take?' David asked.

'The Sea King will take twenty-nine or thirty. A Wessex about half that, I suppose. I'm not sure what is coming.'

He remembered the storm would be affecting more than just them and hoped like hell that the resources weren't stretched. The coastguard would have contacted the office who, in turn, would have contacted Number 10. They would be trying to get what information they could. If they were the only emergency then there would be half a dozen helicopters in range. But if there were other emergencies, then they would only get a limited response, schoolkids or not. These things had to be seen to be fair. They couldn't have extra boats or aircraft coming here if another incident could require them.

'We'll probably be taken to a nearby ship,' he continued. 'If not, then ashore. The Scilly Isles are closest and they would have fuel for the aircraft too . . . so when the time comes, we will cooperate fully and do as we are asked.'

To Carstairs the boy's eyes seemed to have taken on a firm look.

Nichols moved along the canted catwalk in the ominously silent engine room. Dim bulbs threw soft oily shadows and, below him, he could hear the emergency generator and the sound of steel striking steel as huge tools were worked on the engine.

Two levels down McDermott and his team lay on aluminium-lined tarpaulins that were spread over the upper side of the now-sloping engine. The men were split into teams, each working feverishly to extract a set of the clogged injectors. Fuel lines were already clear from their couplings and the whole room stank of diesel.

Nichols dropped off the catwalk level to where McDermott was.

'How we doing?'

'Badly,' the Scot snapped without looking up. 'Topsides?'

'Same. Archie, the skipper has had a heart attack.'

The chief engineer looked up quickly.

'You don't look surprised,' Nichols said.

'I'm not, lad. How is he?'

'Alive. Just.'

McDermott nodded. 'I thought he looked a bit off colour lately, but he's a tough old bastard . . . It's your ship then, boy.'

Nichols nodded. McDermott was technically senior to him so he needed the acknowledgement of his command for what he had to do next. 'How long will you be down here?' he asked.

'Twelve hours. Maybe fifteen.'

'Too long. I think you should move your men topsides. The cargo in number one has shifted.'

'I bloody know that, boy! The fucking ship is lying on her . . .'

'Number four won't be far behind,' Nichols snarled. 'The seas are slamming on to my hatch covers like concrete blocks. We will be shipping green seas into the holds any time now. A lifeboat and a helicopter are on the way. We will take off the passengers and crew.' Nichols jabbed a finger at McDermott. 'Now you decide who you need down here to keep the generator running and you get the rest of your people topsides, you cantankerous old bastard!'

Nichols stood and jumped on to the catwalk.

'Johnny,' McDermott called with a grin.

Nichols turned to face him.

'You'll do!'

He left with the engineer's ragged laugh in his ears and in spite of their predicament he couldn't help his own smile.

Rescue Romeo

Hall lifted his gloved hand off the collective and tapped the display on the inertial navigation system. The winds were violent and unpredictable. They were headwinds one minute, then crosswinds the next. The navigation system, even with working averages into calculations every few seconds, was unable to give a consistent arrival time overhead any of the waypoints.

Hall took a round pilot's slide rule from the seat's side pocket and turned the bezel with his thumb. One sixty-three miles, one ten knots, chuck in average headwind of eighty knots, allow for none, allow for gusts, add the age of your son, sacrifice a dead chicken.

Selby looked over and raised an eyebrow. Hall looked back down at the INS. It was varying its arrival time overhead between 01:39 and 02:24 local. Go for the median, he thought.

'One hour forty odd.' He waved a hand. 'Tell 'em we will try to be overhead at 01:00 Zulu.'

They were at three thousand feet, the height at which the met officer suggested they would have the least headwinds. Outside, the night was absolute, black as pitch; with rain lashing the windscreen and wind buffeting the fuselage, the aircraft was being thrown around by extreme turbulence.

Selby finished the transmission and tightened his four-point harness, looking across at Hall who sat, his eyes on the instruments. He was, Selby thought, as good a rotary wing pilot as he had ever seen. Both hands on separate controls, both feet working, a map unfolded across his lap. Fast jet pilots often likened the flying of a helicopter under those conditions to being a one-armed paper hanger. He smiled at the analogy and bent down for the Thermos in the bag beneath his legs. He knew he could learn a lot from a pilot like Hall.

He waited for a still moment and poured coffee into one

of the cyclist's drinking bottles with the screw top and straw. He finished the exercise and handed it across to Hall, indicating that he would take the controls.

'You have control,' Hall said formally, taking the bottle.

'I have control,' Selby acknowledged. 'What's the plan?'

'Haven't decided yet. Let's see how close this fleet auxiliary gets. We may be able to unload on her afterdeck. If that's too tricky then it's back into the Scillies.'

He lifted the map from his knees and swung the flexible-necked reading light across its surface.

'There's an LZ on St Agnes . . . here,' he indicated. 'I don't know if they have fuel. They certainly do on St Mary's. That's where the S.61 comes in from Penzance.' He was thinking aloud now. He took a sip of the coffee and spoke again.

'We will need fuel. Two trips minimum. Round trip sixty miles. If we have injured it will be there. They have a hospital.'

'Do you want me to get someone lined up to refuel?'

'Affirmative.'

St Mary's

Norah couldn't sleep. She kept thinking about David on the lifeboat and eventually she got up and got dressed. Five minutes later, the hood up on the old oilskin Barbour she was wearing, she stepped out of the front door and began to walk down the street towards the boathouse.

Dickerson was there when she arrived.

'I'm not intruding, am I?'

He looked at her over his glasses. 'No. You are . . . ?'

'My friend has gone out on the boat. I was wondering if you knew what time they would be expected back.'

'Difficult to say. It may be a while . . . You must be David Parnell's friend.' Dickerson smiled at her.

Norah nodded. She wasn't surprised he knew about them. It was the same in all small communities.

'We have a kettle. Would you like a cup of tea?'

'No, thank you. I'll just be going.'

He knew the look. For some the waiting was tough.

'Well. Tell you what. I was going to walk down to Hal Carter's house. Something for his daughter Helen. You wouldn't mind dropping by there on the way, would you? I don't like to leave the boathouse while they are out if I can help it. I would certainly appreciate it.'

'I'd be pleased to,' she replied. 'Where is it?'

He described it to her and stepped back into the office, returning a few moments later and handing her an envelope. She left immediately and as she did so he telephoned Jean Carter. The envelope was empty.

Ten minutes later Norah was sitting by the Aga stove in the Hugh Street house, taking a cup of coffee from Helen.

'Really I must go,' she protested.

'Nonsense, child . . . so you can sit and worry yourself sick on your own?' Mrs Carter said.

'I'm not worried,' Norah replied firmly.

'And I'm a professional wrestler,' Mrs Carter retorted, one eyebrow raised, hands on hips. 'Look . . . we all worry. We just don't let them know that.'

Helen, whom Norah had only met a few minutes before, winked at her from behind her mother.

'Now tell me about your young man,' Mrs Carter said, sitting down at the table. 'Mrs Holly who sees him every other day for some complaint or other thinks he is just wonderful.'

Norah accepted defeat, settled back in the chair and they began to talk.

Carter watched the curl of the spume-covered giant wave, and judged his crossing point with perfection, coming back on course after a sliding juddering broach as they powered up from the deep trough to face the next.

Time to give one of the others a spell at the wheel, he thought. The experience was invaluable.

He reached across and tapped John Timson on the shoulder and, when the big man looked up, he indicated that he should slide into the coxswain's seat. They changed over, Timson's big hands gripping the wheel, as Simon moved up to operate the radar.

Carter moved back down the wheelhouse, his hands reaching from handhold to handhold, the vibrations from the huge roaring engines coming up through the soles of his seaboots.

He looked at Parnell, trying to make a judgement on the man, not as a doctor but as a crewman, albeit temporarily, on his lifeboat.

Most new men got seasick unless they had had many seasons crewing fishing boats. Not just a bit green round the gills. Some got so sick they just lay on the floor, or wedged themselves in somewhere, covered in their own vomit and wanting to die. All were frightened till they had learnt to trust the coxswain and the incredible strength of the boat. He had never taken a man straight out before. There had always been training runs, the chance to watch and evaluate. The chance to see the way they moved on deck.

Good boatmen sometimes failed because they just lacked that magic something that made good lifeboatmen. The ability of a strong individual to settle in and become part of a team, the ability to see something developing before it did and the skill, the courage and the judgement to confront it. Men like Bob Cameron.

They had gone out looking for a small French-registered

pleasure boat. They had found the two adults. Speaking in French, pleading, crying. The woman hysterical. There was a child. A fifteen-year-old girl. Still in the water or in the wrecked smashed hull on the rocks. He remembered the gale like it was yesterday. He had gunned the big Arun in through the exposed shoals. There was insufficient water beneath the hull so he had waited for a wave and surfed in on it. He was standing on the flying bridge feeling the wave beneath them and there suddenly, in his peripheral vision, was a flash of colour in the water. He spun the wheel and the big boat turned on her keel. With props out and cavitating, she half broached on the wave, no time to shout, no time to point.

Down on the deck Cameron knew. He just knew.

As the boat heeled over Cameron swung himself over the stanchions and, holding the guard wire with one hand, reached down into the boiling sea with the other. Carter hit full reverse on the starboard engine. One chance. An image of John Timson crossing the canted deck with two huge strides, and little Bob Cameron, every muscle in his body straining, lifting something from the sea with strength that could only have come from the Lord himself. She had been going under, he said later. She had given up the fight. Her face was down. He had got a hand hooked through her jacket collar and lifted her full weight, sodden clothing and all, against the drag of the boat, clear of the water, the cable cutting into his left hand. Then there was John Timson, big John who could lift fifty-kilo bags of cement as if they were bags full of feathers, taking the girl in one hand and Cameron in the other, pulling them over the guard wire, Cameron's hands locked tight, the muscles clamped solid on both the wire and the survivor. Judgement and courage.

Parnell looked up at him and managed a smile.

'You all right?' Carter shouted the question, patting his stomach.

The boat skittered down the back side of a wave and

Parnell nodded and gripped the seat arms as he leant forward.

'What will we see first?' he asked.

You don't see, Carter thought to himself. You don't see very much on a night like this. Sometimes it's gone. Sunk. You smell the diesel first. The wind carries the smell for miles. Then bits of flotsam. Wreckage in the water. And if people have gone, then you feel it. You feel a sadness. It hangs over the area somehow. You know that some of them have drowned already. Let not the deep swallow me up. Let's hope we are in time.

'Lights maybe,' he said, miming a helicopter rotor in the air. 'Radar first.' He paused as a wave slammed into the bows. 'Then the vessel. The seas break against it . . . looks different.'

The conversation was difficult with all the noise. Parnell nodded. Carter pointed down to the for'ard survivors' cabin.

'Stretcher down there . . . first-aid boxes both ends.'

Parnell nodded again and tapped the bag at his feet. He then pointed at the casualty bunk beside him.

'Straps?'

Carter nodded and leant over his legs to show him the safety straps to hold a casualty on the bunk.

'Thanks,' he shouted. 'How long now?'

'An hour,' Carter replied, waggling his open-palmed hand to signify his answer was approximate only.

'What do you want me to do when we get there?' Parnell asked.

Carter smiled. This boy looked all right. No seasickness yet. No fear he couldn't deal with. Mind on the job. Thinking ahead.

Carter leant forward. 'The lads will get 'em in here.' He spoke loudly and slowly. 'We'll sort them out . . . put the good ones below for'ard and aft . . . You will get the injured, if any, in here.'

Vic leant across and offered the biscuits again. To Carter's

164

complete astonishment Parnell took one and began eating.

'If there is no obvious injury the lads get 'em below and look for hypothermia. Put them in survival bags. Get them strapped in, and we go back in again.'

Parnell looked up at him, his mouth full of biscuit. 'Again?'

Carter nodded. 'We only get two, maybe three, at a time. We back off, get them below, get secured and go in again.' Parnell nodded and Carter continued. 'We don't usually have a doctor on board, so you stay inside and treat them as they come aboard. That will free up one of the lads to be on deck.'

'Any known injuries at this time?' Parnell asked.

'The master,' Carter shouted back, tapping his chest over his heart.

On the mainland, newsmen, alerted by their sources that something major was under way, made frantic arrangements to get themselves down to the scene of the breaking story. Massive amounts offered to helicopter operators failed to entice them up into the storm and the first team to choose a fast car journey had just left London. Back in their offices and newsrooms back-up teams were scouring libraries for background material.

Crews were setting up outside broadcast units in Downing Street, even though they knew that the Prime Minister was in his constituency. It was more for the atmosphere than because they were expecting a statement.

The Lawlers had left Cocking forty minutes previously with their Special Branch escort. They were driving to Penzance, the nearest mainland point to where their son and the other boys were in danger. There had just been the usual police car at the gate, but they knew that within the hour the press would be there.

The Home Office had, out of courtesy, advised the Palace and the Queen was woken and told of the unfolding drama. She had met young David Lawler on two occasions.

She immediately asked to be briefed on the progress.

In the big black Daimler, Heather Lawler pulled her coat around herself. As the driver accelerated out towards the main road, she moved across the seat towards her husband, who was sitting forward talking into the car's telephone, trying like any other father to get information. The first call that had come through had simply relayed a message from the London police. The ship was in trouble. Two of his staff had since been on to the coastguard.

He put the phone back in the cradle.

'Well?' she asked.

'An RAF rescue helicopter has left from Brawdy. And a lifeboat from the Scillies,' he answered. 'There are also two naval vessels in the area. They have turned back to help.'

'Thank God,' she murmured.

He didn't tell her that there was little a big ship could do. Can't get in close. Can't launch boats. Can do bugger all in fact, he thought.

'So,' she said firmly, 'the helicopter will lift them off the ship, will it?' That's what they do, she thought. I've seen it on television. Men hanging below on winches. Trained for this. Tell me it's so. Tell me our son isn't going to be taken from us.

'I think that's the plan. Then they either fly the load across to one of the naval ships, or they can head back to the Scillies. It's only thirty-five miles.'

She drew comfort from the way he said that. *It's only thirty-five miles.* Easy for the big helicopters. Routine stuff.

She tried not to think of it as sea. Ocean. A storm.

But Lawler did. He knew the risks and the difficulty of the rescuers' work that night. Thirty-five miles into the weather might as well be two hundred. It would take anyone hours to get there.

For the first time in twenty years he began to say a prayer and then stopped abruptly.

'I'd better phone the school,' he said. 'No one else will have.'

But someone had. Only seconds before, the headmaster had been woken by a call from a reporter freeelancing for one of the big daily newspapers. It was the first he had heard of the incident. He said he had no statement to make at that time and immediately decided to phone the coastguard to confirm what he had been told. As he reached for the phone, Lawler's call came through.

He then got up and began making preparations for a busy night. He gathered a small staff, the three house-masters and the school chaplain, and they began phoning parents immediately. For most, it was the first they had heard of the danger to their sons' lives.

Many lived quite near the school and the headmaster, knowing the events would draw them together, offered the school as a meeting point. The chapel and the masters' common room were within yards of each other. He would somehow get information channelled back to them. He picked up his telephone and dialled the number that David Lawler's father had given him for the coastguard infor-mation section.

He then tried to phone the chaplain to ask him to get the place opened up. But he had already thought of that.

His wife answered. 'Paul has gone down,' she began. 'He said the parents would be coming. I'm to make tea and I need to get into the kitchens for the big urn and biscuits. Have you got the spare keys?'

When the headmaster arrived down at the school build-ings he found the chaplain in full vestments kneeling before the altar in the small fifteenth-century chapel.

The RNLI public relations department was in hot demand, being asked for everything from file photos of the St Mary's crew, and any footage of an Arun-type boat in action, to

167

morbid statistics of deaths occurring when ships' engines had failed.

It was a slow news day. No major wars, no elections, no scandals, and word that ITN had a journalist on St Mary's escaped quickly. Within the hour, deals were being struck. In the next twenty minutes syndicating rights were sealed and Susan Farmer's next telephone report would go out to nineteen networks with an estimated audience of two hundred million people, mostly in America where the broadcast would support prime-time viewing on CBS, NBC and the cable news networks.

Caledonia

The rafts were heavy. Jarvis, himself lashed to a lifeline, had rigged a heavier line from a lifeboat davit diagonally across the canted deck from the leeward edge of the accommodation housing to the windward edge of the poop deck. He was wet through and a cut across the back of his hand bled freely. He hefted the raft another few feet, slipped the strop ends over the deck line and signalled to the seaman who was with him. Jarvis stood and, clipping his lifeline over the heavier rope that crossed the deck, he moved round the corner into the fury of the wind, holding the rope in both hands as he went.

This was his fourth trip. The last raft. They would only need three of the twenty-man devices, but he wanted to experiment with the fourth. Drop it over the side. Watch it inflate and see how long it would take for the wind to rip it apart or lift it into the sky. Nichols had reluctantly agreed.

'We may need it, Bosun,' he had said.

'We need to try it with one. See if we can lash it long enough to load before it is taken by the seas or something.'

Nichols silently cursed himself. He should have thought of that.

'Sorry. You are right, Bos', but one only. Go ahead.'

'Aye.'

Now three rafts were safely secured on the lower side of the poop deck and he would nurse the fourth down the deck line to the launch place he had chosen. The wind hit him like a solid force, blasting drops of water like pellets against his skin. It was blinding. Just feet below, the waves washed over the hatch covers of number three and four holds, the white surf roaring upwards, snatching at lines, battens and the canvas hatch covers. He turned his broad back to the wind and moved out.

The aft cargo had gone a few minutes before. A crashing shudder had rocked the *Caledonia* and then she had shivered as if she knew her death was now imminent. The list had worsened by a few degrees and she was now down by the stern. Nichols and the bosun agreed on the reason. The steel plate had shifted in layers, the topmost gathering speed as it slid downwards, and a sharp corner had pierced the hull or had stove a plate outwards. Either way she was taking water into number four hold.

If we have to launch rafts, Jarvis thought, it might even help. Her stern lower in the water would provide a more stable platform to launch from.

He wasn't romantic about his ships. It was his work. This one was sinking. Now his job was to help the mate get the passengers and crew clear. But, like all seamen, he was superstitious and the legends said you talked to a dying ship. You have vested in her the qualities of a good woman: beauty, loyalty, courage and the capacity for hard work. So when they die you don't leave them to die alone. Not after all they have given.

Come on, my girl. You have weathered worse storms than this. You have shouldered aside bigger, better waves than these. Don't give in now. Don't give the big cold frothy bitch the pleasure of seeing you go under. You are proud. You have steamed the oceans with the best of them. You can do it. Let's walk through this one together and, when it's over, I will have the lads fix you up and get you bright and gleaming from stem to stern. Don't die out here, my lovely. Not out here in the cold. Not out here in the deep.

He felt the wave hit below him and his big hands closed over the deck line like vices, braced for the surge of water. He knew what to expect. It slammed into him, a wall of water three feet high, snatching his feet from under him, and he clung on with all his strength as gravity pulled the water back, the backflow dragging him downwards. He stood again, checked the raft that was a few feet ahead of him down the line and moved forward, his lopsided jaw set solid. You'll not take me, you angry great slut.

There would be another eight or ten like that before he reached the edge of the poop deck, and, once down there, he would be waist-deep in the seas.

He would have to shift the line later, either that or rig a second above the reach of the waves as they ran up the sloping deck. He could handle the force of the water but the boys could not. In his mind he planned where it would run as he continued along the line. Alongside the rail, the full length of the aft deck, high above the water's reach. He could secure it at the davits and on the aft goosenecks. Then they could move between the rail and the rope. Once at the quarterdeck, they could follow a second line down to where he and a seaman would load them into a raft. He thought for a second about his baby daughters at home in Southampton. As long as they were tucked up safe in their beds, he could handle this and more. Another wave slammed into his legs and he took his weight on his arms, letting the water surge past.

On the bridge, Nichols nodded and the four men hefted the stretcher and tied the final knot. The angle of the floor was now too steep to carry the stretcher up, so they had rigged a pulley up on the wing where Chafney still kept a watch. The stretcher was one of the new variety of moulded plastic with high sides and straps that would leave its occupant safe, even in a vertical position. Captain

Wellbrook was now asleep, having been heavily sedated by the steward medic.

'Move him up to the bridge wing. He will go first.'

The leading hand, a GP1-rated seaman, nodded and Nichols walked back into the charthouse.

'Right. McDermott and his people will be topsides any minute,' he said to Scott. 'We are down at the stern. Won't be long now. A couple of hours at most.'

'Great. The cocoa is cold too,' Scott said laconically.

'What word from Falmouth?'

'A little better. There are a pair of naval ships headed back this way. A destroyer and an RFA.'

Nichols grunted. They would be little use, he thought. Their seaboats would founder in seconds in conditions like this. They could only stand off and watch and do what they could without jeopardizing their own safety unless . . . He turned to Scott.

'Do they have a helicopter aboard?' he asked.

'They did till this afternoon, but it flew ashore ahead of the storm,' Scott replied. 'There is also a ULCC coming down the Channel. He has agreed to do what he can. God knows what that will be. I wouldn't risk a tanker. Anyway, he is a good way away yet. The RAF chopper and the lifeboat will be here well before him.'

'Let's hope so,' Nichols said.

Scott nodded and began to pull on an oilskin. Nichols raised an eyebrow.

'I'm going to relieve Chafney and his sidekick. They will be wet through and frozen up there.'

Nichols felt his blood run cold.

'Chafney? Chafney is still on the bridge wing?'

Scott nodded, pulling up the zip.

'I gave orders that Jeffries was to relieve him.'

'I know, sir,' Scott said formally. 'He didn't. He is, I believe, in his cabin.'

'Wait here. I'll be right back,' Nichols said.

*   *   *

Jeffries sat on his bunk, his back to the bulkhead, wearing one life jacket and clutching a second.

Suddenly Nichols was framed in the doorway.

'I ordered you to relieve Mr Chafney.'

Jeffries's face was petulance, fear and anger.

'You are going to kill us all! God, where are they! They should have been here by now . . .'

'Get on deck,' Nichols snarled.

'Why should I?' Jeffries sat forward, clutching his life jacket, like a child with a teddy bear.

'Because I gave you a direct order.'

'You're not the captain!'

'I am in command. Listen to me. You are a merchant navy officer. Right now you are in breach of article seven of the code. If you are not off that bunk in five seconds, I will have you charged with wilful failure to perform duty, and conduct endangering the ship and persons aboard, under the Merchant Shipping Act. You will never serve aboard another ship again and, if one person dies out here tonight, just one, I will see that charge rolled into a civilian court as manslaughter. Do you fucking understand me!'

'You can't talk to me like that . . .'

'You are a disgrace to the service. On second thoughts maybe we are better off without you. You would just be a liability anyway.' Nichols leant forward. 'But this much I will promise you. When the chopper gets here, you will be last one off this ship. You and me, sunshine. You try and jump the line, you further embarrass your colleagues and I will have you clapped in fucking irons.'

St Mary's

Susan Farmer had filed her telephone report and, asking Ted and the soundman to follow in ten minutes, had gone, through the wind and rain, straight back to the boathouse. The details were important now. Not only the names of

172

the men, their ages, their family details, the elements that made up the human-interest angles, but the other small points that would become important. The history surrounding Carn Thomas would be wanted by a waiting world. As she arrived she made herself a promise: she would do them justice with good professional reporting.

She knocked, then pushed her way into the boathouse and Dickerson looked up from where he sat at the bench in the tiny workshop.

She felt unwelcome. The message was clear in his eyes.

'It's me again,' she said unnecessarily. The pause was awkward. 'Did you know that David Lawler, the Prime Minister's son, is on the *Caledonia*?' she continued.

Dickerson stood up, his jacket hanging off his lean frame as if it was on a coathanger. 'Yes. I have just been informed,' he said frostily.

'Look, I am sorry about earlier on. I apologized then and I meant it.' She paused and walked forward. 'I want to do this story and do it right. I want to understand them and maybe help everyone else understand them too. My material will be going out to God knows how many networks. I want to get it right. For their sakes as well as mine.'

Dickerson's eyes softened. 'Take a seat,' he said.

'Thanks. I was wondering ... It's a nasty storm out there. Just below hurricane force. Just when do these men call it a day? There must be a limit to what they will go out in. What are the RNLI's parameters?'

'We rarely issue parameters with this sort of thing. It's a judgement call. I, as the launching authority, authorize the deployment of the RNLI's resources, but the coxswain decides when and how he goes.'

'I notice you didn't say "if" he goes.'

'They could, of course, refuse. It's entirely up to them. But I have never known an RNLI coxswain not to launch his boat if it was needed. Never. You must realize that they are very experienced men. They have faith in their own ability and that of their crews. They have faith in their boats. Most of all they know that if they don't do it, no one else is going to. Whoever is out there will be on their own.'

He was loosening up, she thought. This was good.

'So. Hal Carter. Assume he gets there OK. Where on earth is he going to put fifty-six people on that boat?' she asked, settling back.

'Someone else just asked me something similar,' Dickerson said dryly, thinking about the call he had taken from a naval commander attached to Downing Street. 'To be perfectly honest, I don't think he will have to. The search and rescue helicopter will lift off as many as they can. Once they are short on fuel on the helicopter they will head back and leave the remaining few to come home on the boat.'

SEVEN

Hall leant forward and turned up the contrast on his radar screen. The warrant officer (electronics) seated behind him had just cranked out his main search radar. The Sea King had very sophisticated avionics, not the least of which was forward- and down-looking search radar, designed to look for things as small as submarine periscopes. Any time now they would start seeing traces as they came down through the storm towards their search height of one thousand feet. They had taken a positive fix from the beacon at Land's End and a second from the navigation aid on St Mary's. The wind had pushed them westwards and now he corrected for the final few miles so that they would come down through the cloud over the exact spot that the casualty would have drifted to.

They would not be that accurate of course. But they would be somewhere close, so it was an excellent start point, and the radar and radio direction-finding gear were incredibly accurate over ten or twelve miles.

He shook the sealed drinking bottle and, feeling the last inch of coffee sloshing around the bottom, he lifted it to his lips and sucked on the straw, his eyes constantly checking the instruments on the panels before him.

The night was black, the rain flat against the windscreen like sheet water in a car wash. As they went lower they would start getting the foam and the froth from the sea. He had seen spume carried over a thousand feet high during storms. It had felt like being inside a washing machine.

The wind strength was increasing as they went lower and he said a silent prayer. Anything over one hundred knots and he couldn't maintain a hover. Even ninety knots would need both of the big engines on full power, with the disc dropped all the way. This would give them an airspeed the same as the wind strength but negligible groundspeed. Even that was better than gusts.

The Sea King had a small computer that was designed to take the controls. It could make millisecond decisions on rotor angle and disc attitude to allow the aircraft to hover where no mortal pilot's reactions could be fast enough. The autohover was good. It had saved many lives. But, like all pilots, Hall liked hands-on control of his aircraft and used the facility to a minimum.

He eased the controls and lowered the aircraft on to the thousand-foot level. His radar screen, a miniature duplicate of the big set behind him, gave a reassuring green glow to the control panels. Its fine resolution was in dramatic contrast to the blurred reds and yellows on the weather radar set below it.

He moved his thumb on to the microphone switch on the cyclic.

'Falmouth, this is Rescue Romeo, we are crossing through one thousand feet at this time and estimate being overhead casualty in one five Mikes.'

'Roger, Rescue Romeo. Be advised that the Romeo Foxtrot Alpha is now five miles to the east-northeast of the casualty and HMS *Defiant* is off her beam at this time. You also have the St Mary's lifeboat approaching from the northeast.'

Hall's eyes flicked down at the search screen. There through the snowy clutter were two contacts. Big ones. Ten miles out.

A much smaller contact appeared intermittently. That would be the lifeboat, he thought.

'Thank you, Falmouth. I have them on radar.'

'Ah, Rescue Romeo, how soon will you attempt to raise the casualty on your VHF?'

'Falmouth, we will commence in two minutes, over.'

'Rescue Romeo, expect contact from the lifeboat any time.'

'Roger.'

Drumbeat

Captain de Villiers stood, while his electronics officer sat at the console and flicked over the VHF bands with deft fingers.

'No go on the VHF yet, sir. We are trying on thirty-two.'

'What's the range on this gear?' de Villiers asked.

'On a good night, sir, maybe fourteen miles. Tonight, could be down to three or four.'

'Try again.'

The rating lifted the telephone-type handset to his lips.

'*Caledonia*, *Caledonia*, this is the Royal Fleet auxiliary *Drumbeat*, over.'

There was no reply.

'I can raise them on medium wave.'

De Villiers shook his head. The only medium-wave equipment on the ship was down here in the communications rooms.

'I want to talk from the bridge. Keep trying. When you have them, patch it through.'

'Aye aye, sir.'

When he arrived back on the bridge his chief engineer was there with his chief officer.

'I'm going to bring us up to lie two cables downwind of her. If they go to their boats or rafts we will pick 'em up as they blow down on us.'

'Scrambling nets?' the chief officer asked.

De Villiers looked away. Easier said than done on an RFA. Her high sides made it a long climb compared to the low freeboard of a destroyer. He looked at his watch. They had just under forty minutes.

'Drop one on each side. I want three rafts readied. She

is lying into the weather. If they lose theirs we will move up to windward and drop ours into the water on lines. Drift 'em in.'

'With due respect, sir, if they lose theirs, ours won't even get close.'

'I know,' de Villiers said. 'But we have to be prepared to try.' He thought about their shaft problem. If it weren't for that they could have come in closer. 'Trouble comes in threes,' he said. 'I wonder what's next.'

The *Drumbeat* was a small ship as auxiliaries went. She topped out at eleven and a half thousand tons. Built in the late seventies, she was fast, able to give her master nineteen knots when both of her engines were running. A Rover-class oiler, she was laden under with more than just fuel. There were thousands of different items below her cluttered decks, everything from frozen meat to rivets. For a ship her size to have twin screws was rare, but her role required it. She needed to have excellent manoeuvrability. Refuelling a pair of warships while under way left little room for errors or slack steering gear. But tonight she had as much manoeuvrability as a barge.

'*Defiant* off the port side, sir,' someone said.

De Villiers walked across the bridge wing and could just make out the destroyer's riding lights through the spume and rain in the black of the night. A jagged fork of lightning lit the sky and illuminated the scene as a monstrous wave washed over *Defiant*'s bows, completely submerging her 115-millimetre gun turret and the Ikara anti-submarine launcher.

'Jesus Christ. She must be doing ten knots at least,' a voice said in awe. *Defiant* seemed to shake herself free with a sickening roll as her massive manoeuvre turbine powered her upwards and the black water fell from her decks.

'Bloody navy. No respect for a ship,' the chief murmured. The comment was a veiled compliment. All who saw her were impressed. A Type 82, she was everything a destroyer was supposed to be. Fast and brave, at only six and a half thousand tons she was a tiny ship, but bold and, like her name, defiant of the storm. Even slowed down to ten knots from her top speed of thirty, she was taking a hammering from the huge waves. As he watched from the bridge of the *Drumbeat* each man forgot the intra-service rivalry between the merchant navy and the Royals and felt a curious pride in their companion ship.

Pegasus

Captain Hawk was now dressed and stood on his vast bridge looking out towards the distant bows. The bridge, with its wings, was so long – long enough to fit in several ten-pin bowling alleys end to end – that the duty crew used walkie-talkies to talk to each other. She was a gargantuan ship. Twenty-eight times the size of the *Caledonia* and fully sixty times the size of *Defiant*. She was four hundred and seventeen thousand tons in weight when laden. Her deck was large enough to fit three football fields end to end and then round things off with a couple of tennis courts. Cameras mounted on the bows and below the bridge wings gave the duty crew and officer of the watch a clear, if miniature, picture of the immediate area of sea on a bank of video screens. She was powered by a pair of huge steam turbines, each turning one vast bronze screw, that could drive her fully laden at fourteen knots.

Hawk walked back towards the charthouse where his yellow waterproofs hung on a special hook. He pulled the pants over his perfectly pressed white uniform trousers, slipped the jacket on and walked towards the starboard bridge wing. A heavy door opened on to an exposed flat and he wanted to get a feel for the storm. To do that he needed the wind in his face.

His ship, moving at three or four knots, with just a little more than steerageway on, would give them a couple of minutes of decent lee. If he could see, he would command from here, using a hand-held radio back into the wheelhouse where the chief officer would be on the tiny stainless-steel wheel that operated more like a computer joystick than as part of a real ship.

They had been pumping on ballast for the better part of an hour now. It would lower her in the water but would make her far more stable at low revolutions and less likely to be blown by the wind. But, as they lowered their marks in the water, she became heavier and less responsive to the helm. The computers had worked out the optimum ballast load. They had keyed in the wind speed, sea state, the ship's own speed and added a congested sea lanes factor.

He had taken every precaution he could. Now it was down to judgement. Seamanship. Now it was down to him. The *marinero*, as his wife called him.

St Mary's

Helen Carter leant forward and stubbed out her cigarette in a saucer. She didn't normally smoke in the house but her mother had gone upstairs for a while.

'What's he like?' Norah asked.

'Who?' Helen smiled.

'Don't who me . . . John,' Norah retorted. They were getting along like old friends, after only an hour in each other's company.

'Nice. He's big and strong and cuddly and he makes me laugh.'

'He sounds good for you,' Norah said with a practical air.

'He is . . . but I'm not sure sometimes.' Helen paused. 'He is a good man but he wants to live here.'

'And you don't want to.'

'I didn't used to . . . I don't know. John hasn't even seen

180

the world. If he had been everywhere and chosen this place then I could accept it.'

'But he's happy here. Happy with it as it is.'

'Yeah. He is.'

'He's a good man?'

'Yes.'

'He makes you laugh?'

'Yes.'

'He loves you?'

She grinned. 'He adores me!'

'And you love him?'

'Yes, I think I do . . . No, not think,' she said firmly, 'I know I do.'

'So what's the problem?' Norah asked.

Helen looked at her and Norah continued, 'Helen, there are only so many good men out there. When you have found one, a truly decent man who loves you, then it is a rare thing. Take him. Grab him with both hands. Don't make the mistake I did.'

'What did you do?'

'I had David. And I ran away to America.'

'He's such a hunk! How could you?'

'It's a long story. Have you ever known any Irish people before?'

'Not to talk to, no.'

'For us, the Irish, America is something magical. It's the land of opportunity, the place where the streets are paved with gold. When we were starving they took us in, literally. It's the place our ancestors went to, we all have relatives there. We look to America more than to Europe. There are more Irish in America than there are in Ireland . . . so I felt that I should go too. David was happy in Dublin.'

'Did you ask him to go with you?'

'At the last second. I was terrified that he would just say no, so I put off telling him until a few days before I was due to leave and,' she sighed, 'that made it look like I had planned to keep it from him all along.'

'And he ended up leaving anyway. He came here,' Helen said.

'Yes, but I couldn't force him out. When he was ready, he moved.'

'You think John might?'

'He may. But it doesn't matter. If he is happy here then why would you want to force him out? When he is ready to move he will. With you or without you. If you forced him to go somewhere he didn't want to be, you would change him . . . What is so great about Penzance anyway? If it was Grand Bahama or Cannes it would be different.' They both laughed.

There was a knock at the door. It was Susan Farmer, wet-haired, tired and unhappy, looking for half an hour with someone else who understood. 'Hi,' she said. 'You said if I felt . . .'

'Of course,' Helen replied. 'Come in.'

South Coast

The storm had hit the mainland with a vengeance. Four people sleeping in a van had been crushed when the wall behind which they had parked their vehicle crashed down on them. Trees fell on to roads and rooftops as wind speeds reached one hundred and ten miles an hour, pulling down power lines. Two pensioners had been killed when a chimney fire, fanned by the winds, had swept through their cottage, and three people had been dragged from an eroded beach by a freak wave as they tried to shore up the front of their prized waterfront home. Police had closed the Severn Bridge after the driver of an articulated furniture truck had chosen to ignore their advice and had had his vehicle blown over on to its side.

In Dorset a stable girl was almost decapitated when a sheet of corrugated iron lifted from the top of a tool shed was spun through the air like a huge Skilsaw blade, hitting

182

her as she chased after a frightened horse. She was strapped up and bundled into the back of a Land Rover. The journey to the hospital meant fording a torrent that was normally a quiet stream.

Hundreds of late-night travellers were stranded when their train lost power outside Portsmouth, and, in a village outside Falmouth, a police constable and a midwife braved falling trees and fallen lines to reach a woman in labour.

The Bude lifeboat successfully took seven Spanish seamen off a two-thousand-ton Maltese-registered coaster that was sinking in gigantic seas and the men of the Mumbles lifeboat rescued a yachtsman and his wife in the Bristol Channel.

Across the Irish Sea the storm flicked its gigantic tail and the Irish counties of Wexford, Waterford and Cork cowered beneath its onslaught. A fishing boat that had snapped her moorings was driven on to the rocks at Wexford and at Arklow a factory wall collapsed across a second-hand car yard, destroying a dozen vehicles.

Maeve Corrigan

Carter had moved up and stood behind John Timson, who was at the helm, as they powered their way into the seas ahead. At times, the spray made visibility momentarily impossible and John, trusting his instincts, kept the power on, relying on sensing the waves rather than seeing them. Carter approved. The younger man's feel for the seas was excellent, almost as good as Simon's. John flicked a look at Carter, his big eyes twinkling in a face which, in the dark, seemed to be all beard. 'Mine's a pint,' he shouted with a laugh.

Carter smiled and moved back to the navigation table.

Across the wheelhouse Vic Collier was slowly turning the dials on the big Furuno radio direction finder. They should be getting signals any time now. Simon had a fuzzy radar contact six or seven miles off dead ahead and two others off to the east. They would be the navy ships approaching.

Carter looked up. Parnell was standing beside him, one hand holding a grab bar like a veteran, looking down at the chart.

Parnell looked at his watch, then down at the chart and, taking the dividers in his hand, pointed to a rough area.

Carter nodded. 'Done this before?' he shouted over the engines.

'A little. I have had a couple of boats,' the doctor replied.

'Sails?' Carter asked.

Parnell nodded.

Better and better, Carter thought. There were increasing numbers of small-boat sailors in the ranks of the RNLI. The old-timers had mocked them at first, but they had proven to be good. The reaction speed and agility exhibited by those who sailed small dinghies had turned out to be a real bonus on the deck of a lifeboat.

Carter moved forward and tapped John on the shoulder, indicating that he should give the wheel to Simon for a spell. He would take over himself as they made the approach. That should be in twenty minutes or so, he thought.

Victor shouted from his radio position as the lads changed at the wheel and Carter moved back to him.

'Chopper is approaching the casualty.'

Carter nodded and indicated to turn the volume up on the speaker so they could listen in. He normally avoided talking to a casualty till they were very close, usually just as they were about to come into sight, leaving earlier communications up to the coastguard. But this rescue now involved other ships and, if he listened in, he could get a feel for the scene before contacting them all.

Vic pulled off his headphones as the VHF speaker crackled into life.

'. . . *edonia*, *Caledonia*, this is Rescue Romeo.'

'Rescue Romeo, this is *Caledonia*, go ahead.'

'*Caledonia*, we are a Royal Air Force search and rescue helicopter and we are approaching you on a radar vector from the north. We should be visual in two minutes, over.'

'Roger, Romeo, we have a lookout . . . We will be very pleased to see you, over,' a voice replied. The voice was canned and metallic. A small hand-held radio, Carter thought. That will make things easier. I wonder if they have any more. Some ships had three or four, some just one, some smaller vessels no hand-helds at all.

'That's good, *Caledonia*. Sit tight. We won't be long.'

Carter moved up to the radio panel.

It was time to talk to the other vessels approaching the casualty. But first the casualty herself.

'*Caledonia, Caledonia*, this is the *Maeve Corrigan*.'

'*Maeve Corrigan*, this is the *Caledonia*, go ahead.'

'*Caledonia*, we are a lifeboat out of St Mary's, now fifteen minutes away from you. What is your situation?'

A new voice came on.

'*Maeve*, engine has failed and we are beam on to the seas, lying east-west with a forty-five- or fifty-degree list. We are taking water into the aft holds at this time. Situation is critical, over.'

'Copy, situation critical, *Caledonia*. Is your deck canted to windward or leeward?'

'Windward, *Maeve*, repeat canted to windward. We have waves breaking over the hatch covers, over.'

'Thank you, *Caledonia*. Can you confirm you have fifty-six people aboard?'

'Roger, *Maeve*.'

'Does your master want to commence a transfer, *Caledonia*?'

'*Maeve*, the master has had a suspected heart attack, repeat heart attack. I am in command. Nichols. John. Chief officer. At this stage I'd like all passengers and crew lifted off with the exception at this time of myself and the chief engineer.'

'My name is Carter. I am coxswain of the *Maeve*. Let's start then. You have had contact with the search and rescue helicopter already. I recommend you talk direct during the rescue as he comes in. We shall stand off for the moment. There are also two other vessels in the area. Did you copy that, *Caledonia*?'

'Roger, *Maeve*,' Nichols replied.

'That's good, *Caledonia*. I shall ask the Sierra Romeo to contact you direct on channel sixteen. All other comms will be on thirty-two. Confirm you copied that, *Caledonia*.'

'Roger, *Maeve*. Sixteen for the helicopter and thirty-two for you at this time.'

'Affirmative, *Caledonia*. Stand by.'

'Sierra Romeo, this is the lifeboat *Maeve Corrigan*.'

'Go ahead, *Maeve*.' Hall's answer from the helicopter was cool and relaxed.

'Did you copy my transmission to *Caledonia*?'

'Affirmative, *Maeve*.'

'Over to you, Sierra Romeo. They are expecting your instructions on channel sixteen. I am going to raise the Romeo Foxtrot Alpha. They have a helicopter deck. You may wish to consider offloading your survivors there. In the meantime we shall stand off half a cable while you make an attempt, over.'

He checked the VHF was on channel thirty-two and lifted the microphone, holding a piece of paper under the small reading lamp to check the name of the vessel. It was five minutes to two in the morning.

'*Drumbeat, Drumbeat*, this is the *Maeve Corrigan*.'

The answer came through immediately.

'Go ahead, *Maeve Corrigan*.'

'Thank you, *Drumbeat*. We are a Romeo November Lima India lifeboat approaching the casualty from the northeast. May I suggest you stand off downwind until the helicopter has had a chance to get a visual on the casualty?'

De Villiers bridled slightly. '*Maeve*, are you assuming situation commander role?'

186

Carter knew the problem. It was not uncommon.

The master of the auxiliary was a professional mariner with twenty years at sea under his belt and he wasn't keen on taking orders from some fisherman in a dinky little boat.

'*Drumbeat*, I believe you have a helicopter deck. I suggest your best contribution will be to stand off and prepare to receive survivors from the helicopter and then radio relay as required. We will support the Sierra Romeo effort in close.'

The suggestion made sense and Carter was being as diplomatic as possible. He waited for their response. If they challenged his authority, Falmouth would step in and formally appoint a situation commander.

Normally that was unnecessary as assisting vessels were quick to recognize the RNLI coxswain's particular expertise and to defer command to him. It was an anomaly, but a poignant one. In a major disaster involving a dozen ships and thousands of lives the ranking commander on scene was the volunteer lifeboat coxswain aboard the smallest vessel. He might well, however, defer command once he was conducting the actual rescue, because he would be unable to concentrate on coordinating whilst actually involved in saving lives.

'Roger, *Maeve*.' The static cleared and the signal came through strongly.

'Ah . . . Thank you, *Drumbeat*. How soon will you be able to take up station?'

'Estimate Zulu oh one twenty, *Maeve*.'

'Thank you, *Drumbeat*. Please advise when you are there.'

'Roger, *Maeve*. We can commence radio relay any time you require. Helideck is clear and ready. We also have a doctor and two medics aboard.'

'Ah, *Drumbeat* . . . thank you. Please note that we also have doctor aboard,' Carter replied.

He went straight into the next call. '*Defiant, Defiant*, this is the *Maeve Corrigan*, lifeboat out of St Mary's.'

'Go ahead, *Maeve*.'

'Thank you, *Defiant*. Did you copy my last transmission to *Drumbeat*, over?'

'Roger, *Maeve*.'

'*Defiant*, can you also stand off downwind for the moment?'

'Affirmative, *Maeve*.'

'Thank you ... Sierra Romeo Romeo, Sierra Romeo Romeo, this is the *Maeve Corrigan*.'

Hall's voice came back immediately.

'Go ahead, *Maeve*.'

'Please advise when you are overhead the *Caledonia*. The Romeo Foxtrot Alpha has a helideck and is clear to receive you.'

'Roger, *Maeve*. We will need fuel soon, over,' Hall added.

'*Drumbeat*, did you copy that?' Carter asked, prepared to relay the message if not, one hand holding the grab bar as the boat took another giant wave over her bows.

'Roger, *Maeve*. We have fuel, repeat, we have fuel. That is an affirmative.'

'Copy that, Sierra Romeo?' Carter asked.

'Roger, *Maeve*.'

Above them in the furious night, Hall looked across at Selby, his hand on the cyclic.

'That's a bit of luck,' he said. 'They have fuel there too.'

Selby nodded. He didn't like landing on ships. They moved too much and the landing decks were always high and exposed to the wind. Tonight it would be a bitch. With your head into shifting, high-velocity winds, you would want all the power on the collective in case you aborted. He jerked a thumb back towards the two crewmen and Hall nodded.

Hall switched his intercom from flight deck over to general.

'You two buggers awake back there?'

'Yeah, boss,' the warrant officer (electronics) replied, hunched over his radar screens.

'We will be overhead any moment. Taffy, come up and have a look.'

'Roger.' The winchman moved up between the seats so he could see out of the windscreen, the wiper blades beating a tattoo across the Plexiglas. The visibility was appalling.

Although Hall was in command he always let his winchman see the casualty, or the cliff, before making any decisions. Very often they had no choice about their approach direction or hover position, so when the situation did allow it, Hall always consulted his winchman. He was the man who would be hanging underneath the aircraft, swinging in the wind, dodging samson posts or derricks, trees or pylons. Taffy Williams was very experienced and could look at a ship and unerringly pick the best place to winch down on to.

Caledonia

Jarvis held the safety line in both hands and pushed the raft, in its hard fibreglass container, down the deck with well-directed shoves of his boot. The timing here was critical. He had to get the raft below wave wash height, where, once it inflated, it could float free, hopefully round the edge of the poop deck and downwind to the leeward side of the ship. If that failed then he had decided to disobey Nichols and try a second raft, this time over the leeward side, down the bulge of the *Caledonia*'s hull. If he could inflate the raft there in some shelter it might survive long enough to load. With people in it, it might be stable enough to cut loose and allow the wind to move them away from the sinking hull. The only problem would be getting them down there.

The raft was near enough. He stopped to take a rest,

turning his back to the wind. His arms were tired and aching.

He looked back towards the weak light at the accommodation door and saw a figure watching him. A seaman appeared and waved to him, holding up a radio. He looked back down at the seas crashing and swirling round his legs. Somewhere below in the turbulent maelstrom was the starboard rail. There was enough water for the raft to clear, so he lashed the securing line to a gooseneck and measured off a similar length of the inflate lanyard. Finally, holding the lanyard, he bent forward and gave the barrel-like fibreglass container a mighty shove so it rolled round the stern into the seas and as it surfaced he pulled the lanyard.

The bright-yellow rubber raft exploded from the canister and instantly was snatched by the wind, the velocity distorting the form of the vessel from a perfect circle to the shape of a teardrop, with hundreds of pounds of pressure exerted on the exposed edges. Jarvis began to count, wondering what would give first, the raft or the line.

He got to six. The rubber mounting gave and the steel ring that secured the mooring line to the raft flicked back towards him, as the raft, now in tatters, was whisked up into the dark night by the wind.

He signalled to the watching seaman and moved back towards the accommodation island.

Jeffries, still sitting bunched on his bunk, threw the spare life jacket against the bulkhead.

His thin face was mottled with fear and anger and each time the ship shuddered his heart lurched and he could feel the bile rising.

'Bastard,' he swore, 'bastard, bastard, bastard . . . I'm not waiting on this deathtrap just because you order me to . . . I've as much right as anyone. If I had a . . .' He stopped his childish ranting and sat up rigidly, his fear suppressed with the brilliance of an idea. Yes, of course, he thought. The captain's locker. That will show them. Let him try and stop me then. Bastard. He got up and moved out into the corridor.

There, he took a fire axe off the wall mounting and moved up towards Wellbrook's cabin and the steel cabinet that routinely contained cash, a sealed bag of papers, morphine, other restricted drugs for the steward medic's use and three firearms for the ship's safety.

The boys were lined up on the steep internal stairs that led to the bridge. It was dark enough to be uncomfortable with just one dim emergency light halfway up. Some of them fidgeted nervously with their life-jacket straps, others leant against the bulkhead in fearful silence. Cadet Officer Fripp, in his element, moved among them, reassuring as necessary, the ship shuddering and groaning as the steel plate shifted in her holds and the huge waves slammed over her decks.

A deck access door opened at the base of the stairs and Jarvis's bulk moved through the space, slamming the door shut behind him.

In the poor light he seemed larger than ever, his life jacket toy-like, his wet hair matted down against his big head.

He carried a coil of nylon rope in one hand, a pair of flares in the other.

''Ow do, lad?' He rumbled the greeting, smiling at David Lawler.

The boy forgot his nervousness and returned the smile. 'Fine, thanks,' he said.

Carstairs, wet through and cold, hovered beside him and Jarvis, as he pushed his way past, looked into the man's eyes. They were hard and professional. The eyes of a man who had seen these things before. Jarvis realized it had been Carstairs watching him while he tried the raft. The bosun moved up the narrow stairs, threading his way past the boys.

Nichols was there.

'Good. You have the rope. Chopper's on its way in, Bosun. Up on the wing, rig me a hand line and something for their feet to get purchase on.'

'Aye aye.'

'How did you go with the raft?' Nichols asked.

'Not good,' Jarvis replied. He didn't say he was going to try again. He just stepped away, dropped the coil and, finding its centre point, he looped the rope over a handrail. He then began working backwards, weaving a scrambling net with half-hitches at a speed that would have made many a seaman from a seventy-four-gun ship of the line envious.

Two minutes later it was finished. Twenty feet of rope ladder, three feet wide, with nice big knots, that when laid down on the deck would provide a series of footholds up the steep wet slope. He hooked one end over his shoulder and moved out of the bridge wing door into the storm, so big and so solid that it seemed to Nichols that not even this wind could move him.

But it did. It hit him like an avalanche and he bowed his head as he moved up the slope, a foot at a time, towards where Scott sat huddled in the wing corner.

Nichols turned back and faced Chafney.

'Let's have Carstairs and the boy up here. I think they should be offered a place on the first trip with the captain and a few of the other boys.'

'I'll get them, sir,' Chafney replied.

A seaman burst on to the bridge behind them, his face a portrait of fear.

'Water coming in, water coming . . .' he said quickly.

Chafney put his hand up. 'Steady the buffs,' he said firmly. The comment was lost on the Filipino but he understood the tone. He took a breath.

'Number four hatch cover is gone,' he said. 'We are taking water into the hold.'

'Thank you,' Nichols said. 'Go and give Mr Scott a hand on the wing, there's a good man.'

The seaman nodded and Nichols turned back to Chafney.

'Get Carstairs up here, Mr Chafney. Thank you.'

The young third officer turned back and faced Nichols. He grinned. 'You're welcome, Skipper.'

Skipper, Nichols thought grimly. Hell of a way to get a command.

A group of the boys were gathered at the head of the stairs watching and standing back to allow two motormen assisting a third on to the bridge. The man they were helping was cradling his left arm that was bent awkwardly above the wrist.

Nichols moved across and arrived at the same moment as the steward medic who had been sitting watching Wellbrook.

'What happened?' Nichols asked.

'Steel door, sir.' The man grinned through his pain. 'My fault, saw it moving and didn't move quick enough.'

'OK. Sit tight. We will get you off on the first load.'

'No, sir. I want to stay and go off after the passengers. Go off with the crew, sir, please, sir . . .'

Nichols smiled at him. 'You are sure?'

'Yes, sir,' he said quickly.

'Good man.'

The conversation had been heard by Carstairs and David Lawler, who now hovered in the background.

'Thank you for coming up,' Nichols said. 'I'll be with you in a moment.'

Jarvis arrived back and Nichols beckoned him over into the soft light of the charthouse.

'I have a problem,' he began.

Jarvis nodded, waiting patiently.

'It involves Mr Jeffries.'

'I heard,' Jarvis said.

Nichols wasn't surprised. Ships were small and word travelled fast, especially word about officers. 'He goes off last. With me.'

Jarvis nodded.

'He may try to jump the queue or cause a scene. I'd rather we weren't embarrassed further.'

'Aye aye,' Jarvis replied.

As they walked back on to the bridge the Filipino seaman appeared from the wing. 'From the second mate, sir, chopper, sir,' he said, a smile beaming across his face, 'from the northwest.'

'Thank you,' Nichols said. He turned and moved up the steep sloping floor to Carstairs.

'A rescue helicopter is approaching us now. It will take Captain Wellbrook who, as you know, has had a heart attack, off on its first trip. It will also take the first group. The boys. How many I don't yet know. I'd like you two on that flight.'

'I won't be going,' Carstairs said, 'but David will.'

McDermott saw the last of his engine-room crew on to the stairs and followed. Seven men had gone up a few minutes before and he had remained with his number two, whose face was now roughly bandaged, and a Filipino motorman. They had rigged an extra fuel tank on to the emergency generator.

The men had stood supporting the forty-four-gallon drum while McDermott had welded it into place on the makeshift cradle, a two-inch feeder pipe making a snug fit into the filler cap of the original tank. Finally, they had made five trips each back into the dark recesses of the engine spaces to the petrol bunker. There they had bled off quantities into five-gallon jerry cans for the generator and its new auxiliary tank. Forty-odd gallons of petrol would keep the inefficient old engine running for two days, the most McDermott could ever remember a storm lasting for. If the old girl was still afloat then they would have emergency lighting and radios working till they could get a salvage line aboard or get her restarted. He knew even that was wishful thinking. He could feel she was down in the stern already. At best they would be aground on the rocks in another twelve hours so it was all academic. But still he did it.

'If it's all the same to you, I think I would rather wait,' David Lawler said. He seemed taller in the soft light, more confident, more mature.

'I'm sorry?' from Nichols.

'I said I'd rather stay aboard for a while.'

'I think we should do as Mr Nichols asks,' Carstairs said firmly, 'and leave whenever he thinks it prudent.'

'I'm sorry to put you in this position but I'd rather go off with the last group.'

Carstairs turned to Nichols. 'We would like to discuss this. Can we use your charthouse?'

'By all means,' Nichols answered, 'but make it fast.'

A figure pushed its way past the boys at the head of the stairs and moved round on to the bridge.

Nichols looked over.

Jeffries, his eyes now tinged with something insane, stood before him. In each of his hands he held a revolver, the one in his right was pointed at Nichols's midriff.

'You can be the hero, Nichols!' he whispered, strangely calm. 'I'm going off on the first helicopter. You try and stop me and I'll shoot you.' The only sound was that of the storm. The tableau was interrupted by McDermott entering the bridge.

'Fuck me,' he said, astonished.

'Put the gun down, Jeffries,' Nichols said in an even voice.

'Try and make me,' he shouted. 'Me and that toffee-nosed little shit are going off together.'

'Have you gone mad?' Nichols snapped. Behind him Carstairs had come from the charthouse. The boy's constant companion was gone and something far more lethal was evident. He stood, feet apart, both hands holding his nine-millimetre Browning in a classic police pose, the gun aimed at Jeffries. McDermott was shepherding boys away from behind Jeffries and the line of fire as Carstairs's voice boomed out.

'DROP THE WEAPON OR I WILL SHOOT YOU WHERE YOU STAND.'

Suddenly Jarvis was there in Jeffries's line of fire, his massive bulk between Nichols and the young man.

'Do as he says, lad.'

'I'll shoot,' Jeffries shrieked, 'I will!'

'No, you won't, lad, you're not the killing kind,' Jarvis said, coming closer slowly. 'You aren't the kind that could do a thing like that.' Coming closer still until he could reach out.

'But I am, lad,' Jarvis continued, the tone now menacing in the extreme. 'You pull that trigger and I'll start breaking bones. I've done it before. Your choice. Make it!'

Jeffries wavered before him and Jarvis reached out with one huge hand and took the aimed gun.

'Now the other one . . . come on now, don't fuck me about, boy. You could have a machine gun and you would still lose!'

Jeffries, now just looking pathetic, held it up and, as Jarvis took it and slipped it into his pocket, Carstairs lowered his own weapon.

'Thank you, Bosun,' Nichols said. 'Put him somewhere where he can do neither himself nor anyone else any harm, will you?'

'Aye aye.'

'Mr Chafney.'

'Sir.'

'The cabinet in the captain's cabin. There should be a third gun. Find it. Then secure the other contents in a waterproof bag and bring it all with you.'

Nichols turned to Carstairs and the boy. 'My apologies. That should not have happened.'

Carstairs grinned. 'Very little of what is happening tonight should be happening.'

'Fucking well say that again,' McDermott said dryly and, as he did so, David's face broke into a smile. He did like that word but was never allowed to use it.

Above their bows, the big Sea King settled into a steady hover at sixty feet, nose into the wind, her computers making the complex minute adjustments necessary to keep her stationary in the face of the screaming winds.

Hall looked down through the Plexiglas windscreen as the nose-mounted spotlight stabbed at the foredeck. The windscreen wipers slapped back and forth, only marginally effective against the rain and spray that filled the air.

This is it, he thought. I have taken the King's shilling and now I earn it.

Taffy Williams, the winchman, leant between Hall and Selby to get his first decent look at the casualty and then moved to look over Selby's shoulder towards the bridge of the stricken ship.

'How many did you say?' he asked into the intercom microphone.

'Fifty-six,' Hall replied.

The helicopter weighed in at thirteen thousand pounds. With full power from the engines and coarse pitch on the blades he could lift a total of twenty-one thousand pounds. Stripped of her anti-submarine warfare gear, the helicopter could lift off with twenty-eight fully armed troops or eight thousand pounds on the external pods. But they had the ASW gear fixed on board. He looked down at his fuel usage notes and, subtracting weight for the fuel consumed, he spoke to Williams.

'They are only kids. We will take twenty-five in the first group.'

'Where to?'

'Unless that ship looks like turning turtle, back to the beach I think. It will be safer landing.'

'Roger that,' Selby replied from the other seat.

Hall flicked a look down at the radar screen. There was no contact blip for the *Drumbeat* because they were too low and the bulk of the *Caledonia* dominated their surrounds. She was there off to the east with her landing deck ready and expecting survivors, but helicopter landings on pitching decks in storm force winds were not something you did unless you had to.

'We will also have a nice fast trip in,' Hall added with a grin, making a joking reference to the tailwinds.

He pushed the cyclic right and eased the big helicopter crab-like along the centre line of *Caledonia*'s deck, allowing the spotlight to work its way towards the bridge and superstructure. Selby took the pistol grip in his hand and began to control the light's direction, sweeping it back and forth across the decks.

'Lots of waves coming right over on to the upper edges there,' Williams said. 'Can we move up a bit nearer the superstructure?'

'Yeah,' Hall said. 'That's where they will be with a bit of luck.'

He pressed the transmit button on the cyclic.

'*Caledonia*, *Caledonia*, this is Rescue Romeo, the helicopter above your foredecks.'

'Very pleased to see you, Romeo. My name is Nichols. We have gathered the first group up here on the port . . . the upper bridge wing. How do you want to handle this over?'

Good, Hall thought. He liked cooperative people. There was nothing more difficult than trying to complete a rescue when someone on the ground or the casualty, however well intentioned, wanted to control things.

Williams, listening on his headset, spoke to Hall as Selby switched the spotlight over to the wider search angle and, looking right out of his side window, directed it at the upper bridge wing.

'That looks pretty good to me.'

Below them, caught in the light but still partially

obscured by spray and spume, someone in a yellow water-proof waved back.

'Approach is clear,' Selby said. 'That derrick is well back.'

Hall leant over for a look himself. The rotor diameter was a full sixty-two feet and he liked at least ten to play with in calm conditions. In gusts like tonight's, he wanted double his rotor diameter area for a safe working zone. The derrick was canted well over and, if necessary, he could increase his height and simply reel out more cable.

'*Caledonia*, the wing looks fine. We will take one person at a time. Our winchman will come down on to the wing and secure each one. Once we have his signal we will move back until they are safely up and then we will come back.'

'Roger, Romeo . . . the first person I would like to get away is a stretcher case, suspected heart attack, over.'

'Roger, *Caledonia* . . . What kind of stretcher is he on?'

Below them Nichols tried to remember if it had a name. He couldn't.

'He's secure at any angle, Romeo,' he replied.

'Ah . . . roger, *Caledonia*,' Hall replied, then said to Williams, 'OK, Taffy, let's start.'

Williams walked back into the main fuselage area and slid back the door to swing out the boom, the incredible clatter of the rotors and the whine of the engines suddenly magnifying the noise tenfold.

He reached up and pressed the manual clutch, reeled off some slack and hooked the main rescue assembly, the nylon strops and harnesses on the cable hook along with his own harness.

He looked back and raised a thumb to the warrant officer (electronics) who moved back to control the winch mechanism. Lastly he turned on the small VHF radio mounted in a waterproof cell on his harness at shoulder level.

'Ready to lower, boss,' he said.

'Roger, Taffy . . . *Caledonia*, we are about to lower our

winchman on to your bridge wing, please have your stretcher case moved up for him.'

'We are ready, Romeo.' Nichols raised a thumb to the three seamen with Wellbrook's stretcher. Two lifted it off the steep deck and the third began to work the pulley. Wellbrook, securely trussed in the moulded stretcher, was moved out into the storm.

'Thank you, *Caledonia*,' Hall said. 'Away you go, Taffy.'

Williams stepped out of the door, the winch line taking his weight and immediately the other warrant officer began to lower him. The wind was not snatching and tugging at him as he had expected, instead it was a solid force, blowing him back so that the angle of the line was not vertical, but at seventy degrees. Looking up, he realized that by the time he was on the bridge wing, he would in fact be below the tail rotors and not the door and the winch boom.

Maeve Corrigan

Carter stood behind his son, listening to the radio talk as Simon steered the big lifeboat the last few miles in to the casualty, taking the huge waves at full power. The windscreen wipers slid back and forth across the five small, square, shatterproof windscreens in a futile attempt to give visibility. During the half-second that the glass was clear, all Simon could see were sheets of spray and foam, the lights finding the monstrous black waves only seconds before they were buried in the wall of water, the boat shuddering to her keel.

They had broached four times already, sliding broadside into the trough on the down side of a wave, threatening to capsize and with only superb seamanship to save them. Simon kept the twin throttles jammed forward and the power going straight back on, in time to surge up the long side of the next angry giant.

The short ones were the problem, steep, solid banks of water breaking over the bows and, on one occasion, burying the *Maeve* under tons of white water before her flared bows broke clear, the thousand horsepower of her sealed engines and her own positive buoyancy blasting her out of the maelstrom like a cork.

John Timson was bent over, his face tucked into the radarscope's soft rubber viewer. Behind him, David Parnell, who had got used to the feel, stood holding grab bars with both hands.

He was thinking about Norah, her warmth, the feel of her against him in the dark before the phone call had come. In the last few days he had never been happier. It was all back there waiting for him. For him, life was good, but for others out there in the dark, it didn't bear thinking about. He willed the boat forward.

Victor Collier, who sat working the radio direction finder, looked up as Carter walked the two steps across to the steep stairs down into the forward survivors' cabin.

He went down backwards, too old to worry about what it looked like, swung the clips back and opened the watertight door into the engine space.

Ernie Coutts sat on the nonslip floor surface, his back to the far door, a beatific smile on his face, the great diesels that were his pride and joy roaring either side of him.

'All right?' Carter asked and, knowing he couldn't be heard, he raised a thumb and an eyebrow simultaneously.

Coutts, wearing his crash helmet rather than the standard issue bump cap, raised a thumb in return and then mimed drinking from a cup. Carter nodded, miming throttle back, and held up both hands with fingers extended, meaning ten minutes. Coutts nodded and moved through the rear watertight door into the aft survivor spaces to get himself a cup of coffee.

Carter returned to the wheelhouse. It was time to take the helm himself.

Hall couldn't see out of the right-hand lower window, his vision blocked by the bulk of Selby's legs, so he had fixed a reference point out of his side window. It was the cargo derrick between the two for'ard holds.

His left hand rested lightly but firmly on the cyclic, his right on the collective, unable to feel the realtime effects of the autohover unit making its micro adjustments every tenth of a second, but rather feeling a hum through the controls, a steady vibration.

'Ten feet, stop lowering, steady . . . steady. I'm being blown back over the rail,' Williams's voice came back. 'Take her forward a few feet . . . about twenty feet forward. Twenty feet forward.'

'Forward twenty feet,' Hall repeated.

Above him, Williams could feel the Sea King move, her blunt nose into the face of the wind, the beat of the rotors deafening above his head.

'That's good, a few more . . . five feet more . . . four feet. That's good,' he said, talking his pilot across to the drop point.

It was then that the high-speed shaft which linked the starboard engine to the gear box, a short connector shaft that revolved at seventeen thousand revolutions per minute, sheared into pieces, throwing shards of high-tensile steel like shrapnel through the moving parts and the hydraulic lines.

Several things happened instantaneously. The starboard engine, without load on the shafts, suddenly increased revs, throwing the torque through the one hundred and twenty-three per cent maximum loading. A red light and audible siren went off in the cockpit.

Hall's hand moved like a blur across the controls. 'Redlining on number two . . . shut down two, shut down two, shaft failure, shit, shit, shit, shit. Get Taffy back in the fucking door . . . watch the gear box temp . . . Shit, we have lost a fucking shaft . . . *Drumbeat*, *Drumbeat*, this is Rescue Romeo. We have a problem. Clear your deck; we are inbound on one engine.' His eyes swept the panel of instruments as Selby shut down the racing engine. 'Sweet Jesus, hydraulic pressure is falling like a fucking stone.

'Losing hydraulic fluid, do you copy, *Drumbeat*?'

Full power on the other engine, the Gnome 1400–1 screaming in protest, collective up, pitch coarse like a Liverpool whore, disc forward . . . Jesus, give me height and I will love you for ever, seventy knots max speed, one shot at this one, if we miss it, then there is no coming back, not into ninety-plus headwinds, gear box temp is rising.

'. . . Get Taffy inside for fucksakes.

'*Drumbeat*, did you copy, this is Rescue Romeo, we are inbound on one engine with hydraulic pressure falling.'

EIGHT

'Rescue Romeo, are you declaring an emergency?' the voice from *Drumbeat* crackled into Hall's earphones. They were gaining airspeed now, Hall getting ready for the dangerous turn downwind on one engine. The *Caledonia* was falling behind and Hall knew that Williams must be almost skimming the wave tops. He had to gain height. He could just hear the hoist winch working through the open door over the cacophony of engine noise and rotor beat as the other warrant officer recovered Williams.

'Affirmative, *Drumbeat*, losing hydraulic pressure.'

After the turn, he thought, we could lose a fucking lot more. They would have the shrieking winds slamming into their beam and then, as they came around with only half engine power and failing systems, there would come a wild careering ride with a sixty-gusting-to-one-hundred-knot tailwind.

'*Drumbeat*, confirm your landing area is aft and you are into wind, over.'

'Roger, we are under way at three knots, the deck is aft, clear and in the lee of the accommodations. You will want to talk to the air ops people.'

'Affirmative.'

'They are standing by.'

A new voice broke through then, clipped and authoritative. 'Nathan here, naval air ops. We have winds gusting to ninety knots but some shelter below twenty feet. I have a fire and rescue crew and four of my best men up there now. We can have you chocked and chained as soon as you want.'

'Don't wait for signals,' Hall replied. 'I will land with brakes on so just get me secured.'

'Roger, Romeo, what is your Echo Tango Alpha?'

'Seven minutes, *Drumbeat*. Commencing turn downwind at this time . . . Sorry, *Caledonia*. Engine trouble. We are aborting, repeat, we are aborting.'

Below the severely weakened machine, Williams swung on the end of the slowly retracting cable. He knew something was drastically wrong with the engine note. He knew that one had failed or had been shut down and that either way, in these conditions, they were in big trouble. Even so, he still managed a thought for the people huddled on the bridge of the *Caledonia*, now watching their rescue helicopter flying away without them, into the darkness and the storm.

Maeve Corrigan

Carter, who was just about to slip behind the wheel, listened expressionlessly to the staccato radio traffic between the search and rescue helicopter and the fleet auxiliary before taking the radio handset from Vic Collier. Around him, the others in the crew stopped what they were doing as the voices crackled out of the bracket-mounted speakers in the noisy, darkened wheelhouse.

John Timson looked up from the radar set and Parnell's face creased into a concerned frown. Only Simon, at the helm, continued to concentrate on the job at hand.

'Romeo, this is the *Maeve*.' Carter didn't wait for an answer; he knew the crew on the helicopter would be pushed to the limit now. 'Do you want us to divert for your location?'

As if to underscore the dangers of a forced landing in the sea, the wave they were climbing broke, crashing across the foredeck, the lifeboat quivering as she broke free of the tons of water.

'Ah . . . negative, *Maeve*. We should make the ship OK. Thanks anyway.'

What he meant, Carter knew, was that if they missed the approach or were slammed into the side of the *Drumbeat* by the wind, there was little the lifeboat could do for them. Although the Sea King was fitted with air flotation bags in its pontoons and could float for hours on calm water, tonight the sea state was way over the maximum limitations. It would take half an hour to cover the nine miles that separated them.

'Falmouth, Falmouth, this is the *Maeve*.' Carter stood holding a grab bar, looking across the wheelhouse to the chart laid out on the table, the mike of the medium-wave radio in his hand.

'*Maeve*, this is Falmouth coastguard, go ahead.'

'Falmouth, the Sierra Romeo has engine problems. They have suspended procedures and are trying for the auxiliary.'

'Thank you, *Maeve*, we copied some of the transmission. Confirm the Sierra Romeo is making for the *Drumbeat* with engine problems. We shall advise Brawdy and . . . ah . . . allocate another Sierra Romeo when available.'

Carter acknowledged and moved up to the wheel and, as Simon slid across, he sat in the coxswain's seat, his hand reaching for the twin throttles. He pushed them forward against the gate as if trying to coax an extra knot of speed out of the big engines. From playing very much a support role for the helicopter they had now moved centre stage. They were it.

Parnell stood beside him.

'I want to talk to the casualty. Talk to whoever is looking after the cardiac case,' the doctor said.

Carter raised an eyebrow and handed him the VHF microphone, thinking, I should have thought of that.

'*Caledonia, Caledonia*, this is the *Maeve*.'

'Go ahead, *Maeve*,' Nichols's voice came back strongly.

'Thank you. My name is Parnell. I am a doctor. Can I

206

speak to whoever is looking after your cardiac patient, your stretcher case?'

'Stand by, Doctor.'

A minute later a new voice came on.

'Varney here, Doctor, the steward medic, over.'

'I believe you have a heart attack patient?' Parnell asked.

'Aye. That's right.'

'Is this your diagnosis?'

'Aye. I've seen 'em before,' the medic replied defensively.

'Fair enough,' Parnell replied soothingly. 'What is his condition now?'

'He's asleep. I forced four aspirins down him and a tranquillizer to help him sleep, like.'

'When was this?'

'Two hours ago,' the medic replied.

'How's his pulse?'

'Weak but steady. Blood pressure is low, over.'

'Thank you, Mr Varney. You are doing everything right. Keep it up and we will get him over here as quick as we can.'

'Doctor, we also have a compound fractured wrist. I have it strapped up and have administered my only morphine, over.'

'I have drugs. We will get him over quickly too, over.'

'No, you won't, Doc.' The medic gave a dry bitter laugh. 'He is crew and wants to stay with the others. Told me to get stuffed.'

Parnell laughed. 'Very well. We will see you soon.'

Caledonia

Nichols, the small Motorola radio close to his ear, looked across at the others as the helicopter struggled to climb away from them and into the storm. There were dismayed faces, some disbelieving, some angry. Some like

McDermott's just resigned to the fact that, tonight, nothing was going to go as planned.

Jesus, what next? Nichols thought. He would have to do something fast now, get their minds on something else while he planned their next move.

'Bring the captain back inside and secure the bridge and wing. Mr Chafney, relieve Mr Scott if you will. Ask him to join me in the charthouse. Mr Fripp, move the passengers back into the mess, please. I will address them in a minuté. Bosun?'

'Aye,' Jarvis answered.

'The lifeboat will be alongside presently. Advise the crew please,' he said, trying to sound like he knew more than he did for the benefit of those listening, knowing that the crew needed to be reassured as much as anyone else.

Scott arrived a few moments later, his clothes and hair sodden, stepping into the charthouse followed by McDermott.

'Engine trouble,' Nichols said. 'They are going over to land on the auxiliary.'

'Not our day, is it?' Scott said. 'So what now?'

'The lifeboat,' McDermott said. 'It's all that's left.'

'It's only fifty-odd-foot at best,' Scott said. 'Some of them are even smaller. Be a bit of a squeeze.'

'That's if they can get in close enough,' McDermott added. 'The deck, which is the only approach area, is to windward and full of sharp things that make holes in little boats. I wouldn't try it . . . one good wave would pick up a fifty-footer and throw her across the hatches.'

'She's our only option,' Nichols said.

'We could try and ride it out,' Scott suggested, full of optimism. 'She might still be afloat by daybreak. We won't be aground till lunchtime. I'll bet there are at least two of those deep-sea Dutch salvage tugs heading to us at top of the green now.'

'Fucking vultures,' McDermott muttered.

'No. The old girl is going down,' Nichols said firmly. He wanted no doubt about who was in command here. Discuss it, Wellbrook used to say, but you decide and you live with it. It's what command is about. 'We have three hours at best. At worst she could turn belly up at any time. When the lifeboat gets here, passengers off, crew off. In that order.'

Drumbeat

Lieutenant Roy Nathan RN stood in the bright hallway beside the flight deck access door. His hair was short and grey and his epaulettes marked him as one who had risen from the ranks. He didn't mince his words to his assembled crew.

'Right, listen up. An air force search and rescue Sea King is on its way in. ETA five minutes. Now, it has thrown a high-speed shaft and is pissing hydraulic fluid everywhere. He is gonna hit the deck hard, brakes on and his heart in his mouth and his arsehole puckering, because if he cocks it up he is fucking dead and so is his crew . . . Once he is on the deck I want chocks in and chains on before his weight has settled! Understood?'

The crew nodded.

'Now don't fuck about. I want more chain over those wheel struts than sweat on a fat lady. Get her chocked and secured. If that driver gets it in safe and one of you fuckers slips up then I throw you in after them, OK?'

'Aye aye,' they chorused back.

'Right, fire team get suited up.'

He watched them disperse, pleased with them and comfortable that they could do what was needed. Nathan knew his job and so did the small team around him. They were the only Royal Navy personnel on the ship, there to serve the helicopter that had flown ashore that afternoon. Their aircraft's normal function was the transfer of spares and equipment to the fleet ships that the auxiliary replenished and that was all done in normal weather conditions. The last thing they had expected was to be back at work on the landing deck tonight.

The system was tried and tested. The helicopter would land, her nose into wind, and, once the pilot was happy with his positioning, he would signal the ground crew who would move forward and chock the wheels. In bad weather they would also chain the aircraft down and, if the landing was in rough conditions with a pitching ship, then the chains would go on at the same moment the chocks went under the wheels, big two-inch steel links over hooks on the wheel struts. But tonight the pilot wasn't going to signal. They would move as fast as they could to get the big Sea King secured, because the wind would simply blow the machine off the deck into the sea if they didn't. Furthermore, thought Nathan, this helicopter might not necessarily be fitted with securing hooks and, even if it was, they might not necessarily be where his men expected to find them. Tonight, they would improvise. Tonight, the helicopter would have to approach over the stern to have her nose into the storm-force winds and that meant that an overshoot would slam her into the superstructure. The wind came round the high accommodations like an express train. No room for mistakes. One error and they would be whipped over the side like a child's toy and there would be no rescue possible on a night like this.

'Lights,' Nathan said to the last departing crewman. 'I want the deck and after areas of the superstructure lit up like Wembley Stadium. If this poor bastard is going to try and land on this deck, at least let him see what he is coming in to.'

210

Falmouth

The senior duty officer now had eight staff in the maritime rescue coordination room, his duty shift of three and five auxiliaries, volunteers who were on call.

It was a busy night. The plotting map on the wall was alive with movement, each case with its assigned officer.

The man coordinating the *Caledonia* rescue called his superior away from the map.

'Problems, boss.'

'Shoot.'

'Rescue Romeo out of Brawdy has lost an engine and is making for the RFA that's standing by. Looks a bit dodgy to me.'

'They going to be all right?'

'It's touch and go. I have advised Brawdy. They are going to scramble their second chopper in about thirty minutes. It is returning from a job now. We will know in about three minutes if they made it OK. If they don't we will divert the *Maeve*. The other problem is that this leaves the casualty to the St Mary's boat. Fifty-six survivors at this time.'

'You want more resources?'

'Yes.'

'Can't. We don't have any at this time. The Sennen Cove boat is still out and so is St Ives. The Penlee boat is still committed but they think they will be available in a couple of hours.'

'Two hours is too long, boss. What about Culdrose?'

The naval air station at Culdrose had two search and rescue Sea Kings based there. Two Culdrose-based winchmen had just received medals for their part in the rescue of the crew of a Pakistani freighter the previous year.

'Both committed,' the senior officer said. 'There's another freighter in trouble off the Bill. You'll get the first boat or aircraft available. It's the best I can do.'

'What about them?' He jerked a thumb at the door that

211

led through to the anteroom where two television crews were already setting up equipment and a group of local reporters was gathered. 'They are expecting to get updates.'

The senior officer shook his head. 'Say nothing about the chopper for the moment.' He thought about the Prime Minister's small motorcade heading towards Penzance. They had asked to be kept informed of developments. 'Where's the number for the car phone?'

'Rather you than me,' the other man replied, handing his superior a slip of paper.

The motorcade was small. Four cars travelling, in spite of conditions, at the legal speed limit with a police escort. The Prime Minister and Mrs Lawler were in the third car, the black Daimler, their driver and a security man in the front seats. Behind and in front of them, in big Ford saloons, travelled their security detail. Up in the lead car, three plain-clothed officers of the Thames Valley Police kept pace with the uniformed driver of the marked car that sped through the night, its blue lights flashing through the driving rain and buffeting wind.

The phone in the Daimler, primarily for the passengers' use, was set between the front seats and as it warbled softly the security man, a ranking Special Branch inspector, picked it up. 'Message from Falmouth.' He leant over and spoke to the PM.

The inspector's voice had a peculiar timbre, especially when bearing news that was unpleasant.

'Falmouth coastguard, sir,' said the voice.

'Go on,' Lawler said, looking across the darkness at his wife who sat tense in the seat beside him.

'The RAF search and rescue helicopter has an engine problem and has diverted to the RFA *Drumbeat* to make an emergency landing. That should be in about two minutes. Brawdy will scramble their second machine when it's back, but that leaves just the RNLI lifeboat out of St Mary's operational for the next two hours at least. She is about to arrive on the scene.'

Lawler was a a keen weekend sailor and, like anyone who knew about boats, he was painfully aware of the inadequacies of big ships for close-in rescues. He hoped the Scillies men lived up to the stories of their skills with little boats. Their son's life and the lives of fifty-five others would depend on them tonight.

'I see,' he said, trying to keep his voice normal. 'Thank them and ask them to keep us informed.'

'Of course.'

The inspector replaced the phone handset on its cradle and sat back in the seat.

Heather spoke, her voice soft in the darkness. 'Tell me what this means. The realities please, James. I'm not some blue-rinse voter to be protected from the truth.'

'The rescue chopper has aborted, but the lifeboat is due on the scene about now, so . . .' he said, trying to make light of it, 'they will do what they can until more help arrives.'

'So the lifeboat is on its own?' she confirmed.

'Yes, for the time being.'

'Ships sink in minutes. It may not be there when more help gets there. Can't they send another helicopter? One from the south somewhere?' she asked, the tears flowing down her cheeks.

'One's leaving soon from South Wales. Nothing closer, I'm afraid . . . A very busy night for them.'

She looked back out of the window, praying silently. Please, God, spare my son. He is so young.

Lawler reached across and took her hand in the darkness.

'It must be hard here. Will you tell me how you wait? How you pass the time?' Susan Farmer asked. She had settled into the last chair around the table.

Jean Carter looked across at her, her eyes old with worry and many sleepless nights.

'Most of us were OK for years. It was not until the *Solomon* that it struck home.'

'The *Solomon* . . . ?' Susan asked.

'The Penlee lifeboat. No one knows what happened. Never will. She went into the shallows to try and get on to the leeward side of a foundering ship. It was every sailor's nightmare. A lee shore, sharp rocks . . . something happened. The entire crew were lost with their boat . . . We had become over-confident in them, I think. New boats, good strong boats. Self-righting. Watertight and some supposedly unsinkable. There hadn't been an accident like that for years. So, we didn't worry unduly. Injury, yes. A man overboard for a while perhaps. But a whole crew? It didn't seem possible any more.'

She took a sip of her tea. 'Hal wasn't coxswain then. He was number two. They were out in the boat. Not the Arun back then, a smaller boat. They were listening on the radio when it all went silent and they joined the search for survivors. There have been others too, but Rye was the worst one before Penlee. In the late twenties. Their boat the *Mary Stamford* capsized in the river mouth when they were coming home. Rye is bad in rough weather. All seventeen of the crew were lost. We don't dwell on it.'

'But the waiting. It must get harder?' Susan probed.

'It's different each time. If it's inshore and close we can listen on the VHF. Towing a yacht is simple enough. Taking a man from the water the same. But a big ship is harder, so they say. It's high and difficult to approach in weather. So I worry more when it's offshore and a big ship. We don't let them know that. Wave 'em goodbye like they were off fishing.'

'At least there are no rocks out there,' Susan offered.

Jean smiled. 'Hal was brought up in these rocks. He knows every single reef, every sandbar, the tides and the wind. He is as at home there as a seal or a gull . . . but deep sea?' Her gaze was fixed for a second, somewhere far away. 'No man is master out there.'

'You know that David Lawler, the Prime Minister's son, is a passenger on the casualty?'

'I heard. They are all the same to Hal. A life is a life. They will bring them all home if they can. There's the helicopter too. It will be there by now, I shouldn't wonder. Helen tells me that your young man is on the casualty too. The mate.'

'Yes,' Susan said.

'And the master is down . . . he will have his work cut out tonight.'

'Yes.' She paused and smiled as if the prospect of John Nichols working, working as hard to saves lives as the men of the lifeboat, made it more normal. 'I hadn't thought of it like that.

'Will you explain a lee to me? Apparently there is a tanker coming through and she is going to make one.'

Rescue Romeo

Hall could see the *Drumbeat*'s lights ahead. The turn down-wind had been touch and go. He had the disc dropped right over into the wind to try and slow it, as the sheer power of the wind twisted the aircraft round like a cock on a weather vane and they began the rushing ride with their airspeed at ten knots and their groundspeed over one hundred. The next turn would be critical. He would come into the wind and allow its force on his nose to slow him down, slashing the groundspeed and giving him lift.

Then bleed off whatever speed is left and just flare out on to the deck. Sounds easy, he thought. He remembered the fixed-wing instructor at flying school: 'Helicopters? Fucking unnatural. All that machinery going round overhead. Can't eject. Helicopters are mutants. Just when you think you can fly 'em one of them will kill you.'

Here we go then. Let's land this mutant. No, I didn't mean that, my baby. I think you are sexy and clever and can fly backwards and stop in the sky and I know you can land on this deck, even though it's rising and falling fifty feet and the wind is trying to throw you to the waves. I know you can do it, even on one engine. Yes, that's what we will do, because I know you are strong and clever, but not even you can fly off for a second chance if I make a mistake. There's no going round again. Please, Jesus, don't let me fuck up.

'I'm going to try and time it so the deck comes up to us. Flare out and attempt a hover and, as she gives in and settles, just hope the deck's coming up to us.'

'Roger,' Selby said. 'Hydraulics going, gear box temp is redlining and we are losing the tail rotor.'

'Roger. Ship's abeam now . . . How you doing, Taffy?' Hall asked.

'Wet through and freezing my bollocks off, Skipper,' Williams replied.

'Get strapped in . . . we are turning now. *Drumbeat*, we are inbound now.'

'Roger, Romeo, you are clear to land and ground crew is ready to secure you.'

The aft deck was ablaze with lights, the beams catching the horizontally driven rain and spume so they looked like shards of clear glass in a frosted window. The ship was hog-backing gently as the huge waves rolled under her, lifting first the bows, then the midsection and, lastly, the stern and her high tumblehomed transom.

The waves weren't the long gentle giants of the North Sea with four-hundred-yard troughs between crests, but steep short angry walls that attacked the *Drumbeat* without ceasing. To try to predict the next rising of the deck would be all but impossible, so Hall, committed by the aircraft's problems, decided to leave it to Lady Luck and his skill on the flare-out.

Airspeed ten knots, groundspeed ninety, full power on the last engine, throw the disc over. As they began to turn, Hall increased the pitch, the rotor at its maximum lift angle.

This converted the engine power and what speed they had left into lift and forward motion, before they were blown backwards by the force of the wind. The helicopter careered round the side of the superstructure, Hall fighting the tail rotors, willing them to perform and line him up. He felt the speed falling away. Please, God, don't let me fuck up here. I am good. I am the best rotor-wing driver I know. Don't let me fuck up, don't kill the boys. The aircraft was settling and the deck looming up at them, wet slick with the spray and the rain drumming against the windscreen, the lights flaring, the deck rising fast, too bloody fast. Flare out, flare out, you big sluggish bitch, fly for me, brakes on, fucking brakes on hard. The deck slammed up into his falling wheel struts with a thump. Then the blur of men, the clang of chains, and the cold feel of fear and sweat and his hands shaking.

Selby cut the power and a length of two-inch nylon hawser slapped across the canopy under the rotors right over his head as the ground crew lashed them down. We are down. Thank you, Jesus.

Hall leant forward and raised a quivering thumb at Nathan through the tiny drop-down window flap, and then thumbed his mike as the crew opened the door.

'*Maeve*, *Maeve*, this is Romeo.' He tried to keep his voice steady, the adrenaline racing through his blood still. 'We are down and secured on *Drumbeat*.'

The sea state was now, if anything, worse than when they had left St Mary's. The waves were huge rolling leviathans, the breaking ones a full fifty feet from trough to crest. It had been a bruising, battering run and they had broached no less than six times already, but there had been no compromise on speed. The twin throttles were hard against the gate, Ernie Coutts's beloved twin diesels roaring and throwing almost a thousand horsepower of torque down the parallel shafts to the big bronze propellers.

Carter swung the bows to take the next wave head on and, as they blasted over the crest, John Timson lowered his big shaggy head to the radar screen.

The RDF, the radio direction finder, was pointing them loosely, but they were now so close that each time they crossed a wave, their radar, its scanner then high enough to see over the seas, gave them a big solid blob on the screen. The MV *Caledonia*.

But hitting each wave at the right angle meant course changes and, without constant corrections, even this close, they could miss the casualty.

Without looking up, John reached across and tapped Carter's arm and pointed his finger round to the right a few degrees.

Carter corrected as they hit the trough and, as they crested the next wave, Timson raised a thumb.

'Close,' he shouted, 'very close.'

Carter nodded. 'Simon . . .' he called. His son came forward and he jerked a thumb upwards.

Simon nodded and moved back down the wheelhouse towards the rear door on to the deck, zipping up his jacket and pulling up the hood as he went. He judged his moment and, as they bottomed out in the next trough, he threw the big handle anticlockwise on its centre pivot. It was connected by visible rods to six clips that rotated downwards off the rubber-lined sill and he pushed the watertight door outwards and went through it, slamming it shut behind him and locking it down as they travelled up the next wave.

Once outside, the noise of the storm and the blast of the wind stunned him for a second. It always did. He caught his breath and, both hands on the white nonslip stair rail, he took the nine steps up to the flying bridge one at a time, his fingers tightening like steel bands as the *Maeve* broached and then gathered her stern under herself once more. He stopped again briefly, halfway along the access walkway beside the life raft while the *Maeve* crossed the next wave. Its breaking crest covered the bows in surf and black water. Spray and foam were snapped up at him and the wind shrieked in his ears. Up here the boat's motion was exaggerated, every roll now a whiplash.

He grinned quickly, feeling the excitement rising. He went forward and took shelter behind the windscreen, his back to the black padded support. Then he took the broad kidney belt and secured it round his waist below his life jacket. Now she could be thrown flat and he wouldn't move more than a few inches from his position below the slowly turning radar scanner. The water cascading off his hood was being blown hard against his skin and into his face by the wind. He pulled the hood back and, through slitted eyes, looked out through the spray. There through the wind-blown water, the foam and the spume, was a break in the wave pattern, a maelstrom of surf and confused seas. The smell of diesel was heavy in the air. A fork of lightning speared somewhere above the clouds and, in the flash, he picked out what must have been her upperworks and port bridge wing, above a sleek blackness that would have been her hull. Further back there was another hint of something solid. Her quarterdeck, he thought. Jesus, she's awash back there over her cargo decks.

He lifted the waterproof intercom phone and pressed the rubber-sealed button with his thumb.

'I see her! Dead ahead. She's hull towards us, listing the

other way, windward. Look for a blob of white. That's her bridge wing.' He looked down at the rudder angle indicator.

'If you want to pass her bows, come round with twenty degrees starboard rudder.'

Down below Carter eased the bows round, watching the waves and taking them on the starboard bow now, bringing the power back to manage her over. He would want to pass wide. The lee beneath her great concave hull would be awash with drums and rope and debris and God knew what else. Lightning flashed again somewhere above as they crested a wave and this time Carter saw her, automatically adjusting his heading.

He reached above his head for the VHF mike and put it to his lips.

'*Caledonia, Caledonia*, this is the *Maeve*. We have you in sight and are approaching your leeward beam.'

Carter looked over at Timson. 'Let 'em see us. For'ard light.'

A grinning Timson stepped up towards the electrics panel. This was always a good part of any rescue, actually seeing them, knowing they were still alive.

Carter took one hand from the wheel and delved into his pocket and produced a flat cap. He took the orange bump cap off and slipped the old blue cap on. It wasn't that he felt it was lucky or an omen. He liked it, it was comfortable and it kept his head warm.

Caledonia

Nichols dropped the torch, scooped up the small VHF hand-held radio and ran for the bridge wing, his right hand on the rope Jarvis had rigged, his feet finding the scrambling net.

Chafney grabbed his shirt front as Nichols lurched to a stop beside him and he reached for the rail to pull himself the last two feet, the wind slamming into his back. He leant to shout into Chafney's ear.

'The lifeboat.' He jabbed a finger at the seas.

Chafney pulled himself up alongside Nichols till he was standing and looked out into the storm.

They both saw her at the same time, her running lights barely visible through the spray, her dark shape against the surf atop a wave as she powered her way round. As they watched, both unsure yet of what they were seeing, a bright light, a searchlight beam, suddenly stabbed the night and then dropped down to illuminate her foredeck.

'There!' Nichols shouted. Chafney gave a whoop beside him, the tension of the helicopter's departure falling away with this new chance. The *Maeve* disappeared from sight into a trough and then rose again, this time closer.

My God, Nichols thought, she's tiny. She's so small to be out here, deep sea in storm force. As if to prove him wrong, the *Maeve* danced round the side of a short breaking wave and took the next longer monster at sixteen knots, shouldering through the surf.

He ducked below the rail and lifted the radio.

'*Maeve, Maeve*, this is *Caledonia*. We see you . . . You are a very welcome sight. How do you want to proceed?'

'Roger, *Caledonia*. Do you wish to commence a transfer of passengers and crew?'

This was the formal bit that Nichols had expected. Some masters were reluctant to accept help or admit they even needed assistance. The RNLI always asked if they could proceed.

'Roger, *Maeve*. We are down at the stern. Situation is critical.'

'Copy that, *Caledonia*. We will take a slow look around the windward and decide where best to begin.'

Hall and Selby had watched from the access door as yet more chain and soft two-inch rope was used to secure their Sea King and they now stood in dry borrowed overalls, drinking cups of coffee on the bridge of *Drumbeat*. She was under way again, back up to six knots, working through the smaller seas and rising with a shudder as the larger waves washed over her foredeck.

'You say she's lying canted into the wind at right angles to the wave patterns?' the master, de Villiers, asked Hall.

'Yeah,' he replied, sipping at his cup, 'waves breaking over the deck, some going clear over her aft quarters. Her poop deck is effectively awash.'

'Quarterdeck,' de Villiers corrected. 'I'm going in closer.'

'With due respect, Captain,' Hall said diplomatically, 'the lifeboat's working area will be all of the casualty's lee and about three hundred yards all round her. He will be darting in and out, timing his approaches between waves . . . He won't want to be wondering where another ship with limited manoeuvrability is currently lying.'

De Villiers turned and looked at the tall helicopter pilot.

'I know the limitations of my command and my helmsman,' he replied frostily. 'It will do everyone good to see another vessel. We shall do a long slow pass along her seaward side, far enough away to be no danger to anyone, but near enough to be seen . . .' His eyes creased then, as he remembered other black nights where the glass had fallen and he had felt the fear. 'This is no time to feel alone.'

'Quite,' Hall replied, accepting the soft rebuke.

Defiant

Defiant, her bows spending more time underwater than above, was standing head into wind five cables off *Caledonia*'s port quarter, her turbine ticking over to keep steerageway on. On her bridge, her captain stood, his eyes to the powerful pedestal-mounted night-vision glasses. The electronics cast a surrealistic green glow over the scene in the viewfinder.

A seaman stood, leaning into the second set at the other end of the pitching bridge, his hands moving across the controls, trying to enhance the images further. He had never seen a sinking ship before. He felt a kinship. He had had his trouble with the merchant navy seamen like every navy man who had ever docked at Portsmouth, but tonight they were all seamen together.

He saw a flash of light, not from the bridge wing but further round. It flared dully in the image intensifier, the equipment's electronics dampening down the effect. There again.

'Lights, sir!' he called.

'Bearing?' the duty officer reminded him.

'Ah . . . one three eight, sir,' he called, hoping he had made no mistake. His captain was swinging the second pair on to his bearing.

'Got it . . . good lad,' the captain said. 'The lifeboat.'

He stood up, straightening his back.

'It's dark out there,' he said to his first lieutenant. 'Darker than a virgin's hole.'

The other man smiled. He was used to informality on the bridge and waited for his captain to finish what he was going to say, watching him take a plain cigarette, tap it on his watch face and finally light it with an ageing Zippo lighter.

'When's the *Pegasus* due?' he finally asked, blowing a stream of blue smoke into the air and picking a stray shred of tobacco off his tongue, his lips mobile in his lean handsome face.

The second stepped forward. 'About fifty minutes, sir.'

'Good.' He smiled. It was a bright raffish smile that usually made their lordships of the Admiralty wince and reach for their bound books of standing orders. The same smile gave the girls at Henley tingles when he directed it at them. 'This is what we are going to do.'

Maeve Corrigan

Simon took the wheel on the flying bridge while his father moved up to him. They were coming round past the raised bows of the *Caledonia*, from the relative shelter provided by the bulk of her hull, back into the full force of the storm.

The first thing Carter felt, as usual, was the sheer force of the wind and all that it brought. It never failed to surprise him. The noise was variable, from a dull moan to a piercing howl in seconds. It was a solid force capable of ripping strong sails into shreds and gear from its mountings.

Out there in the open the waves were gigantic, rolling, crashing monsters the size of buildings, thirty or forty feet high, that hissed as they broke and then rumbled and tumbled their way forward, breaking into their own troughs, booming like thunder. As the boat went up the side of the next one, the wind's roar built again and, as they crested, the cacophony was deafening before they went down into the next trough of black foam.

Carter slid behind the wheel under the canvas spray hood that, remarkably, still stood. The windscreen sheltered him from the full blast of the winds and, as he strapped himself into the body belt that Simon had vacated, he watched his son hook his lifeline on to the backrest's tubular steel frame.

This was the tricky bit. Without her massive engines powering her at any kind of forward speed she was at the mercy of the waves and could be saved only by the skill of her coxswain. They needed to get a good look at the windward side of the casualty, to see where they might come in to take survivors off.

There were two ways of doing it.

The slow pass was something reserved for a gale only, when the wave height was not threatening. In this storm only the other method would work. Move at a decent speed and swing the bows into the waves as each approached. Take the wave under the hull and then turn to starboard and run down parallel in the trough till the next monster approached and, again, turn into it. Zigzagging their way down the length of the ship, they could pause every so often and even stand into the weather with enough power on to keep her under way for short periods, ten or fifteen seconds at a time.

Carter swung the wheel to starboard and, as the *Maeve* answered the helm, he got his first good look at the decks and superstructure of the MV *Caledonia*.

He took in the images with old eyes, eyes that had seen scores of vessels in distress, the eyes of a lifeboatman. For all the wrecks he had seen, it never failed to move him. Half a cable distant across the angry seething stretch of water, a ship was dying. A ship he knew. A brave ship that had crisscrossed the oceans and had tales to tell. On voyages to far-off lands, she had kept her crew safe and shown them tropical sunsets and calm lagoons. She had braved the tempests with them, her mighty forefoot slicing through storms and history. She had seen war and peace, served her country bravely in Aden and the Gulf, and she had been there when the *Atlantic Conveyor* had died in the cold frigid waters of the South Atlantic, her horn blowing a last sad farewell. The red ensign had flown proudly from her staff for ten thousand sunsets and in a hundred ports and now she was lying on her side, her decks awash. After twenty years of battle with wave and wind, reef and rust, she was being pounded into submission at last.

As if warning the little boat not to come closer and suffer the same fate, the *Caledonia*'s horn blasted out, a mournful cry that carried back into the wind.

Carter watched as a wave slammed on to her with a

crash, the surf rolling up her wide deck, its last few foamy feet tugging at the upside rail. Her wide cruiser stern was down, her quarterdeck and small raised poop proud of the water, but the seaward edge of the aftdeck area was under a few feet of water. The waves were rolling over holds three and four between the quarterdeck and the main accommodation structure with impunity.

None of those kids are going off that way, Carter thought. They would never make it over that deck. Above it only, along the upper rail. But a man might. A seaman who could read the waves and judge his moment. He looked back at the seas and swung the wheel to starboard to ease the lifeboat over a wave and then surveyed the *Caledonia* again.

Below him John Timson had come out on the rear deck to cast his own eye over the stricken vessel. Simon moved down to him and together they watched the way the waves hit, the way the water surged and eddied over the hatches and upright structures.

This was a situation where they would have to find the best out of a series of bad choices. The lee of the ship would be easier to approach, but would mean a long, dangerous, exposed journey for the survivors down to the boat, across the bulbous curve of the hull and the hazards of flotsam, drums, rope and the other debris that all ships gave off as they got deeper into trouble.

The windward side was clear of debris, but exposed to the waves and the full power of the wind. Somehow they had to get in there close enough and for long enough to slide a stretcher aboard and maybe to take a couple of the other survivors off on that pass too.

Above them, Carter watched the same waves hitting the same areas of the ship, looking for a way to get the fifty-two-footer alongside for a few brief seconds. The water was deepest over her rail in the area immediately for'ard of the quarterdeck. A man could either jump from the quarterdeck on to the lifeboat or stand down in the surf nearer the port rail and be pulled aboard as the boat came in. A strong man could do that, he decided. A very strong man could manage another into the water. Buoyed with life jackets, they could hang on for a few seconds, sheltered by the edge of the deck housing. Be pulled on to the low-waisted area as *Maeve* rushed in. Two men in the waist, lifelines on, grab 'em, full reverse engines, get the bows round in time for the next wave. Could be done, he thought.

He looked back down at Simon and John on the rear deck and keyed the microphone that was linked to the waterproof speakers at both ends of the wheelhouse.

'Simon, helm,' he said. It came clear and loud from the speakers and he saw his son raise a hand and go towards the wheelhouse door with John and a minute later he felt the familiar three tugs to the left that meant the other wheel was manned. He followed them down.

'I want to start,' Carter said. 'We will go in alongside the port rail abreast of the quarterdeck. Take the first group off there. I'll have them move the first three down.'

'Can I have the cardiac case off, please?' It was Parnell. He had come up behind the other three men.

Carter studied him for a second. There would be no trial runs. Each was intrinsically dangerous so on each run they would go in with the objective of taking survivors off the ship, saving lives. He wasn't keen to have a stretcher in the first batch. Not while he was feeling his way, unsure of the underwater obstacles that could damage his hull.

'I think we can get in aft of the accommodations. Hard against the quarterdeck bulkhead. The problem will be the stretcher in the surf till we get in,' Carter said to Simon and John.

'I'll get him,' Timson suggested. 'Put me aboard along the accommodation bulkhead.'

Carter was pleased that he had volunteered. Seaward approaches were always difficult and he wanted a life-boatman on the other side for the first attempt. Someone who thought like he did, familiar with their ways, not someone desperate to get away, someone who would take unnecessary risks.

'I'll come back down the quarterdeck edge,' Timson persisted. 'A half-dozen life jackets under the stretcher will support it long enough.'

'Would it be easier without the stretcher?' Parnell asked in an easy manner.

'Yeah,' Timson answered plainly.

'Then get him out of it. I'll give you something to keep him relaxed. It will be intra-muscular but the medic can administer it. Just keep water out of his mouth,' he finished.

'What about his heart?' Carter asked. Being nearer the age of heart attacks himself, he was more concerned than Timson who was young enough to think he would live for ever.

'As long as he is relaxed . . . no physical exertion, he should be OK. If he comes to, strapped in a stretcher while the transfer is taking place, he will feel claustrophobic and panicky anyway.'

'Fair enough,' Carter said. 'What about the broken arm? Do you want him off now as well?'

'Not if it's going to create a drama. He will be OK for an hour or so. Besides we can't make him come, can we?' Parnell answered.

'Oh, yes, we can,' Timson said with a grin.

'No. Not unless he is willing. Compound fractures are tricky. I'd like to get a look at him . . . but it can wait.' He thought for a second and then looked at the big man, thinking, I must be mad to suggest this. 'Why don't I come with you?'

'No,' Carter said. He offered no explanation. He was coxswain and his word was final. Parnell was relieved.

Carter stepped forward, stood behind Simon at the wheel and reached for the VHF microphone and a grab bar as the lifeboat powered her way over a wave, its crest dropping foam and white water over the foredeck with a slam.

'*Caledonia, Maeve.*'

He could feel them watching him from the ship, every pair of eyes.

'Go ahead, *Maeve.*'

'*Caledonia*, we are going to put a man aboard you to bring off your stretcher case. We will approach from your windward quarter and put him aboard directly aft the accommodations. Can you drop a line down that area of the deck?'

'*Maeve*, we already have a line for'ard off the quarter-deck, over.'

Carter looked across at Timson who nodded. Rigging a second line would mean risk for someone. Better to avoid that.

'But a man coming over won't be necessary, *Maeve*. You tell us where and how you want to receive my people and my crew will be there to assist, over,' Nichols said firmly.

'*Caledonia*, we will come alongside your port rail abreast the for'ard edge of the quarterdeck. We will have probably two to three seconds in which to transfer the first group. Then we will need to back off. Did you copy that, over?'

'Yes,' Nichols replied. 'Go ahead.'

'My doctor wants the cardiac case over here immediately. Do you have anyone who can carry him down to the edge? One man, *Caledonia*. There will not be room for two at the rail.'

Jarvis, Nichols thought.

'We do, *Maeve.*'

'Suggest one adult helping each of the first group, over.'

'Roger, *Maeve*. We will be ready in five minutes.'

Carter took the helm then, to start the circuit to bring them round to approach the ship from the west. As he did so, he spoke into the intercom.

'Ernie?'

'Aye,' the engineer's voice came back, the roar of the engines louder through the speaker.

'Close manoeuvring starts in five minutes.'

'Aye aye.'

Down in the engine room, Ernie got to his feet and took a final look at the instruments. Close manoeuvring was what the Arun was designed for, but it meant that he would be needed in the wheelhouse. Happy that everything was in order, he picked up his cushion from the walkway floor, stowed it, swung back the watertight door and made his way up to the wheelhouse.

On deck, Simon Carter and John Timson, who had taken the decision that he was to remain aboard with a shrug, were unclipping the guardrail from the low-waisted area along the *Maeve*'s port side. That would give them two points to bring the boys and Captain Wellbrook aboard. One at the usual boarding point and a second up at the bows, where the side rail and the pulpit overlapped. The safety rails ran parallel to each other with room for a person to move between them.

Both men had lifelines, Simon's clipped on to a cable running the length of the deck and John Timson's to a shorter cable set at head height on the orange wheelhouse wall. Collier joined them on the deck as they began their first run in.

Caledonia

'They wanted to put a lifeboatman aboard. Down at the seaward quarterdeck,' Nichols said to Jarvis, 'to take the captain off. I said no. I would like you to do that, Mr Jarvis. Carry the captain down there. Will you do that for me?'

Jarvis, huge in his oilskins, like a great yellow telephone box, smiled. It was a warm solid thing. 'Aye, I will.'

'Thank you,' Nichols said.

Jarvis nodded and began to move aft.

'Mr Scott, have the captain taken down to the aft deck's door. The medic is to accompany him that far. I will meet them there. Have young Fripp choose the first group of boys. Split them up. Groups of three or four. Draw numbers for the order they go off in.'

'Lawler and the sergeant?' Scott asked.

'I'm going to have a chat with him as soon as the skipper is away.'

'If he gets away.'

Nichols looked at him.

'Look, you have seen the conditions back there . . .' Scott said.

'I have. I think that's why they wanted to put their man on board to try the first rescue,' Nichols replied.

'And if it's too rough?'

'I don't know,' Nichols replied tiredly. 'They will try somewhere else, I suppose. Anyway, Fripp and I will accompany the first group down the deck with Jarvis. I will have a VHF. Make sure I can find you.'

St Mary's

Susan Farmer had left Helen and Norah to begin work on the first videotape report she had made up at the boathouse.

The second voice report would go through on tape so she had time to get it right. 'OK, in three . . . one, two, three. The latest from St Mary's is that a supertanker will be assisting in the rescue. The tanker, the *Pegasus*, is a giant of the seas and, weighing in at over four hundred thousand tons, she is so large that if she comes close enough to the rescue scene, she can shelter both the *Caledonia* and the lifeboat from the storm and waves. The expected minute to minute and a half of shelter, a lee in sailor's terms, will allow the lifeboat to stay in alongside the *Caledonia* much longer on each approach and hopefully rescue more people. This is Susan Farmer for ITN on St Mary's.'

Helen and Norah sat at the table, the smoke from their cigarettes curling up towards the ceiling as the last inches in their coffee cups grew cold.

'Well,' said Norah, 'I'll have things to get ready.'

'I'll come and help,' Helen said, standing too. 'I did a summer up there. I know where the kettle and the cups are.'

'Thank God someone does,' Norah replied, smiling at the downplayed local knowledge. Extra hands could well be needed. 'I wonder how they are getting on,' she finished. Please be safe, David, I have just found you again.

Helen looked up at the quiet VHF on the shelf, wishing they were closer so they could listen. She checked her watch. 'They should be in the thick of it by now.'

Falmouth Maritime Rescue Coordination Centre

The coastguard centre was controlled tension. Nine rescues still on the board, five completed and four hours of darkness till the dawn. The officer coordinating the *Caledonia* rescue sat with headphones on, one side pulled back away from his ear so he could hear what was happening around him. He looked up at the red Chinagraph pencil number on the board. Fifty-six, with a big circle round it. One Arun-class boat on service. You boys have got your work cut out tonight.

'Boss,' he called, 'any word on another chopper?'

'Negative.'

Poor bastards, he thought. You would pick tonight to get into trouble. He looked across through the glass of the top half of the door into the reception area where the reporters and their equipment were. As he watched, one of the volunteers walked across and stuck a large piece of paper over the glass section as yet another camera was aimed into the operations room.

He pulled the other earphone across and leant forward, concentrating to hear the incoming signal. He finished writing and looked up.

'St Mary's boat is doing her first approach on the *Caledonia*,' he said aloud. Men began to move towards him, irresistibly drawn, to listen to the drama as it unfolded. This was no ordinary rescue. One boat. Storm-force conditions. Casualty deep sea. Lots of people. Even if she managed to get most of them away she would be loaded to the gun-wales for a long dangerous journey home, running before the seas. Either it was a tragedy in the making or there would be a legend born this night. Of that they were certain.

NINE

They were scattered in scared, apprehensive clusters around the seamen's mess, groups of three boys, selected by Fripp and the teacher. The teacher had been sullen and despondent, more from fear than anything else, and Fripp had taken him aside.

'Shape up. Set the example,' he had said firmly.

'How dare you insinuate . . .'

'It's not an insinuation,' Fripp, barely out of school himself, said to the teacher. 'Your feelings are obvious to the most inexperienced eye.'

The man withered a little, but found strength beneath the dim yellow lights, strength enough to be honest. 'I'm sorry, I am not a sea person,' he responded. 'I am . . .'

'I know,' Fripp said. 'Just hide the truth. Put on a brave face, all right?'

'Are you frightened?' the teacher asked.

'Shitting bricks,' Fripp lied easily. He had never felt so confident in himself. The man smiled and the cadet officer moved away, touching a boy on the shoulder. 'And what group are you in?'

'Seven, sir,' the boy answered firmly.

'Good. And you?' He pointed to another.

'Four, sir.'

'Good. All right, the crew will now come among you and check life jackets. Group one?' Three boys raised their hands.

'Come with me, please.'

Out in the passage, Jarvis and Joe Mangalo, the man who had been on the helm when the engine had failed, carried Captain Wellbrook's stretcher aft down the angled floor.

Nichols followed them, a big waterproof flashlight in one hand and a radio in the other. For the first time he was carrying a life jacket.

Twenty feet further down the passage a door opened to the right, the upper side. It occurred to Nichols that if the ship had listed the other way, access to the aft decks from within would have been impossible. Thank God for small mercies, he thought.

The two men lowered the stretcher to the floor.

'OK. We will move out on to the deck and along the line at the port rail. At the end of the deck drop down the second line. Jarvis, you will take the captain. Joe, one boy, Fripp, one, and I will take one.'

They nodded and Nichols looked back over his shoulder to where Fripp had arrived with his charges and, as he spoke, he put on the life jacket.

'Get a bowline round each. One end over the line and one end round you. If one gives, then there is the other. When the boat comes in he will have three seconds. Get your man aboard . . . and come back for the next group.'

He looked around the group. 'Any questions?'

As Jarvis began to undo the straps that held Wellbrook into the stretcher, Nichols turned to the three boys. He tried to remember their names, their backgrounds, something about each that he could use to try to get them closer, to trust him and his men. He couldn't think of anything so he got straight into it.

'Let me tell you what we are going to do. First we get out the door.' He jerked a thumb at the steel door that was clipped shut. 'I say that because the noise and the storm will be scary, OK? Very noisy, very dark . . . but you are not to worry. We know our way round those decks with our eyes shut . . . Mr Jarvis here, whom you all know, has been across it . . . how many times tonight?'

'Oh . . . ten or twelve times,' the bosun lied. 'It's no problem.'

'But just in case,' Nichols continued, 'we are going to tie you on to the big rope and we will move along like mountain climbers, OK?'

The boys nodded together, faces pale under the emergency lights.

'Do as we say . . .' Nichols began.

'How will we hear you . . . if it's noisy?' one interrupted sensibly.

Nichols smiled. 'Because we will be that close,' he said, holding up two fingers side by side. 'At the other end of the deck we will go up the steps on to the quarterdeck. Mr Jarvis has put another rope there for us. We will move down the rope towards the water and you boys will get on the lifeboat. It will then drive away and come back for the next group.'

The radio hissed in his hand and he lifted it to his ear.

'Thanks,' he said into it and then looked back at the group.

'Jarvis, stay with the captain. They are going to pass some medication to us. He needs that first and will go next trip.

'I'll lead. Then Mangalo, then Fripp. Let's go.'

'I'll come,' Jarvis said, standing. He seemed huge in the narrow passage as Nichols looked up.

'No. Wait here with the captain if you will, Bosun.'

The *Maeve* stood by, her sharp bows into the seas, taking the waves head on, rising forty or fifty feet, then falling like a stone into the troughs.

Carter was on the flying bridge again. It was cold and exposed and, even in his thermals and all-wool garments under the foul-weather gear, he shivered. But from up here he knew he could see what was happening.

Below him on the afterdeck Simon, John and Vic huddled in the lee of the wheelhouse. They would not

236

move round on to the exposed port deck until they were almost on the casualty and, once there, they would grab whoever they could, haul them over the rail, under it, through the gaps at the entry ports, wherever they could.

Parnell and Ernie waited inside, Ernie on the radios and close to his engine panels and Parnell feeling more than a little redundant.

Carter saw the glow as the deck door opened across on *Caledonia*, the night so dark that even the feeble emergency lighting cut through the spray. He flicked the searchlight on and swung it back so it danced across the turbulent water. Each time they crested, it found the *Caledonia* for a second before they plummeted into the next trough. He needed someone to operate the light but he wanted the three men on the deck where they were. He half regretted leaving short-crewed but instantly dispelled the thought.

He lifted the bridge phone and a moment later Parnell stepped from the wheelhouse and moved gingerly up the steep exterior stairs to the flying bridge. As he arrived, bent over by the strength of the wind, Carter grabbed his lifeline and snapped the clip on to the back frame.

'Give 'em the light,' Carter shouted, pointing to the huddle of people moving out on to the exposed afterdeck of the stricken ship. Parnell understood immediately and swung the beam across the two hundred yards of water, creating a bright pool of light ahead of the group.

Nichols held the taut rope with all his strength, his back to the storm, his charge between him and the rail, the rope running between them. They were inching their way along, the bigger waves reaching up across the entire deck to snap and lunge at their feet, the wind shrieking and howling past them. The boy with Fripp had his eyes shut, his face into Fripp's chest, allowing the man to nudge his feet along, his hands holding on to the rope like vices. Joe

Mangalo's boy slipped and the Filipino's hand snapped out like a striking snake and, with wiry strength, he lifted the lad back to his feet and pushed him along.

Ahead of them, a searchlight played on the deck, the spray and foam white and bright in its beam. Twenty feet to go, Nichols thought, then up the steps and down, down into the surf. There must be an easier way. His companion was moving more confidently now and, a minute later, they watched the last pair arrive at the quarterdeck. There was no respite for them there; the wind drove droplets of water like needles against the skin. Below them, the water, channelled by the steel wall of the bulkhead, raced up the edge of the main deck. Keep moving, Nichols thought, must keep moving now. If we stop, they will freeze up on us. He wiped salt and spray from his eyes and looked down into the black watery maelstrom. Keep moving.

On the *Maeve*, Carter watched. Not the group itself, but where Parnell, with younger eyes and more time, played the light. They were at the far end of the deck and about to move down.

Time, he thought. He pushed the throttles forward and the lifeboat rose on to the plane, her flared bows swinging around. This was dangerous. The stern was on to the seas and there were no trailing drogues. She would have to be fast enough not to let any wave catch her or she would risk being pitchpoled, thrown end over end, and even an Arun might not survive that.

Then she would turn, beam on to the seas, and run in alongside the casualty, timing the approach so that, by the time the next wave came in, he had her ready once again, bows on, to meet it, juggling the twin throttles for bursts of power.

Below on the deck, the men felt the change in engine note as she responded to the helm, the big engines roaring beneath them.

Timson grinned and leant forward. 'Here we go, then,'

he called. Simon grinned back and together they moved round on to the port deck, and secured lifelines. John stayed in the low waist and Simon moved up to the pulpit on the wide exposed front deck.

Both men were aware of the dangers. Both were experienced, but each had such faith in their coxswain and his ability that it occurred to neither to doubt they could do an approach. One, at least. See how it goes. John Timson flashed a look up at the flying bridge.

Harold James Carter was many things. He was a father, a husband, a fisherman, a keen sailor and a chess player. But most of all he was a lifeboatman and tonight he was in his element. He knew this was no ordinary rescue. Not the practised retrieval of two wet and frightened people from a yacht, or the rescue of three weekend fishermen from the upturned hull of their small cabin cruiser. It wasn't the sinking trawler where the rescue was manageable and predictable because the people they were taking off were all professional seamen, people who made their living on the water. He knew that this would be the culmination of a career at sea, a career that had seen scores of storms and scores of ships. But never one like this. Never so many people, so far offshore, in such weather, with such a difficult approach. Tonight would need all the accumulated experience of forty years of boathandling and, with his hands on her wheel, the boat seemed to feel that tonight was her night too. She danced over the foam-streaked water, light on the helm, her responses positive in the banshee wind.

Usually the best approach was obvious. There was one way in that was better than the others, safer, faster, with fewer risks to the lifeboatmen or the survivors. One circuit of the casualty vessel was enough to find it. But not tonight. Carter watched the seas break over the aft decks of the *Caledonia*. It was the only way in alongside her, but it was fraught with danger. The second option was just as risky in many ways and would take much longer. That option was to approach to one end, like the St Peter's Port Arun had done in the now legendary rescue of the crew of the *Bonita* in 1981. They had gone in to her transom stern. But the *Bonita* was smaller than this fourteen-thousand-ton merchantman. A lot smaller.

In both cases the waves were the problem. They were so big that even one of the smaller, steeper monsters could dash the small lifeboat against the unforgiving steel sides or deck of the *Caledonia*. One of the big ones would pick her up and throw her high on to the upper sides to be smashed to pieces by the following waves. Airtight chambers and strong hull aside, the key to her survival lay in her speed and manoeuvrability. Dead in the water or caught against a rock or ship's side she was as vulnerable as any boat.

Carter watched the waves come, swinging the bows right in a gut-wrenching turn to meet each one. As they crested back to the left on to track he felt for the broach, correcting, power on, surging forward and running flat out in the trough. The throttles worked constantly, back into the next rolling mountain of black spume-laced water. Zigzagging in towards the confusion of foam, surf and breaking seas that marked the place where a ship was dying.

They were on the edge of the deck now. Nichols and Fripp crouched with the three boys wedged between them and the transverse rail that ran across the ship from one side to the other at the edge of the quarterdeck. From there it was nine feet down to the working deck. Below them, the hatches of holds three and four were awash, with the starboard rail completely submerged under four feet of water. A big wave crashed in on them. Should have stayed up by the poop, Nichols thought, should have stayed above the waterline. Beside him Fripp tightened his grip on the leg of one of the boys as the backwash began, tons of water rushing back into the sea.

Joe Mangalo, crouched beside them, lifted his arm and

pointed and, as he did so, the searchlight found them again, but this time it didn't die like before.

Nichols looked up. There, behind the light, he could see the boat as she powered her way over a small breaker, the final leg of her erratic course in alongside completed, perfectly timed, in the big trough between two waves.

Suddenly she slewed round to the right offering her broad beam to the seas, the power coming off, reverse engines to slow her down. There were figures on her side deck, yellow slickers, one a giant of a man the size of Jarvis, hands signalling to say, wait for it, not yet. The light was lowered to illuminate the seven-foot drop and her deck area, and, then, a wave came from nowhere.

Carter felt it first, not under his feet, not through the hull, but in his blood, in the hair as it rose on the back of his neck. Then he saw it, saw it late because his night sight was impaired by the searchlight so close. Unlike the others it had no curling breaking crest, no flash of foam or white in the darkness to signal its rushing gathering presence. It was big. Very big. A black-walled leviathan without foam streaks because it had risen from the trough.

He turned the wheel in the same millisecond that he felt it, but not all the way, relying on his instincts, not taking it direct under the *Maeve*'s flared bows, but on the starboard bow, deliberately sheltering the port decks. Creating a lee with the wheelhouse, creating a barrier that would prevent his crew from taking the full force of the wave as it broke because it was sure to, as sure as the sea was salty. He hit the throttles in the next millisecond and the boat lurched forward, a thousand horsepower thrusting back into the twin propellers in their recessed housing, a nasty thump underwater as the stern came round, hitting something on the *Caledonia*, and the propellers churning the sea.

On the for'ard deck, Simon felt the wave the same instant his father saw it. His night sight was also impaired so he ran aft, in a low crouching ducking dash, seeking the solid shelter of the wheelhouse. He raised one hand in an instinctive gesture as he began to move, to protect his head from whatever would be falling, his lifeline whipping along the securing cable. John Timson grabbed him as he tumbled down, the bows rising, the boat rolling heavily over to port as she shouldered her way upward. Both men snatched at the heavy bars of the A frame. Anything solid, anything real, grab and hold tight and hold your breath before it's knocked out of you. As the wave broke over them, the force was so powerful that the *Maeve* stopped dead in the water for a second, shuddering right down to her bilges.

The sound was like a cannon shot, a flat crack that slammed against the wheelhouse and the decks all at once and the world seemed to shake. The solid wall of water and foam rushed back down the side decks, split by the wheelhouse, the force knocking her sideways so her rail was in the water. Up on the flying bridge Carter and Parnell ducked as water cascaded over them, not the usual spray and spume, but so much water it seemed impossible for the boat to recover. Yet she did. With her engines set low in the hull providing ballast, she shrugged the water clear, found her keel and snapped upright.

Carter raised his hand to his eyes and wiped them clear of water and immediately looked back to the *Caledonia* to judge the best way for the next attempt.

That was no more successful, Nichols watching in awe again, but this time they met the wave head on and the *Maeve* powered her way over it, her crew safe inside or behind the wheelhouse.

The third attempt at last brought the lifeboat in close enough and a voice boomed over a deck speaker, 'ON THE RISE, JUMP,' and, as if on command, the next slope of water came in and the lifeboat rose, real and there and close enough to touch.

'Now,' Nichols yelled. They each stood with a boy, pushing him up on to the railing. They were all terrified; one yelled something and Nichols hit him with a fist behind the knees and, as his legs folded and he fell forward, a hand below from the boat caught him. The others were across, one having fallen on the narrow deck. The engines were gunning, a deep throaty roar above the wind, and she was turning into the next wave as it came down, full power on. There was a crash as something hit something, an object thrown, a bright-yellow line in the lights. The drugs, Nichols thought, and then the *Maeve* was away, climbing the wave as he watched, up and up and finally battering her way over the crest.

'Sit here.' Parnell shouted to be heard. The boy, bewildered, frightened and shaking with a mixture of adrenaline and relief, sat down and wiped the water from his face. The doctor went to work, running his hands through the boy's hair, feeling for a bump or lump.

The boy had fallen on the deck and Timson had carried him, under one arm, into the warm wheelhouse which, with the instrument lights and the constant roar from the engines, seemed cosy.

'Any pain?' Parnell asked, flashing a light into the boy's eyes, aware that his hand was still shaking, his own adrenaline still in his blood. The pupil's reaction to light was normal enough but Parnell made a note to check on him every so often for delayed concussion. There was no response to his question. He was in shock. Parnell shook him roughly.

'Look at me. LOOK.'

The boy looked up, his eyes focusing, realization there.

'You are safe. I am a doctor.' The boy nodded. 'That's better. Do you feel any pain?'

'A headache,' the boy replied in a flat monotone.

Parnell grinned. 'I'll bet you have. That was a hell of a thump. You seem OK.'

Parnell took off his bump cap and put it on the boy and then Simon took him for'ard to the survivors' cabin, where he was wrapped in a survival bag and strapped on to the bench with the other two.

The bridge phone warbled and John Timson snatched it from the cradle and listened before acknowledging.

'Ernie, Hal says we hit something underwater. Have a look below. Aft cabin.'

'Aye, I felt it,' Ernie said, walking towards the stairs.

'Vic,' John continued, 'Hal says to contact Falmouth. Tell 'em we have three aboard.'

'Aye aye,' from Collier.

'A good start, eh, Doc!' Timson bellowed, a beaming grin across his face.

Parnell smiled and nodded. They had the first survivors aboard and he had beaten his own fear.

Fripp and Mangalo had rested for a moment in the lee of the small poop structure while Nichols forced the lock on the door. The small steel enclosure had been added some years after the *Caledonia* had originally been built, as cover for an auxiliary winch for the aft cargo derricks. Modernization had subsequently seen the winch and engine removed but the garage-sized area remained and was now used as a store for paint and rope, grease and tools.

Once inside he looked about. A couple of paint tins had rolled on to the deck and now lay hard against the lower wall but, other than that, the job of securing the store had been done well. A few moments later he rejoined the other two and they moved back across the main aft deck.

Scott met them in the doorway. In his hand he held a Thermos flask and three plastic cups.

'Well done all,' he said, cheerily handing each man a cup. 'That seemed to go very well.'

'Only just,' Nichols said. 'Third attempt. I was expecting her to pull away and try again.' He handed Scott the plastic-wrapped package and pointed down to the figure who lay still in the stretcher. 'Get the medic to give it to him.'

Scott nodded and passed Fripp the Thermos flask. My God, Nichols thought, looking into the mess. They are quiet in there. The quiet of fear. We got three away. Three only.

Images of the approach flashed through his mind: the waves, the lifeboat, the wavering searchlight, the jump and the timing. Images of failure. Crushed bodies swept into the dark deep waters. If we try three each time, they will have to do that twenty times. With what success rate? Fifty per cent at best? Forty approaches? Maybe fifty? Sixty even?

'We must accept the fact that they will have to do at least forty approaches. Maybe more,' he said firmly.

'One for the captain alone,' Fripp said, dragging on a wet cigarette. Jarvis looked at him, a new respect for the lad, noticing the cigarette for the first time. A few people had taken up smoking that night.

'I want a second chain,' Nichols said, 'to get the groups as far as the poop store. There's room there for three batches. Nine people. Then, if the boat gets two chances inside a few minutes, we have people there ready to go off.'

The medic arrived and bent over the captain, the plastic package open on the floor. He raised a hypodermic syringe and pressed the plunger to clear the air from the chamber and needle. Fripp looked away. He hated needles. Chafney arrived and they shared a grin, no longer deck officer and cadet, but equals, comrades. Fripp had dropped into Jeffries's role as if he were born to it.

Nichols lifted the radio handset.

'*Maeve*, this is Nichols.'

'Go ahead.'

'We will be about five to seven minutes with the stretcher case, over.'

'Roger.'

'*Maeve*?' Nichols had dropped all pretence of radio procedure now, accepting a cigarette from Chafney.

'Aye, go ahead.'

'That was gutsy. Very gutsy, over.' He sneezed then, a mixture of cigarette smoke and a cold coming on.

On the *Maeve*, Vic Collier on the radio was a little embarrassed at the compliment and said the only thing he could think of.

'*Gesundheit.*'

On the flying bridge, Carter waited for a damage report from Ernie Coutts. There had been two thumps down there. She was designed to take hull-to-hull contacts. They were inevitable in a rescue where the boat had to be alongside another in any kind of weather. But even her thick hull wasn't built to be slammed against steel or rock. While he waited for the report and the confirmation that the first survivors were secured in the for'ard cabin, he ran through the approach, over and over in his mind, trying to work out a better way to get alongside the *Caledonia* without risking major damage, without putting his deck crew at undue risk. Each approach that brought them angling in with the seas on their quarter carried risks. Every wave had to come under the bows. That made the zigzag in an uncomfortable tiring approach each time and there was no way out of that. The real danger lay in presenting the *Maeve*'s beam to the seas once they were alongside. Timing was everything. There were two other possibilities. One was to trail a drogue off the bows and run in backwards, letting out the winch cable as they went.

The drogues, big cone-shaped canvas contraptions like oversized windsocks, made effective sea anchors. One secured to the front of the lifeboat meant that, in theory, they could winch back on to the casualty with their bows always into the seas. But someone would have to be on the foredeck manning the lines, two men in fact, and they would be exposed out there, without protection of any kind. Unmanned, the drogue would hold the bows down. That meant they wouldn't rise over the waves as fast as they should. The waves would come over the bows, tons

246

of water moving at phenomenal speeds that would snatch a man from the deck and smash him against the wheelhouse, or simply pluck him off, like a feather, never to be seen again.

Carter had been caught on the for'ard decks several times, holding the winch or the pulpit rails as green seas came over him. It was terrifying. He expected that from no man. Drogues off the bows were not an option. They were for emergencies only.

The other possibility was just to back in, on engine power, juggling the throttles, offering the *Maeve*'s stern and her flat aft deck for the survivors to jump on to. One of the real benefits of an Arun-class boat was that, alongside, it offered fifty-odd feet of length to jump for. Stern on reduced that area to twelve or so. It also meant that her propellers were perilously close to snags and underwater objects. Without props she was a cripple, as much a cripple as the ship they were there to help. He could not risk damage down there.

That left the way they had gone in, beam on for the transfer, men on the port decks.

'Right. I'll go with the bosun. Mr Chafney, Mr Fripp, organize the next group into the poop store. Joe will go with you. We should be back for the next trip after that.' Nichols turned then to the medic. 'Is he ready?'

'As ready as we can make him, sir,' the medic replied.

Nichols looked down at Wellbrook. He was ashen, his face had aged twenty years in the last two hours, his breathing was shallow and raggedy. Hang on now, boss, just hang on and we will get you into a nice warm bunk with a real doctor.

'Let's go,' he said to Jarvis.

The big bosun undid the straps that held Wellbrook and gently lifted him into a sitting position. He slipped a bright-orange life jacket over his shoulders and tightened the straps, hooked a lifeline on to the lifting ring and then hefted the inert man up and over his shoulder. Nichols noticed he was now also wearing one of the lifeline harnesses although he had crossed the deck many times that night without one.

They stepped out immediately, Nichols leading, Jarvis behind him, snapping the lifelines on to the rope as they cleared the edge of the deck and took the force of the wind. Chafney and Fripp watched them for a while, Jarvis with the captain over his shoulder moving steadily out along the rope safety line, sliding one foot then the other.

'Ready?' Fripp asked.

'Lead on, MacDuff,' Chafney answered. Behind him Carstairs had appeared as they moved back into the mess to round up the next group to cross to the poop store. The Special Branch sergeant stood in the open door and watched the two men proceed across the wave-lashed deck towards the rescue point.

'Can't see any real damage, Hal,' Coutts reported. They were all in the wheelhouse now, Carter having come down from the flying bridge. He held a match to his pipe while Coutts finished speaking. 'I had a look over the stern. Nothing there either. I can't think what it was. We were to seaward of the rail. No pipes or intake cowls, no scuttles that low. I think maybe there is flotsam in the water.'

Carter looked over the flame of his match, enjoying the deep satisfying flavour of the smoke for the first time since he had left his dining room table, his eyes creasing in concern. Flotsam was the scourge of wrecks. Timbers, battens, rope, canvas, drums, pallets and tins all found their way into the sea, washed from the ship. They fouled propellers, cooling intakes and rudders. Big objects or sharp heavy objects could even pierce the hull.

If there was something to hit in the water, there could be something to foul the propellers. He drew on the pipe, thinking to himself, weighing up the risks. Whatever was there should have been carried round the hull by the waves or wind. Flotsam was never on the seaward or windward side for long.

'Maybe,' he said, looking at his watch. Four minutes since the radio call. 'It's time. Let's hope it has drifted round,' he finished, putting his pipe in his pocket. Not flotsam, he thought. Can't be. It's something else. Three aboard and fifty-three to go. One group crossing the deck at a time. At this rate, it would take three hours or more. 'Vic, get on to *Drumbeat*. See if they can raise the *Pegasus*. Get a time when she's expected.'

With a big ship sheltering them from the force of the storm they could take maybe fifteen or twenty off at once.

Ernie took the wheel from Simon while Carter and the three younger men moved out on to the deck, the coxswain and the doctor moving on up to the bridge. Parnell would operate the light again. He was ready below, the stretcher laid out, survival bag and blankets prepared.

Once on the bridge, Carter took the lamp for a second and flashed it back at the *Caledonia*, not on the decks, but up at the samson post that held the twin derricks for the aft holds.

The angle was difficult, but he knew what he was looking for.

He picked up the bridge phone and spoke to Vic Collier who was still below by the radio panel. Collier immediately picked up the VHF handset.

'*Caledonia, Caledonia*, this is *Maeve*,' he began.

'Go, *Maeve*.'

'*Caledonia*, we hit something in the water on that last pass. Please check your aft cargo derricks. We think you have lost the topping lift and gear from the for'ard derrick. Please confirm, over.'

'Roger. Stand by.'

Above him on the flying bridge, Carter waited for a break in the wave pattern and turned the lifeboat for the next long approach. By force of habit he looked down at the depth sounder and, with ten knots of speed under the hull, he steered the lifeboat in towards the *Caledonia*. Parnell, instead of trying to follow figures in the storm, had the light fixed on the corner of the quarterdeck and was hoping they would appear there any second. Carter was watching the spot every few seconds but, otherwise, his eyes looked to seaward almost over his right shoulder, turning to meet each wave as it thundered and roared in on them. Then the *Maeve* was back on course, her hull carving through the hissing surf.

The bridge phone went and he picked it up, listened and replaced it. He had been right. *Caledonia*'s for'ard derrick on the aft samson post, the number three hold derrick, was lying on the deck, its topping lift cable and pulleys, blocks and hook all over the side in the water. As it landed, it had also driven a hole straight through the hatch covers and knocked them askew. They would be taking water into that hold with every wave now.

He could see figures at the pickup point: one man, almost as big as Timson, was on his knees, his back to the wind, holding on to the rail and a figure that lay slumped at his feet. Another man flashed a torch at them.

Carter moved the throttles forward and, as the boat gathered herself under him, he watched the approaching seas. The rise was thirty to forty feet as the waves came in. He had to make sure they arrived as one wave broke over the *Caledonia*. There could be no jumping here; they must be high enough in the water to take off a sick man. A big wave, feels wrong, too close. Round again, hitting the power on again, turning her as she hit the trough, a broach back end, correcting, more power, hard over now, the deck heeled like a ski-boat in the turn, line up again, try again, and again and again.

The sixth approach was good. Ready, lads, he thought, as he lined up. The ship was suddenly there, huge in the light. Power off, ten degrees rudder angle, reverse engines, the sea boiling under her counter, the water rising, lifting them. 'ON THE RISE,' he yelled, move, move, move, waiting for Timson's shout, not daring to take his eyes off the waves, come on, come on.

Nichols, who had been willing them in, was standing up on the deck. Jarvis had Wellbrook in his arms like a child, one massive arm under his back, the other under his knees. The lifeboat seemed surprisingly big up this close, bright orange, wheelhouse lights, two men on the deck by the wire safety rail.

Jarvis was looking for the way to hand over Wellbrook, expecting two men, seeing two, but only one leant forward as the boat rose. He was a big man, very big, his own size, like a great bearded bear. Their eyes met. Then there was the thump of the hull hitting steel, big hands reaching across the narrowing gap. Suddenly the weight was gone, the big man yelling, 'GO,' dropping to one knee and the lifeboat surging away, the second man coming up, reaching for Wellbrook's lifeline and snapping it on to the running stay, easy as pie, a classic transfer.

But only on the sixth attempt.

Parnell met them at the wheelhouse door and the sick man was lowered gently on to the fixed stretcher position, almost a sea berth, in the wheelhouse. As Parnell checked pulse, pupils and breathing rate, Simon began stripping the clothing from Wellbrook's body. Two minutes later he was dry and in the heat-insulated survival bag with straps over his legs and chest to secure him in the bunk.

'Anything more I can do?' Simon asked.

'No, thanks,' Parnell answered. 'Their diagnosis was right, it's heart failure. I'd say it's left-side, backward failure. I'm going to give him something that should stimulate action. Until I can get an ECG done we won't know any more.'

'Is he gonna be OK?'

'His breathing is shallow and laboured. Pulse weak and erratic. He could fail again any time. So no. He may die. However, I should be able to stabilize him.' He held up a hypodermic to check the dosage in the light, no longer the

251

first-time rookie crewman, but a physician with a patient. He was back in his own world where he was the expert and the others just visiting.

He leant forward and pushed the needle home firmly, squeezing the powerful digitalis-based drug into Wellbrook's bloodstream.

'Just keep a close watch now. What he needs is an ICU. Can we let Falmouth know? I'd like a transfer from St Mary's as soon as we are back.'

Simon looked at his watch. 'We may be here another two hours yet. Then two home. If the weather lifts, we can get the helicopter. Will he last tha . . . ?'

'Hope for the best,' Parnell interrupted evenly.

'You lads ready?' Collier asked.

'Yeah,' Simon answered.

'Good. We are going in again.'

They had stopped with the group at the poop store. Nichols ran over the way he wanted things to go on the deck. Jarvis remained with him while the seaman Mangalo, Fripp and Chafney returned to the mess to get the next group.

The boys stood in the torchlight, shivering and frightened amongst the paint tins, scrapers and drums of rope, reminders of a time when someone cared about nice-looking paint jobs.

'So. Down the deck. As she comes alongside and, as she rises on the wave, cross over. All right? Wait for my shout. Don't try and go until I tell you, because he may want to come round again. He will only come in if it's absolutely safe.' He didn't use the word jump, or mention the gap, that it was only three feet wide, or the way that the decks pitched. He didn't say that if the coxswain ballsed this up, then a wave would pick up the lifeboat, all thirty-odd tons of her, and drop it right on their heads. He raised the radio to his lips and talked for a moment.

'Let's go.'

*   *   *

'I want you away with the next group,' Carstairs began. 'We didn't draw you a number so you would be able to tag along with any of them.' He was trying to deliver the message as a decision made. Not something up for negotiation.

David Lawler stood opposite him in the chartroom, his thumbs tucked in the life-jacket straps, a posture like his father routinely adopted with his thumbs in his jacket pockets. 'Sorry,' he said. 'I go last.'

'I thought we agreed that we would do whatever the officer in charge wanted, we would cooperate,' Carstairs reasoned.

'It wouldn't be right,' the boy countered.

'What's not right?'

'Are you prepared to leave?'

'No. I am a serving officer in the police,' Carstairs said flatly, 'and this is an emergency. I stay.'

'Well then. We go last. You can't be seen to desert me now, can you? So we stay . . . easy. Anyway, I am the prefect. It would be very wrong of me to cross before any of the others.'

'Let me worry about what that looks like. My first priority is your safety.'

'I am in as much danger there as here. We all are.'

Carstairs looked away for a second then. He was quite comfortable with the prospect of going off in a helicopter. But he wasn't keen on the lifeboat.

'What's this really about?' he asked. 'It's not appearances. It's not that . . .' He trailed off, remembering the conversation they had had. David had been worried about living up to his father's legend. How would he react if it were ever him? My God, Carstairs thought, he thinks this is his burning car.

McDermott who could not help overhearing them from outside the chartroom entered to lend support.

'Why don't you do as he says, lad?' the Scots engineer asked.

'It's OK,' said Carstairs, looking David in the eyes, understanding him, 'he has his reasons.'

'I don't intend to be difficult for the sake of it, chief. I am simply doing what I must do. My decision is final.'

They looked at each other then, the older hard Scotsman and the boy, eyes locked like adversaries in a courtroom.

'Look. Just get on the bloody lifeboat, OK?'

'Why? What makes me more important than any other person aboard?'

McDermott studied him for a moment. Outside the wind shrieked and the seas battered the ship but, in the chartroom, it seemed quiet, deadly quiet, and Carstairs could feel the atmosphere change.

McDermott threw back his head and laughed. 'Ballsy little bugger, aren't you? Just like your old man,' he said.

David Lawler's heart soared with pride.

Chafney was pale. He stood in the door, a lukewarm cup of chocolate, the last of the contents of one of the big Thermos jugs, in his shaking hand.

'Never saw anything like it, Mr Fripp,' the medic said.

Fripp, sitting on the floor, was having his head bandaged and he looked up. He hadn't seen anything. Not the wave, not anything. He just remembered his head hitting the rail and Jarvis's hand through his life-jacket straps and then everything went black.

'It just came out of nowhere. I'd heard about the big ones. But I've never seen one,' the medic continued.

'I didn't see it. I fucking felt it though,' Fripp said, wincing as the medic worked.

'It just hit her and over she went . . . knocked flat like a boxer in the ring. Nothing then. Just foam and the surf everywhere. White surf. And then she came back, bounced back like a punch bag. I'd never seen a boat capsize before. Small boats, yes. But a big boat? Knocked right over? I mean she was right under the water. Came back up like a bloody cork.' The medic had finished and was putting things back in his little tin.

Chafney looked down at Fripp who was lighting a cigarette. In the dim lights he looked older than his seventeen years. 'You are a lucky lad. That wave should have had you.'

'Naa,' Fripp said, finding a grin, his hand shaking lightly. 'I've signed on for seven. No cadet gets away that easy.

'Anyway,' he continued, the grin falling away, 'it was my fault those two were still on the deck.'

'Bullshit,' Chafney said. 'He just got scared and jumped. They were OK, so the number one says.'

'Yeah, well, next time I'm going to sit on the little bastard till it's time.'

Chafney smiled. The little bastards, as Fripp called them, were only three years younger than he.

The approach had been fine. It was the second for that group and Carter had pulled the power off and nudged the boat in alongside perfectly, on the rise. There were three men on the side deck. Simon, John and Vic Collier, one for each of the boys coming over.

Then everything happened at once. The first two boys crossed when they were told, over on to the narrow port deck, risking the drop of a few feet to land near the men in the bright-orange life jackets and yellow foul-weather suits. The third, frightened and panicky, had broken from Fripp's hold and run a few feet forward, leaping the rail, going for the bigger wider foredeck. Carter had seen the wave then. It was a leviathan. Sixty or seventy feet high from trough to crest it had gathered itself gently but now it was steepening. It was no longer a roller. It was going to break. He barked a warning into the speakers as Simon ran down the deck, his lifeline whipping along the wire, snatching the boy up from where he lay clinging on to the anchor that was lashed to the rail.

On the bridge Carter hit the throttles, the big twin diesels roaring. He turned the bows into the wave, but knowing that while Simon might survive the strike bows on, held by his lifeline, the boy never would, he turned back again, offering the boat's quarter to the sea, willing his son to get back down into the lee of the wheelhouse.

Simon pulled the boy behind him and the wave broke with a crack like thunder, a three-storey building falling sideways, slamming broadside into the *Maeve*, tons and tons of water, solid like concrete, driving her over and down.

It seemed to Carter to take for ever for her to come back. As the boat capsized he was thrown to the left, held in place only by the body belt around his waist. It all went black. He had his hands on the wheel, already turning the rudder to bring the bows round, the silence unbelievable. My God! We are under! Knocked flat and the wave has rolled over us. He began to count, knowing that in a couple of seconds she should start the roll back. It seemed like an eternity, but she gathered herself, the airtight wheelhouse buoyant and the massive weight of the twin diesels set low for just such an occasion as this. The *Maeve* began to right herself, tons of water pouring from her decks as the wheelhouse rose from the foamy sea.

On the side deck, Simon had one hand round a stanchion and wrapped in the boy's life jacket and the other over his mouth and nose. He had seen the self-righting tests in Poole and with the wonderful confidence of youth he knew, the water black and salty as he held his breath, that if he held on long enough, she would come back.

Parnell had no such faith. The barked warning from the bridge came a second too late for him. He missed his reach at the straps that held Wellbrook, his fingers scrabbling for the stainless-steel grab pole. Again he missed, falling backwards as the floor tilted under his feet. Collier shouted a warning, grabbing at the collar of one of the survivors. John Timson was holding on tight to a grab bar, the other boy in his other hand, thinking, Jesus, over we go. Simon's out there, hold on, lad, I'll get to you. He turned his head to check the clips on the aft door, knowing Ernie had shut them only a second before, everything in slow motion but checking anyway, the boy heavy under his arm. Then Parnell fell back, crashing into them, as the yells and cries from the for'ard cabin were drowned out by churning props and screaming engines. They were on their side. The blackness at the windows could only mean they were underwater. They all noticed the engines throttling back at the same moment.

'Oh, fuck,' Parnell said.

Someone screamed down in the front cabin. Pure absolute terror.

'We're OK,' Timson said softly for Parnell's benefit, before his full-throated bellow shook the wheelhouse. 'Steady down there. We are OK!'

John looked down at Parnell who lay on the floor, as the world began to turn again, but chose to thrust the boy at Ernie. 'Take him,' he said. 'I'll be needed on deck.' Ernie reached for the boy, but his eyes were on the instrument panels, willing the engines to keep running while they were lying on their side, Timson already at the aft door, waiting for the rollback.

Suddenly they were right side up and the engine note changed as power went on, the bows coming round. Hal's on the ball, Timson thought, not expecting him to have been washed away, but pleased with the boatmanship. The moment the propellers had purchase he used it.

He went through the aft door on to the deck like a tiger through a burning hoop, slamming it shut behind him, throwing the clips and then moving round on to the port deck with a speed and agility that belied his size. There on the deck were two bundles. He ran to them, not bothering with his lifeline, and, as he arrived, Simon lifted his head and then dropped it again, gasping in great draughts of air.

'Everyone all right?' boomed out of the speakers.

'Aye,' Timson bellowed.

He prised Simon's fingers loose from the stanchion, feeling that it was bent where Simon had held on against the force of the water. He lifted the lifeboatman from his position covering the vomiting boy beneath him, checked the lifeline and then snapped his own on.

'Up,' he said, lifting Simon to his feet, one boot on the boy's back to hold him in place. Collier arrived then and together they carried the boy back down the deck, Simon walking unaided, but groggily.

Ernie Coutts took the wheel while Carter came down from the bridge with an assessment of damage. It was considerable. The radar scanner was gone, as was the reflector. The big circular aerial was gone and the upper assembly was buckled and twisted to the right. The lifebelt and inflatable had been washed away as had the canvas overhead spray cover. Luckily the tall whippy VHF aerial still stood.

As he stepped into the wheelhouse and sealed the door behind him, Timson looked up with a grin.

'Mine's a pint,' he said. Carter smiled. They were all alive. The boat was serviceable so far. Maybe they could go on.

Normally that would be unthinkable. A capsize would mean a nice gentle trip home. Other lifeboats putting out to escort her. Could be hull damage, stressed structure, certainly stressed crew, enough for one night, hand over to another boat, thank the Lord for your life, and go home.

Although the boats were self-righting, they all knew that sometimes when they went over the forces at work were so strong they just broke the lifeboat's back. Things happened. No one ever knew what, because no one ever survived.

He shut the thoughts out and looked about the crew.

Could they go on? There were no other boats available. No one else to help. They would have to. There was simply no one else. Forty-nine more people on the casualty. What condition was the *Maeve* really in? The answer to that would take a marine surveyor to find with one of those fancy little boxes that fired X-rays through the hull and the deck joints. She might be ready to take in water along some joint or seam with the next wave that caught her.

He looked around his crew. They at least seemed all right. Even Parnell. A capsize on his first trip out. That should cure him for ever, he thought, that and the sick. It was everywhere below, the smell of the vomit rising into the wheelhouse.

'Well?' he asked.

There was a pause.

'I see,' Ernie Coutts said with a dry smile, 'that you managed to keep that god-awful cap on your head.'

'So I did,' Carter said, putting a hand up to touch the soggy brim. 'So I did.'

'And your boy went swimming by the looks of him,' Coutts finished.

'Aye. He did,' Carter said, looking at his son, his pride obvious, feeling a rush of love, not just for Simon but them all.

Simon broke the spell. 'Ernie?' he called with a smile.

'Aye,' the engineer answered.

'Fuck off.'

The eccentric little man laughed, chuckling out loud, his body bobbing with delight behind the helm.

The boys were covered and secured below and the crew set about clearing up the wheelhouse. Parnell checked Wellbrook who hadn't budged an inch during the entire episode as Carter stood by the radio panel.

'*Drumbeat, Drumbeat*, this is the *Maeve*.'

'Go ahead, *Maeve*.'

'*Drumbeat*, please advise Falmouth we capsized in taking off the last group. We have no medium- or short-wave radio aerials. Radar is Uniform Sierra. Some other damage and loss. No injuries. We now have seven survivors on board, over.'

259

'Roger, *Maeve*. Can we do anything for you, over?' The voice held an edge of awe. A capsize. Beyond ninety degrees. Death for a ship. Yet this man reported it like it was a shopping list.

'Just relay messages if you would, *Drumbeat*,' Carter said pleasantly.

'With pleasure, *Maeve*.'

Carter reached up and, with the inherent concern for batteries that all boatmen share, he turned off the medium- and short-wave radios and then looked back at the five men around him.

He said nothing for a moment, giving any man amongst them the chance to speak, to voice his fears on the condition of the boat and her ability now to handle the elements.

They knew what he was waiting for. He was the coxswain and they would crew for him into hell itself, but they were volunteers and he was giving them the opportunity to say their piece.

No one moved.

No one spoke.

Finally Victor Collier said it for all of them. 'Let's get the rest and go home to our beds.'

At the school parents had begun to gather, seeking comfort from each other and naturally wanting to be where David Lawler's father had promised to keep the information flowing. A handful of others had driven down to Penzance, but the bulk now stood in the master's common room, where the school chaplain's wife poured tea from the urn. A prayer service would begin any minute, but one father had said, 'Bugger it, I could use a drink,' and the head's cocktail cabinet, a hideous art deco arrangement, had been lugged down from his house by two of the senior boys who had been woken up to help out.

The telephone was silent and they stared at it, willing it to ring, willing it to bring good news.

TEN

At the Falmouth Maritime Rescue Coordination Centre frantic efforts were under way to support the St Mary's lifeboatmen. The Padstow boat, now refuelling after a service, would put back to sea immediately and stand by a coaster that was shipping water off St Ives. That would free up the faster St Ives boat to relieve the Penlee lifeboatmen who were finding their service was taking a lot longer than they had anticipated. Once released from their role they could make for the *Caledonia* at top speed. The Sennen Cove boat was still on service but she would also head deep sea to help the *Maeve Corrigan* as soon as possible. Their efforts were redoubled when they heard that the St Mary's Arun had capsized and was still on service. If nothing else she would need an escort home.

Other lifeboatmen and volunteers from the Lizard and Falmouth stations converged on their boathouses to ensure a fast turnround once their boats returned. That meant fresh crews, men to pump fuel, others with bags of sandwiches, flasks of soup and dry gear for the wet, exhausted men to change into if they got the chance.

At RAF Brawdy, the second Sea King, now back from her first mission, had her ASW gear unceremoniously pulled from its racks and fuel pumped into her as she prepared to take off southwards into strong headwinds.

Andy Hall's wife had taken a call twenty minutes before to advise that her husband would not be back that night. She had replaced the phone and then walked into the boys' bedroom where they slept, oblivious to the happenings of the night, and, although not a religious woman, she had said a small prayer of thanks over the snuffling and restless sleeping forms of his two sons. She then turned on the television to wait for news on the satellite channel.

At the Royal Naval air station at Portland, home of two Sea King search and rescue helicopters, standby crews waited for the return of the machines that were still committed, lifting the crew from a sinking freighter.

At the CNN centre in Atlanta an anchorwoman looked up at the camera lens with impossibly beautiful eyes and read from the auto-cue.

'And now for an update on the rescue of a party of schoolchildren from a ship sinking off the coast of Britain, we cross to Christine Jacobs in London.'

The producers then fed on to the screen a sequence compiled earlier. It was a voice-over of Susan Farmer's second telephone report with library footage of a lifeboat in heavy seas, fading out then cutting to a live scene where an older, but still attractive, woman, faced a camera.

'The latest here from Falmouth, a small coastal town in the southwest of England and base of the area's coastguard, is confused but promising. The lifeboat, which is attempting to rescue the fifty-six people, including the son of British Prime Minister James Lawler, on the stricken ship, has now taken off six of the students and the ship's captain, who apparently suffered a heart attack earlier tonight. But, in doing so, the boat was swamped by a huge wave and capsized. She, like all the newer lifeboats, is self-righting but informed sources tell me that it is usual for a lifeboat that has been knocked down in this manner to head home, abort the attempt if you like, leave the rescue to others, to head back to their base for repairs and a survey for major structural damage. No one is sure just how many times a lifeboat can stand being capsized because the forces out there cannot be duplicated in tests.

'So far fate has not been kind to those aboard the *Caledonia* awaiting rescue, nor to those in the rescue parties. A Royal Air Force rescue helicopter was overhead the ship and was about to winch up the first survivors when she developed engine problems and had to make a forced landing on another ship standing by. Informed sources say they were perilously close to needing to be rescued themselves.

'There is also growing controversy over the deployment of rescue resources. One London radio station has been taking calls from people suggesting that British ships and British passengers should be the first to receive help when resources are stretched. This is a direct reference to the continuing rescue of the crew of a Pakistani freighter by navy helicopters, which some people believe should be diverted immediately to the scene where the *Caledonia*, a British ship, is in peril. A spokesman for the Royal National Lifeboat Institution, the privately funded organization that conducts rescues in the home waters of the British Isles, said that they deploy their boats and crews to ships in distress regardless of nationality and without favouritism. In the meantime, there is no news of the identities of the six boys who have so far made it to safety, and police have said that it is not customary for names to be released until survivors are ashore and positive identification has been made. At 10 Downing Street, as at other homes in Britain, the lights are on as the staff await news. This is Christine Jacobs for CNN, live in London.'

The headmaster looked round the room at the parents as someone turned the volume down on the television. Six boys now on the boat, but which six? Which of you have your sons off the sinking ship? He half wished the police would release names so that some, at least, could relax, safe in the knowledge that their sons had made it that far. The other half of him agreed with the rule. Keep the names of the survivors quiet until all is known, until the relatives of any who don't make it have been informed.

In the Daimler speeding westwards, Heather Lawler looked across at her husband. He had seen the look before. Absolute determination.

'I don't care any more. I don't care about the house, the party, the constituency or the bloody country. I just want David home and safe.'

'They are doing their best,' James said. 'Six boys have crossed and there will be more as we speak.'

'If you do nothing else in your term, you change this,' she replied firmly. 'How a country like ours, a country that can field a world-beating army, produce technology and design that is the envy of the industrial nations, can leave a group of our children to six volunteers in a little boat funded by donations is beyond me.'

'It's rather more complex than that,' he said sadly. 'They have avoided government funding lest they become bound to government's whims. What a dreadful statement that makes about our system.'

'Then don't fund them,' Heather replied frostily. 'Scrap one of your precious bloody submarines and give them the money. No strings attached.'

'I will address the issue,' he said and she knew he meant it.

'*Maeve, Maeve*, this is *Drumbeat*.' De Villiers himself was on the radio this time.

'Go ahead, *Drumbeat*,' Collier replied.

'*Maeve*, the *Pegasus* will make her pass in thirty minutes. We have her on radar, over.'

'Roger, *Drumbeat*. Thank you.'

'*Maeve*, *Pegasus* has requested that all ships remain downwind of her, nor'east of the *Caledonia*. In the meantime we will make a windward pass ourselves. We won't give you much of a lee but you are welcome to use it.'

'Stand by, *Drumbeat*, I shall advise the coxswain,' Collier said diplomatically. He knew that Carter would have views on that and he wasn't going to pre-empt them. A minute later Hal Carter, dripping wet, his cap still firmly on his head, was down from the flying bridge standing at the radio panel.

'Just how close do you intend passing, *Drumbeat*?' he asked. If they could get very close then it was worth the effort. Worth holding off his own next approach to try and use her lee, the area of comparative calm as she passed between the prevailing winds and seas and the ship.

If not near enough to be of use, she would simply be in the way of his manoeuvring. Ideally with her bearing problem she should be standing seven or eight cables off, about a mile at the nearest.

'Four hundred yards minimum, *Maeve*.'

That distance, with a ship the size of the *Pegasus*, would give ample cover but a fleet Rover-class oiler was a different proposition. No good to man nor beast. They wouldn't even see her at two cables distance, not in this heavy weather. But let them pass anyway. It would allow them to think they were doing something useful.

'Make it three cables . . . six hundred yards, *Drumbeat*. Then we can continue working, over and out.'

Without giving de Villiers a chance to argue he thumbed the on switch a second time.

'*Caledonia*, this is *Maeve*.'

'Go, *Maeve*. Everything all right over there with you?' Nichols asked.

'Aye,' Carter answered. 'We are going to make another approach now and a second as the fleet oiler makes a pass to try for a lee. In thirty minutes, that is, figures thirty, *Caledonia*, three zero, a Uniform Lima Charlie Charlie will make a slow pass. We shall be alongside when she does. Can you please have as many people as possible ready to transfer at that time, over.'

'Roger, *Maeve*. Let us know as you head in for the next approach and we will have another three at the rail.'

Carter handed back the microphone and went towards the door.

'You game for the light?' he asked Parnell.

The doctor shook his head. 'Rather stay down here with him for a while.'

'You do the radio if it squawks?' Carter asked, pointing to the VHF set.

'No problem,' Parnell answered.

'Vic.'

Collier looked over and Carter jerked his thumb up towards the bridge. As they left, Parnell crossed from his position beside Wellbrook and familiarized himself with the workings of the radio. He was now alone in the wheelhouse, the wheel moving as if by magic, the throttles worked by some invisible force.

The small poop store was crowded. Nichols, Chafney and Jarvis waited for the signal from the lifeboat with nine of the boys, while Fripp, Joe Mangalo and another of the seamen moved across the deck, bringing another group of three. That left only one group and their teacher and Carstairs in the accommodations. Nichols looked round the group, his thoughts on the images of the lifeboat as it capsized, the despair he had felt, then sudden realization that it was a selfish singular consideration, that brave men were aboard her. He had offered a silent mental apology and now stood thinking about the supertanker.

How fast? If it were me I would come past at two knots, make it three in this weather. A ULCC could be anything from three hundred yards to four fifty-odd in length. A mass, let's be conservative and say three hundred yards long, starts to move past a given point at three nautical miles per hour. How long does it take for the other end to pass your given point?

Four minutes. Chop off a bit either end because the weather will be curving round her hull, so a real lee of half that. Two minutes. But she won't be that close and the wind will funnel round her and meet at an apex some distance away. Distance unknown without a scale model and a wind tank. So where will she be in relation to that quiet triangle? Two minutes? Bullshit. We haven't been that lucky tonight. Halve that. One minute at most. One minute of oily swell. No breakers, thank Christ. How many passes could the lifeboat make in one minute?

He won't want to risk taking another wave on the beam again. He'll want everyone below by the time he takes the seas under the bows.

He lifted the hand-held radio to his lips.

'Mr Scott.'

'Sir.'

'Did you copy that last message from the *Maeve*?'

'Yes, I did, over.'

'What's your estimate on the quiet spell?'

Scott, still up in the chartroom of the bridge, was the ship's navigator and had anticipated the question.

'All things considered, we should count on no longer than a minute, possibly as little as forty seconds, depending on how far off she passes and how far she is down on her marks.'

'Very well. I want twenty people here by the time that tanker passes. Get the last group of boys down and then have fifteen crew move across to the poop store. Juniors first.'

'Already on it, Skipper,' he replied.

'Mr Scott?'

'Go.'

'I expect to see Carstairs and his charge in the group. No more fucking around.'

'Aye aye, sir,' Scott replied.

*   *   *

267

It was Ernie Coutts who first noticed they were taking water somewhere, and began an intensive search to find where they were holed or leaking. It was somewhere on the starboard side, the side that had taken the force of the wave that had knocked them over. Small trickles down the bulkhead. He reported it to Carter. The automatic bilge pumps hadn't cut in yet so, as the *Maeve* moved in for the next approach, he moved round the lower areas, trying to assess the extent of the damage. He gave the boys strapped on to the bench seats in the for'ard survivors' cabin a wink as he ran his hands down the bulkheads feeling for anywhere else that water might be running down from the deck. He moved carefully, his feet widely spaced, as the boat danced and shuddered beneath him. The floor was covered in sick and that made it slippery.

'How you boys doing?' he yelled. One of the braver, less seasick ones waved a hand back at him. Another lay down across the laps of the two beside him, his face washed out and pale.

He smiled at them and moved up the steep stairs to the wheelhouse.

'Can you do anything for them? Puking their hearts out,' he said to Parnell.

'Not really,' the doctor replied, his hand reaching for the grab pole as he moved forward to be heard without shouting. 'I can make them sleep, but it will be the sleep of the dead for several hours.'

'No,' Coutts said.

Good, thought Parnell. He knew why. Not with a boat that has gone over and is shipping water.

'Did you find the leak?' he asked.

'Somewhere down the side,' Coutts said, pointing along the right. 'It's nothing to worry about. Bilge pumps haven't cut in yet.'

'Unless we get hit again in the same place,' Parnell said dryly.

'What are we going to do? Turn shoreward and leave 'em?'

'No,' Parnell said. 'I didn't mean that.'

'I know . . . It's like the army.' Coutts said with a grin. 'If you can't take a joke you shouldn't have joined.'

The only thing was, Parnell noticed, that when the engineer smiled his eyes weren't in on the joke. He was as concerned about the leak as anyone.

'Ho, fucking ho,' Parnell said dryly.

'That's the spirit, lad. We'll make an islander of you yet.'

Up on the flying bridge, Carter flicked a look at the *Caledonia* as they ran in the last few yards. The spotlight picked out the wind-blown foam, streaks of white against the darkness in the foreground, while, behind them, the bulk of the ship's quarterdeck angled back up into the night. A huddle of figures cowered in the corner. It would be three crew again, he thought, and three of the boys. The last time he had taken people off a ship, there had been none of this order and discipline. There had just been the terrified Indian and Singaporean crew of a bulk carrier, fragmented by fear and the complete breakdown of authority on the ship. They had struggled and fought for a place aboard the lifeboat as she came alongside each time. Two crew had been lost, falling into the dark seas and, although they had searched until they were low on fuel, they were never seen again.

The wave he had been watching was gathering height, its wall steepening, so he aborted the approach and turned to meet it, but instead of swinging the bows round to the left again, he kept them coming right to run back down the line of the ship for a further attempt. It took five approaches before they could get alongside and then, to everyone's disappointment, two of the lads, seized by some sort of telepathic fear, stubbornly held on to the railing with their eyes shut, only Nichols managing to get one of the boys across.

The next attempt was almost a tragedy.

Carter had taken the boat back after a fast turn, angling in on the back slope of a wave, pulling the power off to await the next rise of water. He could see the crewmen of the *Caledonia* with the two boys, Collier holding the light nice and steady and the surf rolling past their feet. Power on again, nudge up nice and close. He stood, his instincts feeling out for the next rise, watching the seas, listening for the shout that would tell him another transfer had taken place.

One of the boys, his fear beaten, crossed like a deer, fleet-footed on to the deck into John Timson's arms, and the next rose, gaining courage from the example. He shook himself away from Chafney who was holding him and climbed on to the rail as the others had done, his eyes on the pitching deck of the lifeboat five feet below.

He held the pose for a second but the wind took his legs out and he fell hard over the rail down into the turbulent backwash of surf at the edge of the main deck. He was being sucked inexorably back into the dark sea.

Simon shouted a warning to his father. They knew the drill. Vic Collier dropped the light beam on to the flash of orange that was the boy's life jacket and never took his eyes off it for a second. Simon did the same. That was rule number one. Never take your eyes off a person in the water. Carter gunned the engines to pull the lifeboat astern and then threw the throttle forward to get the bows round for the next wave. Simon on the port deck held on, relying on his strength and his lifeline and hoping that Collier wouldn't lose sight of the boy as the wave crest rolled back down the foredeck. Four feet of surf and foam ran back down on him, taking his legs out from under him.

As it cleared and he stood up again, they were coming astern, the wheel hard over to the left, Carter running the boat up beside the bright bobbing life jacket. Simon leant over and grabbed the lifting strap and then Timson was back, his huge hand reaching into the sea, and together they lifted the boy up on to the deck, dragging him into the low waist as the bows came round again.

Only a minute later he was in a chair in the wheelhouse, as Parnell eased his life jacket over his head, his young face white with shock and pain. He vomited weakly, his eyes filled with misery and fear.

'Hold him in gently. Mind the shoulder,' Parnell said. Simon, standing behind the pedestal-mounted chair, eased a hand across the boy's chest, careful to avoid the nasty odd-looking bump on the shoulder.

Parnell stood holding the grab bar and fishing round in his bag. A moment later he was back with a hypodermic syringe and an ampoule.

'This will kill the pain,' he said cheerfully. 'Then you look the other way and we will get things back where they should be.' He administered the drug and, while he was waiting for it to take effect, he stood over Wellbrook's sleeping form and took his pulse. He was in his element. This was the kind of medicine he had trained for.

A few minutes later, with John Timson helping and with a violent tug on the arm, the ball joint was back in the socket and the arm was strapped across the boy's chest over the top of a life jacket and he was helped below.

The coastguard officer pulled off the headphones and walked the few paces to the big whiteboard. He rubbed out the seven beside the *Maeve*'s name and entered a ten. 'Nice one, you bloody little beauties. Capsized, leaking and still taking them off in threes. Carry on, boys. Don't give up now. I have help coming soon.'

He was joined by a volunteer who handed him a cup of coffee.

'Ten now. Good stuff. Word's out about the capsize . . . crews all along the coast wanting to slip to help them.'

The officer with the marker took the coffee and smiled.

'They look after their own, these lads,' he said.

'Aye. Well, the boss has told a couple of them to stay

put. The older slower boats. One bugger up the coast wants to launch his Watson class.'

'What? It only does nine knots! The *Caledonia* is fifty miles off Land's End for Christ's sake. It would take them all night to get there.'

'That's what the boss told him.'

'And?'

'He said, "A boat's a boat," ' he replied, mimicking a Devon accent.

'An S and R chopper has left Brawdy, Penlee's Arun will be free shortly and the Lizard people are ready to turn their boat around. We should have two good fast lifeboats on their way any time now.'

'Fifty miles,' the other said. 'That's . . .'

'Three hours, give or take.'

The news was phoned through to James Lawler's car and, with Heather smiling and feeling good for the first time that night, he called the school to tell them that there were now nine boys safe on the lifeboat.

The *Drumbeat* turned her substantial beam to the seas and, rolling like a barrel, she began to steam past at a sedate three knots. The helmsman was having trouble holding her course and was constantly correcting, coming round towards the wind as the waves slammed into her, some breaking clear over her bows. Even as she drew abreast, de Villiers knew that she would not provide much shelter. The seas were too big, the winds too strong and the distance too great. She was rolling viciously now and he stood, feeling the strain coming up through the deck plates.

This is futile, he thought. Futile and foolhardy.

'Bring her round,' he said.

Six hundred yards away on the *Maeve* they could just make her out, her big outline rolling through sixty degrees from one wave to the next, her stabilizers taking the brunt of the roll, a few of her brighter lights cutting through the spume and foam. As she finally gave up her attempt and the *Maeve*'s crew watched her bows turning into the weather once more, Carter nodded, more to himself than anyone else. It was brave and well-intentioned but not much real use. He turned the lifeboat round and began to move back in to the casualty, trying to remember how many approaches they had now made.

Beside him, Collier found the quarterdeck with the spotlight and Simon and John took up their positions down in the waist, John casually sitting on one of the three steps that led from the waist up to the aft deck, his great head held high, hair and beard drenched and laced with salt.

He remained sitting even as small sea came inboard at his feet, simply dropping his head as the foam and water showered over him. He hated the wet-weather gear they were issued with. It was designed for weekend sailors, he thought, and since the RNLI committees were run by weekend sailors, this was the gear they bought. The Americans had the kit: sealed at the cuffs and neck like a diver's dry suit, inherently buoyant and apparently wonderfully warm, it was the stuff of dreams. One day, he thought, watching Simon, who was equally wet, move to the rail, I'll get some of that gear. They were coming in. He stood and moved down the waist, one hand holding the rail, the other running his lifeline down the wire. Then it can blow a gale and I will be as dry as toast. Come on then. Let's be having you, lads.

Defiant's electronics and maintenance teams had been working feverishly since the orders had come down from the bridge. The gear that had been brought aboard for the fleet exercise was pulled from the stores and re-mounted on the temporary brackets that still stood above the radar housing and the aft superstructure. Small groups of men, in heavy-weather gear and secured by lifelines, worked under their respective petty officers, running the heavy cables back down the open conduits. All the destroyer's deck officers were present on the small bridge and the communications ratings and lookouts were tense at their posts. Every so often the duty officer would motion the radar lookout to one side and drop his face into the soft rubber viewfinder to watch the supertanker's progress as she moved towards them. All other shipping heading west out of the Channel had been moved southwards and they appeared as a series of contacts on the extreme edge of the screen, the nearest being twenty miles to the southwest.

The captain stood near the clear screen watching the storm. Every so often a flash of lightning would illuminate the sky, the scudding clouds flashing white. In the soft diffused light, he could pick out the black hulk of the *Caledonia*'s hull and the upper sections of her port bridge wing. He crossed the few feet to the bank of instruments and read off the wind speed. He was silent. If anything, the velocity had increased.

'I make it force eleven now, sir.'

'An occluded front. It shouldn't be that strong,' he replied.

'It has gusted to twelve,' his number one replied. 'I think they may want to review their conventional wisdom at the met centre.'

As they spoke a huge sea crashed over the *Defiant*'s bows, the water breaking round the sides of the Ikara launcher and cascading through the scuppers into the sea.

'I've seen seas like this up in the Arctic, but never here. That's the bitch I know and love,' the captain said with a wolfish grin, 'always full of bloody surprises. Are we ready?'

'Yes, Captain.'

It was on the third attempt that the *Maeve* managed to get close enough for long enough to take off the next small group of survivors. Chafney, Jarvis and Nichols had the procedure established now. Don't let go of them, Nichols

274

had drilled, don't let them get a hold of anything they can hang on to, and when they go, get them over the rail so they drop into the waist. It was another two feet further to fall but worth it for the protection given by the lifeboat's wheelhouse, and the solid unflappable presence of the lifeboat's crew.

'Both the incidents so far were preventable. The kid on the foredeck and the poor little bugger that went in. Both put the lifeboat at risk. One capsize. One man overboard. Not good enough. Those men are risking their lives and we owe it to them to get it right. No more fuck-ups. Understood?'

The group of men, rank having been cast aside for the purpose of this phase of the rescue, stood quietly while Nichols spoke.

'Right. It's thirteen away. The ULCC is due past in fifteen minutes. We will have thirty seconds. I want twenty people off in that time.'

'There's not room for twenty down there, sir,' Chafney said.

The poop store, where they were gathered, was crowded and Nichols had his back to the passengers who were squeezed in amongst the shelves of paint, turpentine, scrapers and wire brushes.

David Lawler had arrived with the last group of boys, Carstairs close by, as always.

'No. But there is in here . . . cramped but possible. Those who don't fit, crew,' he emphasized, 'will wait outside. I want a line of people moving down the deck one after another. Two of us at the bottom handing them over, throwing them over, whatever it takes. No stopping. No hold-ups. Mr Fripp and Mr Chafney will be here at the head of the line. Bosun, you will be with me. Any questions?'

There were none. The old *Caledonia* was sinking. There was no doubt about that. She had settled at the stern in the last half an hour. Nichols thought they might have another hour, maybe an hour and a half. Then she would either roll over or, tired and weary, just slip beneath the storm into the black quiet depths.

Anyone still on board would go with her, sucked down with her fourteen thousand tons of steel and fuel and machinery.

They all knew it.

Carter held up his lighter to his pipe and sucked the flame down, puffing as the tobacco caught. The RNLI frowned on smoking on the boats but they weren't out here and he was. He slipped the lighter into his pocket and watched as Parnell looked over the last three survivors to come aboard and as Simon and John unpacked survival bags. He had another reason for lighting the pipe. The sick smell coming up from the for'ard cabin was strong, but his tobacco was also strong, a pleasing rich aroma that would do much to cover it.

Coutts sat at the helm, both hands on the big wheel. Carter moved towards him.

'Find anything?' he asked.

'No. Must be all along the wheelhouse deck bond seam.'

'Pumps?' Carter asked. The bilge pumps would cut in when the water level reached a certain point.

'Any minute,' Coutts answered.

Carter looked at his watch. It had only been fifteen minutes since they had gone over. They could manage that. He had finished services on boats that were leaking like sieves. As long as she had engine power and functioning rudders, then her watertight compartments would allow them to stay afloat and do their job.

'Vic, can we manage a cup of tea for everyone?' He meant the boys in the small survivors' cabin as well as the crew. The sheer normality of a cup of tea helped people. Half-cups in plastic beakers or tin mugs, no one minded the effort of trying to keep the fluid in the cup long enough to drink it on a pitching boat. It was a piece of routine. A ritual they could cling to. They all reacted differently once aboard and safe. Some just sat. Some wept. Some talked, pouring out words. Some joked and laughed, glad to be alive. Others sat frozen, the fear still real until their feet were on dry land.

'I think so,' Collier replied with a smile.

Carter left him to it. That was Collier at his best. Taking care of others with a genuine concern. He was their best first-aider; he could splint limbs, dress wounds, and he was the man who could brew tea or coffee anywhere and produce food for those hungry enough to eat it. He said it was the little things that made the difference. He pushed past Carter and dropped down the steep steps into the small aft cabin where a little urn that heated water made up for the *Maeve*'s lack of a galley.

Four minutes later they had completed three abortive approaches and Carter had decided to stand off and rest his crew till the *Pegasus* arrived. He wanted them ready for that.

Andy Hall and Mark Selby stood well off to one side on the bridge of the *Drumbeat*, out of the way of the helmsman, deck officers and lookouts. Captain de Villiers paced back and forth, looking every so often at the big green glowing radar screen that dominated the grey electronics panel. The advancing supertanker was a huge bright-green blob on the screen, approaching them on what seemed like a collision course.

De Villiers made his living by putting his ship perilously close to others, and during refuelling only yards separated the vessels. But that was in good weather with both ships under way, twin-screwed ships, fast and manoeuvrable, running parallel to each other. This was different. He was hove to in appalling conditions, with almost nil visibility, and watching another ship on radar bearing down on his little bit of water. And no ordinary ship either. The *Pegasus* was over thirty times the size of *Drumbeat* and would trample her underfoot without losing a knot of speed. Any miscalculations on the bridge of either ship could result in real trouble.

He remembered the story of the British tanker captain in a VLCC, much smaller than *Pegasus*, making her way under escort up the Arabian Gulf during the Iran–Iraq War. The captain had radioed his escort and said he thought they had hit something, but he wasn't sure. They learnt later she had hit a mine. She was so big that a mine that would have broken the back of the *Drumbeat* had barely been felt on the bridge of the tanker.

He paced the linoleum floor. She should be visible any minute.

On *Pegasus*, Hawk was also on his bridge. The supertanker had a small lookout tower that rose above the bows. Atop the tower, a radar scanner swept the stormy night, giving close coverage to the area that the main sweeping system above the wheelhouse could not see, due to the sheer size of the vast steel deck.

They could see three vessels, the contacts this close differing in intensity. He leant across the panel with his number one.

'If they are to leeward like they should be, those are the two navy ships there and there.' Hawk pointed to the pair of contacts to the right.

'The lifeboat lost her reflector when she went over,' the number one said. He was still chewing his cigar, pointing to a blurred, hazy, indistinct contact hard against another clearer, bigger one. 'That must be her there. She is to windward.'

Hawk nodded, looking at the screen, trying to read more than it could tell him. The weather was so bad that when they passed, it was quite possible they wouldn't even see the *Caledonia*, let alone the tiny fibreglass and aluminium rescue boat. He imagined this scene in American waters. There would be a coastguard cutter in attendance, maybe wo, each one hundred and eighty feet of state-of-the-art, any-weather ship, with a helicopter and full-time professional crew. He only had to leave America for five minutes to learn to appreciate the incredible resources they could throw at a problem, be it military, civil or commercial.

Here, deep sea, in severe storm conditions, was a fifty-footer crewed by half a dozen volunteers trying to do the same thing.

Shit, he thought, walking to the big bridge windows, I have at least three friends who have bigger weekenders than that rinky-dink little boat. But, he admitted to himself, it was some little boat and some crew. Knocked over and driven under a big wave, she rolls back and carries on working. All her weight must be down low like one of those little blow-up men that kids knock over to bounce back.

'I want to come in close,' he said. 'A quarter-mile'. Modern tanker men didn't think in cables. He let his eyes sweep the instruments on the banks of panels. She was moving at 3.7 knots, the minimum for steerageway in good conditions, but tonight it was critical because, travelling in ballast only, she was high and light in the water, presenting her gargantuan beam to the wind.

Behind them a figure stepped on to the bridge. She was slight and beautiful with wavy black hair that cascaded off her shoulders. The pale-pastel pants suit showed her figure without being provocative and she wore sensible training shoes in the same shade of pink.

'Good evening, Mrs Hawk,' the number one said respectfully. Hawk turned in surprise. There were three areas on the ship that were open to visitors on invitation only, the crew's quarters, the engine rooms and the bridge. Juanita Hawk, however, knew that with the right murmured apology later in her husband's bed she could get away with it.

'Good evening, gentlemen. I have never seen a rescue. I would like to watch if I may.'

Hawk looked at her and nodded and a junior deck officer stepped forward.

'I'll get you some oilskins, ma'am.'

The number two stepped forward to stand beside Captain Hawk as his wife struggled into a pair of bright-yellow waterproof trousers.

'Four minutes to the turn, Captain.'

'Thank you. Instruct the helm to bear when you are ready.' And with that he stepped back to the console and lifted a VHF radio microphone, looking at the paper in his hand.

'*Drumbeat*, *Drumbeat*, *Defiant*, *Defiant*, this is the *Pegasus*. We will be coming round to starboard in four minutes. We will pass one quarter-mile off the *Caledonia*'s seaward beam. Do not, repeat, do not come to windward of your present positions until we have passed. Do you copy? Over.'

Two static crackled acknowledgements came back and Hawk lifted the microphone again.

'*Maeve*, *Maeve*, this is *Pegasus*.'

'Go, *Pegasus*.' Hawk noticed the soft Irish accent. He had been listening in for the last half an hour and this voice was new, but it made sense. The master would be at his helm.

'Six minutes, *Maeve*. We will be passing in six minutes. Good luck.'

'Thank you for your help, *Pegasus*.'

'You are welcome.'

On the *Maeve*, Parnell pushed the microphone back into its clip and looked across at Carter. They all held cups, some filled with tea, others with instant soup. Carter wanted this opportunity to let his crew warm up before the tanker made her pass, warm the chill that made fingers fumble. They were all wet through and would not be really comfortable until they were home and in dry clothing, but the hot drinks and the warmth of the wheelhouse helped as they rested. The concentration needed to work the deck was exhausting and anyone who relaxed for a second risked his life and the lives of others. Carter relit his pipe and puffed solidly on the burning tobacco, the sweet rich aroma filling the air, comforting in its familiarity.

Wellbrook stirred in his stretcher and Parnell moved across the cabin, John Timson standing back to make room for him to pass. All were holding cups in one hand and grab bars in the other as Simon, on the wheel, took the lifeboat over another dizzying wave, and dropped her down the back side.

Parnell leant across Wellbrook, taking his wrist in his hand and feeling his pulse. His eyes were open.

'My ship? The boys?' he asked weakly.

'Relax. We are taking everyone off now. They will be OK. Don't try and talk.'

'Save them. They are only children,' he rasped.

'Don't talk and don't worry. We will take them off.'

He closed his eyes again and Parnell smiled and stood. His patient had the strength to speak and was clear and lucid.

A good sign. He suddenly thought of Norah. Get the beds ready, my sweet, we are bringing home some very sick people. Then you can take me home and wrap me in your life.

Carter drained his cup and looked around the wheelhouse at the wet-haired, sodden, cold and tired group of men.

'Let's do it then. I am going to bring her in backwards. Take the swells under the bows while we transfer over the stern rail.'

They all stared at him. A stern approach was enormously difficult in any kind of sea. Impossible in the conditions tonight. The waves would simply pick up the lifeboat and dash her against the casualty. But when the tanker passed they could expect a fifty per cent improvement in conditions for the short time, twenty or thirty seconds perhaps.

They also knew they needed to maximize the time alongside, to get as many people across as possible. The lee would not prevent a swell but, if it reduced the wave height and prevented breakers for thirty or forty seconds, then they knew an outstanding coxswain could juggle the engines, waddle the boat back and forth, taking the seas under her bows, nudging back every time the swell had passed to allow more people over the stern.

'Doc, you stay inside. Simon, John, at the aft rail. Vic, the door, Ernie, you by the aft stairs.' That deployment put each individual where he was best and left the engineer nearest his engines. 'Stick them in the aft cabin. Doc, you watch them come in. Pull any you want to see. Otherwise get them below. If necessary sit them on the floor in here. We can reposition and get things squared away once we are clear again.'

They followed him out, only Simon and Parnell waiting inside. Parnell, because that was his post and Simon, because he was waiting for his father to take the helm on the flying bridge before he moved.

'Stern on?' Parnell said aloud to Simon. 'Surely that's . . .'

'If he says he can do it, he can,' Simon answered simply.

On *Defiant*, the captain, Commander Sir Giles Forbisher, ninth Earl of Warwick, 'Spud' to his chums at Eton, grinned at his number one, a lieutenant commander. He had just lied through his teeth to the master of the *Pegasus* and was now about to compound the situation with the same disregard. There was no way he was sitting still while the *Pegasus* passed. Not while he thought they could be of any assistance whatsoever. But he reasoned there was no point in advertising the fact in advance.

'Are we ready?' he asked. The preparation had been taking place for the last hour. Gear out of stores, cables run, the cruise turbine barely ticking over, the manoeuvring turbine powering the ship.

'We are, Captain . . . Ah, Captain?'

'Speak up. There's a good chap.' Forbisher beamed at his officer.

'When our intentions become clear he is going to be rather hostile.'

'It would be a sad day when the feelings aboard an American merchantman determined the behaviour of the Royals, would it not?' Forbisher said with a glint in his eye.

'It would, sir.' The officer grinned back. 'Just thought I ought to mention it.'

'And so you did.'

'Christ. Look at her.' Selby said.

She wasn't just big, she was a leviathan. The size of a skyscraper lying on its side, she moved forward, lit by flashes of lightning, as if no power on earth could stop her, shouldering aside the huge seas as if they were no more than ripples on a village pond.

As she came round, the waves slammed impotently into her cliff-like sides, the barest roll becoming visible as she brought her beam full on to the seas.

Hall nodded. 'First time I have seen one at this height.'

They were both still on the bridge of the *Drumbeat* and both were feeling seasick as the fleet oiler took the seas under her bows, pitching and falling like a car on some bizarre rollercoaster. In front of them through the clear screen they could just make out the bows of the *Caledonia*, her long black hull out of sight to the right. Above her, spume powered up into the sky as the spray was snatched off the wave tops.

'Oh dear,' de Villiers said aloud. He was looking out of the port wing windows. '*Defiant* is under way.'

His chief officer moved across and lifted a second pair of glasses and tried to focus through the storm. Across the quarter-mile of turbulent seas he could no longer make out the destroyer's riding lights. He swung the glasses up to her bows where he could see hazy flashes that would be her now illuminated bow light. The visibility was dreadful.

You wonderful cheeky bastard, he thought. You have something up your blue bloody Royal Navy sleeve, haven't you? He smiled to himself.

'She seems to be, sir,' he said to de Villiers. 'I wonder why.'

'*Caledonia*, *Caledonia*, this is *Maeve*.'

'Go ahead, *Maeve*,' Nichols answered quickly. He wanted to get in before Cochran, who was still in the radio room. The signal was strong into the hand-held radio, even through the walls of the poop store.

'*Caledonia*, as the *Pegasus* passes we will come in stern on. Please listen for the deck speakers. We will be constantly manoeuvring. Listen for the all clear before each transfer. I will shout "go" each time. Repeat "go". Is that clear? Over.'

'Roger, *Maeve*. We are ready for you.'

Jesus, Nichols thought, stern on. He must be some helmsman.

'*Maeve*, how wide is your aft deck?' he asked.

'Sixteen feet back there, *Caledonia*. Limit your transfer to the area between the crewmen, over.'

Carter eased the *Maeve* round, in a long oval turn, timing her arrival back at the casualty's quarterdeck to coincide with the lee created by the mammoth tanker that was looming out of the storm. He could make out her bow light and he tried to judge her arrival time and the distance she would be from the exposed decks of the *Caledonia*, putting it at the two cables her master had advised.

He put the bows round into the weather as another huge breaker reared out of the dark, its foaming shoulder crashing down on to the *Maeve*'s foredeck, and sluicing round the wheelhouse in a torrent feet deep.

This was now as bad a storm as he had ever been in or

service and as bad as any he had ever seen. The wind shrieked and moaned, the gigantic seas rolled and thundered towards them endlessly.

He swung the wheel back to port and pushed the throttles forward, racing to follow the wave diagonally in towards the casualty without risking his stern to following seas. Correcting and swinging the bows back round, he finally pulled the power back so that the lifeboat sat, her sharp, deep, flared bows into the seas, hove to fifty yards from the *Caledonia*.

He undid the body belt to stand side on. He would need to see over the stern to manoeuvre, and yet be able to turn his head to watch the seas coming at them. But he couldn't work the throttles and the wheel and look both ways and work the intercom.

He lifted the handset and below Parnell answered.

'I need you up here,' he said. It wasn't a request and Parnell made his way up to the flying bridge as he had done in the early stages of the rescue.

Carter watched the tanker coming. They had another half a minute or so until her massive football-field-sized bows crossed his position. He reached across and clipped the doctor's lifeline on to the frame and handed him the intercom phone.

'You relay what I tell you,' he shouted. 'Volume is up.'

Parnell nodded and felt his hand close tight over the back brace. He felt very exposed on the upper deck and, looking back for the first time since the capsize, he saw that the inflatable was gone. He looked up at the buckled aerial mounts and the stubby mounting where the radar scanner had sat.

Carter indicated that he should move back on to the brace and he nodded and pulled the wide belt around his waist. If we go over, he thought, I grab him and hope the belt holds. He looked down and then reached out and, taking Carter's lifeline, he clipped it on to the frame. Carter nodded like it was of little consequence and then, with his hand on the throttles, he put the engines astern and the lifeboat began to move backwards through the water, waves still hitting her bows, foam and water racing back down her decks. Shit, Parnell thought, he remembered mine and forgot his own.

'Stand by on deck,' he shouted. Parnell lifted the handset and relayed the command.

Down on the aft deck, Simon and John moved and unclipped the access cables opening the deck to the rear. Inside, Ernie Coutts turned on the aft deck light which was mounted on the bulkhead by the speaker. The single lamp made a brave attempt at lighting the area but all it really did was illuminate the spray. It would, however, help the people crossing the moving gap between vessels, the people having to judge the drop which could be anything from dead level to ten feet if they misjudged it. God help anyone who jumped if she was in a trough, Simon thought, but the *Caledonia*'s crew should be able to prevent that.

John Timson pointed a huge yellow slicker-suited arm into the dark. Simon looked but his night sight was gone. Then, as if to illustrate her arrival to any so afflicted, the *Pegasus*'s foghorn blared out with one long deep bass blast. I am under way in poor visibility.

Behind them on *Caledonia* someone found the lanyard and there was enough steam left in the head, because she answered the call like a mortally wounded animal to another of her kind, and three shorts were followed by one long mournful blast. Someone with a sailor's soul over on *Pegasus* broke the rules because she replied immediately, and a deeper, richer bass blast cut across the sea and the storm and the shriek of the wind and she seemed to Simon to be saying, I am here now, I am here to help.

He moved right back to the starboard side of the deck and clipped his line on to the rail.

The wave-battered bulk of the *Caledonia* was only twenty

yards behind them now and Carter eased the throttles forward to await the lee.

The *Defiant*'s turbines had separate functions. The cruise turbines were geared to drive the destroyer at her cruising speed for extended stretches, but her manoeuvring turbines could ease her forward with control never dreamed of by those encumbered with diesel engines. It was these turbines that gently moved her forward now, and, making barely a knot of speed, she crept round the bow end of the *Caledonia*'s hull.

Her quartermaster – the position dated back to fighting ships of the line – was the man charged with steering the ship as she entered shoal waters, battle, or danger, and he now stood at the helm, easing the warship round within feet of the much bigger stricken vessel.

Ahead, out in the dark, the massive *Pegasus* commenced her pass and Sir Giles Forbisher turned to his number one.

'Let's go to work. Tell the quartermaster. Forty per cent power for five seconds. Put us half a cable off the lifeboat and half a cable off the *Caledonia*, and hove to in the water. Turbines to remain on pursuit standby.'

'Aye aye.'

Below the decks, the gleaming turbines rumbled and spun, the great shafts throwing their torque into the propellers as the *Defiant* leapt forward like a highwayman into the now visibly calmer waters. Just as suddenly the turbine shut down, whining into silence, and the quartermaster smiled. They were exactly one hundred yards from both the *Caledonia* and the lifeboat's position further down her steeply sloping decks.

No turning back now, Forbisher thought. I could end up in front of their lordships of the Admiralty, protests from the American, her owners and every other bugger with a beef about the Royal Navy. But I'm not sitting back, leaving these poor bastards in the dark.

Not with fifteen thirty-six-inch quartz halogen flood-lights.

They were now arrayed in banks along the upper works as they had been for the night recovery operations off Gibraltar only days before. He was about to offer enough wattage to light Wembley Stadium.

'Light 'em up,' he said and, just for good measure, pulled the claxon lanyard. The warship's high-pitched little siren blared her whoop-whoop-whooping call to action.

'Jesus Christ,' Timson bellowed.

Suddenly, the night became day. He immediately turned his back to the searing light source. An area from one hundred yards out in front of the lifeboat to the high side of the *Caledonia* was bathed in light. Sharp hard shadows were thrown across the decks, and spray, less heavy now in the lee of the mighty *Pegasus*, was highlighted like snow on a Christmas card.

Carter, whose night vision was already impaired by the pool of light on the aft deck, got over his surprise and breathed a quick prayer of thanks. In spite of the flying spume he could see the incoming seas and he could see the *Caledonia* as if it was daylight.

The shelter, however temporary, offered by the *Pegasus* was impressive and the waves were now half their original height and rolled in without breaking crests. A big swell. Thirty seconds and counting. He hit the throttles and the lifeboat waddled backwards for the first stern-on transfer.

The destroyer, Nichols thought. Nothing else sounds like that, can manoeuvre like that, and nothing else would have lights like that. He swung his eyes back on to the reversing lifeboat and saw her for the first time in decent light, the high orange superstructure, buckled aerial frames and the yellow-clad figures on her tiny aft deck. Six feet, four feet, two feet, a burst of power from the engines as they went forward and then astern again, the boat stopping exactly against the side of the ship six feet below, her sharp bows turned into the swells as they rolled towards her.

A voice boomed over a deck speaker and shouted, 'Move.' Nichols felt Chafney lifting a boy beside him as he did the same, their efforts a frantic race against time.

ELEVEN

Carter, his back to the banks of floodlights on *Defiant's*
decks only one hundred yards away, watched the swell
and then flicked his head round to watch the action on
the aft deck. There was a falling frightened bundle of movement in the harsh light as a fourth teenager dropped the
distance to the deck, Timson's huge hand breaking his fall.

'Stop and hold on,' he barked to Parnell. As the doctor
repeated the order urgently into the intercom, Carter hit
the throttles and the lifeboat surged forward as the swell
hit. She rose up the side of the twenty-foot swell, and, just
as abruptly, he threw the throttles astern, stopped atop the
swell and let the water's motion carry them backwards.

The effect of *Pegasus's* pass was indeed dramatic. Her
sheer size blocking the wind had reduced waves that would
have been forty- or fifty-foot monsters to half that size and
rolling more as swells. Even so, Nichols, watching from
the *Caledonia's* quarterdeck, was almost mesmerized by the
lifeboat coxswain's seamanship. From his vantage point he
was almost level with the *Maeve's* flying bridge and he
could see Carter's right hand juggling the throttles, thumb
and forefinger controlling the port engine and little finger
and heel of hand on the starboard, his left hand down out
of sight on the lower rim of the wheel, as the lifeboat
sashayed back in.

In all the manoeuvres since the breakers had become
swells the lifeboat had not moved more than fifteen or
twenty feet from the ship's side. Less than a third of her
own length. The boathandling in the face of the conditions
was nothing less than masterful. Each time he came back
in and the lifeboat gently nudged the side of the *Caledonia*,

people crossed to safety. Nichols turned and looked back up the deck at the straggly line of wet frightened people, their life jackets bright orange, deceptively festive in the floodlights, only their pale stretched faces showing the pressure and the fear.

The bosun, Jarvis, was now down at the waterline, and opposite, on the tiny aft deck of the lifeboat another giant, younger and bearded and, if possible, even bigger than Cecil Jarvis, was taking the boys as they dropped. Passing them like parcels back to a smaller lithe sure-footed man nearer the watertight door that stood back on its clips.

Four across, then a booming voice from the deck speakers, Jarvis's hand closing on a small collar, holding a figure back. Carter, his flat cap on his head, his pipe jutting from between clenched teeth, moved his hand on the throttles. The boat surged forward up the next incoming swell, gave a throaty roar as the engines went astern and the black-blue shiny hull slid back into her own boiling, turbulent wake. Nichols was aware suddenly of the sweet welcome smell of the big diesels working down inside her, blowing back through her three-inch exhausts.

The line was moving again, hands clutching at the two-inch rope. As the hulls touched, Jarvis and Chafney urged sodden figures on to their feet and up on the rail. The plan was working well.

Nichols looked back up the deck and across towards the main accommodations. Below the wind-carried foam, McDermott and four of his engine-room crew were moving across the deck, followed by the remaining Filipino seaman. Scott and Cochran, Nichols thought. They are still at their posts.

The mighty blast of *Pegasus*'s horn crossed the waters. This was no greeting. This was an angry belligerent sound. There was no code here. Intended for *Defiant*, the meaning was plain to all. You are too close. Stand clear.

He heard the speakers again, followed by the engines,

and he watched as the lifeboat cleared the side and then eased back in and the transfer continued.

Forbisher crossed *Defiant*'s small bridge and watched from his vantage, willing calm on the tempest from his seaman's soul. For all his panache and the Oxbridge accent he was as much a simple sailor as the men aboard the *Caledonia* or the lifeboat, and was as much a sentimental, superstitious romantic as any who had ever gone to sea. He was one who loved figureheads, full-rigged ships and the traditions of the navy and the sea. The first rule of the sea was to protect life – and all the superstitions and legends came back to that one fundamental law.

Forbisher allowed his men to placate their superstitions in three ways. Flowers, the bringers of bad luck because they represented a funeral wreath, were banned aboard *Defiant*. Rumour had it that somewhere up on the forest of masts and antennae was a small laminated photograph of a naked woman, a flaxen-haired Viking beauty, who faced forward because the seas loved a beautiful woman and her image could calm the storm, serving the same function as the bare-breasted figureheads on ships three hundred years before. The last superstition was more traditional and one which he personally kept alive. That was the spilling of wine on the deck. The same legend had led to the modern practice of smashing a bottle of Champagne on the bows of a ship being launched and he now turned to the most junior midshipman aboard and nodded. The lad held up a cut-glass goblet of fine Bordeaux and slowly poured it on to the deck. Legend said it was an effective libation to the gods of the sea and, as it splashed down on to the spotless nonslip flooring of the bridge, Forbisher turned his eyes to the floodlit scene across the hundred yards of water, his appeal to the gods not to spare the *Defiant*, but the men and boys aboard the sinking merchantman.

Behind him the quartermaster manned the wheel, his

hand occasionally touching the power controls of the massive manoeuvring turbine engine six decks below.

Forbisher had ignored the horn blast from *Pegasus* five
seconds before and when the radio barked into life he was
expecting it.

'*Defiant*, what the hell are you playing at? Stand off, I
repeat stand off.'

Forbisher crossed to the console and took the radio mike
from the communications rating. His grin in the soft red
bridge lighting was positively wolfish.

'*Pegasus*, *Pegasus*, this is Her Britannic Majesty's Warship
Defiant, assisting with a rescue of the crew of a British ship
in British territorial waters on the request of her Britannic
Majesty's Coastguard. I am assuming on-scene command.
Incidentally we have been close manoeuvring in these
waters for the last six hundred years. I'll trust you not to
tell me how it's done. Proceed on your course for one more
minute.'

Off to his right a rating grinned, the pleasure of hearing
his captain shove it to the Yanks showing clearly, until the
quartermaster glared at him.

Forbisher then crossed the bridge to one of the pairs of
big pedestal-mounted binoculars. He bent over and put his
eyes to the lenses and watched. It was the finest piece of
boatmanship he had ever seen, the control of the fifty-
footer that was inching her way back and forth in the still
big swells.

'Starboard the wheel, sir?' the seaman asked into the small
control radio handset. There was an urgent tone in his
voice, a tone that said, I have been waiting for this order,
now give it to me. On the bridge wing Captain Hawk was
seething.

Damn and blast you, you goddamned limey prick. I risk
my ship and my crew and you want to be a clever bastard.
He stood in the relatively sheltered open wing of his bridge
and superstructure, his mind quickly recalculating the risk.

The destroyer was three hundred yards off their beam, hove to in the water, safe in their lee. If anything she would be blown downwind on to the casualty, not their way.

'No,' he snapped into his radio. 'Hold your course.' He looked across at his chief officer who stood beside him and pressed the earphones tighter to his head as a signal to the other to do the same. 'Get a fix on the auxiliary. If she moves an inch this way I want to know.'

'Aye aye.'

The chief officer moved back on to the bridge, leaving Hawk and his wife, small and slight in the huge oilskins, standing out on the wing to watch as they moved past. Across the water, through the foam and spray, they could see the pool of light thrown by the banks of floodlights on *Defiant*. The orange flash of colour that would be the St Mary's lifeboat was in the centre, the long-listing wave-washed decks of the *Caledonia* up into the dark behind, her white superstructure leaning drunkenly towards them. The lee was working and Hawk forgot his anger for a second and ran a hand along the rail, patting it twice as if she were some four-hundred-thousand-ton dog, thanking her. I'm proud of you, my girl. You are far more than just a huge scary steel thing that moves. Tonight you are the queen of the oceans and they don't fear you. Tonight they need you.

Together, from *Pegasus*'s seven-storey-high bridge, Hawk and his wife watched the Lilliputian drama progress below.

Carstairs, lying flat on the deck like all the others in the line, looked at David, who lay a few feet further down holding the rope that ran down to the rail. Every now and then he ran a hand down his face to clear the water from his eyes. They were drenched to the skin and cold, but, only a few feet from the rail, that didn't seem to matter. David was the last of the boys. They had agreed that much and he had walked from the poop store with a solid smile to take his place in the line. Carstairs watched the *Maeve* as she manoeuvred a few feet away in the glare of the lights.

Once across on the lifeboat he wanted access to a radio. A foot slipped past his shoulder and he looked up. One of the Filipino seamen grinned back. He's glad to be getting off, he thought.

On *Maeve* they had perhaps fifteen seconds of decent shelter left and, as they topped the swell, Carter once again reversed engines and ran the Arun backwards into the *Caledonia*.

The Arun-class boat wasn't the fastest off the blocks but she was powerful and responsive and could stop, turn on a penny and give you change, the makers said. And now she was proving it. Every sleek inch of her award-winning design was doing what she was built to do, and more.

They now had around twenty survivors on board, Carter thought. Numbers were always a problem till you moved off and secured. Ernie would be settling them in below in the aft cabin and the lap-strap-fitted bench seats would be full. They would have to start wedging them on to the floor, two for'ard and two aft until the aft spaces were crammed. Keep the centre of gravity low and aft. Mustn't be heavy at the head. Not in these seas. All the weight aft or we will pitchpole before we can get a drogue out. They nudged.

Aft at the rail, centre stage in the lights, Timson grinned at Simon. This was where they worked best together. Both seeing, both doing, but covering for each other. Very often conditions outside the wheelhouse didn't allow for talk. A shout could be heard over the wind and the roar of the diesels, but not much more, so they had learnt to predict, to see things happening and be in the right place at exactly the right time. Simon was fast and agile like a cat on the deck, John bigger and not as agile, but immensely strong.

It was he who caught the first boy of the next group, passing him back to Simon in time for the second one. Below their feet Ernie heard the first lad hit the deck and he moved up the narrow stairs from the aft survivors' cabin to the wheelhouse to direct him below from where Vic Collier stood in the open wheelhouse door. There was a frenzy about their efforts now. They had but a few seconds before the wind would begin building around the back end of the *Pegasus*.

'Move . . . Come on, come on,' Simon shouted. Above on the bridge, Parnell heard the shout over the wind and without asking Carter he repeated it into the intercom and it barked from the speakers.

A bigger body dropped the few feet and rolled gracefully to its feet and was followed by another, but he fell heavily and slammed hard into the rail. Adults, Simon realized. The boys were all off. These were grown men. Two more followed and then the voice on the intercom halted things as Carter hit both throttles and the lifeboat surged forward away from the unforgiving steel hull of the *Caledonia* as a big swell rolled in. As before, he stopped the boat on the crest of the swell but this time he didn't allow her own drag to pull her back in. Carter pointed and Parnell looked out into the floodlit area in front of the boat. Out on the softening diffused edge of the pool of light there were flashes of something pale, moving, gathering and falling.

There were whitecaps coming in.

The breakers were back.

As they watched they could feel the wind velocity increase and see the waves gathering in size once again as the vast stern of the supertanker came across their bows. That had been their last attempt stern on.

Carter watched the seas for a few seconds before shaking his head at Parnell and taking the intercom microphone. They had had their chance. Time to stand off and get things sorted out before their next attempt at a fast beam-to-beam approach.

'Ernie, the helm. Clear the deck and secure below,' he said sadly.

Carter looked at the figure standing before him, one hand extended, the other holding one of the grab bars.

'I am Detective Sergeant Carstairs. I am with David Lawler. I want to thank you for your efforts tonight. You and your crew. If I can be of any help . . .'

'Oh aye.' Carter glanced at Collier, who looked up from where he stood helping Parnell who was bent over examining the mashed and bleeding face of the seaman who had hit the rail.

'He's down in the aft cabin,' he said, speaking of David.

'Well,' Carter said, as Timson and Parnell pushed past him towards the steps, 'we are not done yet. As soon as the lads have things secured below and have got their breath back we will go in again.'

'Can I trouble you for your radio? I need to advise my people that we have transferred.'

'Won't do you much good, lad,' Carter said, packing his pipe, and moving up towards the radio panel. 'The aerials have gone. We have VHF only. Why don't you ask *Drumbeat* to relay for you?'

He lifted the VHF mike to his lips.

'*Pegasus, Pegasus*, this is the *Maeve*, over.'

'Go ahead, *Maeve*.'

'*Pegasus*, thanks for your help and we wish you a safe journey, over.'

'Thanks, *Maeve*. Hope you get them all off and you get home safe. Over and out.'

'*Defiant, Defiant*, this is *Maeve*.'

'Go, *Maeve*.'

'*Defiant*, thanks also to you. Can you relay a message to Falmouth?'

'Roger, *Maeve*.'

Carstairs took the mike from Carter as he moved forward to the helm to relieve Ernie Coutts. The lifeboat went over the top of a breaker; the water hitting the decks threw a crunching hollow boom around the boat and Carstairs held on tightly as he spoke into the microphone.

'*Defiant*, please advise Falmouth that Marbles, that is, Mike Alpha Romeo Bravo Lima Echo Sierra, is aboard the lifeboat. Over.'

'Roger, *Maeve*. Marbles' – the Royal Navy communications rating spelt the codeword back phonetically – 'has transferred, over.'

'That's affirmative, *Defiant*.'

Across the cabin, Parnell took a curved needle from his bag and, holding it in a pair of forceps, he passed some surgical suture thread through the eye. He wiped the lacerated area of the seaman's face with surgical spirit and then, wedged between the patient's chair and the bulkhead, he pushed the man's head back and went to work. There was local anaesthetic in his bag but the seaman had shaken his head. He said he would take the temporary stitching job without intravenous painkillers and Parnell hadn't argued. The night wasn't over yet and he had only limited supplies. Collier leant over to help him by holding the man's head in the crook of his elbow, as still as the pitching boat would allow, and holding a torch in the other hand. It was going to be a big job. The upper lip was split all the way up past the nose and there was a second bone-deep gash under the eye running down the left cheek. Two teeth had been knocked out. As he worked, Parnell thought he could feel bone grating under his hands. There were certainly fractures in the cheekbone and upper jaw.

While Parnell worked above, Timson moved amongst the people crowded in the aft cabin, checking lap straps for those seated in the few available places, wedging others in between storage lockers and finally seating the last few on the floor. There was nothing to hold on to for those in the centre, so he was relying on them being jammed in like sardines to prevent anyone being thrown against something hard. Four were already being sick and the smell was bad, but they all seemed too frightened to notice, all except one lad who was sitting near the engine room aft access door, who reached across and wiped the vomit-strewn face of the boy to his left with his own wet sleeve.

He then pulled the other boy closer and put his arm round his shoulders, his moves calm, considered and sympathetic. Coutts, standing by his engine-room door, noticed the gesture. He also recognized the lad. He was the last one over.

In the for'ard cabin the scene was the same. Simon started with the handful of adults now aboard and then moved as many of the boys back against the engine-room bulkhead as he could, trying to keep the weight back. This gave the boys seated on the benches at the apex of the pointed cabin a definite space advantage, as the floor at their feet was clear. But that didn't equate to comfort, not in the bows. They were moving vertically by at least fifty feet and the pitching would have made even seasoned seamen sick. Satisfied that the weight was distributed as evenly as possible without blocking the entrance to the engine room, Simon completed the count and moved up.

In the wheelhouse, he compared notes with Timson, while Parnell and Collier stood on the bloody floor and finished their job on the injured seaman. They had taken a total of twenty-six survivors off the *Caledonia* so far and were almost fully loaded. They could fit another four or five in the for'ard cabin. There were thirty people to go.

The radio crackled and Carter, who had just called *Drumbeat* to ask them to advise Falmouth of the count, instinctively turned the volume up. Anything coming in now was VHF and that meant it was nearby.

'Her Majesty's Ship *Defiant*, this is Mobil's humble ship *Pegasus*.'

Timson grinned, the expression spreading like a great gaping hole in his beard. The others stopped to listen; even Carter took his pipe from his mouth.

'Go, *Pegasus*,' came the guarded reply.

'*Defiant*, if it pleases your lordships, may we please proceed about our business, or would you like us to heave to so you can flog us over the gratings?' The question was rich with sarcasm. It could only have been her master.

Everything stopped in the *Maeve*'s wheelhouse. Witty radio traffic was always appreciated, even when things were tense and it looked like these two captains were squaring off.

'You may proceed about your business, *Pegasus*. I think you tanker chaps spend enough time taking it bent over, don't you?'

The reply from *Pegasus* was immediate and reflected the reaction aboard the lifeboat. It was a burst of laughter. Only Parnell was serious as he bent over his patient. Then *Defiant* came on the air again.

'Thank you for your help, *Pegasus*. Bon Voyage.'

Carter broke the spell.

He looked at Carstairs. 'You may secure yourself up here for the moment,' he said, pointing to one of the seats. 'Just stay out of the way.' He put his pipe in his pocket, digging round through the layers of wet-weather gear, and spoke to his crew.

'Let's go get the rest then.'

Carstairs did as he was asked and sat back in one of the pedestal chairs and watched the two lifeboatmen working in torchlight, stitching up another's face. From below, the cries of fear and the sounds of someone vomiting came up, clearly audible over the roar of the engines and the crash of the water against the hull. The red diffused night-vision light in the wheelhouse added to the Dantean feel, with the still form of the *Caledonia*'s captain in his stretcher and the helm seeming to turn itself, perhaps with a spirit coxswain in command.

Falmouth

The coastguard officer took the relayed message of David
Lawler's transfer with professional objectivity. He had been
bent over the radio panel and his working details for three
hours or more now and was as close to the rescue as anyone ashore. But when *Drumbeat*'s message came through,
detailing the total number of survivors now transferred,
he pulled the headphones off his head with glee and
punched the air with one triumphant fist.

'Twenty-six!' he shouted. 'The buggers have taken
twenty-six off the *Caledonia* and they are going back in.
You bloody little beauties!'

His boss crossed the floor as the other duty men looked
up and smiled or raised a thumb. They lost too many ever
to take a successful rescue lightly, let alone one of this size.

'The lee worked then,' the boss said.

'It did that. They must be going back to the side
approaches now.'

'Right. Thank the master on *Pegasus* if you will.'

'Twenty-six. Shit . . . she must be chock-a-block for'ard
and aft.'

'Let's get an update on the Penlee and Lizard boats. If
it's anything like promising, let them know. I want an ETA
on the Brawdy S and R too. Otherwise wait till we have
something definite for them. Have you advised the police
on the boy?'

'Not yet. I'll do it now.'

'Ring his father while you are at it. Let him know all
the boys are across on the *Maeve*.'

St Mary's

Dickerson took the call from Falmouth at the boathouse
where he was waiting, as he normally did, for his boat and
crew to come home. While he was talking, Susan Farmer

wandered around the boathouse. When he hung up he walked over to her and gave one of his dry smiles, his eyes alive. He smiled at her, ignoring the camera.

'Falmouth. The lads have taken twenty-six off so far, that is all the boys and a few adults. They had a supertanker come by and give them a lee . . . make a sheltered area as it passed.'

He blew his nose noisily and then spoke again, his voice shaking with emotion.

'I don't think anyone has ever taken off that many people in one go before. They have capsized once. If they head home now, no one will hold it against them.'

Susan looked up at him, thinking, John won't be off yet. He is the old-fashioned bloody hero type. Please tell me they will stay out there.

'But they won't, will they?' she asked, trying to keep her voice level and professional, knowing that the camera was rolling.

'These men?' He laughed. It was a short dry bark. 'No. They will stay. As long as they have engines and a hull that floats, they will have a lifeboat and they will stay on service.'

She breathed a sigh of relief.

'What will be the drill now? They will finish the job and return presumably to St Mary's?'

'Yes,' he said, reaching out for the door frame. 'Touch wood they won't have any more problems.'

Caledonia

Carter, up on the flying bridge, was strapped on to the back frame as they approached the *Caledonia*. The seas were as big as they had seen before the *Pegasus* had passed by and, if anything, even more confused. Breakers fell into troughs, the white walls of foam were ten or fifteen feet high and spray was being thrown sixty feet high as wave

302

hit wave like colliding cliffs. Water was flung like hail-stones against his skin.

He pulled his hood down over his cap and, with one hand, made the drawstring tight. He needed someone on the bridge with him to control the light and, knowing that Parnell and Collier would be busy with the injured survivor, he used the intercom and dragged Ernie Coutts up from his engine room. As they came alongside, Parnell and Collier would have to stop and lend a hand, but until then, he could work with three men. He silently acknowledged to himself that until they were home, Parnell was a full active member of his crew and no longer just the medical adviser.

Defiant was now steaming away upwind and, although her decks were still ablaze with light, they were angled the wrong way to allow her to heave to into wind and still provide light for a rescue attempt on the windward side of the merchantman.

He flicked the wheel over to take the *Maeve* up the side of a breaker and then corrected back into the trough for the run in.

Coutts arrived and he pointed to the light. Nothing needed to be said.

They were fifteen yards from the *Caledonia* and alongside her stern, the high quarterdeck canted over, making a sharp angle of steel forty feet long, when the wave hit.

It had gathered from nowhere, a rogue in the truest sense. It rose at right angles to the run of the seas, gathering and twisting, until it towered over the lifeboat's beam when it met another incoming wave, and they joined together. The union of goliaths topped fifty feet and collapsed downwards, slamming the lifeboat against the ship. *Maeve*'s bow rail and pulpit were ripped away, and, on the aft deck, tons of water washed over the sides as she slid downwards, tearing away the *Caledonia*'s quarterdeck rail, before hitting the seas again, rolling over and finally righting herself. Gasping for breath, John Timson and Simon

303

Carter were washed against the side rail, their lifelines strained, their bodies bruised.

Up on the bridge, Carter, who was strapped to the back frame, hit the throttles and instinctively brought the bows into the seas, aborting the attempt. Ernie Coutts managed to pick himself up from the deck beside Carter, the lamp in his hand now useless, the lens shattered when he fell.

John and Simon immediately moved back into the wheelhouse where they knew it would be mayhem.

Inside, Parnell and Collier had both been thrown against the radio panels. Their patient, who was strapped in, fared better. As the boat righted herself, Carstairs undid his lap straps and, holding a grab bar, he swung down to help the doctor to his feet. Miraculously neither man had been hurt. Collier's bump cap, that made him look so like a garden gnome, had saved his skull as he was thrown against the big grey Furuno direction finder. The Filipino patient sat stoically, the curved needle and a seven-inch length of suture hanging from his face. The only part of him that showed the fear were his knuckles. They were white as they gripped the armrests on the chair.

'You all right?' Timson bellowed as he came crashing through the aft door.

'Seem to be,' Parnell answered.

'I'll do for'ard,' Simon said, pushing past them, holding his ribs where his lifeline harness had cut into him.

Timson dropped down the back companionway into the aft cabin as the noise reached a new pitch, of cries and confused yells, prayers and someone calling out a name.

'Quiet,' he said. It had no effect.

'QUIET!' This time in a voice that could be heard the length of the new quay, any day of the week.

The noise abated into murmurs and questions as people felt limbs and heads where they had bumped into each other or hard objects. The steady drone of the engines so close by was a comfort for all and the tight packing seemed to have done its job. There were no injuries. Carstairs's head appeared at the top of the stairs, his eyes scanning the room and seeking out David. Their eyes met and, as Carstairs raised an eyebrow, the boy smiled and raised a thumb. He had changed in the last hours, Carstairs felt. Grown. Found confidence. Found his place.

'Everyone all right?' Timson asked. There were heads nodding uncertainly, frightened eyes locked on his, searching for some reassurance that all would be well. They didn't get it.

He nodded once, turned and climbed the companionway steps back into the wheelhouse where he met Simon.

There were two bumped heads and a cut lip in the for'ard cabin and the injured waited by the helm. Then Collier slid behind the wheel to allow Carter to come down from the bridge.

Coutts was down first, going straight to the seals that had been leaking since the first capsize. The bilge pumps had cut in now, their high-pitched whine distinctive over the deeper roar of the main engines. He didn't seem bothered that he had been out on the flying bridge when she had gone over. His harness had held as it had been designed to do. He expected nothing else.

'Oh, shit,' Simon said.

'What?' from John Timson.

He followed Simon's pointing finger.

'Oh,' he said.

There, sticking clear through the hardened glass window beside the radio panels, was a piece of what looked like four-by-two-inch timber, possibly one of the battens from the hatches of the *Caledonia*. They had been thrown over so hard that the flotsam had speared straight through the glass.

But it was more serious than that. The *Maeve*'s ability to self-right was heavily influenced by her watertight wheelhouse. With a smashed window she had now lost her watertight integrity.

The next capsize could be their last.

Carter came through the aft door, his eyes taking in the scene in the wheelhouse, and walked straight to the radio panel.

'*Defiant, Defiant*, this is the *Maeve*.'

'Go, *Maeve*.'

'*Defiant*, we have been knocked down again. Can you go to dead slow. We want to come past in your lights and have a look at the damage, over.'

'Affirmative, *Maeve*.' As he put the microphone down he noticed his hand was shaking. That one was close.

In the harsh lights it looked bad. The pulpit rail was gone, just a few feet were left hanging off the starboard side. The anchor, normally secured on the port-side main beam rail, was gone, pulled away by the force of the knock, down against the ship's hull. The front left-side corner of the wheelhouse no longer had a nice clean edge. It was now crumpled and dented with hairline shatter cracks running away from the four separate impact points along its vertical edge, and the entire port rail was canted inwards twenty degrees. Up on the flying bridge the two glass panels on the port side were gone and the circular front of the bridge was dented and stove in a good six inches. As Carter surveyed the damage, he realized that he and Ernie had been only inches from being crushed.

'Leave the timber,' Carter said. 'Secure the other end on something. While it's there the rest of the glass may just stay put.'

'Aye aye,' Timson said.

The radio crackled and Carter lifted the handset.

'*Maeve*, can we be of assistance?'

'Stand by, *Defiant*.'

Carter was thinking quickly. There would be no more beam approaches. This lifeboat would spend the remainder of this service bow on to the seas. That would mean a frontal approach on to the *Caledonia*'s stern or bows. The stern was lower in the water. The St Peter Port lifeboat had done that with the *Bonita* back in 1981. Memorable because it had been achieved in hurricane-force winds, and her coxswain, Michael Scales, had been awarded a gold medal for the service.

The *Bonita* was smaller, much smaller than *Caledonia*, but with her stern having settled as much as it had, it would be possible. It would be dangerous, that was for sure, he thought. No bow rail now, and it would need at least one man up on the for'ard deck to control a line. He would need to be secured and secured well. But it was possible.

'*Defiant*, we will be coming in to the casualty's stern. Can you come round to her lee and stand to. We may get some benefit from your lights, over.'

'Affirmative, *Maeve*. We only have three that we can direct that far for'ard but we are pleased to be of assistance.'

'Thank you, *Defiant* . . . *Caledonia, Caledonia*, this is the *Maeve*.'

'Go ahead, *Maeve*.'

'*Caledonia*, we sustained some damage that time. We are no longer watertight. We are abandoning the beam approaches from this time. Please move your remaining crew aft. We will come in from the leeward below your transom and heave a line aboard. One or two men at a time, if possible, to tie the line on and jump. We will come astern and collect each in turn, over.'

'Ah . . . Roger, *Maeve*,' Nichols said. He slipped the radio into the voluminous pocket of his sou'wester and made his way from the poop store up across the few feet of sloping steel to the upper edge of the quarterdeck, the wind pressing against his back like a solid force. She was well down in the water now. The usual sixty feet down to the water was reduced to perhaps twenty feet. The big waves thundered past, rolling black spume-streaked monsters.

He moved back to the store and pulled the radio out again.

'Bridge.'

'Go, Skipper,' Scott replied instantly.

'You are relieved at this time,' Nichols said formally. 'Make a log entry to that effect and proceed aft with Mr Cochran and Jeffries to abandon ship. Bring the log.'

'Aye aye, sir,' Scott replied, before saying, 'Skipper?'

'Yeah?' Nichols answered.

'I'm sorry.'

'On your feet, Jeffries.' Scott stood over him, his gaze indifferent. 'I'll only say it the once. I'm going to undo your bonds. The passengers are all off now. Try and keep it together. It would be a shame to further embarrass everyone in front of the crew. OK?'

Jeffries nodded. He seemed to have regained his composure in the last hour and now looked not insane, just young and frightened.

'Make no mistake. You lose it again and I'll clap you in irons again. But you are an officer. I would prefer to treat you like one.'

Jeffries looked up at the second officer. He believed him. He got to his feet, clutching his two life jackets.

'Follow me,' Scott said, turning and walking away.

'I'm scared,' Jeffries admitted, 'shit scared.'

Scott turned and looked back at him.

'We all are, we just aren't allowed to show it.'

'And I am ashamed. What must you all think of me?' he murmured.

Scott wasn't sure what to say to that, so he simply answered, 'Let's go.'

Cochran, the Marconi-supplied communications officer, was still in his radio room when Scott stuck his head round the door.

'We are relieved, old chap,' he said. 'We are to make our way aft and join the others.'

'This is it. Crew are abandoning then.' It was one thing to have your passengers taken off. It was another thing to

308

discuss and plan for the eventuality that the crew may also have to leave the vessel. But when the radio operator was relieved, the talk was over.

'Yes,' Scott said. 'Afraid so. She is going down. Never mind. Look at the bright side. The lifeboat is aft and, as Ratty said to Mole, there is absolutely nothing half so much worth doing as simply messing about in boats.'

'That quote is the benefit, no doubt,' Cochran said, 'of a classical education.'

He leant forward and lifted the microphone.

'Falmouth, Falmouth, this is motor vessel *Caledonia*. Radio room is closing down and we are going off the air now.'

'Thank you, *Caledonia*. Good luck.'

There were half a dozen messages from other ships' operators who had remained silent during the early stages of the rescue, leaving the channels clear for emergency traffic, but now that Cochran was signing off they came in with their own messages and farewells, including the operators aboard *Drumbeat*, *Defiant* and *Pegasus*. Cochran thanked each in turn, the camaraderie between marine radio men as strong as in the days when they could recognize each other's morse signatures.

Finally he switched off the power to each of the sets, the little red system power lights fading in turn.

'Fuck it. Fuck it. Fuck it.' He punched the console in frustration. 'I have never left my ship before. You know what I mean, it's not right. I hate this shit.' He wiped a tear from his eyes.

'Let's go, Corky,' Scott said softly.

Scott moved aft with the two men. One who was terrified and couldn't wait to get off the ship and the other, a consummate professional who felt that, in doing so, he was letting down his colleagues and his craft.

Once on the quarterdeck, they crammed into the poop store and Nichols prepared to pair them off.

'I know you are all sailors, but check your knots. When

309

you go, go together, with your arms down over your life jackets. Make sure your bum-ties are secure. If not, those jackets will whip up and probably snap your neck as you hit the water.'

Jarvis nodded to himself. He remembered the stories of the old Board of Trade life jackets that the merchant marine used in the last war. They were made of cork and very buoyant. They also had no under-the-groin straps. There were lots of broken necks, until the desk-bound idiots in the BOT changed the specifications.

Nichols looked round the gathered men. Cooks, seamen, stewards and motormen, engineers and deck officers. Twenty-nine of them.

'I'll go with Jock, Captain,' the steward medic said, indicating the junior engineer with the broken arm.

'I'll go with Mr Jeffries,' Scott said.

Nichols looked up. He was expecting that duty himself, but in the soft light of the one overhead emergency bulb, he could see from his expression that Scott was sincere. Jeffries stood against the wall simply looking off into space.

'Very well.'

Maeve Corrigan

'Rig a line from the for'ard winch back down each side. Good and tight. Anyone going for'ard will be secured to that. Simon, you will be on the bridge with me, heaving the line each time. John, you and Vic in the waist. Drop the A frame on the port side. The line will be secured at the for'ard bollard. We will come astern far enough to tow them clear, then run in and pick them out of the water.'

The attempts to secure the batten while still in the glass had failed and the wind was now whistling through the broken window, with water coming through every time a wave slammed against her.

'Sounds good,' Collier said, 'but where shall we put them?'

'Four in the aft cabin, six for'ard. Sorry, Ernie, but you will have a couple in your engine spaces. The rest we will have to squeeze in up here. If it comes down to it, the aft deck,' Carter said.

With that the men moved off, John and Vic for'ard to run a line up the foredeck and Simon to select a nice medium-weight line that he could physically heave aboard the *Caledonia*'s quarterdeck. Parnell knew he would have the fractured arm aboard soon. He set out splints and, because he knew the man would now be in some pain, the last of his morphine.

Three minutes later they were running in, nice and slow, bows into the huge seas. Timson was on the foredeck, level with the end of the remaining rail, his lifeline attached to the heavy two-inch nylon line that was taut, three inches above the deck, and ran back from the winch bollard into the low waist on the port side. Ahead of him, the bows dropped away into the darkness and every few seconds water broke over the deck and ran back. He held on with his left hand and, in his right, he held a boathook.

Up on the edge of the quarterdeck they could see a group of men. As Carter eased the lifeboat in alongside the *Caledonia*'s stern, Simon, who was secured with two lifelines and was standing on the flat area where the life raft was usually stowed, swung the line with its weighted end and let go. It spun up into the dark, against the force of the wind, and fell back. He began to pull it back in and, a minute later, swung it again. This time he succeeded and three pairs of hands aboard the *Caledonia* grabbed it.

Thirty seconds later, two Filipino seamen were secured and leapt, a prayer on their lips, from the deck into the sea. As they hit the water and surfaced, Timson had a boathook over the line and had dragged it down. Using

311

the hook like a weaver's batten, he secured the heaving line under the two-inch rope that ran the length of the deck. Carter eased the throttles back and began very gently to come astern, pulling the two men in the water back from the *Caledonia*'s hull.

As soon as Timson felt the engines move into forward gear again, he leant over the side with his boathook. Simon, above him, pulled the line in furiously so as to keep it away from the propellers, ready to slip the hook into a life jacket's lifting loop or anything which he could use to pull them alongside.

Down in the waist, sometimes knee deep in water and surf as the waves surged past, Vic Collier waited at the A frame. The frame, powered by a simple windlass, could lift a thousand pounds from the water, so two men in wet clothing could be managed with ease.

Collier looked up the deck. Timson was moving back towards him, pulling the boathook, and, down in the water, he could see flashes of two life jackets, bobbing in the white surf. The two men were holding on to each other. They didn't need the A frame with this pair. They scrambled up the two feet and on to the deck like trained seals, their faces alive with great beaming grins, delighted to be out of the water.

The system, which they had never practised, worked and as the two seamen were led up the steps to the aft deck and the wheelhouse door, Carter moved the lifeboat in again.

They did eight more approaches in the next thirty minutes, the *Defiant* half a cable off in the weakening lee of the *Caledonia*'s hull. Three banks of lights were angled to shine on the froth and foam where the *Maeve* was coming astern, each time towing two men back through the water. The sixth approach had taken the longest. Simon had thrown the rope four times before cold fingers aboard the casualty could grab and hold it. But now there was a system up on the quarterdeck, a line of men three feet

312

apart, so it didn't matter where the rope fell, there were hands there to grab it.

At the school the news that the last of the boys were across was greeted with jubilation, cheering and handclapping. Many were in tears, tears of relief. The battle was half over. Now they just had to get home.

'How strong are these Aruns?' one parent asked the RNLI member who sat explaining things to a small group.

'Very,' he said.

'Well, I think I shall get on the phone. Get some shampoo over here. We may be ready to drink it soon!' he said with a grin.

James Lawler sat, his arm around Heather's shoulders as the car powered its way westwards. They were both feeling confident now but unwilling to tempt fate by talking about it, so they just cherished the feeling in silence.

'You two next,' Nichols shouted. The steward medic nodded, swallowing hard. He was frightened but, unlike the others, he was prepared to admit it. He knelt beside the engineer still cradling his broken arm, and lifted him to his feet as the bosun moved forward. The rope landed six feet away and was passed towards them. Neither of these two men were sailors in the real sense, so Jarvis tied the knots.

'Ready?' Nichols shouted, leaning forward. The fourth engineer nodded, his face a mask of pain. They were both outside the rail, their feet on the edge; the steward was looking over the side, hesitating. McDermott, the chief engineer, moved up to the rail beside the pair and shouted to his man.

'You did well. I'm proud of you,' and then he pushed. They fell backwards into the sea.

The procedure worked the same, but this time there was no scrambling into the waist and Timson moved back for

313

them. His huge hands reached down into the sea and, applying a combination of brute strength and technique, he lifted the injured man on to the deck. He was in such pain that he could no longer walk and, as Timson carried him round to the wheelhouse like a child, he could feel the bone grating in his arm. The steward medic followed, pleased to hand his patient over to a real doctor with a supply of real drugs and to be relieved of the responsibility.

Within the minute Parnell had a dose of his morphine going straight into the meaty part of the man's thigh. Then he set about immobilizing the joint. There was no way he would try and set it until they were ashore.

The next pair were the second and third engineers, the knots again tied by Jarvis, and they were hauled aboard the *Maeve* without incident.

'Ready, lad?' the bosun bellowed. Fripp and Jarvis were outside the rail and going off together. Fripp looked out at the huge breakers, the tops level with or above their position as they thundered past. The noise was like an express train, bass notes to the wind's high treble shriek, the ship shuddering each time, the big waves throwing water completely over her aft working decks. He nodded. The fear was dry and metallic on Fripp's tongue. This is it, he thought. He reached under his life jacket and adjusted something and then looked up at Jarvis. The bosun set his lopsided jaw solid, grabbed at Fripp's life jacket and jumped backwards, pulling him down into the turbulent surf, the wind driving them back, throwing them clear.

They surfaced, shot upwards by the life jackets' buoyancy, mouth and eyes and nose full of salt water, spray everywhere. Fripp turned his head away from the wind by instinct and took a breath, eyes closed, one hand feeling out for Jarvis, slapping the water, hearing the roaring, foaming approach of another breaker, desperate to feel the bosun near him, when he felt himself being dragged backwards through the water by the heavy rope at his waist. He opened his eyes for the first time and Jarvis was there, his head and shoulders clear of the water two feet away, wild-eyed and powerfully striking out for the lifeboat that was manoeuvring back towards them, pulling him along as he went.

'I am James Fripp, officer cadet of the *Caledonia*. This is Mr Jarvis, the bosun.' He held out his hand to Collier and then wasn't sure what to say next, so the 'thanks awfully' sounded very natural when it arrived.

The wheelhouse was crowded now, the injured on the floor by Wellbrook's stretcher, and Fripp looked them over, the responsibility of being the first officer aboard suddenly real and of importance.

'Everyone all right?' he asked, then turned back to Collier. 'What can I do to help? I'm sure there must be something that . . .' Then he remembered. 'Gosh. How's Captain Wellbrook?'

Collier smiled and to his surprise the boy undid his lifejacket strap and reached underneath. He pulled out a heavy brass sextant and shook the water off.

'Couldn't leave this behind,' Fripp explained with a shy smile.

Collier laughed. He had seen it all before. The relief of being rescued manifested itself in many ways and it was not uncommon for ship's officers to seek normality by resorting to what was most familiar. Command. Being useful. Collier had seen him earlier in the night, up against the rail, helping boys over the side with scant regard for his own safety. The cadet looked all of sixteen in the subdued red light.

'He's fine and, yes, lad,' he said, 'you can make a cuppa for those who'd like one. We only have six cups but we can take it in turns.'

'Right. Show the way,' Fripp replied. Collier pointed down to the crowded aft cabin and, as Fripp took the stairs, Jarvis stepped towards the wheelhouse door with Collier.

'Find a piece of floor,' Collier said.

'You're short-crewed. I am handy on a deck,' Jarvis said.

He was at least a foot taller and four stones heavier than Collier, so the lifeboatman wasn't going to make an issue of it. He was also right. They were short-crewed. As they stepped over the coaming, Collier took a lifeline harness and handed it to the big survivor. Jarvis held up his own, the carabiner still attached.

Half a minute later he was on the foredeck with Timson, pleased to be back in the fresh air. He couldn't have stood another minute in the wheelhouse with the smell and the vomit. They faced each other, two giants, each with recently gained respect for the other, legs braced apart on the pitching deck. Timson grinned, eyes shiny in his great bearded face, and handed the other the boathook, as yet another wave crashed over the bows, the water swirling round their massive legs. Carter was too busy on the bridge to enter discussions on who should be on the deck, so he ignored the newcomer to edge the lifeboat close enough for Simon to heave the line.

Both unwilling to jump, unwilling to admit defeat, Cochran and Chafney finally leapt together, the rope a slender umbilical to safety. Two minutes later they were aboard the *Maeve*, where Cochran immediately made his way to the radio operator's position. He saw the big sets were shut down.

'Problem?'

'Aerials went the first time we capsized,' Parnell shouted.

'I can try to fix it,' Cochran said.

'I said the aerials are gone,' Parnell shouted over the crowd of heads, his patience wearing thin. 'What are you, a fucking magician?'

'No. I'm a Marconi man,' Cochran replied, his expression deadpan.

Parnell realized he was serious. 'Go for it,' he said.

'Tools and some coaxial cable?'

'Engineer's below.'

Cochran pushed his way past people at the head of the rear steps. When he got to the bottom, there in amongst

he vomit-splattered, ashen-faced, fearful people, Fripp
ood by an urn, offered him a cup of tea. 'Plenty of cups,'
e said. 'I haven't got any takers down here.'

On the bridge, Carter, not a religious man, reminded God
r whichever angels he had on this job, and good ones they
ere too, that their work wasn't yet done. He couldn't quite
elieve that they had taken fifty-two people off the *Cale-
onia*, but the boat was telling him he had. She was sluggish
o the feel. The bilge pumps were running flat out, trying to
eal with the leaks. She was overloaded way beyond what
he was designed for, the fast response to the helm was gone
nd she wasn't rising to the seas like she should. Come on,
y girl, he said, talking to her like Jarvis had done to his
hip only hours before, you can take this and more. Just
our more and I will take you home to the pool.

The radio crackled at his side but he left it, allowing
omeone down in the wheelhouse to answer it. Instead he
ust turned up the volume.

'*Maeve, Maeve*, this is Rescue November.'

'Go, November.' The voice was Parnell's.

'*Maeve*, we are the Sierra Romeo out of Brawdy. We are
pproaching you from the north and will be overhead the
asualty and ready to lend assistance in figures two
ninutes, over.'

'Thank you, November. We look forward to seeing you,'
he doctor answered formally.

Carter signalled to Simon to get ready and, moving the
hrottles forward, eased the lifeboat up alongside the now
inking stern. Simon's first throw found its mark and one
f the last four men snatched the rope where it was run-
ing back over the rail.

Scott and Jeffries tied their own knots and climbed
ogether over the rail to stand on the edge, Nichols and
McDermott steadying them from the inside. As the two
enior officers, they would be the last to abandon the ship
nd they watched as the second and third officers leapt
rom the rail.

They watched as Scott hit the water badly and winded himself, and watched as somehow the rope came clear, and they watched as he gasped for breath as a wave rolled over them, the water pouring into his lungs, and feet away Jeffries, blinded by spray and himself coughing water, seemed powerless to help.

They knew they were watching Scott drown.

TWELVE

Carter shouted from the flying bridge and, although the word was snatched by the wind, those outside knew what to expect and were holding on extra tight when he jammed the throttles forward. He spun the wheel over to the right, trying to keep the trailing line away from the props, while he raced the lifeboat round to get near enough to the two men in the water.

Collier, down in the waist, couldn't see but Simon had them in view and, as far as he knew, he was the only one. Never, never, never take your eyes off a man in the sea. As the lifeboat charged up the side of a wave and then curved round, he changed his position on the bridge behind his father so he could keep them in sight.

Below, Timson was moving back down the deck towards the waist where he knew he would be needed. Carter hit the foghorn in short sharp blasts to warn the *Defiant* he was coming round at speed and, with the bow wave curling under her, the *Maeve* took the next wave at eighteen knots, her engines roaring, the line now safely out astern.

Aboard *Defiant*, Commander Forbisher took it all in in a second.

'Full astern, wheel twenty to starboard . . .' He wanted to reverse his destroyer in a curving sweep to place himself across the seas. Beam on to the storm.

'But, Captain . . .' his first officer began.

'THERE ARE MEN DYING OUT THERE. DO IT!' Forbisher snapped.

'Aye aye, sir.'

'And get the other lights on. MOVE IT!'

Ten seconds later the destroyer was coming astern, rolling dangerously in the heavy seas, every bank of her lights blazing out. Forbisher, on the bridge, was calling the orders himself while watching the lifeboat as she danced through the heavy seas, her bow wave bright in the lights.

Jeffries, his hand still through Scott's life-jacket straps, coughed again and, forgetting his own fear, desperately pulled the other man towards him. Scott's head was lolling about.

'Scotty,' he yelled. 'Scotty!'

He's drowning, he's not breathing. He forgot that the rope wasn't there any more, as he tried to remember in flashes what they had been told at Merchant Marine School. It seemed so long ago.

Breathe. I must make him breathe. Don't die, Scotty. Oh shit, please don't die. You were the only one who believed in me. Please don't die. There was another breaker looming. He pulled Scott's head round and covered his nose and mouth with his free hand, before taking a breath and closing his eyes as the wave thundered down on them. His other hand was closed like a wire trap in Scott's jacket straps and he began to count. There was a story told that if you went under a big one it could take ten seconds to come up again.

They hit the surface as he reached six and he remembered that he must start mouth-to-mouth, but it didn't seem to work.

Nichols could see it all from the quarterdeck. The two bobbing heads down in the surf in the almost blinding lights from the warship, Jeffries's pathetic but frantic attempts at resuscitation and the lifeboat bearing down, a bow wave curling back, the bottom of her deep V hull slicing through the water.

*   *   *

Down in the waist, Timson and Collier were on their knees as Simon reached them. He had snatched a second boathook from its rack and stood over them as they came alongside, the engines already going astern, the sea boiling under her broad transom and the big brass propellers churning in her own wake.

His timing was perfect and as he drove the hook through Scott's lifting loop he yelled and, above them on the bridge, Carter put the throttles ahead and brought the boat's bows round into the seas. Timson reached down with one huge hand and rose, pulling Scott's lifeless body into the waist, as Collier got a grip on Jeffries who was yelling at them to do something.

Timson lay Scott on the deck and reached down to help Collier. The moment that he had Jeffries aboard, with his feet still trailing in the sea, he turned back to the *Caledonia*'s second officer.

They still had time. He lifted him quickly over one shoulder and literally ran up the three steps to the afterdeck as Simon got the door open.

'Doc!'

Then, as Parnell watched, Timson dropped the man's head, shoulders and torso until he was holding him upside down from the waist, and, as he began to shake the body, the water flowed from the lungs.

'On the floor. Flat on his back. Quickly,' Parnell said. Timson lowered him without ceremony on to the deck as Parnell reached for his pulse.

'Five cardiac massage to one breath. You blow. Let's go.' The wheelhouse went quiet as they worked, Timson's big shaggy head lowering every six seconds to blow air into Scott's lungs, Parnell kneeling across his stomach, his arms stiff, one hand over the other pressing down rhythmically on the sternum.

They were well into the procedure by the time Collier and Simon came through the door with Jeffries. The third officer sank to his knees beside the doctor and the lifeboatman as they tried to bring Scott back to life. Those gathered in the wheelhouse had fallen silent, the atmosphere now subdued.

The only noise was the roar of the wind and the engines and the sound of Parnell's voice as he counted the cardiac massage strokes aloud. Jeffries took Scott's hand.

'Oh shit, Number Two . . . please don't die . . . Not now . . . We are off . . . I'm sorry . . . Shit, I'm sorry . . . please don't die, Scotty . . . not now.'

Collier bent down and took over from Timson. This was his forte, just as the deck was John's.

Simon lifted Jeffries to his feet and pulled him away to give them room, Carstairs giving up his seat for him. Across the wheelhouse the bridge phone warbled. Simon crossed to it. He spoke briefly and then hung up. He signalled to Timson and the two friends made their way back to the wheelhouse door, where Jarvis waited. As Timson approached, Jarvis seemed to remember something and pulled his wallet from his pocket, shaking the water from it, and checking the contents of the little clear-plastic picture window.

Timson, seeking to cut the mounting tension as the two men tried to save the life of the man on the floor, looked down at the small photograph. It was an amateurish snap of two pretty little laughing girls with a sylph-like serene Asian woman.

'Your family?' he asked.

'Aye,' Jarvis said proudly. 'You?'

'Not yet,' Timson replied with a grin, 'but I have a girl in mind.'

Cochran pushed his way through the people, a length of coaxial cable and a pair of pliers in his hand. He looked down at his friend.

'Oh, Jesus . . . Anything I can do?'

'Three, four, five, breath, no thanks, one, two, three . . .

He arrived up on the bridge with Simon, surprising Carter who raised an eyebrow at him. He snapped hi lifeline on and held up the pliers, pointing to the aerial mounting above Carter's head. Below the mounting, sprouting from a conduit pipe, was the aerial cable from the medium- and short-wave sets. Carter, seeing the tools in Cochran's hand, understood immediately who he was. He nodded and looked back to seaward where the *Caledonia* was still being pounded by the waves and where the last two men waited to be taken off. The Marconi man began stripping the plastic exterior off the cable.

'*Maeve, Maeve*, this is Rescue November.'

Simon took the microphone on the bridge, turning the VHF set's volume up to its maximum, and giving the microphone to his father.

'Go, November,' Carter said.

'*Maeve*, we are a quarter-mile off your stern at this time. How can we assist, over?'

'November, there are still figures two, repeat two, deck officers aboard the casualty. They are aft on the high side of the quarterdeck, over. Stand by please.' He switched channels.

'*Caledonia, Caledonia*, this is *Maeve*, over.'

Aboard the casualty Nichols looked at McDermott and pointed to the helicopter that was now visible by its anti-collision beacon.

'Roger, *Maeve*,' Nichols answered.

'*Caledonia*, we can take you off with the helicopter, over.'

McDermott shook his head and pointed to the lifeboat. Nichols nodded. He felt the same way.

'Thanks, *Maeve*, but my crew is aboard your lifeboat, over.'

'I understand, *Caledonia*.'

Carter changed channels again. It would have been nice to have sent a few of the sick and the hurt ashore, but transfers from pitching lifeboats to helicopters were dangerous at the best of times. They were safer aboard and, providing Parnell agreed, they would not take the risk.

'November, the survivors want to come off with us. I have a suggestion. Please relay it to Falmouth. We have some injured below. Suggest you return to St Mary's, refuel and await our return and be ready to lift seriously injured back to the mainland, over.'

'Roger, *Maeve*. We will relay your request and stand by, over.'

Cornwall

In the Daimler the phone warbled and Lawler snatched it up, Heather stiffening in the seat beside him. He listened for a few moments and then said, 'You must have designated a place for relatives to wait for news. Can you explain it to my driver? Thank you.'

He handed the phone over to the driver and settled back into the seat.

'What?' Heather asked.

'Apparently the boat capsized again. It's now overcrowded and leaking.'

'Are they heading in now?'

'No. They are staying to finish. There are still a handful left aboard apparently.'

She knew it was wrong, wrong to wish the lifeboat to head back for the shore while there were still people aboard but she did and had to justify it to herself as being a perfectly natural wish before saying, 'Are you going to tell them at the school?'

'No.'

Maeve Corrigan

Parnell was delighted. Scott was breathing and they had a pulse. It was weak and erratic but it was a pulse. They had moved Wellbrook in his stretcher from the position by the

324

doctor's seat down on to the floor, and Scott now lay in his place in a second stretcher. He needed an intensive care unit, not this, but it was all they had. He had turned down Carter's offer to fly the man ashore in the helicopter. Even with the tailwind they were an hour from an ICU and the next sixty minutes were critical. If the pulse and breathing were still stable in an hour the worst was over. He was young and fit and very strong and with luck he would survive the journey ashore with the others.

It was time he did his rounds of the others and, knowing that Collier was needed on deck, Parnell spoke to Jeffries. 'Hold his wrist. Feel for the pulse.' Jeffries nodded. 'Watch him breathe, talk to him every now and then if you think he is awake. Any change, if he stops breathing or it gets shallow, call me. If his pulse stops, or gets erratic, call me. OK? I shall be just there for a couple of minutes.' He pointed to where Collier sat with the others, the engineer with the broken arm, the man with the smashed face and their other cardiac case, Captain Wellbrook.

'Make sure the oxygen mask stays on and the air bag keeps inflating. OK?'

Jeffries nodded and Parnell moved over to relieve Collier. They were about to make their last approach.

On the wheelhouse roof and behind the flying bridge, Simon, his lifeline clipped to the inner rail, coiled the heaving line in his hand, leaving the end, with its plastic-coated lead weight attached, lying on the deck. He had lost count of how many times he had swung the line that night and his arm ached. He watched as his father brought the boat in closer and, lifting the weighted end, he began to swing the line, low over the stern end and then high to clear the stump of the radar mast, round and round before letting it fly upwards and across to the deck of the ship. His aim was true and two pairs of hands snatched the line up from the *Caledonia*'s rail.

Down on the narrow deck in the shelter of the

wheelhouse, John Timson and Cecil Jarvis stood, ready to secure the line.

Nichols doublechecked the knot he had tied round McDermott's waist and looked up, raising a thumb. He didn't want a repetition of what had happened to Scott and Jeffries, the image of Scott, lifeless in the water, and Jeffries, poor Jeffries, forgetting his own fear to try and breathe life into him. He hoped the doctor aboard the lifeboat had got to him in time.

The ship's log was wrapped in a waterproof bag and safely secured under his life jacket. He took one last look back up the angled deck, the waves now washing right over holds three and four, towards the accommodation superstructure. He suddenly remembered the photo in his cabin, the one of Susan, and debated, just for a second, going back for it, before dispelling the thought from his mind. It wasn't just the photograph. It represented everything they were leaving behind, the memories, the smells, the steady thump of the diesel, the feel of the old spoked wooden wheel that Wellbrook had salvaged years ago in Thailand.

She shuddered beneath their feet and gave a groan from somewhere deep down inside her. Goodbye, old girl. You did us proud. You kept us safe and sound for so long it just wore you out, didn't it? I'm sorry to be leaving you like this. It will be cool and calm down there. Perhaps it's better. Safe from the wrecker's torch. It wouldn't be right to have you ending up as a couple of hundred Toyotas, so you go now, down where it's deep and silent and you can be the proud old *Caledonia* for ever.

He looked back at McDermott and was surprised. The engineer must have felt the same. He looked most unhappy.

'Ready?' he yelled.

'Johnny . . .' McDermott leant forward. 'I can't swim,' he yelled.

Nichols fought back the urge to laugh. It seemed a

ludicrous time to be either emotional or admitting one couldn't swim, or confusing one for the other.

'Too late now,' Nichols shouted back and, grabbing McDermott's skinny arm, he jumped, pulling the man in after him.

Carter watched them hit the water, arms folded over their life jackets, knees together and bent and feet down just like the experts said to do and he gently put the engines astern as Timson and the big seaman from the casualty waited with boathooks ready to secure the line as he came forward again. As his hands moved on the helm, the boat felt heavy and unresponsive beneath him. He hoped the bilge pumps were coping with the leaks. They were dangerously overloaded now and the last thing he wanted to be carrying was sea water. He swung the bows to correct their heading as a big breaker rolled in and he began to contemplate the journey home for the first time.

The seas would be following, the wind to their backs. If the storm continued at this strength, then, with waves rolling in on to their stern, they would risk foundering. A big wave would either roll over their stern, or as it gathered height, pick up the stern and flip the boat end over end. Of the two alternatives the Arun was designed for the first, and, with the watertight door shut and clipped, she could take any number of waves over her stubby aft deck. To hold her down they would need to trail a drogue. The big three-foot-wide mouth tapering back into six feet of canvas cone that dragged through the water behind the boat. It would act like brakes and would hold the back end down, letting the wave roll by. If it broke over the deck, well, they couldn't prevent that. So be it.

The men were clear of the hull and he pushed the throttles forward and ran the boat in towards them, watching the seas come in and the two men on the deck, one now with a boathook, the other taking in the line to keep it clear of the props. He felt Simon's hand tap on his shoulder, he was moving down to help. To his left Cochran, who was doing something with a screwdriver, stopped to watch them come in for the last two survivors from the MV *Caledonia*.

A nice slow ride home, because without radar they were blind in the storm, relying only on sailors' eyes. They would need to steer nor'easterly, use the RDF if necessary when they got close. Without radar to give them a trace on the Crim rocks, they would rely on a visual sighting of the Bishop Rock light.

Then they would give it three cables of room over the starboard beam, come on to zero four two, and in with the Western Rocks on the starboard beam, direct up the sound and, finally, pick up the St Mary's light.

He watched the two men as they eased alongside them and finally he pushed the throttles into neutral. Simon, who had joined Vic Collier down in the waist, got a grip on the two men in the water. Come on, lads. Come on, come on. He flicked a look back at the seas, wanting steerageway on again. This was the dangerous time and they had had their fair share of luck tonight.

Timson joined the other two and, scorning the A frame, he reached down to lift them up into the waist, one older, his hair thin and grey and one younger, stronger, the life-boatman's hands dragging them upwards, just like on the old lithographs. Let not the deep swallow me up. Carter slipped the throttles forward again, feeling the boat respond to the helm. That's it, he thought. Now we count. Fifty-six. Should be fifty-six alive and accounted for. Thank you, God.

Simon and Vic were helping Nichols and McDermott round on to the afterdeck towards the wheelhouse door and Timson had turned and was moving back up the deck to call Jarvis when the wave came in. It wasn't as big as many that night, but big enough. A steep wall that would break right over the *Caledonia*'s quarterdeck and roll round the stern of the dying ship. Where they were, there was nothing to impede its thundering advance.

Carter saw it coming. There would be no taking this wave on the edge, or the beam, no matter who was on the deck. With the window gone, and damaged as she was, she just wouldn't survive another capsize. With sixty-two people aboard he didn't have any choice. God forgive me, he said, and he swung the wheel to bring the wave over the bows, barking a warning to those still on the decks. Timson heard the warning and, it being a lifeboatman's cry, knew it wouldn't necessarily be understood by Jarvis. He began to run forward.

St Mary's

Norah Madden and Helen Carter worked together preparing the receiving room. The storm had provided other work for the St Mary's Hospital that night: a hand cut by the shards of glass from a shattered window pane, a badly bruised hip, and a fractured ankle, where a man had fallen down on to the deck of his boat while testing the knots on his mooring lines along the wall of the old quay. A senior nursing sister and a second year on duty shift had coped well enough, but had called in the other doctor, a retiree, for the fracture. Now they had split up to prepare beds and take supplies from the store.

The cook had been roused from her bed and a car had been sent to the Atlantic Hotel for more soup and loaves of bread, and the staff at a smaller hotel had turned out and were filling thick slices of bread with tasty fillings to create substantial sandwiches. Others would be gathering up warm dry clothing, towels and blankets and would soon walk down to the quay, like the islanders had done for decades when the lifeboat came home with wet, cold, injured people. And however many people they came home with, they would be prepared to feed them, get them warm and dry, treat those who were hurt and make them welcome at firesides.

They knew they had one cardiac case and Helen knew that there would be others injured. You didn't get transfers without bumps and falls.

'We can set up the dining room for the walkers. Will we need extra blankets?' Helen asked.

'In the hall press,' Norah answered.

'In the what?'

'The . . . sorry. The cupboard. We will need dry clothing too. I'll get the word out.' Norah looked at her watch.

'No need. They will be there,' Helen replied confidently.

Norah stopped what she was doing and, holding the box of sterile dressings, said softly, 'I hope to God they are all right.'

Helen was about to respond with something upbeat and positive when the door opened and Susan Farmer walked in.

'Hello,' she said. 'I've been looking for you both. Heard the latest from Falmouth?'

'No,' they both said.

Susan put on a brave grin. 'Your menfolk had taken twenty-six off the *Caledonia* up till that time. That was a while ago.'

Helen felt a surge of pride and smiled, but Norah knew there was more.

'And . . . ?'

'And what?' Susan said.

'And don't tell us half the story. There's more.'

'Nothing to worry about.'

'Let us decide that,' Norah said firmly.

Susan half regretted coming now but she was here and had been cornered.

'They capsized again. Or rather were slammed up against the side of the ship first. A window or windows are broken in the wheelhouse. They are no longer watertight, so they have begun approaches to the *Caledonia*'s stern. Mr Dickerson says that's so they can keep their bows into the seas.'

'Oh, my God,' Norah murmured, visions of her David on a damaged lifeboat flashing through her mind.

Helen gathered herself, worried for the first time about her menfolk. 'Are the boys all off?' she asked.

'Yes.'

'And they are staying on service,' Helen confirmed.

'Yes, they are,' Susan said firmly, thinking, please, please stay on service, don't come home without him, willing them to stay out with the conviction in her voice.

Maeve Corrigan

The bows had risen, powered up the fore-wall of the wave by the thousand horsepower of her engines, the rest of the boat following, a mad race to get over the top before it broke over them. Timson had moved up the steepling angle of the deck as fast as he could, the light training shoes gripping like glue, his lifeline whipping along the heavy line as he ran. It wasn't far from the waist up to the flat area of the foredeck. It just all happened so fast. Cecil Jarvis moving back from the for'ard bollard and winch, his carabiner snagging on something. Timson watched him fall and kept moving, one eye on the huge towering wave, black-walled behind the spume and foam as it broke. He threw himself down between Jarvis and the four-inch up-standing fire hydrant that stood centre deck, knowing that when the water hit it would slam the seaman back into the hydrant with the force of a juggernaut.

It was not surf or foam. It was solid water, many tons in weight, and the combined kinetic energy was awesome. The overloaded lifeboat was losing speed as she went up the side of the wave, but was still doing eleven knots, and the falling wall of water had at last given in to gravity and the strength of the wind.

It hit Jarvis as he was attempting to stand up again and slammed him into Timson, who had grabbed the rising pipe with both arms. The lifelines, designed to take many thousands of pounds of stress, held firm and as the lifeboat shuddered and broke free of the water, Carter could see both men still on the deck. The darker figure was moving, trying to rise to his knees, but the other in orange, Timson, was lifeless, rolling with the boat as her nose dropped over the back side of the wave.

In the wheelhouse a few of them had been knocked to the floor. The door had just shut after getting Nichols and McDermott inside, when Carter's warning had crashed through the speakers.

Simon and Collier were on their feet and moving as she shook herself free of the water on the decks. They ran out of the door and round the starboard side where there was more room between the rail and the wheelhouse.

When they arrived on the deck, it was black. The for'ard deck light had finally given in but they could see Timson, big strong John, feebly trying to rise, and the other, Jarvis, on his knees, winded, taking great gasps of air, reaching out to try and help. They were like helpless giants.

They clipped lifelines on and bent over Timson as someone in the wheelhouse found a torch and shone it out through the front window. Gently rolling him over, they wiped the blood from his face, as beside them, Jarvis dragged in another lungful of air. As Collier watched, Timson's legs moved and his eyes rolled. Collier quickly ran through his examination. Spine's intact, neck's not broken. There's something wrong here. Don't like this. Don't like this at all. He looked at the standpipe. Its entire front side had been flattened by a blow. Jesus Christ. No.

He bent over and ran a hand under Timson's life jacket over his chest, his fingers pressing and feeling through the thick wet sweater.

He looked up at Simon. 'Get Parnell!' he shouted.

'What's wrong?'

'Just get the doc,' he shouted.

332

It was pointless asking for a stretcher. They didn't make them big enough. They would have to carry him when the time came.

Parnell's first examination was fast and thorough and, in the torchlight, they could see the bright-pink frothy blood around Timson's lips as he coughed. Simon was looking up over the bows every few seconds in case they were again caught on the exposed deck.

'Let's get him aft. I want his chest kept straight if possible.'

Simon bent to try and lift him but Cecil Jarvis, at last on his feet, pushed him aside and, sliding one arm under Timson's legs and one under the small of his back, lifted him and carried him, gently as a baby, back down the narrow starboard deck.

Jarvis stood holding him, his feet spread to balance as the boat rolled and pitched, while they lifted Scott's stretcher off the flat position aft of the navigator's table to make room. Parnell cut the life jacket away and went straight through the layers of clothing with a pair of scissors.

'If that second cardiac case is breathing OK I want the oxygen back here,' he said to Collier. 'And someone get some straps round him.'

Coutts moved up to the helm to allow Hal Carter down off the bridge and he arrived as Parnell was bent over Timson's huge chest with a stethoscope. Timson tried to say something, his voice weak and croaky.

'Don't try to talk, John,' Parnell said. Behind him, Simon stood listening to his lifelong friend's raggedy shallow breathing and watching him coughing blood.

Collier arrived with the small oxygen bottle. 'Five minutes won't hurt the other,' he said casually. 'Besides it doesn't really matter. That's all there is,' he finished, going to take the helm from Coutts, the helplessness turning to anger. Parnell ignored him and leant over Timson. 'John, I'm going to roll you on to your right side a little.

333

Just breathe at whatever rate is comfy. I want you to take a little from the bottle, OK?'

Take a little because that's all there is, and take the pain, Big John, because I have no more morphine. It will not be long, my brave new friend. As he watched the big lifeboatman struggling he made an oath to him. I swear that I will never run out of drugs again. I swear this. Never again will I watch a man dying in pain like I am watching you. I feel inadequate to the task and I feel humble in the face of your courage.

Carter moved forward to help roll his crewman over and, as Timson settled on to his side, his eyes were masked with pain, the sheer effort to breathe immense.

As Parnell straightened up, Carter took him back to the door.

'How is he?'

Parnell looked him in the eyes. They were red, tired and rimmed with salt. He had forgotten about Carter on the exposed bridge. Four hours now, maybe four and a half hours of intense concentration, and the lives of many others in his hands. He was drenched to the skin and, as Parnell put his hand up to his neck, he was cold to the touch.

'You need dry clothing,' Parnell said. 'Move over by the heater please.'

'How is John?'

'Technically,' he replied tiredly, 'he has a crushed thorax. The ribs that have gone, and I can't tell how many without an X-ray, have pierced both lungs. The right one is the worst. He is also haemorrhaging into the pleural cavity. There may also be internal injuries to the heart and oesophagus.'

Carter looked at him, waiting for it, and, as Simon joined them, Parnell just shook his head.

'I'll recall the chopper,' Carter said desperately. 'Maybe if we get him ashore or over to the *Drumbeat* . . .'

'He's dying, Hal,' Parnell said gently. 'He has ten, maybe fifteen, minutes.'

'But you are a doctor! Fucking hell! Can't you do something? Jesus, I mean he's just . . .' Simon blurted out, but Parnell stilled him.

'In a first-class trauma unit, we could drain the lungs, aerate the blood with a machine, keep him alive for hours. But even in a first-class hospital, with injuries like these, he would be listed as critical and be in an intensive care unit.'

Simon stood listening, his hair matted with water and salt, and finally his tired eyes filled with tears. When he spoke again, his voice was thick with emotion.

'Oh, Jesus, Doc, he's my friend, please try . . .'

'Go to him now, Simon,' his father said gently. 'Sit with him a while, lad. We will come round then and we'll want drogues out for the run in.'

As Simon nodded and moved off, wiping his eyes, a figure came up to them. Carter turned to face him and took the proffered hand.

'I am John Nichols, first officer . . .' He smiled. It was a bleak, wintry expression as he corrected himself. '. . . Late first officer of the *Caledonia*. I wanted to thank you. Thank you all, on behalf of my crew, my passengers and my company. We owe you our lives.'

'Your cadet is down aft brewing tea. Why don't you get yourself a cup?' Carter said. He was usually embarrassed by thankful survivors and tonight was no exception, but Nichols wasn't that easily put off.

'Our lives, at some cost it would seem. It was the bravest thing I have ever seen.'

'Aye,' Carter said. 'It was that.'

Another figure joined them, pushing his way through the crowded wheelhouse. It was Cochran, the *Caledonia*'s radio officer.

'Excuse me. I managed to get the medium wave operating, but the short is playing me up. We can raise Falmouth though . . .'

Simon sat crouched on the floor beside his friend,

listening to his ragged painful short breaths. Timson coughed. The oxygen mask splattered with blood and Simon pulled it away and wiped it clean. In the soft light he could see Timson's mouth and beard were red with blood.

'Hell . . . of . . . a . . . night . . . eh?' he murmured through the pain.

'Yeah,' Simon said, reaching up with the mask again. Timson shook his great shaggy head.

'No . . . we . . . got . . . 'em . . . eh?'

'Yeah. We did.'

'Fifty . . . fifty-six.' He coughed then and another bright gout of blood came to his lips. This time Simon didn't try to wipe it away.

'Yeah. Don't talk,' Simon said gently.

'She's . . . wallowing . . . a . . . bit.'

Carter stood over them and Timson looked up. 'Simon, take the helm please. Bring us round nice and careful now.'

Simon looked back down at Timson who smiled through bloody lips.

'Away . . . you . . . go . . . lad. I'm . . . not . . . going . . . anywhere.'

Simon nodded and stepped away and, using strength he didn't have, Timson reached out and touched his hand.

'Mine's . . . a . . . pint,' he said.

As his son walked up to the wheel, Carter looked down at Timson again.

'Silly bugger,' he said fondly.

'I . . . know . . . always . . . have . . . been . . .' He coughed and blood ran from the corner of his mouth. 'The . . . big . . . fella's . . . got . . . kids . . . Tell Helen I love her.'

'You tell her,' Carter said, wiping Timson's hair from his forehead.

'No . . . I'm . . . done . . . for . . . Hal . . .'

'No, you're not. You'll be fine, lad.'

'Take . . . us . . . home . . . now . . . eh?' he finished painfully, coughing blood again.

'Aye, lad. I'll do that.'

Carter stood and began to push his way through the people towards the wheel, asking some to wedge in between the chairs and others, who were sitting in them, to strap themselves in. As he got to the helm, to take the damaged lifeboat and the survivors, the injured and the dying home to St Mary's Pool – it happened.

The port engine stopped.

Ernie Coutts, who had slid from the helmsman's seat only moments before, was still in the wheelhouse and had moved back to check one of the instrument panels, driven by habit more than anything else. He saw the problem the second the engine failed. He shouted, 'Overheating!' and came off his position like a sprinter from the starting blocks, shouldering people aside. Stepping on legs and knees, regardless of whatever was there, he took the for'ard stairs in one leap, shouting, 'GANGWAY,' at the top of his voice.

Carter pushed Simon out of the helmsman's seat and slid into it, his hands running over the throttles, pulling back the port throttle and reducing power on the starboard engine, his heart pounding, counting aloud now, his eyes watching the seas. They had practised this many times. When you relied on engines, then engine failure was a real danger and he had trained his crew to restart in ten seconds. Overheating meant the other engine could follow any second. They were halfway through the gentle turn that would put them on a course for home. Beam on to the seas. Since the port window had gone, the next big wave that hit their side could be their last.

Timson, a lifeboatman to the end, used the last of his strength to sit upright and try to stand. Jarvis caught him as he collapsed, his mouth and lungs now full of blood, the red bubbly mass of it running down his front.

McDermott took the stairs after Coutts, who landed on someone at the bottom and, still shouting, he barged past the people jammed into the standing area by the door and pushed into the engine spaces, throwing the levers and slamming the door back on its hinges with a crash. Two of the *Caledonia*'s crew had found refuge there, engine room men, comfortable and at home in the noise and heat. They were both coming to their feet off the grating, one swearing as he tried to work out where the sea water cooling lines were on this miniature version. The other had begun a prayer out loud.

Coutts yelled and pushed one to the floor, leaning past him to reach into a dark area that he only knew by touch, swearing ancient sailors' curses, his face against the hot engine, his knuckle scraped. 'Please let it be this fucking line coupling. I hate you, you fucker!' Behind the joint lay the last of a series of filters.

Up in the wheelhouse, Carter had brought the boat slowly round to face the bows into the seas and had given the problem some thought.

'My fault, Hal. I should have seen the temp rising,' Collier said. 'I was thinking about John and . . .'

'I should have seen it too,' Simon said.

'No one's fault,' Carter said. 'Here's what I want to do. Stream a drogue off the bows. A sea anchor, but I want the tow line round the winch. Then we slacken off and let the bows ride. As we drop, I'll take up the slack. One of you tailing, the other on the tripping line. Double lifelines on each of you.'

'We still have one engine, Hal,' Collier said.

'Not for long.' He indicated the temperature on the helmsman's instruments. 'I'm going to shut it down to let Ernie get at the intakes. If we shut down now, before she fails, we can always restart if we have to.'

The drogue was dropped from the bows. Its thick towing line was spliced every twenty feet to indicate the length over the side. It was trailed out on a second line, the tripping line, which was secured to the narrow end. Once the desired towing distance had been reached, the towing line was secured. Then the tripping line was extended another few feet until the open end of the drogue swung around and faced the seas.

Simon ran the tow line round the winch drum five times and then a sixth for luck. He sat down behind the winch with the end of the rope tailed off into his hands and lying out behind him on the deck. He adjusted his lifelines and, with his legs hooked under the main rope, he raised a thumb high. Collier kept the tripping line running out while Carter eased the overheated, but still firing, starboard engine into neutral and shut it down.

They felt the drogue bite and Carter immediately started the generator to power the banks of batteries which, in turn, powered the winch.

Each time a wave rolled in, Simon, lashed to the bollard and secured by a lifeline, ducked his head and let the pressure off the tow line. Released from the incredible drag of the drogue, the bows rose over the wave and the line ran out through Simon's thick leather-gloved hands and around the winch drum. The moment the boat crested, Carter, in the wheelhouse, started the winch. At the same time Simon reapplied pressure to the drum and tailed the rope as it came back inboard, pulling the boat straight again, her high sharp bows turned safely into the heavy seas.

Inside, Nichols, having lost his reservations, stood alongside Carter, watching the two men on the deck. Sixty-two lives now depended on the skill of three men, a winch, some canvas and a length of rope.

'Incredible,' he said and when Carter flicked him a look he added, 'You can be on big ships so long, you forget basic seamanship.'

Twenty minutes later, Coutts coupled the intake pipe back together and gave it a turn of the wrench. He bent down to bleed the port side. He finished and looked across at McDermott who sat on the other side of the small pile of fluff – strands of rope and seaweed that had been clogging the sea water cooling intakes. 'Prime the other,' he called, 'and let's get the hell out of here!' His finger worked the tiny hand pump ten, eleven, twelve, jumping back up to the panels, eyes checking the battery levels. The book said never start simultaneously, generators running. Procedures said start one, give it ten seconds, start two. Fuck it. There was no time. His greasy filthy thumbs reached up together and, as he hit both the starters, he said, 'Please God.'

Up in the wheelhouse, a blast of noise sounded from below. As both engines fired, developing a thousand roaring horsepower, Coutts ran them straight up to maximum power on the throttles below. Carter pushed his throttles up into gear, swung the big wheel round and brought the power setting back to idle again.

'Retrieve drogue,' he said calmly into the intercom.

Five minutes later Simon and Collier re-entered the wheelhouse and Carter pushed the throttles forward, willing her to respond, to get up on the step, to fly like an angel round to face the waves. Damaged, leaking and overloaded she was, but she answered the call like a thoroughbred, leaping forward as the big propellers bit the water, coming round on the hard starboard helm.

Cheering broke out from both the packed survivors' cabins as the engines settled into their familiar sweet rhythm. In the wheelhouse, the atmosphere was more subdued because of the blanket-covered form by the doctor's seat, and the big silent bosun who sat by its side like a faithful hound.

Parnell moved among them, crew and survivors, watching for signs of hypothermia. There were not enough survival blankets to go round and, even with the heaters blowing, the risk was there.

Three minutes later, at 05:23, they trailed the drogue again, this time out behind the stern. The *Maeve Corrigan*, St Mary's' fast-afloat Arun-class lifeboat, was homeward bound.

Defiant's offer to escort her home was gratefully declined.

owing a drogue, she was stable enough. Carter had been embarrassed when the warship's captain had said that the rescue was the finest piece of seamanship he had ever seen, as he wished them a safe journey.

Collier raised Falmouth to advise that they were returning from their service. For the first time in hours they had a direct link with the coastguard and they used it to update the shore-based officers and request an ambulance to meet them. The Penlee boat, which had been on her way to support them and was now just six miles off St Mary's, maintained her power setting and swung in towards her heading, to escort her home. The other boats, not as fast as the Aruns, would make their way to Broad Sound to lend assistance and escort as needed.

Carter gave the wheel to Simon and moved to the radio to ask the coastguard to raise Dickerson on the telephone. He needed to get a message to Jean to break the news of John's death to Helen or stop her coming down to the quay. He didn't want her seeing him like that, not with all the blood that had seeped through the blanket round his face.

Nichols sat for a while with Wellbrook when he woke up, and they talked softly in the dark crowded wheelhouse, Nichols telling the captain of the rescue, the accounts of Scott and Cochran, Jeffries's courage in the sea, trying to save Scott, the accident on the foredeck, the pass of the mighty *Pegasus* and the coxswain's skill with his lifeboat.

Carter stood behind his son and smoked his pipe, carefully blowing the smoke away from the *Caledonia*'s second officer who was breathing steadily in his sleep, the young third officer still sitting by his side. They had stopped the spray coming through the smashed window with judicious use of ducting tape and a black rubbish bag and now the wheelhouse was at last warm.

Parnell and Collier sat on the floor against the door, while Collier prepared French bread, cheese and biscuits and offered them to those who weren't seasick. Fripp and

341

Chafney sat opposite them and dozed, their chins on their life jackets, Fripp still holding his sextant. Collier made up a thick wedge of bread and cheese and took it below for Coutts and McDermott who sat in the engine space.

Carstairs was sitting on the steps, his eyes never very far from David who was by now, like many of the boys, in an exhausted uncomfortable sleep, oblivious to the motion of the boat, the crowded conditions, or the vomit.

The Penlee lifeboat picked them up on radar nine miles off the Bishop in the soft light of a stormy dawn and came round to intercept their course from the west. The coxswain was the first to sight the *Maeve Corrigan*.

'Jesus Christ . . . would you look at her!' he said in awe, his own tiredness falling way.

There across the waters – down on her marks, her bow rail gone, window broken, inflatable washed away, her wheelhouse panels stove in, her radar mast just a stump, and aerials gone – was the St Mary's lifeboat. She was down almost to her gunwales in the waist, the seas washing forward over her flat aft deck, the drogue line stiff out astern.

She was battered, leaking and broken, but she moved with a pride and a dignity that said she had done her best that night and her crew was proud of her.

'Shit, she's a bit buggered up,' the mechanic, a practical man, said.

The coxswain was more romantic.

'She is magnificent.' Then he remembered she was carrying a dead lifeboatman, one of their own, who had given his life on service.

He gave the helm to his assistant and moved up on to the flying bridge. When they finally took up escort station two boat lengths astern and to starboard, those aboard the *Maeve* could see that the RNLI flag, which was snapping out astern, was flying at half mast.

When they were just two miles from the pool the Penlee boat pulled out and moved ahead at full throttle.

None of her crew asked why they were going on ahead. They knew. The *Maeve* had fought the storm alone, rescued people alone, capsized twice, been damaged and still gone on and rescued the rest. She was bringing everyone home and she would have that honour to herself.

Carter, dog-tired, barely acknowledged that she had left her station, and kept the *Maeve* running in under the drogue for another mile, when Simon and Collier tripped it and hauled it in. Two other lifeboats were there when they arrived. The Lizard boat and a Watson were hove to at the entrance to the pool and the Penlee boat stood off to one side. It was daylight now on St Mary's, and the islanders and some visitors, wrapped in coats and wet-weather gear, were gathered on the quay to see their lifeboat coming home, bags of dry clothing and blankets at their feet.

As the *Maeve Corrigan* limped round Bacon Ledge, past the quay wall and into the pool, one of the St Mary's boatmen aboard his launch stood and looked at the damage the lifeboat had sustained during the night. He saw the crowded wheelhouse, the faces of survivors peering outwards, and he felt the same sense of pride they all felt. With a lump in his throat and wet eyes, he dropped into his own wheelhouse and pulled his horn lanyard. The sound cut out across the waters, a welcome home for a hero. That was the start.

All across the pool, from the carn to the old quay, others did the same, launches, yachts, barges, foghorns and sirens calling out, along with deeper, louder notes from the three other lifeboats drowning out the car horns that blared from the street as they welcomed the *Maeve Corrigan* home.

Susan Farmer was on the quay and her camera crew caught the events from right above the lifeboat, as Carter brought her in alongside the steps. The police moved people back to let the ambulance and the island's three taxis through, and one by one the survivors were helped up the steps to be dried and changed and driven to the hospital.

Nichols saw her at the top of the steps and froze, uncertain of what to do. She fixed that. She ran into his arms and held him, and only let go to tell Parnell that Norah was waiting for him up at the hospital.

'Where are you going now?' she asked.

'I don't know,' he said. 'I will have a few days' leave I think, before the inquiry.'

'I have a suggestion,' she replied with a smile.

'What about the story?'

'It will only take a couple of hours,' she replied. He held her hand and hushed her as, below them, Cecil Jarvis pushed others aside and alone carried John Timson's body up the steps that, in life, he had climbed so often.

They stood with Carstairs at the top of the steps to pay their respects, and, when the policeman got into the car that someone had borrowed for the drive to the hospital with David Lawler and Parnell, Nichols looked down at Hal Carter and Collier, Simon and Ernie Coutts.

'Can I buy you gentlemen breakfast?'

'Thank you but no. Got to get her refuelled and cleaned up.'

'Later then,' he said.

Someone nodded and, as John Nichols and Susan Farmer walked arm in arm down the quay, the four remaining crew began to handpump diesel into the *Maeve*'s big hungry tanks.

It would be a couple of days before her replacement boat arrived and someone might need the lifeboat again before then.

EPILOGUE

ohn Timson was buried on St Mary's and today his simple
headstone is surrounded by daffodils in the spring, bright
sprays of yellow and primrose. He was posthumously
awarded the George Medal for bravery. The medal,
accepted by Helen Carter, who lives in Penzance, now sits
in the boathouse at Carn Thomas.

All the members of the crew were awarded the Royal
National Lifeboat Institution's gold medal for their valour,
the reverse of which shows a bas-relief scene of three men
pulling another man from the sea into a small boat, below
an inscription that reads

LET NOT THE DEEP SWALLOW ME UP

Parnell decided to stay on St Mary's and accepted Hal
Carter's offer of a full-time place on the crew. His wife
Norah is an enthusiastic fund-raiser for the RNLI and they
can often be seen, much to Ernie Coutts's ongoing amusement, windsurfing by Newford Island.

The *Maeve Corrigan* is back in the pool, and when the
winds come from the north, she tugs impatiently at her
mooring line, bows facing out into St Mary's Road and
beyond to the islands of Tresco and Bryher and the wide
Atlantic Ocean.

Sometimes, when people see the man in the blue coat
and flat cap, pipe jutting from his mouth, checking the
mooring lines on his punt, they point him out to their
children and begin to tell the tale of the stormy night when
the engine failed on the MV *Caledonia*.

To Kill the Potemkin
Mark Joseph

In the ocean's deepest waters, a silent, deadly war of nerves is under way . . .

USS *Barracuda*, pride of the American fleet, is one of the fastest, deadliest hunter-killer submarines ever. But now she's caught up in a terrifying, potentially fatal war game with an enemy more powerful, more lethal than herself, and until now top secret. Somewhere below her, beyond the reach of her sonar, deeper than any sub has ever gone before, lurks the *Potemkin*.

Tracking this state-of-the-art killer is Jack Sorensen, *Barracuda*'s chief sonar man, whose extraordinary skills are matched by a true submariner's sixth sense. Sorensen can almost feel where the *Potemkin* is hiding. He knows that this is the real thing. And he will do everything to make sure that if it comes to it, the next time the *Potemkin* dives to the ocean bed, it will stay there, for ever . . .

'A taut, seaworthy, and extremely plausible what-if thriller . . . builds up to a high-tension confrontational ending'
Kirkus Reviews

'A remarkably gripping and infinitely researched first novel . . . the final dénouement is a nail-biter' *Publishing News*

ALISTAIR MACLEAN'S

Dead Halt
Alastair MacNeill

A privately owned schooner is caught in a hurricane off the coast of Nantucket and blown ashore where it breaks up on the treacherous rocks. Next day, a group of children picking over the wreckage discover a case of brand-new Armalite Assault Rifles.

According to its log, the schooner had embarked from New York and was headed for Dublin. The arms were meant for the IRA.

UNACO agents Mike Graham and Sabrina Carver, their own working relationship as volatile as ever, are plunged into an investigation which tests all their skills, all their courage, as their quest takes them from America to London, to Switzerland to Ireland, to unravel a web of deadly intrigue. Arms, drugs, the Mafia and an international power game are at the centre of a complex and compelling story which moves at a cracking pace from start to shocking climax.

ISBN 0 00 647310 5

Star Shot
Douglas Terman

The electrifying thriller from the
bestselling author of *First Strike* and *Shell Game*

Shot down over Vietnam, US pilot John Bracken is
interrogated, tortured and broken by Lu, a cold-hearted
Eurasian KGB agent. Finally he returns home, only to find
himself forced out of the service in disgrace. Twenty years
later, on a charter trip to Florida, Bracken's peaceful new life
as a yacht skipper is shattered when he is dragged into the
world of international terrorism.

With the US space shuttle and its payload of top-secret Star
Wars technology standing sabotaged on the launchpad,
Bracken comes face to face once more with his hated former
tormentor in a heart-pounding battle of wits on the high seas
. . . racing to prevent the most devastating act of terrorism
ever conceived.

'This is a *must* read . . . spies, Star Wars technology, revenge,
hate and heart-stopping suspense, all carefully crafted into a
taut zinger of a tale.'   Stephen Coonts

'A page-turner . . . pulls you headfirst into a world of danger
and intrigue.'   Larry Bond

'A stimulating, totally captivating thriller.'   Ernest K. Gann

ISBN 0 00 617809 X

In Honour Bound
Gerald Seymour

Barney Crispin, SAS Captain, is sent urgently to the Afghanistan border on the direct order of the Foreign Secretary.

His mission – to organize the destruction of one of the new Soviet helicopters and to bring its secret parts back to Britain.

But the guerrillas he trains and sends in are killed, and in defiance of his orders he goes in himself to challenge the Russian gunships in the remote Afghan valleys.

'Action is what Mr Seymour does best . . . terse, clipped, sometimes brutal . . . genuinely exciting.'   *The Times*

ISBN 0 00 617196 6

Kingfisher
Gerald Seymour

There were few who had seen the student arrested. There was no siren, no flashing light. There was nothing of it in the Kiev news. But for the other three, all Ukrainian Jews, it was a signal to try for freedom. They hijacked a plane and made for the West.

One country after another refused to help – they could have no truck with hijackers, least of all Soviet dissidents. Almost out of fuel, the plane landed in England. Political refugees or murderous criminals? While the authorities took their time to decide, the students chose the only route left to them . . .

'Gerald Seymour's accomplished thriller turns the tables for a change. Instead of enemy terrorists preying on us or our friends, it is a trio of Russian Jews who hijack an 'enemy' plane . . . and this state produces palm-sweating tension – tension so taut that the smallest development explodes in the reader's head. Seymour builds drama within drama both inside the plane's cabin and outside.' *New York Times*

'Full of suspense . . . all too credible.' *Daily Telegraph*

ISBN 0 00 616614 8

HarperCollins Paperbacks – Fiction

HarperCollins is a leading publisher of paperback fiction. Below are some recent titles.

- [ ] DEAD HALT Alastair MacNeill £4.99
- [ ] THE SCORPIO ILLUSION Robert Ludlum £4.99
- [ ] POINT OF IMPACT Stephen Hunter £4.99
- [ ] NIGHT SOLDIERS Alan Furst £4.99
- [ ] WHISPERS IN THE DARK Jonathan Aycliffe £3.99
- [ ] DUNCTON STONE William Horwood £5.99
- [ ] CORMORANT Douglas Terman £4.99
- [ ] DEEP BLUE Gavin Esler £4.99
- [ ] MORNINGSTAR Peter Atkins £4.99

You can buy HarperCollins Paperbacks at your local bookshops or newsagents. Or you can order them from HarperCollins Paperbacks, Cash Sales Department, Box 29, Douglas, Isle of Man. Please send a cheque, postal or money order (not currency) worth the price plus 24p per book for postage (maximum postage required is £3.00 for orders within the UK).

NAME (Block letters)_____

ADDRESS_____

_____